Tim Connor Hits Trouble

Frank Lankaster

Clink
Street

London | New York

Table of Contents

1. Getting There...1
2. The Interview..15
3. Goodbye, Hello..31
4. Out of the Frying Pan..45
5. The Beginning of Term Party...60
6. An Unexpected Start to Term..72
7. The Team Meets..85
8. A Place to Live and a House Warming...........................96
9. Home Again..107
10. Henry on the Rocks...122
11. Mending and Upending Fences....................................137
12. The Psychology Lecture Interrupted...........................147
13. Thank You for Coming...155
14. Henry and Tim Play Golf...172
15. The Fight..181
16. Henry Receives an Invitation......................................186
17. Aisha's Party...194
18. Thank God for a Conference.......................................206
19. Ladies Evening...221

20. Decisions Have to Be Made..234
21. In Some Other Lifetime...249
22. The Grand Tour Begins...264
23. The Lord and the Lady...275
24. The Grand Tour Continues... 282
25. The Calm: Phoney or Funny?.......................................296
26. The Great Disappearing Acts...307
27. Moment of Truth..317
28. There's a Price You Pay...327
29. It's Staring You in the Face...337
30. On Bognor Sea-Front...348
31. A Get-Together at Rachel's Place.....................................357
32. Great Transitions.. 369

Chapter 1
Getting There

He wiped a splatter of sweat from his forehead and glasses. He was hot, late and lost. He tried again to relate the map in his hand to the surrounding countryside, shifting it about urgently. No chance. Whatever angle he chose failed to match to what was around him. Cursing, he hurled the map into a nearby field.

Not by habit punctual, Tim knew that on this occasion he had to make it on time. He had good reason. He had been trying to get a job in higher education for almost ten years. Averaging roughly one rejection a year, morale and belief were beginning to dip... But this was his best chance yet. The job description played to his strengths; he could almost have written it himself. Unusually at university level this job required teaching experience in psychology and sociology, the subjects he had been teaching to senior high school students.

Time was running out; he was thirty-eight years old and part-time tutoring with the Open University was his only higher education teaching experience. This was his first interview in nearly two years and his chances of getting a full-time job as a junior lecturer were fast disappearing. He was already too old for 'new blood appointments'. This one he had to get. The alternative was to reconcile himself to a career in school teaching: worthy, maybe, but as he was beginning to discover, dull. He had drifted into school teaching after a succession of bit jobs and it now threatened to turn into a life-sentence. A separation from his partner, the maintenance of his daughter, and his own rising life-style expectations meant that a return to the semi-bohemian lifestyle of his twenties was no longer realistic. Besides, as he reluctantly acknowledged, he was beginning to feel just a bit older.

He looked around for help, few people were about. Wash University was a couple of miles outside of Wash City, but where exactly? He began to curse himself for not taking a taxi from the station, indulging an idiot notion that a brisk walk would sharpen him up for the challenge ahead. The bright countryside around him seemed to mock his frustration. Suddenly he spotted what looked like a student passing on a bicycle. He flagged the helmeted androgyne down. The cyclist, a young woman braking suddenly, almost cannoned into him. For a moment she looked annoyed but replied helpfully enough to Tim's enquiry.

'No problem. Cross the roundabout, carry straight on along the big hedge and you'll come to a large ornamental gate on your left, go through and it's a couple of hundred yards to the main university admin centre. It used to be a country house but it's been modernised now. You can't miss it. You ok?' She added as Tim spluttered his thanks.

'I'm fine now,' he said. 'I was just a bit lost.'

'I can see. Don't worry. It's easy from here. Follow those instructions and you can't go wrong. Straight and then left.' She smiled, re-engaged the stirrups and swiftly moved off.

Tim watched her lycra clad rump rotate into the distance, too stressed to register even routine appreciation.

He set off to follow her directions. It was already past two o'clock, the time he was expected to arrive. He broke into a jog, gasping in relief as he reached a large wrought-iron gate. To one side was a notice board, the college's name emblazoned above a list of sponsors, mainly large corporations, their names almost as prominently displayed. He quickened his pace as he turned into the drive, barely noticing the parkland on either side, still substantial despite chunks being sold off to private developers. Following the drive through a cluster of trees he arrived within fifty yards or so of a complex of older and newer buildings. The drive morphed into a circular strip with an ornamental fountain in the middle, providing a one-way loop for traffic. A more recently built road, angled off to the left sign-posted to a car park and teaching area.

Tim slowed as he approached the buildings. A gust of wind lifted a tiny spray of water from the fountain, splashing it coolly onto his face. 'Good omen,' he thought, as he reached inside his jacket pocket for his tie. He fastened the top button of his shirt, knotting the tie round his neck. It felt uncomfortable, tight and obdurately off centre; it would have to do. He regretted not buying a fashionable kipper tie instead of exhuming his old bootlace one. Knackered from his shuffle-sprint from the station, he felt like a sack of spanners tied with a piece of string. For a second he contemplated ducking his face into the fountain to clear the sweat and flatten his hair. Common sense prevailed and he hurried towards the main building.

Several students were hanging around on the front steps, some of them smoking. Still breathing heavily he was caught in the acrid fumes. His allergy to cigarette smoke flared into a sharp sneezing fit, his mucus membranes instantly pricking and swelling. According to his doctor the allergy was psychosomatic. Just now that diagnosis seemed perverse, though he knew the mere sight of someone lighting up could trigger an instant reaction. Wheezing and dishevelled he leant against one of the columns that flanked the steps. This was not how he had intended to arrive. The students eyed him with mild interest.

'You alright, then?' A tall Asian young man asked.

'Yeah ...well ... err ... no ... I'm a bit late for an appointment. Can you direct me to Reception?'

'Sure. Go up these steps and it's pretty much in front of you. You can't miss it. Maybe you should take a breather before you go inside?'

'No ... No ... That's ok. Maybe after I've registered at Reception.'

'You here for the Social Science job then? I think I saw a couple of other candidates arrive about half-an-hour ago.'

Tim gasped his thanks. He stumbled up the steps with all the poise of Jarvis Cocker on ice. Clattering his way through a pair of period doors, he found himself in a large hall. The angular Georgian elegance of the room and its cool pale blue and white décor had a calming effect. He reminded himself of his determination not to let the tension get to him. Nothing definitively awful had happened so far; he had not even met the interview panel yet. He looked around for Reception. It was neatly signed directly in front of him, sitting between two wings of a double stairway leading to a balcony that in turn accessed the building's first floor. He wiped his face with the back of his tie and smoothed down his jacket. Adopting a composed and purposeful demeanour he approached Reception and knocked firmly on the door. Off-balance, he found himself lurching towards a startled receptionist. The door had been slightly open. 'Sorry ...' he began.

Startled, the receptionist, a severe looking woman swiftly reasserted her professional poise.

'Oh ... You must be Mr. Connor,' she said, quickly correcting herself, 'I do apologise, I mean Dr. Connor. We've been expecting you.'

'Yes, I'm here for ...'

She scrutinised him more closely adding 'If you want

to use it there's a gentleman's comfort room under the left-side stair way.' Tim decided to remain uncomfortable rather than risk further delay. *Funny word – comfort room – one of the odder American euphemisms.*

The receptionist's directions took him to the first floor balcony and from there into a large room at the back of the building. Its solid but worn furniture was more early twentieth than eighteenth century, failing to match the impressive Georgian interior. It was only on a second scan of the room that he noticed an Asian woman sitting on a highbacked, heavily upholstered couch towards the end of the room. She looked about thirty, perhaps slightly younger.

He blinked in surprise. From his extensive experience of the job circuit he assumed there would be two or three other candidates waiting for interview. On a bad day, and he'd had a few, even more. Buoyed at the prospect of this depleted opposition, he approached the young woman.

'Hi, my name's Tim Connor. You must be one of the other candidates.'

'Oh, hi, that's right. I'm Aisha Khan. 'Nice to meet you. I'm glad you've made it. Are you ok? I think they've almost given up on you. They seem quite concerned.'

'I'm fine, just had a few problems getting here.' Tim looked around the room again. 'So you, me and whoever's being interviewed now are the only candidates?'

'Yes, I'm pretty sure. Two of the short-listed candidates have withdrawn. They've got jobs elsewhere apparently. There are only three of us now. The other candidate is Barry Hobsbawn, you know? The social psychologist. He's written something on the psychology of racism. He's in there now.' She gestured towards a dark panelled door some yards adjacent to the couch.

This information revived Tim. Two withdrawals seriously improved his chances of getting the job. One in three from one in five was a massive shift in the odds. He eased into an armchair opposite the couch. He'd briefly considered sitting next to Aisha Khan but quickly decided against.

Better to keep a civil distance from a competitor. And getting too near her might well distract his focus. She shone with a well-groomed but unaffected beauty: cascading jet-black hair and long glossy legs bare to above the knees. Glancing into her face he found that her eyes were not dark brown as he expected but almost hazel. She returned his gaze with a look of unapologetic intelligence. His optimism dimmed again. He sensed serious competition. Professional qualifications aside, she was way ahead in the personal presentation department. He felt a tremor of paranoia, not for the first time wondering why he persisted in believing that by looking downbeat he was somehow showcasing his integrity. *There's not a snowflake in hell's chance I'll get this job if the men on the panel fudge the rules of gender impartiality.*

Even if the panel avoided a Sharon Stone moment, the clause in the job advertisement that women and minority ethnic candidates would be preferred (other relevant matters being equal) could leave him adrift.

His mood dropped another notch as he suddenly remembered why Barry Hobsbawn's name had seemed vaguely familiar. He was the author of a recent, well-reviewed book on ethnic relations. One chance in three or not, he would still need a ton of luck to get past Hobsbawn. He looked again at Aisha. Sat just a few feet away he found it difficult completely to disengage from her. His over-sensitised hooter swam in a haze of subtle perfume that inconveniently threatened to fire his imagination as well as precipitate another sneezing fit. Determined to keep his focus he was about to make an attempt at polite conversation when Aisha remarked, 'Your nose looks rather red. Would you like to borrow a lightly medicated tissue? I have some Vaseline as well if you think it would help.'

The panelled door abruptly opened, sparing Tim the need to reply. Two men emerged. He assumed the younger one was Barry Hobsbawn. The other, exuding executive poise, Tim guessed was Howard Swankie, Dean of the Faculty of Social Science. He moved quickly towards Tim, his hand outstretched. 'Ah, you're here. I'm glad you've made it. Transport from the station can be a bit tricky. Even taxis are not always readily available at this time of day. I'm Howard Swankie, Dean of the Faculty of Social Science. I'm chairing the panel today. This is Dr. Hobsbawn,' he briefly laid a hand on Hobsbawn's shoulder, a little patronisingly Tim thought.

'Anyway, welcome. There's an automatic drinks machine on the ground floor should you need it. That's where the loo is too. You've got twenty minutes to half an hour before we call you in.'

Swankie turned to Aisha Khan.

'And no doubt you've already introduced yourselves,' he said, smiling at Aisha a little too enthusiastically for Tim's comfort. *Fucking done deal,* he cursed to himself.

'Ms Khan, I take it you're ready for the next interview as we agreed?' Turning back to Tim he added, 'And then it's you Dr. Connor.'

Aisha Khan followed the Dean leaving Tim with a drained looking Barry Hobsbawn who wearily lowered himself onto the couch. At this point Tim usually pumped a rival candidate for information on the interview set-up but Hobsbawn started talking first.

'Shit! That was a nightmare. Easily the worst interview I've ever had. I completely lost it.' He ran his fingers through his hair. 'I've absolutely fucking blown it.'

Tim looked studiously sympathetic. 'It was that bad, was it? Maybe it wasn't as awful as you thought? What do you think went wrong? Are they asking really tough questions?' Maybe he could nudge Hobsbawn into spilling some useful information.

'No, well yes... I can't really remember. It was me. My head was swimming. I don't usually panic. Not to that extent. I've seriously blown it,' he repeated.

Tim was well aware that candidates often understate their performance immediately after interview: a superstitious avoidance of hubris. But Hobsbawn's angst seemed real enough. Tim's response was mixed. He certainly didn't want a tough interview. But if Hobsbawn really had blown it, then his own chances had soared to a tantalising fifty-fifty, always assuming that Wash did decide to appoint. But Aisha Khan was still in contention. Short of her having an unexpected seizure, she was almost certain to get the job. There seemed no other outcome.

He wondered vaguely if he should try a vote-winning, politically correct pitch hinting that he was gay. He rejected this on the ethically and factually sound grounds that he wasn't gay. Probably best to play it straight and be himself, whatever that was. Looking at the disconsolate Hobsbawn, he felt a pang of sympathy. He knew well that totally trashed feeling in the wake of a catastrophic interview. 'I'm sorry you had such a tough time of it. But you can't always tell what impression you've made. You might have done better than you think.' He sounded blandly unconvincing even to himself.

Reverting to the hard win-lose dynamics of the situation he probed again for information, trying to keep the optimism out of his voice. 'Are you sure it was that bad?'

'Believe me, there's no way back from that. I blanked out on my specialist area. And then the Dean threw me a question about some Eastern European theorist whose name was completely unfamiliar to me. It sounded something like 'Scissors'. He probably came across him in Sunday supplement. I'm ditched as far as this job is concerned.'

Tim pumped Hobsbawn once more. 'Was it only Professor Swankie that was difficult? What were the rest of the panel like?'

Hobsbawn shot a quick glance at Tim as though only just connecting with him. Why should he help out a competitor? Fuck it! He'd nothing to lose now.

'Henry Jones, the subject leader was ok. In fact he tried to be supportive until I got hopelessly enmeshed in intellectual spaghetti-land. There are a couple of women academics on the panel that kept banging on about teaching methods. That's not my thing. I didn't go down well with them at all. They seemed to think that using a sheet of A4 as the only aid for my presentation was a bit feeble for a media specialist. The external, Fred Cohen was friendly enough but he went for the light touch. He left most of the heavy questioning to the others.'

He paused weary and disconsolate. 'Look I'm frazzled. I don't know whether they intend to let us know the outcome while we're here but I'm not hanging around. They can give me the bad news by phone. In fact I might as well withdraw – more dignified than being dumped.'

He got to his feet. 'Anyway, best of luck to you. Watch out for those two women.' He left the room, his stiff leather interview shoes squeaking plaintively on the hard, stone floor.

'Best of luck,' Tim called after him. He checked his watch. He had about ten minutes to figure out how to use Hobsbawn's information.

Teaching methods? This was an area where academics were often at their most opinionated and dogmatic. Whatever he said was likely to offend someone. But maybe his experience with the sixteen to eighteen year olds could be made to count. His strategies for keeping mid-teenagers engaged or at least occupied for two-hour sessions might translate well into higher education, now that it was almost fully comprehensive. What were the buzz words and ideas? There were plenty of them: student centred education, resources based learning, individualised learning. Tim had tinkered with all these approaches but what he most enjoyed was face to face interaction with the students, trying to spark and respond to curiosity. He knew this could sound old-fashioned; not the image he wanted to create, but perhaps he could put his own views as an add-on after he'd spouted all the 'best practice' patter? Risky. It was the techno rather than the humanistic line that usually went down well these days. The education mechanics were taking over. He decided he would cover both angles, appealing to the nuts and bolts lobby but also defending divergent and critical thinking. Should he risk a joke referring to his 'default survival kit of read, summarise and discuss among your-selves?' *Forget it! Don't go there.*

The tension was getting to him. His dismal interview track record nagged at his self-belief. Usually laid-back and self-confident, despite his gangly clumsiness, he was becoming neurotic about this pesky blockage to his life's progress. Yet the fact that he was still called to interview meant that he remained a serious contender. What was he doing wrong? Did he talk too much as one interviewer had unhelpfully implied in the middle of an interview? Or too little? Did he freeze up, sounding wooden and boring? Or, did his attempts at originality come across as too adventurous, even wild? Maybe he just tried too hard. Whatever the answer to the riddle of selection he needed to find it now. An unlikely combination of circumstances had thrown up a real chance, probably a last chance. He'd better take it. He felt momentarily exhausted. He hadn't slept much the previous night. Then the chaotic journey: what a buffoon to try to walk from the station. A band of tension gripped across his temples. He hooked his glasses over his knee and pressed the heels of his hands against his eyes; sweet oblivion!

The sudden click of a door returned him to the moment. Aisha Khan emerged alone. She smiled at him. Tim smiled back, a blank goggle.

'How did it go?' he found himself asking.

'Not bad, well ok, better than I expected,' she replied hesitantly, reluctant to sound too optimistic.

'Well, oh, good.' He half meant it. It was not easy to wish ill luck on this lovely woman, even if her success was to be at his expense. 'So you think you might have got...' He stopped mid-sentence as the door clicked open again. It was Howard Swankie.

'Dr Connor, we're ready for you now.' Without waiting for a response he turned to Aisha Khan and said, 'Don't forget to pick up your expenses claim form, Ms. Khan.

You can get it from Reception.' With what Tim interpreted as a meaningful smile, he added 'You'll be hearing from us very shortly.'

Tim got up and walked towards the oak door of the interview room. It was at this point at previous interviews that his brain fled to a remote part of his cranium where it lodged irretrievably until the ordeal was over. He breathed deeply, determined to remain if not calm at least coherent. Swankie held the door open for him. As he entered the room he got a whiff of expensive eau-de-toilette. With a gargantuan effort he managed not to sneeze.

Aisha Khan skipped down the stone stairs two steps at a time, almost losing her balance as she arrived in the Reception Hall. She felt disoriented from the intensity of the interview but high with relief and optimism. The Dean had gone out of his way to sound encouraging, congratulating her on her 'exceptional performance' and expressing 'the hope and indeed the expectation' that she would accept the job if offered. He added that 'of course the interview process had to be completed' but he was confident that he would be able to phone her with firm news within the next couple of hours. They agreed he would use her mobile rather than terrestrial number.

But suppose she was wrong. Her limbs turned heavy as a wave of anxiety surged through her. So much depended on her getting this post. It could give her an escape from domestic work and boring filler jobs. And Wash University was barely fifteen minutes drive from the house. It was ideal but ... She reminded herself there were other candidates – probably with decent publications. Had she read more into the Dean's parting remarks than he intended?

She hesitated for a moment in the entrance hall. It was pointless to fill in a claims form for the price of a four-mile journey. She decided to take a walk before returning to the city to collect her son Ali from nursery. In a phrase of her mother's she realised that she also needed 'to collect' herself.

Once outside, the fresh air had a sobering effect. She had not seriously expected to get this job or perhaps even to get as far as an interview. Sure she wanted a decent career but initially this application had been little more than a gesture of intent – as much to her sceptical husband Waqar as to herself. Now she was slightly fazed at the stark immediacy of a previously distant goal. 'Be careful what you wish for,' she spontaneously mouthed the cliché.

Did she really want all this? To teach? To write? For it to be assumed that she was ambitious? To compete with smart, confident types who never questioned their motives? What might be the effect on her family life? On her friends? It was seven years since she had started her part-time degree in Social Science. She had gone on to complete an M.A. in Ethnicity and Gender Studies. Part of her dissertation was to be published as a chapter in a collection on the experiences of third generation Muslim women. Write about ourselves – that's what we feminists do, she mused. And if we're Muslim we write about our Muslim selves. The interview panel had been impressed with her plans to develop her research. She would increase her research sample from ten to sixty Muslim women and stratify into three distinct age groups. There might even be a book in it.

Yes, this *was* what she wanted. And so much the better if it came more quickly and easily than she had expected. But Waqar was a problem. He was ambivalent at best. He had not been keen for her to do the part-time degree, arguing that a better way to fill her time would be to manage one of his restaurants. She doubted whether he was really serious, even about this suggestion and in any case it had little appeal for her. But his concerns about her taking on a full-time academic job became stronger as the possibility became more realistic: it would take up too much time, they had a young physically handicapped child, he needed her support with clients as his business continued to expand, they didn't need the money. She had quietened him by insisting that the chances of her getting an academic job were remote, especially as she would only take one within a thirty-mile radius of Wash.

Ten Years ago she would have organised her life according to Waqar's wishes. She was twenty-two when they married, fifteen years younger than him, impressed by his vitality and apparently effortless material success. A princess in her own home; becoming the richly indulged wife of the besotted Waqar had involved minimal transition. He loved to show her off, although the trophy wife phase satisfied neither of them for more than a few years. In the longer term what he wanted and expected from her was a 'good wife and mother.' He conceded that when the time was ripe she might develop a career of some kind, but it was not a matter he gave much consideration.

He was still a dominant figure but she had changed. She was now almost as old as Waqar was when they married and by now she had accumulated her own experiences. She quickly concluded that trophy status offered diminishing returns, but the seismic shift came when she realised that being a wife and mother might not be enough for her either. Yes, crucial to her identity but not the whole of it. And yet it was the experience of motherhood that first jolted Aisha out of her naïve youthful narcissism. They had found having children difficult. The doctors were unable to discover why. Their one child had been born prematurely at seven months and had suffered bleeding from the brain. Now four years old, Ali's left side weakness showed in a pronounced limp and a limited ability to grip with his left hand. Mercifully his language development had not been affected and his basic cognition seemed to be intact. Aisha had lived every moment of his perilous and often painful existence. The early discovery of the extent of his physical weakness had been an agony but the gradual evidence of his lively brain and personality, her greatest joy. But if she was always to put herself second to Ali, she knew that it would be better for everybody, including Ali, if she also had a life outside the home. Yes, she wanted this job alright.

Lost in her thoughts, Aisha abruptly realised she had also lost her way. She had wandered well beyond the campus boundary onto a lower stretch of land. Turning round she was unable even to spot the university. Getting back to a higher point, she looked towards the City. The view was unfamiliar, but Wash despite its city status, was no bigger than a medium size town and she could just make out her own neighbourhood. Why not walk the remainder of the way home? As she set off her mobile burred lightly against her thigh. Her hand trembling, she took the phone from her pocket.

Chapter 2
The Interview

Members of the interview panel were sat on the far side of a long polished wooden table. Tim took the lone chair opposite them. His head was buzzing but he felt slightly more focused now the action was about to begin. He made an effort to remember the names of the panel members as the Dean introduced them. It was unlikely he would forget Swankie's, but recalling the latter's reputation for vanity he decided to give both his titles of 'Professor' and 'Dean' a good airing.

On the extreme left of the panel sat Henry Jones, Head of the Social Science Department. Sociology was the largest subject but recently a degree in psychology had been set up in response to growing demand. Jones himself was a sociologist. Tim had already talked with him on the phone so remembering his name should not be a problem. He had been mildly concerned that he had never heard of Henry Jones before applying for this job. On asking around it turned out that Jones had published little, despite his relatively senior position. Now in his early sixties, he had been a youthful high flyer, getting a first class degree at the London School of Economics and going on to do research at the same institution. Although he had completed his doctorate he had never published anything from it. Eventually he had found a job at Wash College of Arts and Technology where he had acquired the reputation of something of a sociological savant and a brilliant if erratic lecturer, very much in the old discursive style. When WCAT amalgamated with a local college of higher education Jones found himself leading a small sociology team within a sprawling Faculty of Social Science and Humanities. Chance, the Buggins principle and a slightly higher salary had trumped his disinclination to take on any managerial work, however modest. If Tim got this job, Henry Jones would be his immediate boss. He quickly took in Jones' long thinning hair, thick glasses and purple mottled nose, prominent against the light raspberry colour of his face. A drinker. Tim was not too displeased, preferring characters to careerists.

Next to Jones was someone Tim did not immediately recognise. It turned out to be Fred Cohen, who had written widely on youth and crime. Cohen was of the same generation as Jones, but much better known. Some of his interests overlapped with Tim's and he might be a potential supporter. Cohen, in all denim with matching blue shades, looked even more of a sixties throwback than Jones. What was left of his hair was dyed an aggressive shade of bright chestnut, set off with highlights of sunset orange. He gave Tim an encouraging smile as Swankie did the introductions. It occurred to Tim that if he could win over either Cohen or Jones, the other might sway in his direction too.

If Cohen and Jones were a possible mini-bloc vote for him, the two women sitting to the right of Swankie looked set solid against. Or so he imagined. Physically they contrasted sharply. The one sat closest to Swankie, though perhaps deliberately not that close, was the older by a good fifteen or twenty years and by far the larger. Her tent-like dress increased the impression of volume. Her eyes and complexion were dark and her grey-flecked, curly copperish hair shot out almost at right angles but was oddly flat on top. A touch ethnic Tim thought, maybe Eastern European, or perhaps Celtic. Her expression on being introduced to Tim was not exactly a scowl but it was certainly not a smile of welcome either. The other woman was equally striking, although in a quite dissimilar way. She was wearing a sharply tailored, slim-fit, dark blue suit and had pulled her thick blond hair tightly away from her face. She barely acknowledged Tim as she was introduced to him, seemingly preoccupied with the papers in front of her.

Swankie introduced the older women first. 'This is Ms. Rachel Steir, a senior member of the department.'

Rachel Steir's brow corrugated in annoyance. 'Dr. Steir, please, Professor Swankie. It took me eight years to earn my doctorate so I think I *will* insist on the title if you don't mind. Good afternoon Dr. Connor,' she added attempting a softer tone.

'I do apologise, *Dr* Steir,' Swankie gave exaggerated emphasis to her title. '*Dr* Steir,' he repeated before continuing smoothly.

'And this is Ms. Erica Botham, at least I think Ms. *is* her correct title unless she's also been a recent recipient of a doctorate.' He smirked, appreciating his own sarcasm.

'No, that's correct,' she replied brusquely, un-amused.

'Good, glad I got that right,' said Swankie.

Having then introduced Henry Jones and Fred Cohen, he continued briskly. 'Now that the introductions are over we'll move onto the main business. I believe you have a brief presentation for us, Dr Connor.'

Tim's topic was 'masculinity' or 'masculinities' as social scientists usually refer to it, recognising that there is no single form of 'masculine' behaviour. This was not his main area of research, that was youth as a period of psychological and social transition. He had chosen to talk about masculinity, anticipating that it would interest a mixed gender panel. Glancing at the two women, both keenly poised to

17

decide his fate, he wondered if he should have opted for a safer topic.

He had time for a second fleeting regret before beginning his presentation: his choice to use overheads rather than PowerPoint. He attempted to pass this off with a nonchalant opening quip. 'Err ... well ... they say that if you want to avoid being up-staged don't work with animals, children or PowerPoint. So I won't.' He paused briefly to allow for tension-breaking laughter. A chill silence rippled across the room. He looked up quickly to see a row of puzzled expressions. Not a great start.

The pressure was on to make sure that the rest of the presentation went well. In an attempt to get the two women on side he was careful not to over-egg his main argument that in certain ways gender relations are as difficult for men as for women, especially for young men. He acknowledged that young men are generally far more violent than young women but pointed out that most of their public violence is directed against each other. A sizeable minority spend much of their time knocking each other about and otherwise winding each other up in an edgy friendly-competitive but combustible kind of way. Smiling wryly he suggested that if this was patriarchy, it is almost as damaging to the budding patriarchs as to women.

Glancing up from his noddy-sheet he noticed that the two women were not smiling with him. He decided to dispense with any further attempts at humour. Hastily moving on, he stressed that the violence of young men, particularly in domestic and relationship contexts, is disastrous for young women, not only because of the reality and threat of physical damage but because it controls and traps them. He added that over the life course, patriarchy can systematically oppress and block the opportunities of women of any age. Dr. Steir nodded wary assent. Tim sensed that despite his genuinely felt arguments he was creating an impression of insincerity. He was never at his most convincing when mouthing what he dubbed 'political correctitudes' even when he agreed with them. There was something in his character and appearance that didn't square with conformity, any kind of conformity.

Erica Botham leaned forward eagerly, about to ask him a question.

Swankie cut in before she could get started. 'Right perhaps we'll come back later to Dr. Connor's... em...' his hesitation seemed contrived, 'interesting if challenging arguments.' He paused, holding centre stage for a moment before turning to Henry Jones. Henry, will you kick off the next part of the interview?'

It soon became clear that Jones intended to give Tim an easy ride, going out of his way to feed him questions on topics Tim was likely to be well informed about. A dolly question on the iconoclastic nineteen sixties American sociologist Charles Wright Mills enabled him to showboat from his Master's thesis that dealt with Mills' influence on the American New Left of the nineteen sixties. Playing the interview game, he also took the opportunity to make reference to his recently published journal article – his second so far - arguing that Mills' work was still relevant in 2010. Mills' rebellious and confrontational style was not to the taste of all his professional colleagues neither then nor now. He guessed that Swankie was likely to be in the anti-Mills camp. Without doing a disservice to Mills' ideas, Tim made sure his account of Mills' damning analysis of the 'American power elite' was not uncritical. However he concluded by suggesting that a similar analysis to Mills' might be applicable to the rich and powerful contemporary global elite. Henry Jones nodded agreement. Howard Swankie listened with close but inscrutable attention.

Tim's tension eased and his head cleared as he talked about his favourite social scientist. Fred Cohen seemed genuinely interested and picked up the thread of questioning from Henry Jones.

'So what do you think is the main similarity between the America power elite of the sixties and seventies and today's global elite?'

Tim paused for a second. Cohen was probably trying to be helpful but was leading him into controversial territory. Out of the corner of his eye he saw Swankie lean forward, anticipating his response. Swankie's patrician manner, bordering on arrogance, suggested to Tim that he might be some kind of an elitist himself. Tim's gut response to Cohen's question was that both the American post-war elite and today's global elite were 'greedy' and 'selfish'. He was not going to say otherwise, but he could use other language.

'The main similarity is that both elites exercise power in their own interest at the expense of the public good, the contemporary global elite especially. For instance in Britain and the United States inequality is greater than at any time since the nineteen thirties. And the richer people are, the faster they are getting even richer. It's a combination of technological and financial control that...'

'Have you any criticism to make of Mills' ideas,' Swankie interrupted, adding sarcastically 'or is the great man beyond criticism? Remember, he was regarded as 'the big daddy' of the nineteen sixties New Left and that ended in a mess, partly a violent mess, in the early seventies.'

Swankie regarded himself as a progressive reformer, committed to working within the system to improve it along with his own prospects. He was an enthusiast for what he termed 'techno-administrative led' change. He believed violent political action within a democracy was illegitimate, tending at worst to what he referred to as 'left Fascism.' Tim sensed that Swankie was more interested in flushing out where he, rather than Mills stood on these matters. His response was careful but uncompromising. He stated his agreement with Mills that there were circumstances in which violence could be justifiable as a means to change. He gave a few examples from British history and from the developing world where violent regime change appeared justified. Swankie looked thoughtfully at Tim.

Trying to get on a roll, Tim moved quickly on to pick out a put-down that Swankie had slipped into his question. 'And no, I don't think academic hero worship is very helpful. In fact it can mislead. Actually that was one of the worst things about the sixties; the tendency to generate cultural idols. It's got even worse now with the cult of celebrity. At least then there was sometimes a relationship between heroes and causes. Some popular heroes were also meaningful role models, like Martin Luther King but also a boxer like Muhammad Ali or a musician like John Lennon. They didn't merely articulate their principles, they acted on them. Today there is little meaningful link between the celebs and their followers. The celeb's lifestyle is disassociated from most young people's lives ... irrelevant ... It has little or no positive role model value at all. The celebs distract young people from the good and useful things they might do. It's often little more than mutual cultural masturbation. Pointless.'

He stopped, immediately he realised some of the panel might find his 'masturbation' analogy inappropriate if not offensive. He could be talking himself out of a job.

Swankie shot a concerned glance in the direction of the two women. Both looked less concerned than Swankie himself. 'Hmm ... perhaps I can move us on. Dr Steir, I think you wanted to ask Dr. Connor a couple of questions about teaching methods?'

'Yes, indeed, Professor Swankie, moving on seems a good idea. Dr. Connor, you're no doubt aware that in an institution such as ours teaching has become an even more important yet difficult task than in the past. What can you bring us from your extensive experience with younger students?'

She paused for a moment, moving her head rapidly up and down in apparent approval of her own question, her hair gyrating like a giant tomato plant caught in a cross-wind. 'By the way I was surprised that you didn't use PowerPoint for your presentation, it makes things easier for both the audience and the presenter.'

Tim had anticipated a tricky ride from Dr. Steir, but this was decidedly hostile. For a moment his concentration faltered and he flannelled to buy time. 'I wouldn't presume to tell colleagues here how to teach if I were appointed. I'm sure most of them have developed their own methods. Of course, these days there's an expectation colleagues will exchange ideas, and I'm sure I'd be part of that.'

Regaining momentum he gave a routine run-through of his use of a variety teaching techniques and resources, concluding with a more subjective note. 'What I try to do is to keep a working dialogue going with all students or as many as possible. There are many ways of doing that. Face-to-face is usually best but I use whatever means seems appropriate to the student or students in question.' Again he had the odd sensation that although his comments were sincere, they felt strained and even false. Momentarily distracted by this thought he barely noticed the Dean bringing Erica Botham in.

Her tone was prickly and challenging. 'Dr Connor, that all sounds quite plausible but I'd like to return to the issue of gender, have you considered that teaching itself might be a gendered activity? And, if so, how do you respond to that?'

So far Erica Botham had been up-staged by her more substantial and (Tim assumed) senior colleague. He focused fully on her for the first time. Despite her attempt to adopt an impersonal, business-like persona, he found it impossible not to notice she was startlingly beautiful. This was a Bridgitte Bardot, an Ana Ivanovich moment. The film or the game of tennis becomes subsidiary even irrelevant in the face of the overwhelming beauty of the performer. Despite himself, what gripped him about Erica Botham was not her question but Erica Botham herself. It got worse. From a remote part of his over-stimulated mind sprang an image of her dancing in a swirl of diaphanous veils with no under-cover back up. He was in severe danger of becoming terminally distracted. Mercifully his instinct for survival asserted itself and he managed a shot at answering what he thought might be her question. He battled on as the surreal image lingered. 'A gendered activity? Of course. Most activities are. I aim for a balance of involvement from both sexes. I mean all genders,' he said, swiftly rephrasing to avoid any offence to the two women who he suddenly and for no apparent reason intuited might be lesbians.

Unconvinced by this piece of bland twaddle, Erica Botham was poised to launch a follow-up question when Howard Swankie interrupted.

'Thank you Ms. Botham, I think Dr Connor has given us a pretty good impression of where he's coming from as far as gender is concerned.' He paused for a moment, fixing Tim with a searching expression.

'As Chair I want to ask him just one question arising from his earlier comments on political violence. Dr. Connor do you have a view about the use of political violence in mature democracies? When it might be legitimate I mean. I wasn't quite clear from your earlier comments what your own view is?'

Stinking fish! He's still trying to catch me out. Best keep playing it straight.

'I don't think political violence is justified in a functioning democracy ... By which I mean a society where there is substantial freedom of expression. In various forms of autocracy, it might well be justified.'

'What about non-violent civil disobedience? Is that ever justified?

'Again it depends on the regime and the nature and extent of the grievances and repression. I see it as a last resort in democracies but more often justifiable in autocracies. Of course, the protester would have to take ...'

'The consequences ...' Swankie finished the sentence, sounding slightly relieved, Tim thought.

He knew he needed Swankie's vote but wasn't prepared

to hang his arse out for it. He assumed the women were a no-no, if not from the start, certainly by now. He had some rapport with the other two men but not much with Swankie. Maybe this was the moment to tilt for his support by showing he could compromise.

'I'm no brick-thrower, never have been. People have a responsibility as well as a right to negotiate and compromise.' Keen to secure his integrity he added 'but I do think individuals and groups also have a right to protest and, of course to self-defence if they are the victims rather than the perpetrators of violence.'

Swankie leant forward again, resting his chin heavily on his right fist. He gave Tim a long look, almost as if for the first time he was taking the idea of appointing him seriously.

'These are important questions and obviously we could all spend a long time on them. However, I think we've covered sufficient ground.'

He leaned back, opening his arms in a concluding gesture, as he addressed Tim directly. 'We hope to come to a decision within the next half-hour. You're quite welcome to wait outside if you wish and we'll let you know the outcome shortly or, if you prefer, Dr. Jones can call you later at home. That's something I would usually do but I have another pressing engagement late this afternoon.'

Tim preferred to learn his fate sooner rather than later. Waiting for the phone to ring with the result of a job interview was mini-torture undiminished by familiarity. And the moment of rejection never got any better. 'I'll wait, if that's ok.' He got up, still stiff with tension.

As he turned to leave, Henry Jones went to open the door for him.

'That's fine. Please, don't bother.'

'It's no bother.'

Tim caught a whiff of alcohol as he passed Jones. And was that a wink or an involuntary tick? 'Maybe he knows something I don't,' he thought optimistically. 'Or, maybe he's just pissed.'

Back in the anteroom he slumped onto the couch. No point sitting there for half-an-hour. He got up and walked over to the floor-to-ceiling Georgian windows. Beyond the new building blocks the countryside rolled fresh and green. His head cleared. As he relaxed, his biological needs temporarily parked, reasserted themselves.

I need to hit the pot. And get a cup of tea and a bun. He checked his watch. He had twenty minutes max, just about enough time.

Once back in the anteroom pessimism had set in. Aisha Khan seemed a virtual shoo-in, a perfect identikit fit for this job, whereas his own best pitch of 'rising young star' was well into its twilight. Not that he believed the job was a 'PC' fix – Aisha Khan didn't give the impression of needing unfair help.

His glum train of thought was broken by the sound of the interview room door opening. He looked up anxiously. Swankie was walking briskly towards him, his hand outstretched. 'Congratulations Connor, I'm glad to be able to offer you the post. I take it that you still intend to accept.'

Tim was momentarily disoriented by the Dean's words: life-changing for him. He barely remembered the shake-hands-firmly-to-show-what-a-strong-character-you-are rule as his big, clammy hand closed round Swankie's soft, manicured one. He confirmed his acceptance with a grateful croak.

'Excellent. You'll receive a formal offer in the post during the next few days. Shortly after that Henry Jones will be in touch with you to discuss academic matters. Feel free to contact me if ...' he checked himself, glancing quickly at his watch. 'So congratulations. You know where to pick up your expenses claim form.' With another swift handshake, he hurried off.

Tim's return journey to the station was a good deal pleasanter than his journey out. At this point he couldn't give a flying fuck how or why he'd got the job. So what if it was too late for them to re-advertise the post? At least he hadn't blown his interview. It must have been a 3-2 win for the boys he thought. Thank God he had managed to keep Swankie on side despite their lack of rapport. However it had come about, he was through the door. He felt a stab of concern for Aisha Khan, although he was sure she would get an academic job without the kind of the long wait he had experienced.

He celebrated by ordering a taxi back into town. After a mini pub-crawl he searched out a café where he could indulge in his favourite cream-tea. He wolfed down a plate of scones heavily stacked with cream and black current jam. A second quickly followed, the third he took his time over, savouring the moment. On the way to the station he stopped to knock back a couple of pints.

He spent much of the return journey in the train's tiny tin-box lavatory, his euphoria surfing waves of nausea and tsunamis of vomit. Not for a moment did he think it wasn't worth it!

Aisha Khan pressed the engage symbol on her mobile. For a few nervous moments she heard only the crackle of static. Swankie's cultured voice, straining to connect, broke through. 'Hello, am I speaking to Ms. Khan?'

'Yes, is that Professor Swankie?'

'Good, Swankie here. I'm delighted to be able to offer you a post as a lecturer in the Social Science Department. Can I take it that you accept?'

'Yes, of course, I'm so delighted. Thank you. I hadn't quite expected it.'

'You underestimate yourself. You interviewed exception-ally well. Every member of the panel was most impressed.'

The post-successful-interview phone call is not an equal exchange. Abject gratitude can plunge the newly anointed into spluttering incoherence. Having again expressed her delight, Aisha left it to Swankie to make the running.

'You'll shortly receive a formal offer including information about your salary. You're fortunate to live locally already – that will save you a lot of trouble, either moving house or commuting.'

'Yes, it's amazingly convenient to get the job I want so close to home.'

'Oh, I should say that in fact we made two appointments today. Dr. Connor is the other successful candidate although ...'

'I'm glad,' she interjected. '... he really seemed to want the job.'

'Yes. A second post became vacant after a colleague in the faculty received a late job offer – a promotion to another institution. So we're making a double-appointment. I expect Dr. Jones will want you to come in together at some point. But is there anything you want to ask me?'

Aisha was sure there was but her mind registered a complete blank. 'Not ... not just at the moment, thanks.'

'Well, given that you live so close by, do come in and see me some time before you start if there is anything you want to discuss. You can make an appointment through my secretary.'

'Thank you, that's very helpful.'

'Not at all. I'm sure you'll find everyone will be very supportive. We realise this is a big change in your life.'

Swankie continued on another tack. 'Oh, and, yes, the social scientists along with the rest of the faculty will be having a get-together, a party, just before term begins. You'll get an invitation to that.'

'Thank you,' she said. 'I'll really look forward to meeting other colleagues.'

'Well, congratulations again. As I said, feel free to get in touch with Henry Jones or myself if you have any queries. You're sure there's nothing you want to ask now?'

'No, I don't think so. Thank you.'

'Goodbye for now then.'

'Goodbye.'

'Yeeeeeeeeeeeeees,' Aisha shouted as she triple-pirouetted across the grass, brown legs flashing as her pleated skirt whirled waist high.

'Yeeeeeeeeeeeeeees... Ahhhhhhhhhhhhhhh,' jubilation turned to panic as she tumbled into a nest of nettles.

Brought back to earth she carefully extricated herself.

Who should she share her news with first? With Waqar? Not yet. Best start with Caroline, her best friend and owner of the small pre-school play group that Ali attended. Caroline would share her delight. Caroline had supported her all the way.

Her mobile was still on. She brought up and pressed Caroline's number.

'Caroline, hi. Guess what!'

'What? Tell me. Did you get the job? You didn't.'

'Guess.'

'You did!'

'Yeah ... I've just had a phone call offering it me. I turned it down of course.'

'You're joking.'

'You bet I'm joking.'

'Whowee... Well done, What a genius! Come over. We must celebrate. I'll buy us something special at that new place in Cathedral Square. You know the one. We went there a couple of weeks ago. I'll bring Ali with me, it'll save you having to pick him up. Most of the other kids have already gone home by now. Look, I'll finish up quickly and see you in about forty-five minutes. Is that good for you?'

'That's great, no problem. See you then.'

Aisha made her way back to the road and decided to call Waqar.'

'Waqar, Darling.'

'Aisha, petal-dust! How did it go? Have I finally lost my wife to the world of education or are you still all mine?'

'I'm still all yours but ...' she hesitated slightly. 'Yep, I got the job.'

'Fantastic, my brilliant baby.' Aisha could catch no sign of ambivalence in Waqar's voice. Maybe he was on side, after all. He continued to effuse.

'Look, I'll get home early tonight. Seven to seven thirty. We need to talk ... to celebrate. Make sure Ali is in bed. I'll bring in something from one of the restaurants so you don't have to cook...one of your favourites...'

There was a brief pause before he continued in his more familiar, busy man tone.

'Listen, I have to go now. It looks like there's been some embezzlement at one of the restaurants and I want to crack it without involving the police. Unfortunately it's happened at one of our London places. That's where I am now. Um... I guess seven thirty will be a bit tight, maybe eight o' clock? Anyway, well done, darling. I'll phone when I'm on my way back. We'll talk later. Bye for now then.'

'Bye, Waqar see you soon, miss you.' 'Soon' was more in hope than expectation.

Typical Waqar; always up to his eyeballs in his own concerns. Softening she decided that maybe she was being unfair. In his own way he cared. Still on a high, she left unacknowledged the whisper of worry about the way their relationship was going.

Caroline and Ali and Caroline's child Danny were already in Cathedral Square when she arrived. She saw them before they saw her. They were punting an inflated multicoloured ball between them. She paused briefly to watch. Ali doggedly ignoring the drag of his leg brace was just managing to keep up with the others. For a moment he stumbled. Danny rushed to steady him. Caroline moved over, smothering the two four year olds in a giant hug. Sweet Caroline more like a sister than a friend; better than a sister, because there was no sibling or any other kind of rivalry between them.

Caroline was a British-African who still had family in Northern Nigeria and like Aisha, a Muslim. They had met on an Access course some years ago and remained friends since. Aisha had supported Caroline through a fraught marriage and divorce, since when they had become close confidants. Caroline's energy and optimism in opening a pre-school play group had been part of Aisha's inspiration to pursue a career herself. She was glad to be sharing this moment with her.

'Hi, you guys,' she announced herself.

'Aisha!'

'Mummy!'

The three of them rushed over, almost bundling her to the floor as they bounced into her.

'Your mum's a hero, a star, Ali,' shouted Caroline.

'I know! Will you buy us an ice cream Mum? Caroline said we had to wait for you.'

They found a table and began their small celebration. The boys were not quite sure why it was a double helpings day but weren't asking questions. Aisha and Caroline enjoyed a rare bottle of champagne, quashing their residual religious scruples.

'I'm sure Allah will understand,' suggested Caroline.

'I think so,' replied Aisha who in any case indulged from time to time.

If life wasn't quite perfect it had definitely taken a leap in the perfect direction.

Chapter 3
Goodbye, Hello

Once he had recovered from his hangover Tim enjoyed his remaining time at Peyton College. The perennial schadenfreude of some of his colleagues at his struggle to break into higher education evaporated as they adopted the new wisdom that really he was better suited to that sector. Most were pleased for him and most of the few who weren't pretended to be. In an increasingly competitive and stressful working environment, he was not universally loved but he had made few real enemies.

Some mild speculation hung on about why he had found it so difficult to crack higher education. He was better qualified and published than many successful candidates, although the increasing flood of youthful PhDs onto the job market raised the entry bar year by year. His own opinion was that the problem was mainly an image one: he was too easily labelled as 'potentially troublesome' at a time when university managers were increasingly wary of trouble. This was not merely a defensive response on his part; his handful of published writings were radical. Out of conviction but also for clarity, he had stated even in his first publication, an introductory psychology textbook, that his beliefs were libertarian and progressive. This was not likely to improve his career prospects. At a time of financial cuts, universities were more likely to appoint staff that would generate income, typically by winning research grants than someone who believed in democratic reform, inclusive of the higher education system. There was no necessary conspiracy about it. There was no need for one. The new finance-driven culture was soon embedded as 'common sense'. The pressure was to make safe and manageable appointments. Nobody would apply those adjectives to him. Even an open testimonial from a former tutor did no better than describe him as 'a risk, although possibly a risk worth taking.'

Despite his strong self-belief, serial rejection sparked occasional paranoia. He began to wonder if even his physical appearance counted against him. At a big-boned, slightly cumbersome six-foot three he looked and moved more like a building site worker than an academic. His interview outfits rarely met expectations that were becoming more standardised as higher education succumbed to the corporate ethos. At eighteen he had reluctantly acquired a suit for his university selection interview and had worn it for interviews ever since. Job interviews in higher education are not fashion parades, but this item, made of ninety-five per cent acrylic, did attract attention. When he sat down the trouser legs would shoot up to his calves while his hairy forearms protruded several inches out of the jacket sleeves. This distracting arms and leg show had probably cost him most of the jobs he had applied for, even before he opened his mouth. Topped off by a sweep of long black hair and usually sporting a pair of leather boots at the other end, he invited the killer observation that 'I think we're all agreed that Dr Connor is not quite what we're looking for.' Doggedly and with only a twinge of self-doubt, Dr Connor disagreed. He wanted prospective employers to know what they were getting. And he sensed that if he tried to please 'the suits' by attempting to look like them he would soon start to think like them as well. His was a perverse kind of integrity but finally luck had sprung him from a catch twenty-two of his own making.

One of the traditional farewell rituals for staff leaving Peyton College was a one-to-one glass of wine with the Principal Tom Gardner and another was a night out with colleagues at a local pub. Tom Gardner had enough personal strength and vision to make the progressive regime he had introduced at the college work well. Even so he was feeling increasingly constrained by the stream of relentless government initiatives. He could see no end to them; whichever party won the next election. At over sixty he was beginning to find that looking backwards offered a pleasanter view than looking forward – a sure sign, as he well recognised, that it was time to go.

A bottle of red wine and two glasses were already on the coffee table in the corner of Tom Gardner's office as he welcomed Tim. 'Sit down. And congratulations! We're sorry to lose you but I know from several references I've written for you over recent years that it's what you want. Here, have a last glass of wine at the college's expense.' He poured a glass of Malbec and passed it over. 'Have some salted nuts as well if you want. I don't eat them myself. They get stuck in my teeth.' He sat down across the table from Tim.

'Thanks. That's right. I've always liked the idea of working in an academic environment. Also I need a change. I've enjoyed this place but I wouldn't fancy being here for the next twenty-five years.'

'You're lucky that you've been able to make a change. You'd be surprised how many people here have tried to move on and not been able to, especially older colleagues, the younger ones do usually find it a bit easier. Anyway I'm glad you got the job.'

Gardner paused, getting up from his chair he walked over to his office window. He gazed out thoughtfully, ignoring by dint of long habit the grey expanse of the staff car park.

'Actually I thought of moving on myself a few years ago but it's not easy to get a good promotion outside of this sector and there are few better jobs than mine within it. Most of the higher-paid jobs are in national or local educational bureaucracies and these days they don't seem to be appointing progressives of my ilk.'

Tim listened in mild surprise. He'd come to regard Tom Gardner as a permanent and essential fixture at the college, almost as a part of its foundations. It hadn't occurred to him that Gardner too might feel career blocked. He left his seat and joined his senior colleague at the window, a gesture of egalitarian solidarity he would have hesitated to make on any previous occasion. Allergic to hierarchy he nevertheless respected this man's personal authority as well as his achievement in establishing a liberal educational regime in contrary times. 'I doubt that I'll work under such an enlightened boss again. Not many would have given me the opportunity to develop that you did ten, almost fifteen years ago.'

'I don't know about that but times are changing, as they always do,' said Gardner. 'The pressure is to produce results and to a prescribed format. There isn't the scope now to shape things according to your own vision.' Glancing at Tim he added 'I should warn you that's also becoming the case in higher education as well.' Then dropping the serious tone he looked directly at Tim and grinned. 'So, don't imagine you're going to escape into an ivory tower paradise, young man.'

The conversation moved briefly to more personal matters. Gardner expressed concern about the break-up of Tim's long-term relationship but didn't want to pry. He suggested that once Tim was established in his new job he might come back to explain the mysteries of higher education to the college's students. They drained their glasses in unison, shook hands and said a warm goodbye.

The farewell booze-up was on the last day of term. *The Highwayman* rocked as excited voices competed against the thudding music. A premiership game between Manchester United and Liverpool showing on the pub's giant television screen added to the hubbub. Tim was sat with a group of sports-types who had launched into a rowdy argument about which of the two teams had the best claim to the nickname of 'The Reds'. A chunky northern émigré, the college's first team goalkeeper, offered an opinion:

'Whichever one of them but not those clowns down the road.'

'And who might they be?' This came from an indignant-looking female student wearing an Arsenal shirt.

'Depends which way you're facing: Southend to the East or the Arses the other way.'

'Stop insulting my favourite team! Arsenal is called after guns not bums. As for Southend United, they don't count. People only watch them when they want a break from football.'

A sudden roar swamped their conversation. The group's attention swung to the big screen as a dubious penalty was awarded to the Manchester side, a regular occurrence at Old Trafford. Tim's attention was distracted from the kick as someone pushed a fourth pint into his hand. He looked up. It was from Ted Sidebottom, the bluff, diminutive Head of Physical Education.

Tim's attention was drawn back to the screen as the crowd erupted again, divided by reactions of pain or relief as the ball smacked against the crossbar and sailed impotently into the stand. Tim was in the relieved camp. There was a riff of laughter as the camera caught United's managers hopping about apoplectically in the technical area.

Grinning Tim turned again to Ted. 'Hey, Ted, I haven't finished this pint yet.' He gestured towards a half-empty glass. 'I don't want to get too blotto, I'm on my way tomorrow.'

'Come on … I've bought it for you now. It'll soon disappear down a big lad like you. You'll be as fresh as a daffodil tomorrow.'

'Daisy'

'You're no daisy.'

'I'm no ... Listen this is a silly discussion. Sit down for a minute and say something sensible to me.' He turned to the students. 'Can someone give their chair to Ted for a few minutes so we can have a chat?'

The young Arsenal supporter got up and perched herself on the knee of an athletic looking mixed race guy. 'You don't mind do you?' He didn't. 'No problem, stay as long as you like,' he said shifting her into a more central position on his lap.

Ted was the physical opposite of Tim who on balance was glad things had turned out the way they had. He was barely five foot six, bandy legged and bald in the style of Bobby Charlton. But he was strong and nimble with low centre of gravity that enabled him to bustle past opponents when playing his favourite game of hockey. Unfortunately Ted failed to recognise his inability to achieve a similar level of performance at football by far the most popular sport at the college. He was as bad at football as he was good at hockey. Therein lay the cause of a recurrent clash with Tim. Bizarrely Ted fancied himself as a striker, countering the fact that he almost never scored with claims that he was a creative fulcrum responsible for numerous assists. Mysteriously these remained unobserved by others. Tim also preferred to play striker and had a decent goal tally. Crucially Ted picked the staff-student team that played in a regional league. Faced with their comparative goal statistics Ted had little choice but to play Tim as striker. That was until the team got hammered, physically as well as in the score-line, by Thunderstone Police. Ted saw his opportunity, blamed Tim for the defeat and dropped him from the squad. He moved himself to striker from his previous position that he described as 'libero' and from which he had orchestrated havoc for the rest of the team. Wherever Ted played, it seemed impossible that he could inflict even more damage on the team. This proved not to be the case. The change of position precipitated a ten-match losing streak in which Ted scored one goal, a world-class header that left his own goalkeeper helpless. Frank opinions were exchanged during and after this match. Finally Ted announced that he would give Tim 'another opportunity'. The next game was a 1-0 victory in which the proud goal-scorer was Ted. Never mind that the ball had cannoned off his backside from a defender's clearance. 'Told you so,' he said, 'I saw it all the way'.

A minor source of needle between Tim and Ted was about the correct pronunciation of Ted's surname, Sidebottom. Ted insisted that the correct pronunciation required the separate enunciation of four syllables: thus, 'Sid'-'e'-'Bot'-'tom'. Tim refused to oblige. In the spirit of taking the piss he usually pronounced the 'Side' and 'Bottom' parts of Ted's unfortunate name separately. He insisted that this was the only sensible pronunciation. By serendipity this pronunciation evoked Ted's oddly lateral gait, no doubt caused by constant stooping to connect with a myriad of hockey pucks. The two men never quite resolved this matter although Tim eventually conceded that Ted had a right to have his name pronounced as he wished however ridiculous it might sound.

In a mood of putting past differences aside, Ted had approached Tim. Well tanked up he was in expansive mood, his Yorkshire accent even more pronounced than usual, 'Ye know Tim, you're not such a bad bugger as ye crack on.'

Always ready to listen to an opinion about him-self for good or bad, Tim encouraged Ted to go on.

'How's that then, Ted? I've didn't realise you'd become one of my fans.'

'No, ye're right there. I 'aven't. Ye can be a bit of a tart. I mean why are ye leaving yer Gina and yer young daughter. Everybody likes Gina, ye know.'

'Listen Ted, you don't know what happened between us ... As a matter of fact ...' Tim was about to defend himself when Ted backtracked.

'Look ... sorry ... I came over to pay ye a compliment, not to criticise.'

'Ok. Go ahead?'

'Right ... The truth is that the reason why ye get sum flack is that a lot of the guys envy ye a bit. Not in a nasty way, though it can come out like that. I mean you're a free floater. The system doesn't seem to have grabbed as much of ye as it has of sum of uz. Ye do what most of uz only think about doing, if that. Ye write books, seem to pull attractive women, and instead of serving yer life-sentence out 'ere like the rest of uz idiots ye go and get a job in 'igher education. That's what I mean, yer not afraid to be different, ye go yer own way and show it can be done.'

Tim looked at Ted in surprise. The half-cock eulogy seemed genuine enough. It hadn't occurred to him that the jocks among his colleagues might subliminally admire and envy him. It had taken Ted in a mood of drunken reflection to work it out. In so far as Tim thought about the jocks at all, he took them pretty much at face value. He had never aspired to be one of them, gathering to play cards at break time or getting pissed together when they could get collective dispensation from their wives. They took his demeanour and life-style as an implicit rejection of their own. In response they were often jocularly aggressive towards him. Occasionally this triggered a frisson of irritation, but that was a small price to pay to maintain the identity boundary. He tagged them 'the fat table' and to them he was 'a bit of a weirdo'. It came as a shock that he might be their subterranean role model. But he enjoyed the irony of it and even felt slightly flattered.

'Your wife's just come in Tim,' a voice shouted above the noise.

Ted lurched to his feet. He spun forward, almost landing in Tim's lap as he attempted to clap him across the shoulder. 'That's it, sunshine. Enjoy the rest of yer life. Look after those ye're supposed to.'

'Thanks, you too.' Tim's attention turned towards the disembodied voice.

'I doubt if she still believes she *is* my wife.'

'Partner, then.'

'I haven't got one of them either, ex-partner. Where is she?'

He looked towards the pub entrance. Standing up he spotted Gina's head of curls bobbing through the crowd.

'Relax, man, she's heading your way.' The disembodied voice again.

Tim waved, hoping Gina would pick him out.

'Gina, over here,' he shouted into the crowd.

He caught sight of her, as she returned his wave followed by a hand-signal that he interpreted to mean that she was pausing to exchange a few words with friends. *Keeping me on a string even tonight.* Gina always dressed smartly even on less formal occasions. Physically she benefited from her mixed race heritage of African, French and Portuguese. The colourful clothes she liked to wear enhanced the sheen of her light coffee-coloured skin. Tonight she had put on a favourite blue satin dress matched with shiny maroon heels. As usual she wore several bracelets and more rings than Tim had ever bothered to count, her lean bare arms catching the gleam of silver and gold. A thin chain bracelet accentuated the fineness of her ankles.

Finally she reached him. With difficulty she resisted his usual smothering embrace. Now that their relationship was over, she was determined to maintain her distance. She kissed him lightly on the cheek and gently pushed him away. He looked crestfallen.

'Tim, are you ok? You look a bit drunk.' She was already adopting what had become her default tone of concerned disapproval.

'Well, this is my official send-off so I'm allowed to get pissed. Anyway, thanks for making the effort to come. I guess that you got Joy in to look after Maria. Let me pay for that. What can I get you to drink?'

'Tim, I'm aware it's your send-off. That's why I'm here. Don't worry about the child minding, it gets done on an exchange of favour basis. I thought you knew that.' She paused for a moment, scanning the crowded pub. 'They've really turned out for you. You must be more popular than you think,' she added partly reassuring, partly teasing.

'Not really, it's not just for me. Don't forget it's the end of term. Anyway, you haven't said what you want to drink.'

'I'll have a glass of red wine, just one drink. It looks like I might be driving you back – to your digs that is, not home,' she added, keen to avoid any ambiguity.

They had promised each other not to argue about their relationship problems tonight. This was not the time or place. There was much that was unresolved between them, far more than they yet recognised. They had blundered into a break-up through a series of mistakes and failures of communication. Who was wronged and who was guilty remained ambiguous as they spiralled downwards into chronic mistrust. Gina had become convinced that Tim was having a full-blown affair with a woman he had met at a conference. He swore that what had happened was a romantic flirtation that both parties had decided to pull back from. But self-indulgently and confusingly for Gina he kept open the possibility of further involvement in the weeks following the conference. Gina tried to believe his protestations that it was 'just a friendship' but was eventually unconvinced. The messages she read on his mobile were not conclusive but to her they indicated something more than 'just friendship.' Insecure and unsure of him she began to distance herself.

As the atmosphere in the home began to tighten, their decision to hide their rift from their daughter Maria rebounded. Maria began to pick up on the suppressed emotion and double-entendres. Formerly an easy child she was becoming anxious and demanding. Both parents agreed that they needed to resolve the situation for her sake. They tried to restore trust in their own communication. But distrust had caught hold of the relationship like a virus in the blood.

With the ties of commitment beginning to fray Gina found herself half responding to the persistent attentions of a slightly younger man she regularly came across in her role as a delegate to the regional committee of the National Union of Teachers. His intelligence and charm offered some respite from her disillusionment and loneliness as well as a change from Tim's less polished style. Their occasional drinks after meetings became more frequent and eventually developed into a habit she looked forward to. At the umpteenth time of his asking she agreed to sleep with him.

At first it was Gina's need for comfort and reassurance that drew her into the relationship, but it slowly became more serious. She had never been able to separate sex from attachment. Nor on this occasion could her lover. They carved out opportunities to meet, but with a child to manage Gina found it difficult to hide it all from Tim, particularly as he usually looked after Maria in her absence. In any case Gina was unconvincing in deceit and unconvinced that she should allow herself to deceive. The gathering tension between them detonated into a fierce row ending in an out-of-control spillage of hurtful information and declarations on both sides that things had become unbearable. Gina announced that she didn't think she still loved Tim and now had a new partner who she intended to try and make a go of things with. Angry and upset, Tim's reaction was confused. He continued to deny that he had slept with 'his friend from the conference'. He implored Gina to 'stop playing the blame-game' and insisted that he still loved her. Gina simply did not believe him.

It was the damage they feared they were inflicting on Maria that finally convinced them that they had to separate. Gina was a step ahead of Tim, asking him to move out and insisting that of course Maria was going to remain with her. Dispirited, he agreed to go, provided that he was given an absolute guarantee that he could visit Maria regularly. Gina saw no problem with that but insisted on access being properly organised. Emotionally drained, they struggled to shift from six years of love and intimacy into a workable separation. Their moods swinging between anger and regret, at times they spontaneously reached out to comfort each other... *Please don't tell me this is how the story ends.* But this was only the beginning of it. They would go through these emotions many times before they could feel that the break was real. And still the pain of loss would linger.

For years the idea of Tim getting a new job was to have been a change for the family, a shared adventure and a new beginning. He had not quite given up that hope following his successful interview. But now he faced the prospect of a lonely exile.

Tim handed Gina the glass of red wine she had asked for. He looked at her thoughtfully for a few moments. There was something he wanted to get off his chest.

'I know that I said goodbye to Maria earlier today but I'd like to see her one more time before I go. I'm off early tomorrow so I won't be able to see her then. What about me taking a peek at her tonight?'

Gina hesitated.

He persisted. 'Last night favour.'

She continued to look reluctant.

'Please. She's my daughter.'

Still doubtful she agreed. 'Ok, but it's nearly ten already. You'll have to slip quietly into her bedroom. We'll have to leave as soon as we've finished our drinks.'

Back at the house he could no longer call it his home, he slipped quietly into his daughter's bedroom. As usual she had pulled the duvet up over her face. Only her mouth and nose poked out. He lifted the cover. She was a perfect replica of her mother, apart from the wide sensual bow of the mouth that was his. Her eyes opened, wide and surprised. Her lips flickered into a soft smile of recognition.

'Bye Maria, see you soon.'

'Bye Daddy, love you.' Her eyes closed and she was asleep again.

'I love you, too' he murmured.

Downstairs Gina had just closed the door on the childminder.

'I suppose I had better offer you a cup of tea.'

'I'd prefer something else.'

She looked at him sceptically.

'And what might that be?'

'A goodbye present … maybe.'

Gina was used to his habit of reverting to basics in matters of sex. 'Idiot, Rupert is moving in tomorrow. '

'I know but … he's not here now.'

'No chance.'

'Maybe you could take me in hand, as it were.'

She stared at him astonished, but impressed despite herself.

The decision hung in the balance for several moments.

'Open your trouser zip.'

His hands trembled as he did so.

She pulled his cock out, teasing it until it was ripe and firm.'

Kneeling down, she took it in her mouth, sucking it rhythmically as she manipulated his balls. Her teeth closed around the head of his cock. For a moment he feared the worst as she played the groove between pain and pleasure. Then pure sensation took over.

He exploded like Vesuvius on Speed. She joined in the wild laughter of his release. Reaching for a tissue she wiped the remaining semen from his cock. He leaned heavily against the kitchen wall, sated, tension gone. She stood up and they embraced and kissed gently.

'Strange man you are.'

He smiled down at her through half-closed eyes. 'Not really, we're all like this, we men.'

'Not quite, some men make love before they make sex. Or even at the same time.'

He winced and she regretted her remark. But she couldn't believe what she had been persuaded to do.

'Look, you must go. This isn't sensible. I can't drive you back now. It's still warm outside ... the walk will clear your head.'

She steered him towards the front door. He turned to kiss her goodbye. Instead she pressed her forefinger to his mouth. 'Be good, and call us when you get there. Maria will miss you.'

'And you?'

She gave a wistful smile as she opened the door. 'Who knows,' she said, as he stepped outside.

Chapter 4
Out of the Frying Pan

Tim looked closely at the possibility of commuting from Peyton to Wash but the distance was too great. His temporary accommodation in Peyton, little more than a glorified B and B, offered no long-term appeal. It was obvious that once work got underway he would have to move into Wash or close to it. Wash University provided him with a list of local rented accommodation and within two days of checking out of his digs, he had signed a three-month lease on a first floor flat in the restored Georgian terrace of Calcott Place. It was located in the Western part of the city, about a mile south of the River Wash. A short lease suited his plans. He hoped to be able to raise a mortgage on a small house, made possible by the salary hike from his new job. It would stretch his finances, but he wanted the freedom of owning his own property as well as the possibility of a long-term profitable investment. And he planned to have his daughter over to stay, if not her mother.

The flat consisted of a tiny entrance hall, two large square rooms - a living room and a bedroom, both painted in plain white, a small kitchen and even smaller bathroom. The walls of the main rooms were decorated with cornices that were clearly recent additions, possibly replacing originals. He noted the large king-size wooden bed with approval. It was more than big enough for his lanky frame and better than what he had recently been used to. The living room overlooked a main street separated from the block of flats by a surprisingly broad terrace that softened the traffic noise to a murmur. 'Pretty good for now,' he concluded.

Once he had sorted out short-term accommodation he responded to an invitation from Henry Jones to meet. There was no response to his call to Henry's mobile, so he tried the house phone. His call was answered by a sharp female voice that he took to be Henry's wife.

'I'll get him,' an irritated staccato. The phone clattered down before he had time to give his name.

Henry's voice came on, friendly through the catarrh. 'Tim, good to hear from you. So, you're down here. When can we meet up?'

'Yeah, I've fixed up a place to live … temporarily … from next month. I'm free to get together whenever it suits you, anytime in the next couple of days. Where do you want to meet?'

He was not surprised when Henry suggested a pub.

'Why don't we kick off with a drink? There's a pub with decent ale down by the river, the *Mitre*. It's easy to get to. Let me give you the best route. Get onto the footpath by the riverbank just below the Cathedral and then walk westwards. It's about quarter of a mile from there, just back from the river. We could meet today. How about in a couple of hours, say four-o'-clock?'

'Fine. Do you want me to bring anything … any notes for modules that I might introduce?

'You could do. All you really need is a notebook or a diary. To be honest we're so near the start of term that you'll have to teach to the existing curriculum. But we can talk about all this later. So, see you in the *Mitre* at four.'

'See you then. Cheers.'

The *Mitre* turned out to be an old Tudor-style pub, with an open forecourt that extended to the river pathway. The battered timber of its outer shell looked original. The interior clearly was not, although the low wooden roof beams and wall paintings of rural scenes were a decent stab at retrieving tradition. Hampered by the low-key lighting and thick support columns Tim struggled to pick out Henry. Finally his attention was caught by the flapping of a newspaper to the accompaniment of assorted incoherent noises.

'Hey ... ay ... ere ... hey.'

Behind the newspaper was Henry. Two pints of bitter were already on the table. One was half empty, the other untouched. Tim greeted his new Head of Department.

'Hi. Nice pub but not the easiest of places to find someone in. I guess this pint is for me unless you're drinking two at a time.' Tim grinned at his own chancy humour but nothing about Henry suggested the need for formalities. He sat down opposite him.

'It's yours. Yeah it is a bit dark inside, but I like that. You found this place easily enough then?'

'No problem. It was only when I got inside that I got lost. Is this your regular watering hole?'

'One of many.' Without too much difficulty Henry adopted an expression of mock decadence. 'And before you get too comfortable, why don't you bring in your round? I'm about done with this pint,' he picked up his glass, emptying it with a gulp.

It soon became obvious that Henry had no intention of providing Tim with a detailed job description. He pushed a timetable across the table, mentioning that he had left most of Thursday blank so that Tim could continue with his research. That was more or less it. What he really wanted to talk about emerged soon enough.

'You know, I don't usually talk about job interviews; why somebody gets a job or not I mean, but in this case it's a bit different. You need to know how the wheels of power

and decision making turn in our small world. You've probably worked out how the panel split, anyway.' He glanced
at Tim, gauging his reaction. 'You don't mind me talking
about this? I suppose it is a bit unethical but I don't always
go by the rulebook; there are so many rules and procedures
these days I don't even know most of them. Anyway more
was going on in that panel than just straight interviews.'

'Really? Go ahead, feel free. I'm no ritual conformist
myself. Some rules do more harm than good.' He checked
himself. It was a bit early in his career at Wash to start
unloading his opinions. And he was more interested in
hearing what Henry had to say. 'Fire away I'd be interested
to know what kind of impression I made on the panel.'

'Good point, you're entitled to a feedback session. This is
it. Straight and above-board. The two women, well, originally it was only Steir on the panel with the other three of
us. But she insisted on another woman - a fair gender balance she called it. In fact she wanted three and three but
Swankie refused to set a precedent. But he caved in to the
extent of letting her bring her mate along. As it turned out
the two women wanted to block your appointment. It was
mainly Steir. They might have got their way if Aisha Khan
hadn't already been appointed. They were determined that
a woman should be successful.'

'Regardless of merit?' Tim was sceptical.

'Well, they seem to see more merit in women than men.'
He hesitated for a moment, uncertain that Tim was on side.
'You need to understand they want to take over the subject. They've been moved from the Ridgewell site to Green
Park. The college is being re-structured, at least that's what
they call it since it got university status. They ran Social Sci-
ences at Ridgewell but it got closed down. Lack of numbers,
I'm not surprised. Rachel Steir treated the students like they
were school kids. Everything was regimented and over-or-
ganised. She's trying to do the same thing at our site. Over
my dead body! Erica Botham is more open-minded but she
usually goes along with Steir. In the end the students voted

with their feet. Some of them decamped to our place. Steir says that the drop in numbers was because they'd exhausted local demand. I think that's BS.'

By now Tim was uneasy at Henry's vehement and no doubt biased account of departmental politics.

'You guys don't seem to get along that well,' he said hoping Henry would change tack.

Undeterred Henry carried on in the same vein for several minutes. Tim couldn't tell whether he was genuinely threatened or paranoid. He was an odd mixture of vulnerability and belligerence. He'd wait and see. He attempted to nudge Henry onto less emotive ground.

'What about the rest of the department? How many more full-timers are there?'

Henry took a moment to shift gears. 'Oh, sorry. I should have said. Just one apart from Aisha Khan that is - Toby Woods. But he's on an exchange this year. Normally you would be sharing an office with him. You'll like him when you meet him. He used to be in Human Resources but got out when it became more about resources and less about human beings. He was our only full-time psychologist. You take over part of his timetable in addition to your sociology. Toby's exchange is Brad Purfect, an American from the mid-West. I've only met him a couple of times. He talks a lot, seems a bit opinionated. He's says he's a Marxist but his thinking seems to stop with Lenin; a bit rigid maybe. Early days though, he'll probably loosen up.'

'Quite a small core staff, then?'

'Yeah, Swankie does a lecture a week, probably more to keep an eye on the rest of us than because he really wants to do any teaching. We've got several part-timers or 'visiting lecturers' as they're now called. The management seems to think a fancy name compensates for low salaries. Not their own salaries of course. They find reasons to keep increasing them.'

'Aren't you management?' Tim wanted to shift Henry from his attack-dog comfort zone.

'Management? There's management and 'management'. If you can call what I do management. I try to mitigate the damage done by the bloody bureaucracy. At my level I can still treat people as human beings. It's possible, easy for me to communicate with people individually. I actually know the people I'm dealing with.'

Henry tailed off and looked across at Tim. 'I hope to Christ you're not one of these new managerial types. I'm shafted if you are. That's not how you came across. And I read one of your articles. All that stuff about grass-roots democracy is right up my street.'

Tim felt more comfortable now the conversation had moved away from the personal stuff. 'No, you haven't mis-read me, at least not in that respect. I'm no managerialist. Definitely one of us not one of them.'

Henry's face lit up like a Hogmanay pumpkin.

'Let's drink to that, my round.'

Tim gazed thoughtfully at Henry as the old academic weaved an unsteady path to the bar. It was difficult to know what to make of him. He came across as a man of convic-tion yet also as a clapped out, gossipy old gonzo. Whatever else, he was clearly an alcoholic or so close that the distinc-tion wasn't worth making. Good judgement and reliability were unlikely to be among his salient qualities. Regardless, Tim found him perversely likeable.

Returning to his seat, Henry changed tack, revealing a still embattled intellectual behind the surface shambles. Abseiling on an alcohol-fuelled surge of inspiration, he talked with drunken fluency for the best part of an hour across a range of classical psychology and sociology, seem-ing to grow in coherence the more he drank. He then began to expound on his own political philosophy. Drinking more than usual, Tim's head began to spin as he found himself on the end of a seminar on popular democracy. Tim could see why Henry had been keen to appoint him; they shared simi-lar social and political views. If anything, Henry's ideas were sharper and more worked out, perhaps too much so for Tim who recoiled from anything suggestive of political dogma. Maybe Henry did too. Tim had not quite figured him out in terms of his political views or as a person. He didn't sound like a Marxist but more like some kind of radical democrat convinced that greater social equality won't happen without a massive extension of democracy into all parts of society. He used the phrase 'institutional democracy' several times to describe his belief that just about all major institutional areas of society should be 'run by the people.'

'So, you're a participatory democrat,' Tim interjected.

'It's more than that Tim. I believe that in their own interests the people should have decisive power, not merely participation in the main institutions that run the country; public and private. That's a step on the way to them getting a fair share of what's produced. Practical democracy, not just representative democracy would reduce the terrible inequality we're seeing across the globe; increasing inequality.'

He paused for a moment suddenly apologetic. 'But you know all that. I shouldn't keep rattling on.'

Tim found Henry's ideas interesting, but was conscious that the afternoon was melting away. He gave Henry a non-committal look. Henry took this as a cue to continue, arguing that the introduction of democracy beyond parliamentary and local government was necessary to control elites, and that once the majority of people had access to 'real power' they would surely use it to distribute wealth and resources more fairly. 'Liberty before equality' he concluded, 'and if we can get real liberty, equality will follow.'

Tim was becoming impressed with the intensity of Henry's conviction and decided to test him where it counts.

'So is that how you run your department?'

Henry was quick to reply. 'Firstly it's not my department, it's our department. No, it's not run in that way but only because Swankie won't allow it. If you're in a bureaucracy and you want to radically reform it like I did ... do,' he corrected himself, 'you have to bide your time to change things.

But I have to admit that I've spent too long biding my time. The opposition has taken over while I've been dreaming.' A shadow of regret crossed his face. He shrugged his shoulders, returning to the present. 'To be fair I think Rachel and Erica might like the idea of democratising the department and in fact the whole bloody place. Principles aside, it would reduce Swankie's influence and even mine, pitiful as it is. Rachel thinks I shouldn't be in the job anyway.'

Not wanting to return to the personal stuff, Tim decided it was time to go.

It was almost as an afterthought that Henry finally gave him a short briefing on teaching allocation for the coming year. The key information for Tim was that he would teach his specialism, the life course, as an option module, using psychological and sociological perspectives.

'I'll post a final version of the timetable to you,' Henry concluded. 'We can employ part-timers to cover any gaps. That's if they'll give us the money to pay for them. Otherwise we'll have to jam groups together. Efficiency savings they call it. They keep citing some piece of research supposedly showing that class size and learning outcomes don't even correlate. I've become highly suspicious of that phrase 'research studies show.' Tim was relieved that Henry had a basic plan for the delivery of the subject, however cobbled together it might be.

He turned down an offer to return home with Henry for a spot of tea or 'maybe a couple of whiskies,' making the excuse that he needed to chase up some books and buy a few domestic items in town. They shook hands and Tim left Henry to his paper and pints. 'Bloody Tories, it looks like they're going to cut everything in sight now that they've got in,' Henry mumbled into his paper as Tim left the pub.

In fact Tim did have things to do in town. Relaxed, he ambled back along the embankment. The late afternoon sunlight danced on the water and glowed mellow on the Bath-stone buildings. It all melded gently with his alcoholic high. He felt an urge to poetry. Nothing came. But 'this is not bad' he thought, 'it's pretty damn good.'

The centre of the city was lively. Street entertainers and traders, a few lingering tourists and some early returning students as well as shoppers swelled the streets and squares. Apart from a mild addiction to supermarket 'special offers' and 'bogofs', Tim was hardly an advertiser's image of a 'happy shopper.' Even the prospect of becoming a home-owner had failed to stimulate an interest in furniture and DIY products. He once joked that he had so little interest in the décor of his home – at the time a rented bed-sit – that he couldn't even remember the colour of the wallpaper, only to realise with a shock that this was actually the case. His indifference to consumption did not extend to books. He spent serious time in bookshops. He remembered notic-ing that one of the city's main streets, Miller Street, had a Waterstones and he headed off there.

As usual, he arrowed towards the Social Science section. Then came a J.P. Hartley moment as he checked the shelves for a copy of his own introductory textbook *Psychology for Everyone*. There was just one. Tim grunted in annoyance. He pulled the book from the shelves and placed it promi-nently on a display table. A lone copy was not encourag-ing. Three copies or more would suggest a decent level of demand. Less than three and he would collar a shop assis-tant and strongly recommend that a substantial order be made: at least a dozen. He would reassure the usually scep-tical assistant that sales would be brisk. In Wash he could be optimistic that this might happen. He intended to list the title under the 'Essential Texts' section of his module outlines ... *if you can only afford one or two books* ... His stu-dents would be beating a path to Waterstones in droves. He hoped.

He approached an assistant, a tall, spare young man who in his pale, hirsute way sported a passing resemblance to Che Guevara. Odd, Tim thought, how often young male bookshop assistants resemble Guevara.

'Scuse me, I'm a local lecturer. Do you mind if I recommend a couple of books you might order for my students?'

'No, no, we like suggestions from academics, it helps us in selecting stock. Please, go ahead.'

'I notice you've only got a single copy of Connor's excellent *Psychology for Everyone*. It's a book I intend to use as a core text. You might order a dozen or so copies of it. Oh yes, and could you order a few copies of Mills' classic *The Sociological Imagination?*'

Sub-Guevara looked surprised.

'*Psychology for Everyone,*' he repeated apparently struggling to recall the book. 'Ah, yes, I do know the title. It doesn't sell *that* well Sir. Are you fairly sure we will be able to move that kind of quantity? There's a text by, er... Harry Ambulance that's...'

'Ambulant,' Tim corrected him. 'Yes, I know that's popular but you're overstocked. I mean, you're well stocked with that already. Connor's text really is ...'

'Yes, it really is a useful book,' the voice came from behind Tim. He spun round. Instant embarrassment. It was Erica Botham.

'Oh, it's Erica Botham, isn't it? I'm... eh... just suggesting a couple of titles for my courses next term.'

'I noticed,' she smiled slightly mocking but not unfriendly. 'What else were you going to suggest besides your hero Mills' book and your own... er... blockbuster?'

'Well,' Tim spluttered his mind suddenly blank of any title. Erica Botham rescued him from further embarrassment.

'Listen, you're not the first author to push their own work. Make sure this guy has got your recommendations and then why don't we have a coffee? I was going to contact you anyway. It seems we're teaching on some of the same modules.'

'Don't worry. I've got the recommendations,' said the Guevara look-alike battling a smirk. Straightening his face he added brightly 'By the way, there's a coffee and cake shop upstairs.'

Tim was grateful to exit from the ludicrous situation he had created.

'I could use a coffee. Why don't we give upstairs a try?'

'Ok, let's do that. I know the place. It's a bit twee but quite pleasant.'

'I'll buy,' said Erica as they entered the coffee shop, 'why don't you grab that table by the window before it gets taken. What would you like?'

'A double espresso.'

'And a cake?'

'I feel more like a sausage roll if that's ok?'

'It's ok, but you look more like a cake.'

They both smiled, Tim ruefully fearing that Erica had decided that he was, indeed, a bit of a cake-head.

'A double espresso and sausage roll it is then.'

'Actually I could manage a couple of rolls.'

'Just this once, then,' her lips pouted in simulated disapproval.

Usually he preferred to take the initiative with women he was attracted to, but he found himself drawn in by the confident way Erica teased him and took control. It helped that she was every bit as beautiful as he remembered from his interview.

Tim watched her as she waited in the queue. Her physical impact aside, she seemed quite different than in the semi-paranoia of his interview. Then, she had come across as coldly beautiful, a not quite human, perfect replicant. Now she was engaging and weirdly enticing. Her hair, a pure, natural blond, was streaked pink and green to the nape of her neck from where, caught in a tight band, it cascaded half way down her back. It was so thick and glossy that Tim found himself wondering how it felt to touch. Her eyes were a light metallic blue under violet make-up. She wore a tight purple synthetic jacket and matching skirt.

The gleaming fabric stretched against the high points of her breasts and buttocks. *Christ Almighty that is a shape from heaven...* Lifting his gaze he found himself looking straight into her translucent eyes. She winked and smiled, her mouth a purple-painted rosebud on a bed of pearls.

She must know the effect she creates. His balls stirred appreciatively and his cock began to stiffen. Not now, he tapped the bulge in his trousers reprovingly, *not appropriate.* The response was stiffer still. He buttoned his jacket and shifted his chair further under the table in search of cover. He picked up the menu and began reading it with fierce concentration.

Erica made her way from the counter and placed the coffees, cake and sausage rolls on the table. 'We're lucky to get a table by the window. You can see most of Miller Street from here, right down to the cathedral.' She noticed that Tim appeared more interested in his sausage rolls than in the prime view of Miller Street. One carnal appetite had taken over from the other.

'You look like you're ready for those.'

'Yeah ... I had a couple of pints earlier on an empty stomach. Beer always makes me feel hungry. I met Henry Jones in the *Mitre* for a chat about next term's teaching. We didn't talk much about work but at least I got a rough outline of my timetable.'

'That sounds like Henry. He'd still be doing his teaching in the pub, like he did thirty Years ago, if he thought he could get away with it. He and Howard Swankie don't get on, as I'm sure you'll find out. Rumour has it that they got involved in a brawl a few years ago, but that was before Swankie was elevated to Dean,' she sounded disparaging about both men. 'Anyway I'll leave you to form your own impressions of your new colleagues.'

'By the way' she continued 'have you received one of these?'

She produced a large white envelope from her bag.

'What is it? No, I don't think so. Maybe it went to my old address in Peyton.'

'Well it's a surprise of a kind. It's a notification from Howard Swankie that he wants to meet with the Social Science team in week five. Usually the meeting with him is much closer to the end of term taking the form of a review of how the Social Science group has performed over the period. This seems a bit different. Maybe it's because of the two new appointments – you and Aisha Khan. And Rachel and I have only been at the Green Park site for a few months. So there's been a lot of change and maybe Swankie felt he had to give feed back earlier than usual. But maybe it's something else. I guess we'll just have to wait until later to find out. He must have something big on his mind to notify us so early.'

Taking this as a cue to change the subject, Tim waved the remnants of a sausage roll in the direction of the street.

'You're right about the view. You can see some of the most impressive sights of the city from here. It sure beats South Essex, at least the part I lived in. The A13 out of London passes through the armpit of the country. The other is the A12 which isn't much better. And it gets worse. Both roads end in Southend, home of candyfloss and permanently incontinent sea-gulls.'

Because of his recent family traumas Tim was keen to avoid too much personal chat with Erica and, for that matter, with other new colleagues. He was still feeling his way at Wash, finding out rather than giving out. In any case Erica seemed happy to do most of the talking, filling him in on some of the less obvious aspects of life in and around Wash. She showed no inclination to reveal anything about her current personal life, but it wasn't long before she began to talk quite openly about her life before Wash.

She was the only child of wealthy parents, her father a defence contractor and her mother a fashion journalist. Amongst their careers and moneymaking, they found little time for her. They also found little time for each other. Her father was often abroad setting up deals which he considered to be of the utmost urgency, and her mother was an obsessive participant in a London literary set of bohemian tendencies. Erica usually found herself at home with at best one or other parent, rarely both, and sometimes with only a paid minder.

Things changed as a result of an incident between herself and her father. She did not specify what exactly this was and Tim did not press her. He guessed that some kind of abuse was involved. The incident provoked a fierce row between her parents and precipitated the messy dismemberment of a long-dead marriage. By this time Erica was fourteen and when fully painted up, could pass for three or four years older. Her mother began to take her on a circuit of high living rather than leave her alone in the large house now occupied only by the two of them. This was no solution to either of their problems, expanding Erica's worldly experience at the expense of her stability and education, and hampering her mother's increasingly frenetic and hedonistic lifestyle. Her father for once intervened effectively and stumped up the money for a Catholic boarding school, Catholicism being his nominal religion.

Surprisingly, the school worked out quite well for Erica. She had emerged from the rough waters of her sink or swim childhood with a maturity that was not mere precocity. Amongst the other girls she was a leader, on one occasion successfully organising a protest against the school's attempt to extend 'out of bounds' to include the nearby village, that sixth formers had previously been allowed to visit without a 'chaperone.' By the time she was in her final year she had passed well beyond the influence of the nuns. When she was discovered in bed with another girl in what the nuns coyly described as 'suspicious circumstances' she was asked to leave, but with the concession that she could return to sit her 'A' levels the following summer. Her results were exceptionally good.

Deliberately choosing not to go to a traditional university Erica opted to apply for and got accepted at Oxford's modern university of Oxford Brookes. It proved the better choice. She graduated with a first and followed it up with an M.Phil at the same institution. After that she took a year out to travel and write. On the strength of a couple of pieces in national newspapers on gender relations in pre-modern cultures and one well received academic article, Rachel invited her to apply for a job at Wash. Erica was already aware of the emerging feminist group there and this was a major reason in persuading her to apply. The job was formally advertised but the process was essentially a head-hunting exercise and she was duly appointed.

As Erica and Tim talked, an undercurrent of mutual attraction began to develop. At least Tim felt it was mutual and in matters of sex and love he usually trusted his feelings despite recent discouraging outcomes. As they concluded their conversation, Erica gave a hint that her interest in him might extend beyond his literary achievements.

'You must come round to dinner sometime after you've settled in. Maybe I'll invite one or two other colleagues as well.' She gave an arch smile. 'But maybe not.'

Tim wasn't quite clear whether 'maybe not' referred to his invitation or to the colleagues'. He preferred to go with the second interpretation.

They said goodbye outside Waterstones. His inhibitions lowered by alcohol, Tim felt an urge for physical contact. He could risk no more than a handshake. To his surprise Erica took his outstretched hand, raised it to her lilac lips and slowly and he thought sensuously kissed it twice. The roots of his hair pricked up in unison with his reactivated John Thomas.

'Thanks,' he gasped. 'I mean goodbye, see you soon.'

'Bye Timothy,' he had never heard the three syllables of his name pronounced with such erotic suggestion.' *Could she be taking the piss?*

Tim gazed after her as she walked quickly away, her athletic legs and muscular behind, utterly magnificent. *Just shows that first impressions can be misleading. I'm beginning to enjoy this place, and the job hasn't even started yet.*

Chapter 5
The Beginning of Term Party

Aisha took a taxi onto campus for the beginning of term staff party. The idea behind the occasion was for staff to meet up in an informal setting before work took over. Well before the cab reached the university gates she heard snatches of guitar music and youthful singing. This was unlikely to be her new colleagues. She guessed that some kind of student event was also taking place. As the taxi drew up outside the main building she felt a shiver of excitement very different from the hyper-anxiety of her interview. She wanted to belong here and was eager for things to begin. The journey cost the thick end of ten pounds. Aisha handed the driver a note waving aside his feeble fumbles in search of change. Pleased, the driver decided to be helpful.

'I think the student do is in the Union – that's the big building over there, Miss. You're a bit early though.' He pointed to a square concrete and glass structure some fifty yards behind the main administrative centre.

'Many thanks.' Aisha was flattered to be mistaken for

a student. She checked her watch. It was almost an hour to eight o' clock when the party was due to begin. In her eagerness to be on time she risked being amongst the first to arrive and perhaps not knowing anybody. She could hear the music more clearly now and decided to pass the time by tracking it down. It had been a hot day and a soft haze was beginning to settle over campus. Several buildings were already lit up, their light merging with the sun's early evening glow. She was happy to be part of this enclave of civilised enquiry and human relations. Or so she supposed it to be. She glanced towards the student union and near-by residential blocks. The music was not coming from that direction. She turned to look further up the campus. Beyond the teaching blocks on an open stretch of ground was a period-built mansion circled by a high, solid wood fence. She guessed that this might be the Vice Chancellor's residence. The voices and music seemed to come from some way beyond. As she strolled up the campus the fragments of music began to cohere into recognisable melodies, unexpectedly more sixties than noughties.

High up the campus she wandered onto a stretch of grassland not visible from the main drive. Students were scattered around in singles, couples and small groups: reading, writing, lost to lap-tops or mobiles, playing cards, conversing, some intently, some light-heartedly. One couple seemed to be making love. No one appeared to be expecting rain. It was a scene deserving of a campus Lowry. A frizbee whizzed towards Aisha. She plucked it nimbly from the air. Applause broke out from a trio of young men. One of them must have launched it.

'Good catch,' this from a gangly youth with an American accent.

She threw the frizbee back to him.

'Wow, man. Good throw.'

'Thanks.'

'So why don't you join in? We need someone that can

throw straight. These guys can't keep it off the ground.' He gestured dismissively in the direction of his two companions.'

'Thanks but not this time, I'm heading for the music. I've walked across most of the campus to get to it.'

'Right. You're on track. It's all happening on the other side of that red brick wall, in the ecological garden area.'

'Great. Thanks,' she replied.

Aisha made her way over to the wall, threading her way through a gap strewn with a jumble of battered and decaying bricks. The 'garden' turned out to be an uneven stretch of semi-cultivated grassland interspersed with shrubs, a few trees and some small beds of flowers. It may once have served as a place of quiet retreat but was now given over to informal socialising. It was quite densely occupied by several dozen students and a handful of older adults that Aisha took to be academics. In the centre of the garden was an ornamental fountain with a stone rim and surrounding patio. The fountain was dried out leaving streaks of oxidised rust across its metal surface. Everyone's attention was fixed on two figures sitting on the stone pedestal, guitars slung around their necks. Both looked faintly familiar to Aisha. Intrigued she eased her way through the crowd that thickened as she got nearer the fountain. Finally close enough, she recognised Henry Jones and Fred Cohen. Not wanting to interrupt the flow of their performance, she decided to watch incognito. Retreating several yards she found a spot under a cedar tree. There was a pause in the music and some banter started up between the two musicians and a section of the audience.

'Give us *When I'm Sixty-Four*,' shouted a youthful voice.

'What! So you think I'm sixty-four,' responded Henry with mock indignation.'

'At least.'

'Cheeky bugger.'

Aisha winced at her boss's language.

'What about *The Long and Winding Road?*

Henry turned enquiringly to Fred Cohen who shook his head.

'Appropriate, but not one I can do.'

'*All You Need is Love*,' shouted another voice.

Henry and Fred exchanged a smile.

'Ok, we think we can manage that,' said Fred, 'but we might need some help.'

'Right, here we go. Make sure you lot join in, the lyrics shouldn't stretch you too much,' shouted Henry.

After a couple of practice chords the two men launched into the optimistic chant. The students joined in with raucous enthusiasm swelling to total cacophony as they attempted to vocalise the erratic trumpet sequences of the original. They clattered to a chaotic climax as they tried to keep up with Henry and Fred's manic fade-out. Laughter and ironic applause greeted the end of the song. Merry-making and self-piss-taking hung in the heavy, late-evening air.

Red faced and panting slightly, Henry began to unhitch his guitar. 'Ok, that's it. We have to go somewhere now. Don't you guys have something going on tonight as well?'

'One more song before you go,' someone shouted.

'One more song, one more song,' the rest started chanting.

A lone voice shouted above the din.

'Henry, Fred, tell us what you think of the banking crisis and the protests. What can we do about those selfish bastards?'

Henry was about to reply when Fred cut in.

'I'll answer that, don't set Henry off, it's more than his job is worth.'

'Shame! Free speech!' a voice interjected.

Fred carried on. 'Look, in my view your generation needs to push on from what we did. We freed things up culturally, I mean. But it's pretty obvious we didn't manage to do much about inequality. In fact it's getting worse. Not that it will be any easier for...'

An agitated Henry burst in.

'Listen. I agree with Fred. But this might surprise you coming from an old leftie, be careful, think before you act. My generation; those of us who were involved, anyway, in the end we threw it away. We fell out among ourselves. Keep your discipline and keep together. Keep the protests going but don't imagine that violence offers a short cut. We have to win the intellectual and moral arguments, then the system will lose credibility. Look at the Soviet Union, never a genuine socialist society by the way. Look what happened there: the system collapsed because it was rotten from the inside, rotten to the core. It can happen to Western capitalism, not in the same way, but it can happen.'

Some of the audience broke out in spontaneous applause. Others looked uneasy.

Fred came in again. 'Yeah, Henry's right. One thing we oldies can contribute is to help you avoid the mistakes we made. It's that old cliché - the value of experience, but unfortunately it doesn't always stack up well with youthful idealism. I hope we don't sound too parental. In any case the world in the next thirty or forty years will be the world you make. The best of luck with it.' He hesitated for a moment, unsure whether he was connecting with the crowd.

A spare looking youth with closely cropped hair dipped in with a comment. 'You guys sound more like poets than revolutionaries. We have to be realistic. In the sixties and seventies you could move in and out of the system, more or less when you wanted to. Lots of us guys can't even get into the system in the first place except into low-paid, shit-work. Places like this just keep us in storage for three years.'

A young, hippie-looking, woman interrupted. 'Don't be so negative, man. It's bread *and* roses. Can we get back to some music? It'll soon be dark. Give us one more song? Do either of you guys know anything written after nineteen seventy-five or did the Beatles have the last word?'

Henry and Fred grinned at each other self-deprecatingly. Fred decided to take the opportunity to tie things up.

'Well, we're not exactly rap specialists. We can probably

just about do *Common People* if you all join in with the lyrics. Is that cool?'

There was a murmur of approval.

'Ok,' said Henry, 'but I don't really know it.' He looked out at the audience. 'Can any of you guys hack out a tune?'

A student sat on the rim of the fountain waved his hand. 'Great.'

'Anyone want to take over from me?' asked Fred.

The hippie woman waved enthusiastically.

The ageing minstrels passed over their guitars to the two volunteers. Fred found a place to sit a few feet away inside the bowl of the fountain. Henry must have noticed Aisha arrive because he went straight over and sat next to her.

'Terrific stuff,' she smiled, 'the music, I mean, I'm not sure about the teach-in.'

'Good to see you again. The whole thing is for fun really but it was good to have a bit of political rap. I guess you didn't expect to meet up again quite like this.'

'Not really but you're right, people really seem to be enjoying themselves and for me it's interesting. It is a bit different.'

'Look, it's great to see you here. By the way you remember Fred from the interview panel. He's here for the party, creature of pleasure that he is. He's staying at my place for a couple of days.'

Henry shouted to Fred to join them. His voice was lost as the crowd hit the chorus of *Common People*. Eventually the message was passed to Fred who squeezed his way over. He greeted Aisha with an enthusiastic double kiss. Slightly taken aback, she managed a smile.

'Time to go time,' said Henry. 'It's getting dark and anyway I'm in serious need of a drink. Let's get to Swankie's party. Is that ok with you?' He turned towards Aisha.

'That suits me fine. I'm in your hands,' she replied, hoping that she didn't sound too keen to please.

Henry left a message for the two musicians to leave the guitars at the main reception. Fred who had a sentimental attachment to his old guitar looked slightly concerned but went along with it.

They arrived at the main building to the sound of a party already in full swing. To Aisha's surprise security insisted that they produce their identity cards before entry. She had imagined academics were not subject to such inconveniences. To get Fred in at all required a couple of minutes' lively negotiation. He was issued with a visitor's card only after being primly advised that he 'ought to have arranged this ahead of the event.' Finally, they were inside the entrance hall.

'Ms Khan ... Aisha Khan isn't it?' A high falsetto rose above the din.

Dropping an octave the voice continued, 'and oh, Henry, Fred, glad you managed to make it.' An innuendo of disapproval implied that somehow getting themselves to the party might have been beyond them.

The owner of the voice, a tall, expensively dressed, middle-aged, women emerged through the crush. Aisha took her outstretched hand and answered her question.

'Yes, that's right. I'm one of the new appointments.'

'Welcome, I'm Heather Brakespeare; I'm married to Howard. We use our birth names for most purposes. I'm delighted to meet you.'

'It's good to meet you, too.'

A further exchange of pleasantries established that Heather Brakespeare worked at the University as Director of a recently established research and teaching unit on health and nutrition. While this brief conversation was going on, Henry and Fred contrived to disappear. Heather took the opportunity to offer what Aisha interpreted as an oblique warning about Henry.

'Henry's a bit of an old roué, you know. Apparently he created some serious trouble for the previous Dean. I think he imagines he's still living in the nineteen sixties. I heard from one student that he can scarcely operate a computer,' she added unnecessarily. 'Anyway, don't let me hold you up from enjoying the party. I must go and welcome a group of colleagues that have just arrived. The food and drinks are by the wall on your left and afterwards you'll no doubt want to join in the dancing. Oh, by the way, I can see Dr Connor by the food on his own looking rather neglected. As you probably know he's also a new appointment. Why don't you go over and say hello to him?'

Aisha watched Tim for a few moments. He was leaning against a wall clutching a plastic pint glass in one hand and a plate piled high with food in the other while trying to kick away a chunk of salmon mayonnaise that had dropped onto his shoe. Aisha was about to go over and suggest that he put down his plate and pint before trying to remove the mayonnaise when a familiar voice broke in.

'Aisha Khan, here you are... How good to see you.'

It was Howard Swankie.

'I hope you haven't been on your own for long. I must introduce you to some colleagues.'

Aisha tensed slightly as she braced herself for more formalities. She would have preferred to chat with Tim Connor who she was beginning to find oddly diverting.

'Oh, good evening Professor Swankie. No, I'm fine. Actually I've just been talking to your wife. I was about to go over and say hello to Tim Connor, my fellow initiate,' she said attempting to sound relaxed.

'I'm sure you'll catch up with him later. Perhaps I can find Rachel Steir or Erica Botham for you to chat with.'

He looked around the room in an unconvincing attempt to spot one or both of them. The more appealing thought that he might spend a few minutes with Aisha had occurred to him. She would meet other colleagues soon enough. He had better be careful though. He had not completely out-lived his old reputation as something of a philanderer, even though it was several years since he had risked seri-ous indiscretion. His affair with a young and exotic post-graduate student from Brazil had almost broken his mar-riage as well as undermined his performance and credibility at work. The liaison had begun light-heartedly enough but had become increasingly passionate and out of control. It had dislocated both their lives. Despite or rather because of the intensity of his feelings he had decided that such dalliances were simply not worth the possible fall-out.

Since then Heather had been on permanent orange alert and he was keen to avoid trouble from her direction. He needed her to be on side. And it was not only Heather he had to think about. Sexism had become a cardinal sin in academe. Rightly so as he had come to understand, though he believed that the policing of behaviour could be as oppressive as the problem it was intended to solve. In any case, he could not afford to behave ambiguously. According to his own progress chart he was about ready to launch a bid for a career defining promotion, possibly, given his increasing prominence on the national scene, at Deputy Vice Chancellor level. Still, a few moments with a new appointment hardly amounted to a capital offence. With a bit of luck it would go unnoticed.

'Look, it's impossibly loud in here. Why don't we pop out for a minute onto the terrace? I need to catch a breath of fresh-air, I've been pressing the flesh for the last couple of hours,' his invitation hung awkwardly but he knew that Aisha Khan had little option but to agree.

That was how Aisha saw it, too. They threaded their way towards the French windows that opened out onto the broad terrace. Swankie gestured Aisha ahead of him, stumbling slightly as he followed her through. As he guided her towards a carved wooden bench his hand rested fleetingly longer than appropriate on her slender shoulders. It occurred to Aisha that Swankie might be drunk; no more than slightly she hoped. When he sat a little too close for comfort, she got up on the pretext of straightening her dress and sat down again a good couple of feet from him... If there was a problem this seemed to kill it. Swankie stayed put and resumed the conversation in impeccably bland terms.

'This is one of the great advantages of a rural campus.

We have this splendid view across the countryside with the city lights in the distance; magical really. The urban campuses have nothing to match it. Few of the out of town universities are quite as richly endowed. Aesthetically I mean. They talk about Keele as "the dream on the hill" but its landscape is a little contrived and now more or less obliterated by the decision to build so intensively. And beyond its campus, the terrain doesn't compare to what we've got. But, of course, as a local resident you're familiar with the natural beauty of the locality.'

Swankie was beginning to relax again, confident that he was erasing any impression of over-familiarity. He conceded to himself that Aisha was also more at ease now that civil distance was re-established. Still he did feel slightly light-headed, due no doubt to a combination of three or four glasses of wine and what he sensed was a slightly raised heartbeat. He continued with friendly, if less than compelling conversation.

'Have you always lived in this part of the country, I can't quite recall from your CV?'

'No, not at all. We – my husband Waqar and I only moved here about ten or twelve years ago shortly after we married. I'm a Londoner, from Southall originally. My parents came from Bangladesh in the seventies. We were quite poor when I was very young but my father built up a small chain of restaurants. I met my husband through the restaurant business; he owns a much larger chain than my father ever did.'

'So what brought you down here? People usually leave the great metropolis in late middle-age, if at all.'

Aisha continued, happier now the prospect of futher awkwardness had receded. 'We visited the West-country for a holiday and fell in love with it. The idea of living in Wash was to have a family life as far away from work as was practically possible. Waqar, both of us that is, we haven't even opened up a branch of the business in Wash. We don't want the distraction. It's worked out quite well but

Waqar does have to spend a lot of time in London which is difficult for us. We have a flat there.'

Swankie interjected in what he hoped was the measured tone of a helpful senior colleague. 'Yes, I can see the problem; some people would find that situation a little lonely. But at least you've used your time effectively, admirably in fact, in view of what you've achieved academically.'

He felt a sudden urge to flutter his academic feathers.

'What you describe is a nice example of what the post-structuralists refer to as contingency: the unpredictable effect of one event or circumstance on another. Or, in more everyday terms an unexpected positive outcome has emerged out of a difficult situation, namely your academic success achieved in time fortuitously made available by the absence of your husband. Of course that formulation doesn't address the issue of agency, the ability of individuals to make a difference. Not many people would have turned ill fortune to such excellent effect. You did. And of course many other good things might flow from you doing so.' What these 'good things' might be, Swankie opted not to suggest.

He was concerned that his flurry of poststructuralist theory was over the top for the occasion. He wanted to sound interesting, learned even, but not pompous. And anyway he wasn't quite sure that he fully understood the 'post' theories. He hoped that Aisha Khan was not about to rumble him.

He needn't have worried. Aisha had listened intently to his remarks. Having come into academia the hard way, she was eager to learn more, and Swankie was supposed to know.

'Umm... that's interesting. I've been thinking about agency in relation to the subjects in my research sample. I know ten women is not a sufficient basis on which to generalise, but contrary to some people's impression of Muslim women, most of my subjects were quite assertive in searching out their life options. I'd like to develop the agency theme more when I expand my work. Maybe you could recommend some key literature in the area?'

Swankie was about to confirm that indeed he could make recommendations and would shortly email her accordingly, when he noticed his wife and Ruth Steir emerge through the French windows. Heather looked agitated. Instantly the smile of friendly engagement disappeared from Swankie's face. Abruptly he leaned away from Aisha and gave a pre-emptive wave to attract his wife's attention. Spotting his gesture, the two women walked briskly towards them.

'Howard, no wonder I couldn't find you. The Vice-Chancellor has dropped in for a few minutes. I'm sure he'd like a word with you. He's just inside the French windows talking to Henry Jones and that ancient bohemian friend of his. They seem to have cornered him. They're making rather a nuisance of themselves. Do go and prevent them from doing anything too embarrassing. We'll stay here and chat with Ms. Khan.'

The two women, one large and wide and the other tall and thin sat down on either side of Aisha.

'Lovely to see you again,' said Rachel Steir. 'It's absolutely wonderful that the department has recruited another woman and doubtless, as I picked up from your research, another feminist. You've probably realised that Henry is somewhat unreconstructed and we tend to look to younger colleagues to supply energy and inspiration these days.'

They were interrupted by the crash of breaking glass and crockery from inside the building.

'That's probably Henry falling over,' she commented smiling sweetly at Aisha. 'Let's leave them to it and chat.'

Chapter 6
An Unexpected Start to Term

The start of term was even more hectic than Tim had anticipated. An initial surge of energy carried him through the sessions of introductory guidance he was expected to deliver to students, even though at first he scarcely knew more than they did about how things worked.

Like most higher education institutions, Wash was in a period of cost cutting through the use of technological innovation, 'strategic' redundancies, and whatever 'efficiency gains' looked viable. Along with restructuring came a flux of new rules and procedures: 'ebureaucracy' Henry dubbed it. Tim could see Henry's point and itched to get started on 'the real job' of teaching. Difficulties were magnified in smaller institutions as managers and administrators sought to match the sector's big hitters. As the Wash system struggled to cope, Tim spent much of his time chasing up confused and distressed students, some the victims of his own mistaken advice. In a couple of cases he found himself negotiating the return of students from their parental homes where they had fled in panic. Generating calm and confidence was challenging when he doubted his own assurances that it would all get sorted in the end. But on the whole, for most, it did.

Things slowly settled once teaching got under way. Most of his work was in preparing and delivering lectures and seminars, although administration was almost as time-consuming. As he had discovered in his previous job, email was not always a time-saver. Time saved from face-to-face communication and phone calls was lost sorting through jargon-ridden emails from the bureaucracy. On top of official stuff, his in-box was swollen by frequently unnecessary and incomprehensible emails from students, although these became more coherent as term went on. Then there was the spam: spectacular legacies from unknown benefactors; get-rich-now deals and offers of sex with self-proclaimed beautiful if distant and impoverished women. In the end he zapped his email arrival alert system and set aside a couple of dedicated periods each day to deal with work-related emails. Serious problems he dealt with face-to-face.

Somehow he managed to make some progress with his book on generational conflict and resolution. The topic had become a hot one as the media picked up on a sharp debate between some prominent intellectuals of the 'baby boomer' generation and a group of young professionals. The latter blamed the boomers for many of the difficulties of young people. He pushed himself to keep writing, hoping to get the book out before public interest subsided. His view was that blaming the boomers for the problems of the current younger generation was simplistic. The real issue lay with the concentration of wealth and power in the hands of selfish national and global elites. To that extent he agreed with Henry. He was getting to like his older colleague whose eccentric 'couldn't give a damn' behaviour was an antidote to his own busy intensity. They had struck up a budding friendship and occasionally met for a wind down or barn storming session about whatever came to mind.

Getting to and from Peyton once a week to see Maria, pushed him at times close to exhaustion. Sometimes the effort seemed entirely wasted and left him feeling empty and ineffectual. At first having a 'part-time' dad intrigued Maria but the novelty soon began to wear off. Gina was keen for Tim to maintain a relationship with his daughter but her new partner, Rupert Eccles, was less enthusiastic without openly opposing it. He was coolly polite, but made it clear he did not want Tim to remain around the house with Maria for more than half an hour or so. Predictably, soon after Tim's arrival he would ask some version of the question 'So where are you taking your daughter today, then?' On some occasions, Tim didn't even get as far as the house. Instead Maria was dropped off at whatever venue Tim had decided to take her to. He did his best but soon visits to adventure playgrounds, parks, movies, and, in desperation, even McDonalds began to appeal less and less to both of them.

The lack of a stable base where they could spend time together began to take its toll. Maria became increasingly moody and temperamental. She wanted to know why Daddy had gone to live so far away, and why Mummy and Daddy didn't like one-another anymore? After several weeks she asked whether he was still her Daddy or if she'd got a new one now? Her confusion turned into sullenness and withdrawal. It didn't help much when Gina assured him that Maria was getting on quite well with Rupert. It even felt double-edged when she added that domestic disruption had apparently not adversely affected Maria at school. It all made Tim feel marginal and irrelevant. Slot in, slot out dads. He understood Maria's happiness was what mattered most but that didn't lessen his own hurt and anxiety. Understanding was not enough. He determined that whatever else he had lost, he was not going to lose his daughter.

One Thursday evening about half way through term the

build up of stress suddenly imploded. It hit physically. A wave of darkness surged across his consciousness. His eyes lost focus. His chest went momentarily into spasm. He clutched his temples as he struggled to regain stability and control. The episode lasted no more than a few seconds. Slowly he massaged his face and head, calming himself. He opened his eyes. The computer screen stared primly back, neither mocking nor concerned just stubbornly, unflinchingly there. He got up from his chair leaving the icy machine suspended in mid sentence: 'The two generations have more in common than...' *Time for a change of scene.*

He decided to respond to this scary moment by taking a walk into town. It might clear his head. Then he would wash away the accumulated tension of recent weeks with a few drinks. If he was honest with himself, he had to admit that he was lonely, just a little. He thought of calling Henry to join him, but decided he was in no mood for one of his colleague's more baroque performances, diverting though these could be. He needed to get away from anything and anyone connected with work. He wanted to ground himself again, to get back in touch with what passed for the real world. As he walked through Wash the city seemed solid enough. It was the space between his ears that had taken an ethereal turn. Not that he entertained the possibility of anything so time-consuming or self-indulgent as a breakdown.

He deliberately let himself get lost, wandering over to the eastern outskirts of the city and then meandering haphazardly through the back streets. The suburban sameness of this part of the city felt reassuring. Here the housing was plain and unpretentious, mainly red brick or concrete rather than the sandstone or granite of the city centre and wealthier neighbourhoods. By now, most adults had returned from work and children had gone in off the streets, curtains were being drawn as people closed up against the encroaching night. A few teenagers were still hanging around waiting for something to turn up, but without much optimism that it would. A handful of couples were making their way into the city centre. Arm in arm, a pair of young women passed him, their tall shoes clicking briskly on the hard paving stones. A freshening wind ruffled his long hair. The haunting melody and lyrics of Van Morrison's legendary ballad drifted into his mind - *the cool night air like Shalimar.*

Pensive and reflective, his mood was rudely broken.

Two young lads, short of something to do, decided to amuse themselves at Tim's expense. Noticing that his trousers stopped an inch or so above his ankles one of them shouted, 'Aren't ye a bit old for short trousers?'

Tim made no response.

'Don't ye think you need a haircut Mate?' asked the second youth.

No answer. The lads had kept a wary distance from Tim and he reckoned he could get out of this spot of bother by ignoring it – cautiously. Something along the lines of 'talk quietly and carry a big stick'. All he lacked was the stick. Maintaining his pace he continued to walk on. The lads trailed after him without much conviction.

'Give us a fiver, mate, and we'll leave ye alone.'

Irritated, Tim abandoned his strong silent strategy. He turned to face the lads. They looked no more than fifteen or sixteen years old and quite small and skinny. Both had carrot coloured hair, aggressive freckles and features that were too large for their thin faces. They were clearly brothers and probably twins. He guessed they were jokers rather than thugs. It was no great risk to face them down – unless, of course, they were carrying a weapon.

'You guys taking the piss?'

'Looks like ye've already had the piss taken out of ye mate.' It was reassuring that this remark was made as the two were backing away from Tim, ready to beat it should Tim go for them.

'Very funny... You two are not contributing much to my evening. You could do worse than go missing.'

'Posh ain't we? Do you mean you'd like us to fuck off?'

Tim bristled. He didn't like the 'posh' comment. It disturbed some distant, unpleasant memory. But by now he had concluded that the boys were not a threat. He kept his cool and decided to redirect their surplus energy.

'Look I'll give you a fiver if you can take me to a pub with decent beer,' adding after a moment's thought, 'and maybe a few decent looking women as well.'

The offer had instant appeal to the carrot heads. 'Yeah,' they knew a couple of good pubs, though they couldn't often afford to drink there themselves. Tim sealed the deal.

'Ok, two quid now and three when we get there.'

The ill-sorted but picaresque trio set off towards the city centre. They exchanged names or, as the lads announced themselves as 'Light-bulb' and 'Dipstick', in their case, nicknames. Tim had attracted a few nicknames in his time, the one he was most coy about being 'Spare Parts.' He decided to pass on mentioning it on this occasion. The banter continued in a more friendly tone as they approached the river. They stopped just short of a bridge leading into the main commercial and entertainment area.

'We'll leave you here, Sir, if that's ok,' said Dipstick the noisier of the two, suddenly respectful as the pay-off moment neared. 'When you cross the bridge you'll find yourself in a main street, follow it round for about fifty yards and you'll come to a pub called *The Bombadier*. It sells real ale, the stuff people like you like.' He paused for a moment. 'Can we have the rest of our money now, Sir?'

Tim searched his pockets for three-pound coins. Nothing doing. Keeping a tight hold, he pulled out his wallet from an inside pocket and extracted a fiver.

'Give me two and I'll give you this.'

Dipstick hesitated. 'How about we give you one back so we get three each?'

'You drive a hard bargain.'

'Definitely... one of them.'

Tim handed over the fiver and was half surprised to get

a pound back.

'Ok, see you around.'

'Not if we see you first,' said Dipstick.

'He's only joking, he doesn't know when to stop,' was Lightbulb's farewell contribution.

Tim walked briskly to the pub. His head was clearer now, and his thirst sharper. *The Bombardier* faced flat-fronted onto the street. From outside, its only notable feature was a large pub-sign that sported a muscular red-coated gunner about to fire a cannon gun. It seemed an odd image for a student city. Then he recalled the army garrison that he'd noticed while house searching.

Inside, the pub was half empty. The décor maintained the martial theme with garish pictures of miscellaneous British military victories on the walls that were also festooned with ancient rifles and cutlasses. This did not appear to be quite his scene. Only a pressing thirst prevented him from executing a quick about turn to search out an alternative watering hole. It was no wonder the kids made sure they got their money before he'd seen this place. He scanned the portrayals of martial glory wondering if the artist's intention was perhaps ironic. Looking around the notion of parody seemed plausible, the pub's clientele appeared more boho than military.

He made his way to the bar. Behind were two burly bartenders wearing identical yellow tee-shirts printed with a pink-coloured cannon gun with pink cannon balls on each side. The image did not suffer from over-sophistication.

One of the bartenders approached him, smiling broadly.

'Lovely to see you Sir. What can I get you?' His voice was an octave or so higher than Tim had expected and sweetly pitched.

'A pint of your best bitter and do you do cooked food?'

'Certainly Sir... We've still got curry left or sausage and mash. Green salad if you want it. Oh yes, and in the spirit of multiculturalism we've adopted a hybrid dish called toad in the chapati.'

'I'll have a curry please, the salad and a round of bread on the side, brown if you've got it.'

'No problem. Except that the bread would be white, sir. Is that ok?'

'That's fine, I don't discriminate.'

'I'll bring it to you, Sir.'

Tim found a seat at an empty table. As he glanced around his impression that the pub was gay friendly was confirmed. Several people wore tea-shirts with gay pride slogans and one muscular young man wore a jacket proclaiming his support for Stonewall. Nobody had gone for the cannon-ball t-shirt favoured by the bartenders and prominently on sale behind the bar at twenty-five per cent off half-price. Most of the couples seemed to be same-sex but a number of apparent cross-dressers made it difficult to tell.

Tim was beginning to feel his dip into the real world was taking a decidedly surreal turn. Not that he considered queers surreal. He was simply bemused by the gap between his intention at the start of his 'sortie' and what was emerging. But bemusement was a lot better than the bombed out state he'd been in earlier.

His musings were interrupted by the arrival of the bartender with his meal. 'There you are Sir. Is there anything else you might want?'

Tim took in the bartender's fifteen stone of beef packed into a frame of about five feet six inches. *Nothing you can give me* - was the un-P C thought that popped up. Out loud he said, 'No. That's excellent. Many thanks.'

When eating alone in a pub Tim usually read the newspaper. He found the two activities relaxing although they did not always combine elegantly. On this occasion he didn't have a paper with him and couldn't spot one in the pub. No matter, there was plenty here to interest him. As he ate he peered into the pub's soft rose light. He amused himself by trying to establish the biological sex of the cross-dressers. He did so to his own satisfaction in about half-a-dozen cases. Eventually his attention settled on three people at a table a few feet from his own. Two were definitely males. Occasionally they touched and fondled each other more freely than Western heterosexual norms usually allow to adult males except in peak moments in sport and some other entertainments. He assumed they were partners.

Where did the other person fit into the dual system of biological classification he had adopted: male or female? He or she had achieved a highly convincing cross-dress whatever the biological starting point. The fine, long dark hair and strong, regular features would sit attractively on anyone. The clothes offered few clues; a long, embroidered shirt hanging over a pair of baggy trousers obscured the contours of the body. Tim was torn between embarrassment at his clunky need to categorise this individual and the intriguing challenge of doing so. He genuinely could not decide. Subliminally – very subliminally - he sensed the answer to his question might explain some riddle in his own identity. He leaned forward to get a better view.

'Hi, can I help you? Have you lost something?' Tim had managed to make himself the object of attention of the object of his attention, the observer observed.

'No ... no, not at all. I'm just looking around the pub. I've never been here before.'

'So, what do you think?' The tone was friendly, even encouraging.

'Well it's certainly got its own character. It's a bit different than my usual watering hole. I don't usually...' He stopped mid-sentence.

'You look a little different yourself. Do you mind if I come over for a minute and take a closer peep?' This was said with a teasing and, Tim had to concede, despite his category dilemma, gorgeous smile.

'Be my guest. My name is Tim.'

'Hello Tim. I'm Georgie.'

No clues there then.

'Georgie boy or Georgie girl?'

'That's for me to know and you to wonder.' Georgie pointedly touched an androgynous nose.

Tim decided on a more conventional line of conversation.

'Georgie, can I get you a drink?'

'No thanks, I'm driving and I don't want to push the limit.'

'Ok. It's nice of you to come over and talk to me. As I say I'm new to these parts.'

Perhaps Tim was lonelier than he recognised. His self-image was of habitual self-reliance bordering on self-containment. Yet, as he talked, he found himself opening up to this stranger in quite a personal way. It was not so much emotional release as an unloading of the weight of recent events, a jettisoning of accumulated clutter. It was a relief to share his story of chance and change with another. Perhaps better with a stranger than with someone he knew. Like the confessional, an anonymous encounter offered a screening from consequences. It also helped that the distraction of sexual attraction was in abeyance. His non-negotiable notion of his own sexual identity precluded him from making any ambiguous sexual connection. Or, so he assumed. Uncharacteristically he continued to do most of the talking, almost as if to him-self.

Georgie listened, smiling occasionally and making encouraging interjections. Then the mood changed abruptly.

'Tim that's all very interesting but do you realise what I am?'

'A...' he hesitated flustered, apparently suddenly required to come to a decision on what had been fascinating him.

'You're either a...'

'I'm a prostitute.'

'A prostitute?'

'Yes. I'm enjoying talking to you but I need to make money. It costs eighty pounds.' The tone had suddenly become businesslike.

'Eighty pounds?' Surely he was not negotiating. Yet tak-en-off-guard, the stark offer of sex for money had excited him.

'Tim, are you deaf? Are you up for it or not?' The smile was still friendly yet utterly free of embarrassment.

'Look, I've never paid for sex before.'

'They all say that. Anyway, 'before' is history. Listen, you look pretty fit so I'll make it sixty. Let's go now.' Geor-gie stood up and took Tim's hand. He got up slowly in a show of reluctance more for his heterosexual self-respect than because he wanted to back out. He recognised that he was becoming hooked. He just wasn't quite sure what was hooking him and why he was letting it happen.

The guys at Georgie's table gave a friendly wave as the pair left the pub. Tim avoided their gaze. Georgie's car was in the pub car park. In a couple of minutes they drew up outside a large eighteenth century block recently converted into residential accommodation. Tim followed Georgie up some stone steps eyeing the rear view speculatively. Trim buttocks moving against the soft cloth. *Definitely... defi-nitely, maybe.* They exited the stairs coming to a second floor flat. Inside they passed through an entry hall into a recep-tion room. Tim followed Georgie straight into a bedroom. Georgie went to a bank of electrical equipment and touched a couple of switches simultaneously flooding the room with a soft red glow and the low steady beat of an Indie track.

'Maybe you could give me the money now? I like to get that out of the way.'

Tim was still not sure what he was paying for or what if anything he was about to do but he took three twenty pound notes from his pocket and put them on a dressing table. This seemed to release Georgie.

'Time to strip.'

'Go ahead. That's the least I'd expect for sixty quid.'

'You first. I'll help you.'

He was soon naked.

'Your turn now.'

'Let's dance for a couple of minutes.'

As they did so Tim's remaining inhibitions dissolved. He undid the buttons on Georgie's shirt bending to rub his own hairy chest against small firm breasts. Reaching lower he found a welcome space between smooth firm thighs. She gave a wide-eyed 'now you know' smile.

'Hey, that's a bit of a stretch for you, ain't it, big man?'

'Jump up here then,' said Tim.

He lifted her from her waist and she eased her thighs across his.

His cock quivered as she wriggled towards it.

Suddenly they collapsed, Georgie landing plum on Tim's John Thomas.

'Ouch! Fuck! That can't have been what I intended,' he cursed.

'I'm sure it wasn't, but I was going to get a condom anyway.'

'How romantic.'

'Tim this is not romance.'

And it wasn't. But when at last they did fuck, it was such a thunderous release that the block moved. Or so it seemed to Tim.

After they'd recovered, Georgie suggested that maybe Tim might have been a bit sex-starved. He agreed that that this was a possibility.

'In that case you can have a freebie.' They did it again, shifting the block back into place.

Afterwards they drank some red wine and chatted for a while. Georgie offered Tim a lift 'to wherever.' That was 'lift enough' he replied. He was beginning to enjoy this city, *flâneur* style.

As he ambled home he wondered vaguely if Georgie might be related to the Madame George, of Van Morrison's eponymous song. A star-spangled granddaughter that would be. For years he had thought the title of the song was 'Madame Joy' and its subject female rather than male. It didn't really matter. But he knew his own tastes. Or thought he did.

Chapter 7
The Team Meets

The morning of the Social Science team meeting with Howard Swankie, shaped up badly for Tim. It was a humid early autumn day torn by sharp high-voltage thunderstorms. His car refused to start, even with the help of jump leads. Either the spark plugs were sodden or the battery had gone. For some reason the university mini-bus service from the city had been cancelled and he made his way in by public transport. He narrowly avoided a downpour as he hurried from the bus stop onto campus. By now the initial euphoria of his new job was wearing off, but he was glad to have made it to Wash, even though in the galaxy of higher education it was more black hole than twinkling star.

The notification of the meeting had been sent on to his Calcott Terrace address. It contained a map of the university campus with the relevant building indicated by an arrow. The meeting was in room 261 of the Sheikh Salah building, one of the biggest and most modern on the campus, located in an area unfamiliar to Tim. He made his way along a recently rebuilt access road that cut through a jumble of demountables that wore the weary look of temporary teaching accommodation gone permanent. The Sheik Salah was the central and dominant of several newer administrative buildings that formed a fat T with the access road. Behind the buildings was an acre or so of roughly kept university owned land separated by a wire fence from the countryside beyond.

The glass doors of the Sheikh Salah building opened automatically as Tim approached. Immediately inside was a square metal and glass reception point. It was fronted by a sharply dressed young woman wearing what looked like a platinum blond wig but could have been her own, brightly dyed, stiffly set hair. Behind her were two large black men who Tim took to be security. In the way of a natural anarchist, he decided to by-pass Reception and head straight for room 261.

'Excuse me Sir, you won't be able to get through an entry gate unless you have a building specific swipe card.' Tim swiftly back peddled. The voice came from the dubious blond.

'Are you staff or a visitor, Sir?'

'I'm a new member of staff. I'm here for a meeting in 261.'

'Have you been issued with a building specific swipe card, Sir? This is a high security building, and today we have visiting dignitaries from the Middle East.'

Arriving at the Sheikh Salah had been relatively easy. Getting in was proving more tricky.

'No, not a specific card for this building.'

'Wait a moment Sir. I'll just call 261 to let them know you've arrived. Then security will let you in. Perhaps I could see your staff card?'

'OK.' Tim flashed his card and watched, glumly patient as the receptionist made the call.

'I'm afraid the phone seems to be dead in 261, Sir. Are you sure that's where your meeting is? I don't actually have a record of it on today's events list.'

Tim checked his documentation. 'Definitely.'

'Do you mind if I look at that, Sir?'

Tim pointed to the room number.

'I see.' She turned towards the more senior looking of the security staff. 'I think it's ok to let this gentleman in, don't you?'

'This time, yes. But in future he needs to make sure he has the right card.' He turned to Tim. 'Go ahead. I'll swipe the gate for you.'

Now a few minutes late, Tim hurtled up the stairs two at a time, fighting gravity as he scaled the final few. He propelled himself along the corridor with all the elegance of a can of garbage in full flight. Room numbers in the main corridor ran out at 250. He turned sharply into a short corridor leading to a nest of rooms that as far as he could see were not numbered in any logical sequence. Zigzagging at speed he eventually found 261 in an obscure cul-de-sac. Late or not, he paused briefly to compose himself. It would hardly enhance his image to burst into the room as though he had been launched from a canon. Opening the door he was met by a smatter of welcoming voices, one or two of which sounded mildly reproving. He spluttered a brief apology as Howard Swankie, looking distinctly unimpressed, gestured him towards the remaining vacant chair.

'I'm glad you've managed to find us. This isn't the most accessible of rooms, which is why I had a plan of the building sent out to you all. Do pour yourself a glass of water, if you wish. There will be tea and biscuits later.'

He paused with exaggerated deliberation, waiting for Tim to settle before continuing the meeting. 'Now that Dr. Connor is here I can formally welcome both him and Ms. Khan to the faculty and department. I'm sure colleagues will give them all due assistance in settling in. Full staff details have already been circulated to you so I won't repeat them now. I'm also delighted to extend a special welcome to our American exchange partner Dr Brad Purfect from Ocado

State University. I understand Dr. Purfect wants to be known by his American title of Professor which as you know is the standard way of addressing academics over there.'

'Sure... thanks for that Professor Swankie. 'Professor' is just for the students. Colleagues can call me Brad, or whatever they like within reason.' Purfect let out a vast, bellowing laugh, apparently under the impression he had cracked a joke. His new colleagues did their polite best to indulge his misapprehension.

Purfect looked set to continue but Swankie cut back in. 'We're glad to have you here, Professor. Do feel free to ask any of us for whatever support you may need.' Swankie managed to force a smile in Purfect's direction before resetting himself into business mode. Looking serious he explained that no agenda had been circulated because he wanted to keep the main purpose of the meeting confidential. After summarising recent changes in the department and briefly outlining a five-year plan that he was still working on, he paused and looked up.

Henry Jones took the opportunity to interrupt.

'This five year plan? Sounds a bit Stalinist to me, Howard. Why five years? Two or three would be enough.'

Swankie passed off Henry's outburst with a dismissive wave. He did not intend to be distracted by his perennial tormentor. He looked slowly and deliberately round the table, holding his gaze on each colleague until he obtained eye contact. Tim resisted the impulse to wink when his turn for the beady eye came. He wondered from where Swankie had got this clunky manoeuvre – perhaps from a military manual on techniques in small group leadership. Henry Jones was less successful in exercising self-control, appearing to purse his mouth in a kiss as he met Swankie's gaze. Unruffled, Swankie again ignored him.

Finally, satisfied that he had everybody's attention, Swankie spoke.

'I have an important announcement to make. As you

know the Green Park and Ridgewell departments merged from the beginning of the last academic year with Green Park as the single site. After a year of the merger it has become clear that the lead roles in the department do not quite match the talents of the individuals concerned, Rachel and Henry. I've decided that Rachel will take over from Henry as Head of Department and that Henry will take on a brief to research new developments in educational technology, a crucial area if we or rather you are to compete with departments in other universities. I will line-manage both and additionally, I will assume responsibility for vetting applications for research funding. I'd like to thank Henry for his efforts as Head of Department,' he concluded minimally acknowledging Henry's work.

Tim was caught by surprise at Swankie's public humiliation of Henry. The change of departmental leadership could have been made with little fuss at the beginning of term. But the fact was that Henry had been demoted and his supposed new role was flimsy camouflage to expedite the fact. Henry was a notorious and vocal technophobe. It was obvious that his supposed new 'brief' was designed as a way of simultaneously humiliating him and kicking him into touch. Whatever the justification for the changes, Swankie had set out to make Henry look incompetent, making the most of an opportunity to land a heavy blow in the personal feud between them. Perhaps he was trying to force Henry's resignation. Tim looked across at Henry, his now ex-Head of Department. The pulse on Henry's left temple flickered irregularly but otherwise it was impossible to read his reaction. He glanced in Rachel Steir's direction but her expression also gave nothing away. What she said was sweetly diplomatic but with just a touch of spice.

'I'd like to add my thanks to Henry for his many dedicated years as Head of Department. We all know how extensive his knowledge of the subject is, and I'm sure he can inspire us to do more research even if he is unable to find the time to do much him-self.' She paused. 'I don't want to burden you with more information now but I'll shortly email the agenda for the next departmental meeting to everybody.'

Henry, shoulders hunched, remained silent.

'Thank you Rachel,' said Swankie swiftly moving on without inviting any further comment. Maintaining his directorial tone he launched into a fierce criticism of the department's 'embarrassingly' low place in the various national league tables. He intended to monitor closely all performance indicators, particularly 'customer satisfaction', in his drive to improve the department that was now 'in a total market situation.' He was confident that Rachel would provide the right sort of leadership, adding with a gratuitous dig at Henry that she was 'someone he knew he could work with'.

He was interrupted by a contemptuous snort from Henry. It was the first sign that Henry might fight back. Swankie glared at him and they eyeballed each other angrily for several seconds. Henry still said nothing.

Flushing slightly, Swankie continued in business-speak for a few more minutes, his momentum wavering only when Henry got up noisily, apparently to serve himself from a side-table where several steel drink containers and plates of biscuits had been placed. Swankie's irritation increased a notch or two as Henry fiddled noisily amongst the crockery and urns, but determinedly pressed on.

'I must also urge you to compete for the new prizes for good teaching established at the faculty and university level. I trust none of you consider yourself above competing for...'

'Shit... aah!' Henry exploded gutturally as hot tea cascaded down the front of his trousers. 'Aah ...aah ... my fucking dick!'

Noises of anxiety and hilarity erupted around the table. Henry swiftly grabbed a couple of tissues and exited the room at speed, contriving to barge into Swankie's chair he shouted 'And you can stick your f...ing five year plan where the sun doesn't shine, you pathetic drone!'

Swankie's annoyance turned to thunder.

'Jesus wept!'

Puce and with fists clenched, he lurched to his feet taking a couple of steps after Henry. His colleagues looked on incredulous, as for a delicious moment it seemed that he might charge off down the corridor in pursuit of Henry. Rachel Steir got up swiftly and laid a restraining hand on his arm. Swankie stood quivering, before slowly returning to his chair.

He looked around angrily daring further contradiction. Tim surprised himself by answering the challenge.

'Dean, I can understand why Henry reacted like that even though it was over the top. I think he was shocked by what you said to him.'

Swankie's surprise at Tim's intervention seemed to refocus him. He responded with a put-down.

'Dr Connor you're hardly in a position to comment. You'd be better advised to concentrate on your own work and establishing your place here.'

Tim stifled a combative response. It was a little early in his appointment to start mixing it with his boss.

Shelving the rest of his agenda, Swankie closed the meeting with the minimum of formalities. Brushing aside his colleagues mumbled expressions of concern he left without joining them for a snack.

Immediately after Swankie's departure there was an outburst of mirth and astonishment at Henry's dramatic exit, nevertheless conversation over snacks soon became more subdued. Not much sympathy was on offer for Howard Swankie but Henry wasn't winning many votes either. There was a sense of let-down that what had been anticipated as an important meeting had been turned into a farce. Concerned that their new colleagues might be disoriented by their chaotic initiation into the Swankie-Jones feud, Rachel and Erica made some effort to re-establish an atmosphere of normality. The weight of events was against them.

Only Brad Purfect seemed unperturbed by the bizarre

turn the meeting had taken. Apparently oblivious to how the others were feeling he launched into a monologue on the global economic situation. His obtuseness to the prevailing mood added to the sense that lunatic forces had hijacked the occasion. It made matters worse that Purfect seemed unaware of just how loud his voice was. He banged on spouting the sort of doctrinaire, vulgar Marxism that most people dump shortly after graduating (if they were ever naïve enough to believe it in the first place). A hint from Erica Botham to stop went unheeded. Finally Aisha Kahn broke in.

'I'm afraid I have to leave now. I'm due to pick up my child Ali from pre-school. It's been good to meet everybody. Do say goodbye to Henry and the Dean for me if either comes back. By the way, does anybody want a lift into Wash? I'm in the car today.'

Tim leapt at the opportunity. 'Please, yes. I'm car-less at the moment. I'd really appreciate it.'

'Fine, you're ok to leave now?'

'Sure, thanks'

Outside in the car park the fresh air had a sobering effect.

'Phew! That was quite an initiation. What did you think?' asked Tim.

'I don't know. Maybe the Dean was just trying to get some of the unpleasant stuff out of the way early on in the academic year. He obviously wants drastic improvements. It's a pity for Henry though. He seemed almost demented. The Dean did quite well to keep himself more or less under control. To be honest my main concern is teaching at the moment. All this managerial stuff flies past me but I suppose I'll have to get on top of it. I don't want to get involved in departmental politics though. What do you think about it all?'

'Umm...' Before Tim could answer they reached Aisha's car. She clicked open the central locking. The car was a Renault Clio and he had to bend almost double to get into the front passenger seat. He slid the seat back to make room for his legs. Aisha slipped easily into the driver's seat several inches in front of him.

It turned out that Aisha lived quite close to Tim's place. She suggested that he come in for a quick coffee before she dropped him off on her way to collect Ali. He was glad to agree. The meeting had left them both feeling deflated and looking for some support.

Aisha parked in the stone courtyard in front of the house, a detached, walled Georgian property. She led Tim straight through into a modern kitchen, big and pleasant enough to serve as an informal dining room as well.

Sat at a large walnut table watching Aisha brew up the coffee Tim was again struck by her calm self-possession as well as by her charm and slender beauty. Looking around he noticed a framed photograph of a man and young boy that he guessed were Aisha's partner and son.

Catching the direction of his gaze Aisha commented, 'That's my son Ali and my husband, Waqar. We've been married fifteen years now but we only had Ali about four years ago.'

'He's a good-looking kid. But you must have been very young when you got married. You hardly look out of your twenties now.'

She smiled, mildly embarrassed but pleased. 'Believe me I am and by a few years. We Asians keep our complexions well; the wrinkles don't show up until we're really ancient.'

She handed him a coffee and sat down at the opposite side of the table.

'Please put sugar and milk in to your own taste.'

'Thanks, I like it black.'

'Fine,' she hesitated a moment before pouring the coffee, 'I... I'm a bit concerned about an area of my teaching. Well, it's one module in particular. It has some psychology in it that I'm not really familiar with. Henry says you're quite good in the relevant area. If you could do a couple of sessions for me I'll do a couple for you in return? I don't want to bother Henry, especially after what's happened today.'

Tim was happy to help. 'No problem. It's beginning to look as though we'll have to do our own networking. I think the others are friendly enough but pretty much into their own specialities. Mind you I've met Henry Jones a couple of times. Despite what's happened today he's quite helpful in a general sort of way. He's a bit bumbly, but I'm more comfortable with him than I am with Rachel. We could meet up with him some time.'

'I'd like that. I'm not sure I'd want to meet him on my own just yet. I haven't quite worked him out. I can't believe his behaviour today was typical. You were quite brave to speak up for him.'

'I don't know about brave, foolish more like it. I certainly haven't endeared myself to the Dean. I hope he's not the kind of person that bears a grudge. But going back to Henry, he behaves erratically at times although it's obvious that he's massively knowledgeable about some areas of social theory. He treated me to an hour-long lecture in the pub the other day; really stimulating. I hope he finds more time to get himself published now that he's been dumped as Head of Department.'

'It was tough on him today, but I suppose the Dean knows what he's doing. I think I like Henry but Rachel will probably make a better Head of Department,' said Aisha.

'Maybe... but what do we know? I guess we'll get up to speed with faculty politics before too long.'

They talked for a little longer, relaxing as they shared experiences of their first few weeks at Wash. A day that had begun badly for Tim and then accelerated downwards had tilted again to the upside. If relations with colleagues at work were going to be problematic, here at least was someone in the same situation as himself: a potential confidant and ally in times ahead.

Later Aisha dropped Tim off at Calcott Place.

'Thanks for the lift and don't worry about those lectures, I'm happy to do them for you.'

'Thanks Tim, that's a real relief. But the support is mutual. Let me know if I can help you out whenever.'

On an impulse she held out her hand. Tim was about to kiss it, checked himself, and instead shook it warmly.

Chapter 8
A Place to Live and
a House Warming

Tim combined his search for a place of his own with an exploration of Wash and its surrounds. Every route out of town ran into open countryside. Even the road to the M4 wound northwards through several miles of lush undulating hills dotted with outcrops of craggy white rocks of sandstone and lime. The early autumn colours blended warmly with the soft tones of the stone-built country villages. He briefly considered buying a rural retreat but dismissed it as a retirement option. He was still tugged by the latent possibilities of urban life, a yen his adventure with Georgie had done nothing to diminish. The dull ache of what he had lost never left him but the demands of his life in Wash allowed little opportunity to mope or even for much personal reflection. Activity became his anaesthetic.

He decided to find a place within walking distance of the city centre, although the period properties were beyond his means. Eventually he settled for a nineteen sixties semi in a suburban development in the east of the city not far from where he had bumped into Light-bulb and Dipstick.

The house was a brisk walk from the city centre with good access to the M4, useful when he needed to link up with life beyond Wash.

He didn't have to worry much about fitting the place out. The couple he bought it from were about to start a family and wanted to move on to bigger and they hoped better things. For five hundred quid they agreed to leave all the basic furniture including an old but comfortable suite, a kitchen table and chairs, and a huge floor-level double bed frame filled with a firm bouncy mattress. He already owned all the leisure and communications equipment he needed but added an extra television for the bedroom. He spent the thick end of a month's salary on a four door, second hand Volvo. The bodywork was beginning to flake and even rust in a couple of places but an AA inspection assured him that the engine was in good condition. Buying the car stretched his budget but it provided wheels to visit Gina and Maria in Essex and his mother in Lancashire.

Caveat emptor. According to popular wisdom a buyer discovers what's wrong with a house in the weeks after moving in. In that respect Tim was lucky. He had cut costs on the house survey, trusting the place had been as well maintained as it appeared. That turned out to be the case. Even the ancient central heating system gave no serious trouble, although it didn't provide much heat either. Neighbours can be another risk for a new homeowner. Pick the wrong ones and they can turn daily life into purgatory. That possibility hadn't even entered his mind. The elderly couple in the adjoining semi were pleasant enough but evidently had no wish to go beyond an occasional acknowledgement of mutual existence. That suited Tim. Polite chat had never been his forte. As it turned out, polite chat didn't last long with his neighbours on the other side either. Darren Naylor was a builder who used his house as a base for his business, ambitiously named 'Premiership Builders.' When Tim introduced himself as a social science lecturer, Naylor responded with a semi-literate diatribe about how too many people in the Britain were doing 'useless jobs.' In the brief period in which civil communication survived, Tim learnt that Naylor's wife kept the business's accounts and that both his dad-identikit sons had severe learning difficulties 'due to the fucking education system.' Naylor shook his thick fist to within a few inches of Tim's face as he delivered this damning verdict, implying that Tim was personally implicated in his boys' predicament.

Only a few days after he had moved in, Tim got a taste of Naylor's rough entrepreneurial spirit. He answered an early evening knock on the door.

'You settled in then?'

Tim nodded, 'Fine... definitely getting there.'

Naylor wasted no more time in coming to the point.

'Good. Ye've probably seen that the fence between our two driveways is rotten, falling to bits... I could put up a really nice one if ye'd split the cost. Now's the time to do it while ye're still into making things how you like them. May as well include the fence. I can do a good one cheap 'cos I got access to materials at trade price.'

Tim was well aware that according to the house deeds the maintenance of the boundary between the two properties was his neighbour's responsibility. But for the sake of good will and perhaps a say in the type of fence that went up he opted to make a contribution. Negotiations about how much this should be went on for a couple of minutes. Verbals got a bit edgy as it became clear to Naylor that he was going to get less than he wanted. In the end Tim's best offer of sixty quid was reluctantly accepted. When Tim pointed out that legally he didn't have to contribute anything Naylor's response was a sour 'Yeah right.' Naylor found his way back to his own property by route 'A' stepping over the old fence. He turned with sudden aggression, placed the sole of his shoe against the fence and pushed his weight through it. The rotten timber splintered and cracked. 'See it's fucked.' Tim agreed that it was one hell of a fucked fence.

The two men stared at each other, their mutual dislike setting hard.

Following this incident, Tim decided to limit conversation with his neighbour to a polite minimum. For a few weeks this worked, although it became increasingly obvious that Darren Naylor was no shrinking violet. He managed to inject a surly aggression into their brief exchanges. Tim responded with what he liked to think was his trademark cool. It was a potentially incendiary mix. Naylor liked to 'piss people off,' 'cool' was what annoyed him most.

Meanwhile Tim waited for signs of the fence to go up, cursing him-self for giving Naylor the full sixty quid up-front.

The fence aside, managing to buy a house without too much trouble was doubly convenient because work continued unrelenting. Life in higher education was more impersonal and fragmented than he'd expected much more so than in his previous job where everyone came into work daily, dropping into the staff room at break-times for chat and refuelling. There was usually someone to talk to and maybe a few people around after classes to have a drink with. His social life seemed to roll out fairly effortlessly. Wash University was different and it took some getting used to. Opportunities for socialising didn't arise so naturally. It didn't help that he was a lone rather than a team-based researcher. Swankie insisted that all full-time staff undertake and publish research. Tim disliked his officious tone but he was anyway a keen researcher. Like teaching, it was part of his chosen career of opening minds, not least, his own. Getting lost in his research also contributed to his 'escape' from the demons of regret.

Still, if he had come to Wash to work, work was not enough. He was caught in a tangle of contradictions of his own making. He wanted to remain available to Gina should she change her mind about him, yet he needed some sort of social life and human contact. Tempted by the unexpected opportunity of a period of no-strings hedonism he knew that the excitement and satisfaction of one-off encounters of the kind he had with Georgie was fleeting. His need for a more meaningful relationship was growing. But either way, he was open to possibilities. He was beginning to muse increasingly about the problem when the problem began to solve itself.

One early morning towards the end of autumn term, the phone rang. It was Erica Botham.

'Hi Tim, I thought I'd give you a social call. I hope you don't mind. I got your number from admin.'

He didn't mind.

'No, not at all. It's good to hear from you. I've hardly seen you since we bumped into each other in Waterstones. Sorry if I sound a bit grainy, I don't seem to get my wheels on before ten o'clock.'

'Wheels?'

'Just a figure of speech; I haven't quite revved up yet. What have you been up to anyway?'

'Not a lot. According to Henry you've been creating the news. I believe you've bought a house.'

'That's right. I invited Henry round but he hasn't made it yet.'

'I see. Actually I've called to ask you out for a drink. It's not often we get a new appointment in the department. We need to look after you.' She paused for a moment. 'If you don't fancy that I could pop round to see you and take a look at your new place?'

Tim hesitated for no more than a nano-second. Erica's approach was direct but he liked the direction. He quickly agreed. 'Ok. Why don't you drop by for dinner this evening? Bring a bottle with you, anything except sweet white wine.'

Even as they talked, his libido began to wake. How might the evening ahead pan out? Would Erica be as coolly self-contained but tantalisingly almost within reach as she had seemed when they met in Waterstones? How lucky might he get? She was one of the most beautiful women he had ever come within touching distance of. He wanted to touch.

Erica's voice interrupted his imaginings.

'No problem. I'll bring something for afters. And maybe a surprise.'

'Sounds great. Is eight o'clock a good time for you?'

'That's fine. Gotta go now, I'm teaching in a couple of minutes. See you later.'

'See you then.'

Throughout the day Tim tried not to think too much about the evening ahead. But he was feeling the pinch of abstinence. The episode with Georgie was several weeks ago and he had decided not to repeat it. Erica switched on all his lights but it was too early to second-guess what if anything might happen with her. He had to micro-manage so much of his life that it was almost a relief to leave one area open to chance. As he waited he couldn't ignore the anticipatory warmth and occasional involuntary throbbing of his loins and cock. *Down, hooligan, time you were taught a little self-control.* He was closer to the truth than he imagined but not that close.

The doorbell rang at eight precisely.

Opening the door Tim was dazzled by a vision of blond and blue. Erica's thick hair cascaded almost halfway down her dark blue, ankle-length off-leather coat. Her face was pale in the cold, accentuating the intensity of her unfeasibly light blue eyes.

He stifled an impulse to gape.

'Hi. Glad you made it ok. Come in, you must be frozen.'

'Hi. It *is* cold' she gave an exaggerated shiver as she stepped inside. 'I'll be fine when I warm up.'

Inside she handed her scarf and coat to Tim, her figure as shape perfect as he remembered. On the table, for once clear of books and papers, she off-loaded a large, eco-friendly Waitrose bag.

'A bottle of wine and a homemade trifle. My contribution.'

'Not *Blue Nun* or *Mateus Rosé*, I hope.' Tim eased into the small talk.

'No. It's a red burgundy. I hope that suits. Does *Blue Nun* still exist? I must say I've had my fill of nuns, blue or otherwise. I was educated in a convent. Not much fun, believe me. Well,' she reconsidered, 'there was plenty of fun but the nuns had nothing to do with it.'

Tim decided to move on swiftly from the nun theme, although not for the first time he was struck by how often he was drawn to ex-Catholic convent school girls. Their fall from grace seemed to lend an explosive abandon to their bedroom performances.

'Great. Red burgundy should go well with my trademark Irish stew. I'll put the trifle in the fridge.'

Once they began eating and drinking, conversation came easily. Tim had a line in sixties/seventies American folk/blues music and put on some Kris Kristopherson and early Dylan. Anxious not to appear 'all our yesterdays' he followed up with some Mumford and Sons and the latest Leonard Cohen – the thinking woman's Bing Crosby. None of this was quite Erica's top taste – Cohen, as she pointed out, was old enough to be her granddad, but the music melded into a rising mood of erotic attraction and sexual tension. He could have put on the national anthem without seriously interrupting the flow. By the time they finished the first course there had been enough friendly eye contact and 'incidental' touching for Tim to sense that Erica's interest in him might stretch beyond his Irish stew.

'Why don't we have the trifle in the lounge?' He wished he had found a smoother way of moving things on from the kitchen to the sofa.

Erica gave him a teasing smile. 'Is that where you usually have your trifles?' Embarrassed at her pun she quickly agreed with Tim's suggestion. 'Yeah let's go in there, but why don't we finish off the wine and smoke a joint before the trifle? A joint always puts an extra edge on my appetite. I've brought some stash with me.'

She glanced quickly at him. 'You do smoke don't you?'

'Not the killer tobacco, but yeah I enjoy the occasional joint.' He was beginning to feel that if a seduction was under way Erica was orchestrating it. She took a made-up joint from her bag.

Sat together on the sofa, she lit the joint and took an exploratory pull before passing it over. Tim rolled it tentatively between his fingers before taking a shallow drag. He coughed sharply as the dry smoke hit the back of his throat. This was strong stuff. He drank some wine before taking another pull, deeper this time. He felt a surge of pleasure in his lungs and brain. As the joint passed between them they became increasingly tactile, their hands brushing together. An aura of easy intimacy enveloped them as they began to revel in a sense of mutual discovery.

'Hello, then, Tim.' Erica reached across and gently caressed the back of his head and neck.

'Hello, Erica.' Now well in the zone, he added, 'I guess you know you're very beautiful.'

He had almost broken the spell.

'Tim, please.' She took her hand away from his neck. '*Nobody* knows they're very beautiful. Not really. Nobody's *that* secure.'

Tim leaned back, surprised. Surely she must be kidding him. Haloed in a soft psychedelic haze she was beautiful whether she knew it or not.

'Believe me, you *are* beautiful,' Tim insisted.

Drifting pleasantly, a spate of philosophical ponderings suddenly hijacked his brain. *But what is beauty? Is beauty in the eye of the beholder? Am I beautiful? What is the purpose of...*

Sensing she had lost him and keen to change the subject Erica brought him back to earth:

'Tim, haven't we forgotten something?'

'Have we? What?'

'The trifle. Why don't you get it from the fridge while I roll another joint?'

Tim did as he was told. He took the trifle from the fridge

103

and, never one for fancy presentation, stuck a couple of spoons in it.

Back in the lounge he was startled in a half-stoned kind of way to find Erica had stripped off her skirt and top. Her sheer black stockings, attached to a lace girdle by suspender straps, accentuated the bare flesh of her thighs. Below the girdle around her waist was a heavily corrugated, leather belt, decoratively suggestive but serving no obvious purpose. She had removed her panties and bra or perhaps was not wearing any in the first place. She still had on her platform shoes, her long legs as firm and defined as an athlete's through the tight silk fit of her stockings. Tim swiftly put the trifle on a coffee table. But it was Erica who made the next move.

'Let's dance' she said.

As they did so Tim's hands roamed freely, his sense of touch heightened by marihuana and alcohol. He ran his fingers through her thick, soft hair pulling gently against her scalp. She gave a low sensuous murmur. His hands brushed across her shoulders moving down to her breasts. Her nipples stiffened, hard as bullets as he rolled them between his fingers. Pausing to fondle her smooth, flat belly he gently tugged her pubic hair. Bending slightly he searched out her clitoris. It was moist and engorged, quivering at his touch. She held his hand guiding his rhythm as he began to massage it. She looked up at him, her eyes wide with pleasure, her mouth an open invitation. For the first time they kissed, ravenous with desire. Tim groped to unzip his trousers releasing his aching cock. He pushed hard towards her.

Erica pulled away.

'Mmm,' she fingered his cock, 'but take your time, Timothy, you're not even undressed yet.' She made the full complement of his name sound throatily sexy. 'Why don't you let me do that for you?' she said, not waiting for an answer.

'Lie on the couch.'

Sexual passivity had never been Tim's thing but this was

going too well to interrupt with rigid position taking. He decided to go with the music, Erica style.

Slowly, she undressed him. Straining with lust he attempted to pull her towards him. She gently pushed him back.

Her next remark seemed to mock his urgency.

'By the way, if you want any of that trifle you'd better have it now.'

Not waiting for his reply she reached over for the bowl.

'Here let me feed you. Open your mouth.'

Too far gone in this burgeoning ritual to protest, he did as he was bidden.

'There's a good boy. Open wide.' She slowly fed him half a dozen spoonfuls of creamy trifle pausing only to slip a condom on his cock.

'What a beautiful perpendicular. Now stand up.' She led him by the cock into the centre of the room.

'Stay here for a minute while I go and get something.'

Suspended somewhere between lust and apprehension, images of whips, handcuffs and shackles raced through Tim's mind. Erica returned with a woollen scarf.

'Crouch down a bit.' She deftly tied the scarf round his eyes.

'Hey,' Tim offered nominal resistance.

'Quiet.' She gripped his cock and kissed him full on the mouth.

'Now get down on your knees, find my feet and kiss them.'

'Alright, but... '

'Do it.'

He bent down and slowly began to kiss her feet and ankles, awkwardly conscious of his exposed buttocks.

'Erica I'm not...'

'Now tongue my clitoris.' As he raised his head she grasped a fistful of his hair and pulled his face between her legs, controlling their rhythmic rise and fall. His servicing was punctuated by the swish of leather across his arse as his resistance disappeared in a surge of pure sensation.

'Ahh... Ahh, stop,' she wrenched herself away from him.

Both were now agonising for release but she continued to hold back.

'Tim, you look strong, how strong are you? Can you lift me onto your cock and fuck me in mid-air?'

Tim could.

They came together in a roaring cursing frenzy. When they had finished they sank entangled to the floor.

A poet of the ancient world once wrote that after making love all creatures experience a feeling akin to sadness. These two felt emptied out, exhausted but joyful and happy with each other. Emerging from his semi-conscious drift, Tim pulled the scarf from his eyes. He found himself looking straight into Erica's baby blues, a quizzical half-crescent smile playing around her lips.

'I'd like to do that again,' he said, 'but without the props.'

'I know but not tonight. That was terrific but I'm going to go soon.' She gave him a warm, teasing smile. 'Thanks for letting me have my wicked pleasure with you. I've had fantasies about you ever you since you turned up for interview.' She smiled again in her candid, unembarrassed way before asking, 'Do you mind if I use your shower before I go?'

Erica was as good as her word. After she had showered and dressed, she kissed him and was gone, pausing only to say, 'I'll call soon.'

I sure hope you do.

Chapter 9
Home Again

Whitetown, Blackburn, Burnley, Nelson, and Colne. The names of this crescent of old North West industrial towns signalled home territory to Tim. From the warmth of the car he could see that a late autumn frost had hardened across the landscape. The fields and low-slung hills gleamed dully in the faltering sunlight.

He was born in Whitetown and his affection for it was refreshed by regular visits to his long widowed mother. But the demands of his life in transition had prevented him from making the journey north for several weeks. Now he was on his way, he found himself looking forward to returning to familiar territory. From the moment he thudded into his armchair, always vacated for his arrival, he felt at home in a way that he never quite felt anywhere else. This was the timeless place before which he remembered nothing. Here nothing should change, forever the beloved son. Yet in the twenty years since he had left Whitetown, imperceptibly but relentlessly, the mother/son relationship had transformed. At almost eighty Teresa was ageing fast and was now on the threshold of senility. Her dependency on him had begun to take on an air of desperation. The child had become the parent, his mother the child.

Home is where they have to let you in, he mused as he shifted the car into the fast lane, overtaking a big, bullying lorry that had been blocking him for several minutes. The house he and Gina had bought in Peyton was no longer his other, different home. She was reluctant to invite him inside even for a few minutes when he visited Maria. Too painful, she said, although he guessed she was also falling in with Rupert's wishes. When he stayed overnight it was at the local B&B, where he had briefly lived after their separation. Yet Gina had chosen to come with him now, insisting that her relationship with his mother would not end 'just because of their break-up'. The 'just because' hurt him, but he was grateful that Gina wanted to keep this remaining shared ritual going. And maybe it was also an oblique signal that she still cared for him. The two women had grown close and he and Gina agreed that they would not trouble his mother with their own problems. Not that he had intended to. He had long shielded her from anything in his life that might cause her anxiety.

Glancing in the driver's mirror he saw Gina was asleep, squeezed across the rear seats of the car. She claimed exhaustion at the double burden of work and childcare. Fair enough, he thought, but he sensed she was also pricking at his feelings of guilt.

As always he was glad to spot the signpost indicating twenty-one miles to Whitetown. The 'white' in 'Whitetown' was something of a misnomer. Some of its buildings were still marked by industrial smoke and grime although like many northern towns, Whitetown had been largely cleaned up and gentrified. After years of lying semi-derelict, the docks had been converted into a marina and leisure-park and one of the big cotton mills had become a mail order depot. Many of the old council estates had changed in character. The right to buy policy had edged some households and estates towards lower middle class respectability while others became the last rough refuge of those who could not or would not make out in the new winner-takes-all Britain, a fragmented underclass, some of them not having seen employment through two or three generations.

Tim's own childhood in the late nineteen seventies and early eighties coincided with the dying spasms of Britain's industrial age. His local primary school mainly drew children from a couple of large, run-down public housing estates but also some, including Tim, from lower middle class neighbourhoods for whom St. Patrick's was the only option if their parents wanted them to have 'a good, Catholic education.' This was certainly what Teresa intended for Tim. Ironically, what this meant was an education that owed as much to 'the mean streets' as to the classroom. Even before he had reached double figures Tim occasionally ran foul of would-be hard-nuts who baited him for being 'posh' or otherwise riled him in a childhood play of status and power.

'Posh' was a sure-fire insult used by the kids from the council estates on the West side of the Royal Longchester Road, to ruffle those from the mainly private housing on the East side. Tim contemptuously rejected 'posh'. He knew how hard his mother struggled to keep their house going after the early death of his father. There was no way they were well off or snobbish, no way 'posh'. But he sensed that he wasn't one of the rough kids either. Usually he didn't get on with them. They were often restless and disruptive. A few were threatening. For some reason, maybe because he was tall, the mass of non-fighting kids would put him forward as a kind of protector or perhaps it was just that they needed a decoy target for the bullies. He was a reluctant champion but he wasn't going to bottle out if things edged past the verbals.

He remembered one fight (he was about nine or ten) when he came up against a big bruiser of a lad whose early maturity was well captured in his nickname of 'Ding-Dong'.

Ding-Dong had baleful, pale-grey, almost colourless eyes, one menacingly half-covered by a drooping, thickened eyelid. His calves looked almost distorted they were so huge.

The fight sprawled all over the schoolyard. In the bicycle shed at the bottom of the yard Tim got caught in a neck-lock and was wrenched to the ground. The lock held and Ding Dong pushed his free fist into Tim's face.

'Give up or I'll punch yer face in.'

Tim winced as a thick wart-encrusted fist ground against his mouth. He played for time.

'I can't breathe,' he gasped, 'gerroff mi neck.'

Ding-Dong increased the pressure. Tim's neck cracked painfully.

'Ye've one last chance to give up or I'll mash ye.'

Whether Tim would have given up, risking permanent dishonour was never put to the test. He could not quite recall how salvation came. Maybe Ding-Dong was turned over by some of the crowd causing him to loosen his hold. But Tim preferred to think that he had shaken him off in a moment of Herculean exertion. That was possible. It was too long ago for him to remember exactly. Either way as Ding-Dong's grip slipped Tim wrenched free and reversed the neck-hold.

Now it was his turn to ask the question:

'Are ye gonna give up now, or do ye want me to bash yer face in?' He let go a half-punch to assist Ding-Dong with the decision.

To his relief, Ding-Dong quickly spluttered surrender, offering no more than a threat to 'do in' Tim next time.

Chaired around the schoolyard and acclaimed 'cock of the school' Tim was giddy with triumph. The sound of the bell to end break swiftly returned him to planet earth. The noisy hubbub dropped to an excited murmur as the kids lined up to file into school. Tim tried to look inconspicuous. No chance, the teacher on duty pulled him out as he attempted to shuffle un-noticed into school.

'What on earth have you been doing to look like that, Connor? You're filthy from head to toe.'

'Playing football, Sir.'

'Very likely. Go and see Mother Superior just as you are.'

'Yes, Sir. Can I go to the toilet first Sir?'

'No, you've had plenty of time to do that. Go and see Mother Superior and tell her exactly how you got into that shameful state. Tell her Mr. McKie sent you.'

Tim found Mother Superior outside her office in conversation with a pupil's parent. He decided brevity might work to his advantage.

'Please Mother Superior, Mr McKie wants to know if I can have a wash?'

The nun turned to him, irritated at the interruption. Immediately deciding that he was no sight for parental eyes she quickly dispatched him on his way. A wash she agreed would be a good thing and the sooner the better.

Tim didn't hang about. He skipped the wash and the rest of the school day. On the way back home he bought himself a celebratory stick of liquorice and a giant gob-stopper. Thinking about it he decided he didn't really like fighting, but it was ok when you won.

Tim jerked back to full consciousness as the traffic suddenly slowed. He braked heavily coming to a stop no more than a couple of feet behind a glossy Mercedes.

'What's up?' Gina cried in alarm from the back of the car.

'Nothing. It's only a build up of traffic. Don't worry. You can go back to sleep. It's still a good twenty minutes to home.'

'I might just do that but it would help if you stayed awake. It wouldn't be the first time you've banged somebody from behind.'

'Elegantly put! But stop worrying, it distracts me from driving.'

A groan from Gina signalled an end to the conversation.

Tim appreciated the need to stay fully focused as the

rush hour traffic thickened in the last few miles to White-town. But a mood of reminiscence had taken hold of him. 'Posh!' He knew he had never been posh. The only reason his mum could afford a semi on the bright side of the road was because his dad had left just enough money to cover the cost. Had he not been an only child things would have been stretched even further. Even so Teresa had needed to work as a seamstress and a shop assistant to make ends meet. 'Brave old girl' he thought. He appreciated that now and regretted how much he had taken her for granted as a kid. At least he was starting to make up for it. No chance to do that for his father. Despite his psychological studies, he could never figure out how his father's death might have affected him. His father, Dominic had been a professional footballer and hadn't lived long enough to do much else. He remembered the headline in the local paper as if it were an inscription on a gravestone: 'Dominic Connor: Dead of a brain tumour at forty-one'. Dominic had played at the highest level but despite trying to stay in the game as long as possible had just missed the big money times. Still, he had left enough to set his family up.

Tim idolised his father or at least the image of him that he had conjured up in his mind. At the age of seven he had no previous experience of loss. Until then tragedy was always something out there, remotely dreadful but part of the big wide grown-up non-world of 'the news.' In his own world nothing more terrible had happened than losing the front door key, or booting a football through the front window, or getting bloodied up in a fight, or riding his bike into the local canal. These events could be nerve-racking for a young kid but were no preparation for the death of a parent. He went through the rituals of loss and separation in a trance. His sense of detachment was sealed by the whis-pered words of his uncle as his father's coffin was lowered into its grave: 'Try not to cry, it will upset your mother.'

He didn't cry. He hadn't cried since. Big boys don't cry. On the outside no tears, inside the hurt seeped like a wound.

'Tim!' His mood was suddenly broken.

'Tim, we've just gone past the first exit to Whitetown. If you miss the next one we're on our way to Longchester.'

Gina frequently took on the role of organising Tim. He had found it helpful but was now beginning to resent it. In the post break-up phase of their relationship she was less patient with him, less amused and more often annoyed by his vagaries and zany humour. He had to work hard to avoid triggering outbreaks of mutual irritation. It didn't help that in practical matters she was usually right, as she was this time. He had day-dreamed his way past the first exit to Whitetown. He dropped a gear and shifted the car into the inside lane as the sign for the second exit came up. He mustered the best defence he could.

'Don't worry, Gina, it may be a bit further, but this way we get better views and we can stop at that fish and chip shop we went to once before. You know, the one at the top of the hill arched by trees.' He had almost convinced himself that he had intended to by-pass the first exit.

'Well, I suppose we'll have to buy something to eat. Your mum is way past being able to cook for three. She can't even look after herself properly now. No wonder the social worker thinks she'll need to go into a care home sooner rather than later.'

Tim winced. His mother had long since laid down the battle lines about moving into a care home. She was not going to and it was his duty to ensure that it did not happen. Her determination to resist was set solid by the grim experience of a two-week 'respite break' she had been persuaded to take in a local convent that doubled up as 'a retirement home.' She hated it. After over thirty years of being her 'own boss' she found it impossible to have her life ordered by others. She was so alienated by the regime of rigid wake-up and bed times, regular sessions of worship, and constant cajoling to take her pills that she was driven to make an 'escape attempt' before the first week was over. Carrying a light case and a plastic bag containing her possessions, she failed even to make it past the front door of the convent. The irony was that she had the right to leave. But to her, the nuns represented the authority of the church and she lacked the confidence to face them down. By the time Tim arrived to deal with the situation her two-week 'respite' was almost over.

The incident had been a warning. Teresa was becoming unpredictable, a danger to herself. A rogue parent in Whitetown was all he needed. He was beginning to see where he got his own independent streak from, stubbornness even. He could understand her finding the nuns 'bossy and interfering.' What he hadn't anticipated was that her miserable sojourn in the convent coupled with God's apparent indifference to her increasingly panic-driven pleas to restore her health and happiness would begin to take the gloss off her life-long Catholic faith. Though not a believer himself, this was far from what he expected or wanted. He was worried that any loss of her sense of religious security would accelerate her decline. As the gap between Teresa's increasing needs and her isolated domestic situation grew, matters began to spiral. Managing things from Wash was becoming almost impossible.

'The fish and chip shop comes up on our left in about four hundred yards,' Gina reminded him.

'I know, I know.' It annoyed him that Gina took control even in his home territory. He liked to think that he held his ground on the big issues especially when they concerned his mother. Or did he? Their break-up had shaken his confidence. He was beginning to think that conflict-avoidance had become his default position. But self-doubt wasn't really an option... A mini-breakdown perhaps? Don't even think of it. There just wasn't time to fit one in.

The shop came into view and he pulled the car over to the curb. The shop sign read:

FISH AND CHIPS AND CURRY

'Curry, that's new,' said Gina. 'I think I'll go for one.'

'It's fish, chips and mushy peas for me and Mum. She's not into curry.'

'Surprise, surprise,' smiled Gina, perking up at the prospect of food.

Inside the shop smelt of fried fat, salt and vinegar and hot sugary spices.

'What can I get you?' the young woman behind the counter spoke with an Eastern European accent. 'All food are freshly cooking this evening.'

Tim gave the order and was quickly served. Minus the thick end of twenty quid he returned to the car nibbling on a hot juicy chip.

'We should wait to eat with your mum,' suggested Gina.

'Of course, but if I don't have a couple of chips now, I might flake out before we get home. I'm famished.'

Gina looked like she was going to contest the point. Instead she changed tack.

'Ok. Pass me a chip then, you can have a taste of curry later.'

Score draw thought Tim. No, better than that, positively friendly.

A breath of fresh air and more than a few tasty chips livened Tim up. As usual his faculties came on stream as he drove the last few miles into his home town. Familiar landmarks replaced the endless samescape of the motorway way. First up after the chip shop was the old pub, the *Yorkshire Arms* just off a roundabout that channelled traffic one way into the centre of Whitetown and the other towards the North West. Tim swung the car northwards to skirt the town. Within a minute the football stadium where his father had played came into sight; a shiny monument to the team's glory days and hoped for triumphs to come. But for the moment, a temple of failure. *Can't put two wins together or if they do, they lose the next four.* Not far from the ground was a temple from a different epoch, St. Thomas's church, its unusual broad hexagonal tower solid on the skyline. His dad had occasionally attended mass there.

It pleased Tim that his father had never been a 'good Catholic' in any formal sense. He was sure his dad had been a decent man but without concerning himself much about religion one-way or the other. Not so Tim who had spent much of his early adolescence in pious agonising. Puberty brought a deluge of scruples. God or masturbation? Tim smiled at the sad irony of it all as he gazed from church to stadium. He'd certainly got more out of football than religion, but not as much as his dad. Football was his dad's life. He was proud of Dominic's achievements. A losing cup final, though he'd scored in every round, and a victory playing for Scotland against England when he'd also scored. Tim had wanted to emulate his father and had shown some serious talent before he'd lost the plot in his tangled early-teen years. *Be honest you were never a patch on your father.* But if his father had lived long enough to coach him, maybe...

Next the road passed a long stretch of parkland, the grass and a few shrubs broken only by a dowdy ornamental pond, host to a dozen or so bog-standard ducks and a couple of bored looking swans. Dale Park was one of the first municipal parks in England and even now was held in great public affection though few spent much time in it. There had been an outcry when the council announced its intention to grant planning permission for a residential development on the parkland. The struggle resulted in a popular victory celebrated by the unexplained appearance of a large block of concrete next to the pond. On it was carved a clenched fist with the words 'Power to the People' etched across it. Shortly afterwards at the arrival of spring, swathes of daffodils appeared for the first time along the park's edge. The Council denied any knowledge of who had planted the daffodils and declared the victory block illegal. It was duly removed, only to be mysteriously replaced by another one similarly inscribed. This happened several times until a smoother looking erection appeared inscribed with the words 'The People are Powerful.' That was how the matter rested, with both parties seeming to feel that they had made their point. It was never discovered who carved out the compromise.

At the end of the stretch of road passing alongside the park, came the first of two sets of lights, next they crossed a railway bridge, before passing through the second set of lights, then they took a sharp right, then a left, from where they were only a few tarmac covered yards to home. It was a good sign that the house gates were open. It meant that his mum had remembered that they were due to visit. Last time they were up Teresa had forgotten to carry out the gate-opening ritual – a sure sign that she was fading.

'Looks like she's looking forward to our visit,' said Gina. 'What's the betting she's got the tea-tray laid out just like she used to?'

'That would be nice but I doubt if she's up to it these days.' Tim squeezed the car into the tiny driveway, leaving Gina just enough space to get out on the hedge side. They picked up their travel bags and a bunch of carefully wrapped flowers from the boot of the car. Gina had bought the flowers as she always did. She handed them to Tim. 'Here, you give them to her. She always appreciates them more coming from you.' Tim took the flowers with only a minimal show of reluctance. He had long since become shameless in taking advantage of Gina's practical caring.

They gave the front door bell an extended ring. It had been fitted with a sound amplifier to combat Teresa's serious deafness. They retreated from the raucous noise and waited. A couple of minutes passed. Tim moved forward. Pressing his face against the frosted glass section of the door he was able to make out the shape of his mother edging towards them. She was pushing something in front of her.

'Christ! I think she's using a Zimmer.'

'I'm not surprised. Look don't make too much of it. It will only upset her.'

By now Teresa had reached the door. She was struggling

to unhitch the safety chain, trying to open it while still clutching her zimmer-frame. Tim pushed gingerly from the outside.

'Ooh... careful or you'll have me over.' His mother's voice sounded weaker than at their last visit.

'Mum, move back a bit and leave me to open the door.'

Teresa inched slowly backwards dragging her zimmer-frame with her. Finally there was enough space for Tim and Gina to get in.

'Good to see you, Mum.' He eased her from her zimmer-frame and gave her a careful hug.

'Thank God you're here. I was out of my mind with worry. I thought you might have crashed. That motorway's not safe.'

Gina took Teresa's anxious tone as a cue to engage.

'Teresa, hi. You haven't forgotten who I am, have you? I've been so looking forward to seeing you again.'

'No. It's you Gina, isn't it? It's my eyes. They're not as good as they used to be. I'm always glad when you come. You're such a kind person, not like that woman who brings me my meals.'

They made their way slowly into the living room. The tea tray was conspicuously absent.

'Tim, you chat with your mum for a few minutes and I'll make us all a pot of tea.'

Gina was used to Teresa's kitchen being in a mess but what she found this time was a shock: several half-drunk cups of tea, some caked with fungus, a couple of cans of soup already opened and beginning to smell, crumbs and stains everywhere, an unsealed loaf of mouldering cheap sliced bread, and most worrying, the ancient gas cooker thick with inflammable grease. In the fridge was a carton of curdled milk and not much else. This was mess turning to decay. She went back into the living room adopting as positive a tone as she could muster.

'Tim, I'm going to pop to the shops at the top to buy a

few things,' adding in an aside, 'just take a quick look into the kitchen while I'm gone.'

The chaos in the kitchen and the rest of the house galvanised Tim and Gina into a flurry of phone calls and visits to social services, including Teresa's 'dedicated' social worker, and two remaining friends from her own generation. Neither of the latter was able any longer to manage more than an occasional visit to Teresa and even then they might not be recognized. One thing had become clear. The argument about whether Teresa should go into residential care was over. Hate it or not – and she hated it – she would have to do so. 'I'd rather die than be put into a home,' she had often said, 'but Catholics aren't allowed to kill themselves, are they?' *Holy mother church, where are you when we really need you?*

The decision that Teresa should go into full-time residential care was unavoidable but it proved more difficult to organise the transition than Tim anticipated. Apart from the problem of Teresa's resistance, a suitable place had to be found and eventually the family house would have to be put up for sale. In the short term the best he could do was to increase meals on wheels from one to three times a day and set up a morning and evening visit from a carer. As it turned out all this was nothing more than a band-aid to a steadily, sometimes scarily deteriorating situation.

But it was not all bleak. Teresa had not completely lost her capacity for simple pleasure. Sometimes even forgetfulness was a help, allowing her to live in the moment. She was at her happiest when the three of them went out together. Tim and Gina got reflected pleasure from the old woman's enjoyment of the meals they shared, sometimes driving out to country pubs familiar to her. Most of all she looked forward to the short walks they took together, mere tokens compared to what she had managed even a few years ago. Whitetown had several parks all of which Teresa knew well. Taking an arm each they would support her on an assisted totter for a few hundred yards in one or other of them before finding a pub where she could sip what she still referred to as 'a gill of ale.'

For a change they would sometimes walk by the local canal or go down to the renovated docks. There on one occasion, Teresa briefly threw off the manacles of age and dementia. The three of them were relaxing, leaning against the iron rails of the harbour as they watched the evening sunlight play on the water and boats. Gulls wheeled and glided, occasionally crying eerily as they swooped down, skimming for fish or settling softly on the water. Tim began to reminisce about how the docks had once been a vibrant hub of the town's international trade. For many years Whitetown had been one of the country's main importers of bananas that were then packed at the local Fyffes plant before distribution. Not, he mused, that bananas ought to need much packing. Drop them into a cellophane bag and they're ready for off, presumably minus a few substandard ones. His train of thought brought to mind a calypso that he thought might be called 'The banana boat song.' Inspired by the warmth and well being of the evening he half spoke, half sang the old dock workers song: 'Hey Mr Tally man, tally de bananas.'

He was struggling to recall the lyrics when Teresa interrupted. 'Bananas! What a funny topic for a song. I know a nice poem about daffodils. I'm going to recite it for you.'

She turned her back to the water, leant against the railings and cleared her throat. Tim and Gina respectfully withdrew a couple of yards, taking up their position as audience. In a quiet but firm voice, moved but composed, she began to recite Wordsworth's famous poem: 'I wandered lonely as a cloud...'

She smiled, proud and happy as she completed her recitation. It wasn't the whole poem, but the lines she remembered from Wordsworth's famous verses were delivered word perfect and without a moment's hesitation. Tim and Gina applauded enthusiastically, impressed and moved by Teresa's recitation. Like the poem itself the incident hovered precariously between bathos and the sublime. Another of the poet's phrases came to mind, his definition of poetry: 'emotion recollected in tranquillity.' Thanks for the memory.

The rest of their stay was spent trying to find suitable residential care for Teresa and in doing their best to ensure that she would be safe and comfortable until it became available. They tried gently to get Teresa used to the idea of the move and to nudge her towards some kind of consent to it. What little progress they made was soon reversed. Teresa could seldom remember what she had agreed to from one day to the next.

She was even more edgy than usual as they packed the car to leave. They had done their best to explain the new regime of care and safety now in place, including providing her with an outline of the main points in double-sized print. But Teresa was beyond reassurance. Her response was to become more anxious. She had lost the ability to maintain her old routines and was unable to grasp new ones.

Tim stopped the car outside the front gate to wave a last goodbye. His mother, stood at the front door, somehow found the strength to smile.

Chapter 10
Henry on the Rocks

Henry Jones woke up feeling more than usually lousy. His mouth was dry and furred and pain was pulsing through his eyes and temples. His stomach, normally durable against abuse, gurgled and groaned. For once, even he was nauseated by the smell of stale alcohol and excremental gases. He peered through the semi-darkness at the bedside clock. Five thirty! He needed a piss and probably a shit if he could manage it. Then he would go back to bed.

He rolled over slowly to the edge of the bed, levering his legs onto the floor one at a time. He sat for a moment, recovering, cupping his hands over his eyes. *Sweet fucking oblivion!* But not for long. He lowered his hands planting them on the bed and pushed hard. He shot quickly into a standing position. Even more swiftly he catapulted back onto the bed. A repetition of the routine was more successful. Apparently upright he aimed himself towards the bathroom. As usual he broke his resolution to avoid looking into the bathroom mirror before breakfast. *Didn't you used to be?* He didn't bother to finish mouthing the cliché.

The once handsome visage resembled a fruitcake inadvertently left out in the rain. Was this the face he now deserved? Probably. He thumped onto the toilet. *All energies seek release.* Thank God for that! Relieved he stood up, more easily this time.

Once out of the bathroom he got back into bed. He knew he wouldn't sleep again. He rarely slept well without the help of alcohol. Afternoons were an exception when he seemed able to sleep anywhere, most particularly in his office. Even that privilege was now denied him. Swankie had 'requested' him to move out of his old office following the so-called job rotation with Steir and now he had to share a room with another colleague also considered to be on the way out. He shifted around in bed for a few minutes, his head still throbbing and his chest tight. Should he risk going into Annette's bedroom and slip into bed beside her? He knew that would be the last thing she wanted. A couple of years ago she had insisted on separate bedrooms claiming that 'his erratic habits' kept her awake. After a few months of sleeping separately she announced that their sex life was over. He replied that he had worked that out for him-self as they hadn't had sex for over three years. But he had learnt to avoid sarcasm with Annette. She always hit back with twice the vitriol. And she was lethally clever with words. Sometimes the full import of her put-downs only dawned on him much later, like the delayed impact of a physical injury. Her crueller remarks could upset him for days. He felt he ought to hate her but knew he still loved her. Why? It was beyond logic. He was trapped. His dogged attempts to rekindle communication only increased his feelings of hopelessness as he met an ice-wall of rejection. He concluded none too cleverly that Annette didn't want to know. He was now depressed most of the time except when he was on an alcoholic high or sometimes when he was with friends. But there seemed to be fewer of them these days. There was Fred but he was in London. He liked the new guy, Tim Connor. He thought they had got on well when they met in the Mitre before term started and on the handful of times they had met-up since. But Connor was of a different generation. Things were pretty desperate if he had to trawl for friendship among new appointments. *What kind of mess am I in?*

His thoughts slipped back to Annette. They had first met over twenty years ago when both had arrived in Wash, she as a postgraduate student and he as an academic. He had been appointed as research supervisor to her thesis on gender in the work of Marx and Engels. Back then the institution was a large college rather than the small university it had become and attracted only a handful of research students. Few staff could plausibly claim adequate credentials for research supervision. Henry was at least thought to be 'brilliant' and on the cusp of making a name for himself. Even so he was a little insecure in the role of research supervisor and compensated by playing the charismatic don with his new student. And in those days he was attractive in a chunky De Niro kind of way. More importantly from Annette's point of view, they clicked academically. Their tutorials fizzed along as they contested the merits of radical feminism, Annette's perspective, with the socialist communitarianism that Henry favoured. These days he was less certain of what he did believe, although emotionally and in public he clung on to his radical image. If he was less sure of solutions, he was certain that all manner of evils flowed from the triumph of global capitalism already re-establishing itself, as he saw it, after the financial crash of 2008. Once in a while in the lecture room he could still produce a bravura critique of 'the system' but the charisma that used to draw his young audience to him was gone. Most students liked him well enough and found him entertaining, but few related much to the content of what he said.

It had all been utterly different a quarter of a century ago. His lectures were invariably well attended and he was in great demand among students for small group and individual tuition. Most of all he looked forward to his tutorials with Annette. Their energy and intensity spilled over into sessions in the coffee bars and pubs of the city. Ideas and events seemed all important then – from wrestling with the subtleties of structuralism to celebrating the deliciously heartless dumping of Thatcher. Then they believed that somehow they could change things or be part of change. Now he doubted it. And he was beginning to feel his age. Time had been called on his personal hopes and political dreams. Things were falling apart and he could not see how to put them together again. A cultural ethos of dynamism and expectation had somehow transformed into one of confusion and uncertainty. If he understood it, he certainly did not like it. Much of what he had believed in had become a standard political and media reference point for irrelevance and feeble idealism and was perceived as such in the popular mind.

Despite their growing mutual attraction, Henry held off from making a definitive move towards Annette. He did not particularly buy the conventional wisdom that academics should avoid becoming personally and sexually involved with students although he had more than once witnessed the emotional mayhem and professional disruption this could cause. As he debated and flirted with Annette he was not even sure that he wanted to take their relationship to a more intimate personal and physical level. Was he being cautious, playing a waiting game or perhaps not playing any game at all? He had some notion, half-baked he admitted, that if you stood outside the power games, things came more easily to you. Yet almost two years passed and, for all their pleasure in each other's company, nothing of a romantic or sexual nature occurred.

In the end it was Annette who made the decisive move although he was a willing enough accomplice. Late one night they had gone to her flat after seeing a movie. In her no-messing-about way, she had asked him whether it wasn't time that they slept together. Taken by surprise he found himself readily agreeing that it was. Yet the sudden prospect of transition from friends to lovers momentarily seemed to non-plus them. They undressed separately and got into bed. From then things slowly gathered momentum. He still remembered her cool nakedness as their bodies closed together, first awkwardly and then eagerly. They made love with tenderness and affection into the quiet of the morning. That was a long time ago.

Sometimes Henry persuaded himself that he had not changed much from those days; that his 'real self' was still intact, that he was still worthy of attention and affection. As much as ever, he needed to share his love with Annette. But he knew that she did not feel the same. He might persuade himself that there was no good reason why their relationship should have changed but he could not persuade her. How often had she told him 'to stop kidding' himself? As he stuttered and declined she had grown in confidence and found fresh challenges. Their lives arched off into divergent directions. What they had imagined to be their future together proved simply to be an illusion spawned at a point when their trajectories had crossed. She had now begun to articulate their early relationship almost in psychoanalytic terms. At first she had mocked her mother's sharp comment, offered without the aid of Freudian theory, that he was 'nothing but a father figure.' Even now, she could not accept that their relationship could be reduced to such a banal proposition, but she had come to realise that Henry had been something of an archetype for her, the intellectual as sage and fearless iconoclast. The reality was a straw man, a vacuous old windbag. How could she have been so fooled?

She made no attempt to keep her disappointment to herself but occasionally even she was shocked at how harsh she could be. The best she could do was to pity him. Poor Henry. She had endowed him with far more heroic qualities than he possessed. Yet he had once had a certain presence and conviction and even now could occasionally cut the figure of the ancient savant, especially when he was drunk. But that was about the size of it. She conceded that there was an element of tragedy in his decline. His failure, as she saw it, was due to flaws of character rather than lack of talent. His ability to analyse 'the system', albeit with little reference to leading thinkers of the last twenty years, was at times still dazzling. But not only had he become almost completely politically inactive, he was unable even to manage his own career effectively. When she was twenty-seven and he was in his early forties his title of 'Senior Lecturer' had seemed rather grand. Now the same title was annoyingly unimpressive. At first she had assumed the world of academe would rise to Henry's brilliance. When this didn't happen she encouraged him to publish and otherwise put himself about. As he seemed unable to respond, doubt slowly began to set in. Finally she lost faith that he would fulfil his potential and loss of interest followed. She could perhaps have lived with his career failure and physical decline, repellent though she now found him, but she could not bear the sense that he was a wasted man, a pathetic human being. Love, if that was what it was, had turned first into doubt and anxiety and then into disillusion and contempt. She could barely look at him without wishing she didn't have to. Increasingly she saved herself the trouble.

Her own academic career had developed as his stagnated. She had found a job at South of England University, a more established and higher status institution than Wash University. By the time she was thirty she had published a couple of articles in highly rated journals, followed a few years later by a book based on her research thesis. There had been other publications and she had recently been appointed to a Readership with a brief to promote feminist research. Currently she was working with a joint group from Wash University and South of England University on a collection of essays on the theme of 'why feminism is relevant to the current generation of young women.' Later in the day she had a meeting planned with the Wash section of the collective. Feminism aside she had come to prefer working on publishing projects with women rather than men. Her experience was that women were more cooperative and more supportive: friendship and work seemed to integrate more easily.

Still in bed, Henry stared bleakly at the ceiling. Dark blotches and thin spidery lines danced before him. Lurching forward in an attempt to grab a dense looking giant floater, he was left squinting into his empty hand. He let loose a fart, strident with discontent but faintly comforting as it wafted across his backside. Suddenly conscious of his half-addled state he felt a surge of frustration. It was time he asserted himself. If he did intend to steal into his wife's bed he better do so soon. Once fully awake she would certainly repel him. Even if he succeeded in getting into her bed he realised that his options would be limited. She called the shots between the sheets these days and they were few and far between. What he really wanted was a cuddle, some affection. *You sad old fart.* He stumbled out of bed again. He briefly considered taking off his pyjamas, contemplating a *tour de passion.* Instead he opted for caution, leaving his pyjama trousers on and replacing the top with his cleanest dirty shirt. Fortified by this compromise he stumbled towards his wife's bedroom.

He opened Annette's bedroom door softly. She was still asleep and conveniently facing the wall on the far side of the room. Defying his hangover Henry managed to cross the room unheard and slip unnoticed into bed beside her. For fully fifteen minutes he was able to gaze at the back of her head: the blond hair shading in places to grey, the slim, vulnerable neck and the lean, determined shoulders. Should he seize the moment and gently wake her or stretch out his fragile fantasy of intimacy for as long as possible. As ever the choice was taken from him. Abruptly Annette spun to face him her hazel eyes cold.

'Henry, what the hell are you doing? Separate beds remember. Otherwise it just leads to complications. We've both got to function at work today. I don't want another row. They exhaust me.'

'I don't want a row either. I still have feelings... I just thought,' Henry knew he sounded desperate and pathetic. He attempted to embrace Annette. She jerked away from him.

'Henry, you stink. You're probably still drunk. Where's your pride? We can't go on like this.'

'Annette, please. Let's talk. Why are you doing this?'

'Why am *I* doing this? You've got to be bloody joking. Go and take a look at yourself in the mirror.'

'I already have.'

'Well?'

'Well what? I can't help getting older?'

'You know quite well it's not that. Henry you're an alcoholic. You're a fucking shambles.'

Annette paused, softening slightly.

'Look, I'm sorry. I really am. Maybe I shouldn't have said that. It upsets me to see you like this. But it's been upsetting me for years now. You won't change. I need to live my own life. I'm only just waking up to what I can do, to what I want to do.'

'But Annette, I'm not stopping you. I want you to do your own thing. Haven't I supported you in building up your career?'

'You *are* stopping me. Things are completely different from the way they used to be. You know that.'

She focused again on the dishevelled and demoralised figure of her husband. The spectacle confirmed that there was not an iota of hope for them. Better to seize this unsought for moment to end their relationship, definitely, finally and no going back.

'Henry. I'm sorry. This is it. I've already decided that we should split up. At least we don't have kids to worry about.

We can sell the house. Rachel has said that I can move into her spare room whenever I need to. But I want fifty percent of the value of the house, no messing about.'

'The cunt.'

'What did you say?'

Henry flinched.

'Not you, her... I'm sorry I shouldn't have said that. I'm sorry.'

'You better be. Now please leave me to get ready for work. You ought to do the same. And I suggest a shower. Wash your mouth out while you're at it.'

'Annette.'

'I mean it. Leave me alone. I've got to get ready. Please go.'

Still unsteady Henry heaved to his feet. As he reached the bedroom door he turned to plead again. His partner lifted her hand to silence him.

'No... no more.' For a fleeting moment she was caught by the sadness of unfulfilled hope and expectation and added in a softer tone, 'I'm really sorry Henry, no more.'

They made their way separately into the university: Henry to teach and Annette for her pre-arranged meeting with Rachel Steir and whoever else from the writing group that could make it. Somehow Henry managed to deliver his lecture. Playing the lovable old soak he even exchanged light repartee with a couple of students. One of them pushed it a bit, asking if Henry could confirm that Marx frequently used to get drunk after a hard day's work in the British Museum Library. Henry replied that as far as he knew Marx started drinking at lunch time and his work was all the better for it. He backtracked from this piece of fiction when he noticed that some of the more diligently literal students were writing it down.

Once he had finished his lecture, Henry went over to the new senior common room. The term 'senior common room' was something of a misnomer because very few senior academics and managers ever went there. The old common room was a haven of deep leather chairs and solid wooden tables, where newspapers and magazines were provided and tea and cake breaks put on two afternoons each week. That would now seem like unacceptable luxury to the cost-cutters thought Henry but the old common room had served as a popular meeting place for staff from across the university: at times a buzzing forum of informal democracy and ideas. It was no surprise to Henry when the Estate and Planning Committee had claimed the room for conversion into a lecture theatre. The replacement was a small converted seminar room barely able to accommodate more than a twenty people at a time. The plate on the door of the old common room bore the initials ' SCR' whereas the new plate sported the number '119a' in shiny aluminium. It had been furnished, if that was the word, with a strident collection of bright carrot coloured plastic seats and tables that would not have looked out of place in a primary school classroom. Drinks and snacks were now delivered from a machine or not, depending on whether it worked or had been stocked or whether 'customers' happened to have the right change.

In his politer moods Henry referred to these developments and others like them as 'reverse progress.' At first most of his colleagues found his attitudes amusingly droll if distractingly irrelevant. But as 'efficiencies of scale' slowly proliferated at the expense of small freedoms and comforts, more began to see Henry's point. But most of them were too busy or quiescent to support his sporadic protests to and about the management. 'Mogadon men,' Henry once called some of them to their faces, but that didn't persuade them to his way of thinking either.

Henry found himself doing less and less to oppose 'reverse progress.' But he diligently continued to make a nuisance of himself to the university hierarchy and occasionally to carry the fight to the wider society, known to 'the suits,' he ironically observed, as 'the real world.' He still supported union actions and turned up at any available local anti-capitalist protest, but he did so with diminishing belief that any of this would make the slightest difference. He was more pessimistic than at any time since the early days of Thatcherism. Now what little impetus he could muster came as much from his gut as his brain. Like the time he took a swing at Swankie during a clash about the marketisation of higher education. He had got away with that because it had happened off-campus but Swankie smoothly won the practical argument in terms of university power politics.

Swankie could play and even manipulate the fast changing university system whereas Henry offered sweeping suggestions for reform that had little or no chance of being taken up. At the everyday level, Henry struggled to cope with change, surviving as best he could. Some innovations he sidestepped or took at his own pace, like PowerPoint, whilst others he let bounce off him, like the down-grading of staff room facilities. A plastic sofa was much like a leather sofa to his sainted arse and he was more than happy to provide his own liquid refreshment. He was relieved rather than offended that the remoter echelons of the hierarchy ignored the new staff room although he resented their expensively refurbished private offices and conference rooms in the main building. Still he didn't miss their self-important and patronising presence. They could 'fuck off' and the further off the better.

Having cajoled himself into just such a mood of intransigence, Henry entered 119a in a better state of mind than he had started the day. His spirits were raised another couple of notches on finding that Tim Connor and Aisha Khan were there.

'Hi Henry, good to see you. We're just working together on some teaching issues. How are you, anyway?' said Tim.

'Hello Henry,' smiled Aisha.

'Hi Tim, Aisha, I'm fine, rarely been better. I've just had a good session with the third years. They're quite eager, lots of questions, most of them daft admittedly. Can I get you two a drink, tea or coffee or something else?'

'I'll have a tea if that's ok,' said Aisha, 'milk, or powder to be more precise, and no sugar.'

'Sweet enough,' murmured Henry, instantly cursing himself for his crassness. For him flirtation, especially with junior members of his department or what *had* been his department belonged to another era.

'Nothing for me please, Henry. I have to leave soon. I've got to get across the country tonight, preferably before the weekend rush gets really under way,' said Tim.

'That's to see your daughter? Quite a journey. Let me pull a bottle of water for you. Not that I touch the stuff myself.'

Tim and Aisha smiled at each other, resigned more than amused.

'Don't bother, Henry, I've got plenty in the car.' Tim looked at his watch.

Turning quickly to Aisha he said 'relax about the psychology lecture. I'll fill in for you next week. It'll be basic introductory stuff... Listen, I must go now, otherwise I'll end up spending most of the rest of the day becalmed between Swindon and Reading.'

'Best avoid that,' agreed Henry. 'In the middle ages they used to send criminals to live in Reading as a punishment.'

Tim resisted the impulse to query Henry's historicity. He cleared his stuff from the table and exited purposefully.

After some sparring with the drinks machine, Henry picked up Aisha's tea from the porous metal plate and handed it to her. For a moment he thought of filling the seat next to her just vacated by Tim. Instead he sat a couple of seats away. There was a composure and self-containment about the young woman that he thought better than to intrude on.

'So how have things been going for you? Everything I hear is that the students love your teaching.' Henry had reverted to his default avuncular role, uncomfortably aware that he had been so self-preoccupied that he had failed even to ask Aisha how she was settling in.'

'I'm fine. Things were a bit scary at first but I'm really beginning to enjoy it now. People have been great, very supportive. Starting at the same time as Tim has helped; we've been a kind of reality check for each other, as well as swopping a bit of teaching. Rachel and Erica have been very good too. Rachel seems to know all there is to know about feminism including lots of stuff in my area. Not that I always agree with her. So... yeah, no, things are fine.' She hesitated for a moment. 'How are things with you? You look a little tired.'

Henry glanced defensively at Aisha. Her enquiry was routine enough, but to his surprise there was genuine concern in her voice. It disconcerted him. He had become unused to serious enquiries about his welfare. Her eyes held his gaze. Still raw from the events of the morning he wanted to unload emotionally. But he could not trust himself. He had no idea whether he could trust her. *There's no fool like an old fool.* He ignored Aisha's enquiry and tried to keep the conversation at a safe level.

'So, have you found any time to carry on with your research?'

Aisha's expression of concern relaxed. 'A little, not really, there's just been so much else I've had to do. It's not just work. As you know I have a child, not to mention a husband. Waqar is finding it more difficult to adjust to my career than I am. He really wanted me to work in his family business. But in some ways I think having separate jobs is better; there's more to share when we get home. He's more conservative than me and we have interesting times challenging each other's views. Do you have strong views Dr. Jones? I believe you are or used to be quite a radical.'

Henry blinked, her directness, politely, almost formally expressed caught him off-guard. Clearly superficial chit-chat was not Aisha's style. He remembered that what he had liked about her at interview apart from her obvious intelligence was her focused energy, powerful if not necessarily informed by experience. Not in the mood for an in-depth discussion of his political ideas, he responded with an adapted Wildeanism.

'Like me, my radicalism has a great future behind it. I'm good at critiquing capitalism but come up short on changing it. It's not just me. The left in general has got to rework its strategy. It's unfortunate that it isn't more effective because capitalism itself looks ready for the taking. It's an organisational shambles itself and chronically unfair. Anyway all that's going to fall to your generation if you have the mind and stomach for it.'

Henry gave Aisha a world-weary glance. He now seldom made eye contact in conversation but he felt almost a compulsion to do so with Aisha Khan.

'Dr. Jones...'

'Please, it's time you called me Henry.'

Thank you. Henry. You know I was talking to Tim earlier. We were saying how upset you were at the departmental meeting. We both think you should have been briefed earlier about the role changes.'

Despite himself Henry was drawn by his colleague's empathy. It washed over him like balm. His voice shook slightly as he struggled with his feelings.

'I... maybe it was time that someone else... It gives me the chance to catch up on my research, I...' to his embarrassment, he was suddenly in danger of tears. 'Look, thank you. It's very kind of you. Thank you, but don't let my troubles keep you from your work.'

Henry's resistance ebbed from this point and he began to discuss his problems more openly. He was not a great believer in 'the talking cure' but as he let go, tension he barely recognised began to ease from him. As he spoke he began to appreciate more clearly the depth of his personal crisis. This was not a crisis like those of his youth – at a crossroads – but a crisis in a cul-de-sac: an old man's crisis. *It ain't dark outside but it's getting there.*

But if he saw no way ahead, he had at least found momentary comfort. As they talked Aisha shared something of the new challenges in her own life but mainly she listened. When they parted it was with a quantum of affection.

Chapter 11
Mending and
Upending Fences

Tim was in a mixed frame of mind as he left Peyton. His visit to Maria had gone better than usual but he was concerned at what lay ahead on his return to Wash. He pulled out onto the A13 which looked its usual drab and polluted self. People must have found the post-war East End pretty rough if moving here represented progress. Perhaps pastoral bliss lay off the road somewhere between the A13 and the A12 but he doubted it. Still, the attractions or otherwise of the local countryside were not his concern. Maria was.

He had taken his daughter and one of her friends to see the latest Harry Potter and driven by guilt had bought them more sugary treats than was healthy. The presence of Maria's friend seemed to act as a buffer and to dissolve the anxiety that sometimes marred their time together. After the film Tim watched relieved as the two girls, still high on excitement, ran shouting and skipping ahead. Clearly 'bring a friend' was a strategy for the future. It certainly worked better than his lone attempts to 'have fun' with his daughter whilst trying to ignore the turmoil of their conflicting feelings. And Gina was leaving them to it, believing that it was Tim's responsibility to work out his relationship with his child post-split. If anything she had closed up over recent weeks. Perhaps that was her way of coping with the feelings she still had for him. Or, perhaps it was a sign that these feelings had further diminished. He couldn't tell.

His visit to see his daughter had been shorter than usual. Arriving late on Friday, he was returning on Saturday evening to leave Sunday free to prepare the following week's lectures. He had extra work having agreed to do a session for Aisha with the first year social scientists. She had asked him to give a basic introduction to Freud's 'map of the mind' and to describe how it had influenced one or two later thinkers. For long fascinated by Freud he decided to include himself in the latter group, partly to add a lighter, self-deprecating tone to the lecture. He was determined to do a good job for Aisha and that was going to take serious preparation time.

On top of work commitments, he had set up a meeting with his increasingly troublesome neighbour, Darren Naylor. Naylor had now made a demand – he didn't do requests - for what he insisted was 'a proper contribution' to the cost of the still only half-assembled fence. His tactic was to delay completion of the work in an attempt to pressure Tim to come up with more money. Tim was having none of it. What Naylor had so far assembled was an ill-fitting row of cheap concrete posts loosely connected to planks of plywood streaked with brown resin. If this was not yet a complete mess, Tim was not looking forward to a complete mess turning up. He was certainly not going to pay to hasten its arrival. But he had learnt not to underestimate his neighbour's ugly determination to get his own way. He knew about bullyboys. They kept on bullying if you didn't stop them early – if you could. But this was a tricky situation: worse than a feud at work. Civil avoidance was no longer possible and Naylor was not about to go away. But if he couldn't put the stoppers on him, maybe he could outlast him. Staying power, keeping on keeping on, was one of his qualities. Not matinee stuff exactly, but effective, maybe.

His mind was still scanning through his bunch of problems when the traffic thickened at the junction with the M25, compelling his full attention back to the road. The traffic only began to thin again as he passed the big city north of Barnet. He grimaced slightly as he recalled that Barnet was Thatcher territory, where she was regularly re-elected in 'leafy Finchley.' *God eternally be damned for letting her loose on this green and pleasant island.* He mused that without Thatcher Britain might have developed like Norway. Norway! What the hell did he know about Norway? He remembered that he had once almost attended a conference in Bergen but was put off by the high value of the Norwegian kroner against the pound. He reaffirmed his intention to read a book about that country.

He circled down south of Watford making good time towards the M4. He hit heavier traffic as he approached Heathrow. Once past the airport, the traffic thinned again. People were heading eastwards to the bright lights of London rather than to the comparative quiet of the West Country, though he knew he would run into knots of traffic around Reading and then Swindon. He hammered the old Volvo close to its limits as he attempted to gain time. He watched the speedometer touch a hundred. Better ease off. So far the police had never stopped him on his trips across the country. Perhaps they preferred to nail the drivers of posh new cars than battered old ones. But this was not a light-hearted game of hide-and-seek. He knew he couldn't be sure his brakes would hold up if he had suddenly to stop at top speed.

Years ago he'd been at fault in a nasty crash. The memory of the heavy thud followed by an implosion of metal and glass as he smashed into the back of a truck still turned his stomach. As he lost control his grip froze to the steering wheel, jolting his right forearm permanently out of precise alignment on impact. His brow furrowed and his mouth went dry as the image of the crash reformed in his mind. To injure himself he could live with, but he did not want the serious injury or killing of another person on his conscience. Luckily the only mangling then had been machinery. Maybe now he should give luck a helping hand. He dropped back to between seventy and eighty, the informally permitted zone for those in a hurry. A lesson half learned.

As he accelerated into the long, westward bound stretch of the M4 he began to mull over his first few weeks in Wash. Whatever else, the place was no kind of escape hole. Balancing the demands of a new job with visits most weekends either to his daughter or his mother in Lancashire was barely manageable. To cope he often found himself defaulting into a neutral state of mind or trying to; just getting things done. On the plus side, life in Wash had begun to take on an acceptable shape, the core of it built around work: teaching and research. And he had not been as alone as he had anticipated. Erica continued to drop by from time to time. Her liking for emotionally distanced, ritualised sex had not blocked the gradual emergence of a guarded affection between them. The sheer pleasure they found together made it easy for them to like each other. It was a relief to him that Erica only occasionally tried to play the dominatrix outside of their sexual performances. It wouldn't have worked with him. As well as the frequent sex, still the centrepiece of their relationship, they talked and laughed a lot. Erica, it seemed, found Tim 'amusing and funny' although he wasn't always clear why. Yet, she seemed uncomfortable when the conversation touched on her own personal life and Tim did not persist. However he saw no point in being evasive about himself and Erica proved an interested and sympathetic listener.

Despite their growing affection, an unspoken understanding emerged to keep separate their personal and professional lives. Erica framed the terms. Without her needing to say so Tim quickly realised that at work she preferred that they behave only as colleagues, politely friendly but giving no hint that there was anything more between them. When she wanted to see him she called him to say so. Usually he could arrange his life accordingly, especially as their liaisons had so far always been at his place. For now this set-up also suited him. Logically he knew that his relationship with Gina was over but he still felt emotionally tied. Far from looking for another deep involvement he was open to a period of hedonistic encounters. Despite his unsettled state of mind, he was confident that he could compartmentalise his feelings pretty well.

His concentration on auto, he reduced speed as the traffic fed in from the Reading conurbation. His thoughts drifted to Aisha, the other of his younger female colleagues. He found himself reflecting that physically there was some resemblance between Aisha and Gina. Both were gifted with a satin beauty and lean athleticism that played on his consciousness whenever he was with them. He wondered vaguely whether such reactions could be described as sexist? He didn't think so. Unbidden feelings were not corrigible to PC regimentation, although he understood the protective role political correctness could play. But it was his habit to question orthodoxy, particularly if it came in moral wrapping. His commitment to the equality of the sexes did not mean he thought they were the same. He found no problem in reconciling equality with difference and he perceived most women as different, at least from himself. But if he was drawn to difference he had also learnt caution. He was not sure he understood women. He realised that as far as Aisha was concerned he had better respect the difference, not only of gender but also of culture and religion and so of expectation. He had better behave himself! He remembered that as a student an intense attraction had developed between himself and a young Muslim woman. Tim's tutor, who took a guiding interest in his promising but wayward charge, had warned him 'not to mess with her' unless he intended very serious commitment. There was an edge to his tutor's voice new to Tim. It persuaded him to think of consequences – for others as well as himself. He backed off.

As he reached the final few miles of his journey he again refocused on his driving. It was easy if not advisable to drift day-dreaming along the M4 but to do so on the narrow, winding road down into Wash invited disaster. And here the world beyond his windscreen was worthy of attention, the steeply contoured countryside and farmland on either side of this stretch of road. When he had the time, shortly after leaving the motorway he would park the car, stretch his long limbs, breathe deeply of the fresh air and enjoy the view of the city in the valley. At other times, his appetite sharpened from the journey, he would pull into a farm-shop and buy a homemade ice cream for immediate con-sumption and a dozen fresh farm eggs for later. But not this time. He needed to get to his meeting with Darren Naylor.

He was beginning to regret agreeing to meet at Naylor's house rather than his own. His sporting experience told him that there was a better chance of a good result on his own turf. He swung into his driveway and parked the car, not bothering to unload his luggage. Slipping through one of several large gaps in the semi-erected fence he knocked on the Naylor door. No response. He knocked again more loudly. This time the bull-like form of Naylor appeared. Not for the first time Tim was struck by his neighbour's seamless blend of ugliness and menace.

'Ye trying to knock the bloody door down? Ye fink we're all deaf or somefink?'

Naylor stepped out into his driveway. Evidently tea and biscuits were not on offer.

Tim was already feeling drained. Normally confident in his ability to keep his temper and even to weave a bit of diplomacy he was irritated. He came straight to the point.

'Look if you want to finish the fence off I'll live with it. Or you can take it down and I'll put one up. The money you've already had from me is a lot more than that,' he paused for a second, 'shambles is worth. That's it, no more money.' Naylor's boorishness and his own tiredness were straining his patience.

Naylor moved to within a couple of feet of him.

'Listen, ye gangling pansy. There's somefink ye need to know about me. I'm an arse 'ole. I'll mek yer fuckin' life miserable if ye don't fork out for what ye owe me. I want that fuckin' money now or that fence stays the way it is.'

Tim eyed the beefy form of Naylor, taking his measure. He was not going to back down or back off. He moved in closer. They squared up like a pair of dinosaurs, tall and angular, short and wide. Tim responded to Naylor in kind.

'You're fuckin' right you *are* a fuckin' arse 'ole. You can stick that monstrosity up your fat backside as far as I'm concerned. And don't waste yer time threatening me my friend, it won't work. I don't give a flying turd whether you leave the bloody thing up or take it down. I've had enough. Good night, arse 'ole.'

He was about to turn round to go but thought better of it. It was safer to keep Naylor in his sights. He moved off sideways and stepped through a gap in the fence. 'Are you planning to charge for the gaps?'

'Fuck off Connor. Don't worry, I'll get ye.'

They exchanged further insults as Tim unloaded his car. Once inside the house he opened a can of tomato soup and a tin of sardines. He made a sardine sandwich of doorstep dimensions and spun the soup for a few seconds in the micro-wave, wolfing them down before collapsing for half-an-hour's kip on the couch. Then he settled down to work. Busy as he was, it did occasionally cross his mind that Naylor was unlikely to leave things as they were. A self-described arsehole well positioned to let fly. Expect a shower of shit. It was unfortunate that Naylor brought out Tim's macho side. What was that daft Wayne quotation? – *Never explain, never apologise, it makes you seem weak.* He knew this was rubbish but it matched his mood. He would certainly have managed his meeting with Naylor more calmly if he hadn't been so exhausted. There would be consequences. Even so, when he hit the sack that night he slept soundly, comprehensively knackered from a tough weekend, undisturbed by thoughts of his imbecile neighbour.

Over the next few days the shape of Naylor's revenge emerged. He would try to wear Tim down by making his life so unpleasant that Tim would either give in or sell up and move out. The strategy was the drip-drip of attrition rather than a frontal attack. Tried and tested delinquent that he was, Naylor was not going to risk arrest unnecessarily. Tim had to concede that for such an apparent bone-brain his neighbour was not without a degree of evil cunning. Naylor's first move was to park his van, with its absurd slogan of 'Premiership Builders', on the grass verge fringing the footpath outside Tim's small front garden, blocking the view from the window. Tim's response was simply to avoid looking in that direction but it was more difficult to ignore the muddy mess that the van made of the verge. These manoeuvres brought the two men's conflict into to the uneasy if fascinated attention of the neighbours. Several pulled disapproving expressions at the churned up tyre-tracks but none showed any inclination to intervene. Under siege Tim got some light relief when the van got stuck in its own mess. He offered to help bump the van back onto the road, never short of a sense of irony. His offer was declined in predictably florid terms. Meanwhile Tim patiently waited for an opportunity to land Naylor in as big a mess as his van.

For his next trick Naylor shifted from the nasty to the sinister. Several times each day, usually when he was at home in the evening, Tim's landline would ring. When he picked it up he would hear 'death music'; slow deep drumbeats punctuated by wild shouts and agonised cries. It might have been frightening if it hadn't been so ridiculous. But it was inconvenient. To counter the move Tim transferred as much of his phone communication as possible to his mobile. Thank God for modern technology. Generally he took the landline off the hook or ignored it. When he did pick it up he remained steadfastly unfazed by the music but it was a warning to him how far Naylor was prepared to go. In this war of wills and nerves his strategy was to hang on. He made no direct accusation to Naylor. That would only have pleased his would-be tormentor. In any case there was no proof.

On one occasion he did go to the police. This followed an incident that seemed to offer some prospect of incriminating Naylor in a clear case of intentional damage to property. The issue began with a note pushed through Tim's letterbox in which Naylor claimed that the gutter of Tim's garden shed was leaking 'loads of water' onto Naylor's property. Naylor would 'summon' him if he didn't 'sort it quickly.' Tim checked out the alleged problem several times, including in a period of heavy rain, and concluded that this was just another case of troublemaking. He decided to leave it at that. Another note came through the letterbox. Tim 'better do something about it this time' or Naylor would 'see him in court'. Checking again he found that the gutter and its supports were hanging loose, splintering part of the shed itself. It was obvious that Naylor had deliberately damaged the guttering given that the rest of the shed was sound. Tim reported the incident to the local police. The police did at least turn up and interview both parties. In the event, they were more inclined to believe Naylor's version of events perhaps because it required no further action on their part. They passed on his story to Tim: Naylor hadn't touched the gutter and his wife and children had been soaked by water from it several times. When was Connor going to 'pull his finger out' and put in a new gutter or get a decent shed? The police were unimpressed when Tim pointed out that it was more likely 'pigs might fly' than that water could spontaneously leap four feet from the gutter to the other side of what passed for a fence. The police remained unconvinced, warning him 'not to do anything silly.' Finally they suggested he consider civil action if he really thought it worth taking the matter further. Tim didn't.

It was stalemate for the moment. Meanwhile the fence hung like a row of emaciated cadavers, shifting and flapping in the wind.

Chapter 12
The Psychology Lecture Interrupted

Although Tim mostly managed to block out Naylor's activities there were times when going into work was the best escape. Not that life on campus was without incident. He had been looking forward to doing the lecture for Aisha and perhaps meeting up with her again. As it turned out she didn't make the lecture, instead using the opportunity to visit an osteopath with Ali. This was a first year 'theme' lecture under the general title of 'Minds that Formed Modernity.' On entering a large lecture theatre Tim found well over a hundred, possibly closer to two hundred students already there. There was a buzz of expectation as he stepped onto the platform at one end of the theatre and settled behind a podium. Aisha must have given him a good build up. He decided to play into the high mood by challenging his audience as much as possible. The topic of Freud and the psychoanalysts he had influenced offered plenty of scope.

He began the lecture by pointing out that, according to Freud, for much of the time humans don't fully understand why they do what they do. This proposition seemed to catch his youthful audience's attention. Encouraged he continued up-beat. This lack of self-understanding occurs because apparently conscious motives may be and perhaps always are influenced by the unconscious. For instance we might believe that we are helping an attractive person because they need help but the 'real' and unacknowledged motivation may be that we are attracted to them and want to get closer. To make the point Tim took a straw poll of his audience, asking them to vote on whether they would help a very attractive or less attractive person first, given equal need. Roughly half indicated comparative attractiveness would not make any difference to their choice, but nearly all the rest, some looking slightly uncomfortable, said it would. After some discussion arising from the vote Tim resumed the lecture.

Continuing his opening theme, he observed that, according to Freud sex or the suggestion of it (and most things suggested sex to Freud) is a constant preoccupation of the unconscious mind. Tim paused and looked out at his audience. There was a scatter of sceptical expressions, but no sign of a mass switch-off. Encouraged he did a quick introduction to the id, ego and superego – quick because he assumed that nearly all of this youthful audience would be aware of this foundational piece of psychoanalytic theory, although he knew from experience that any given student might draw a cognitive blank on any given topic. Most first-year undergraduates had heard of Darwin and most of Marx but not necessarily of Freud, a consequence he suspected of a 'cook book' approach to learning, focusing on exams at the expense of seminal thinkers and ideas. He had decided to use the trusty technique of creative repetition to keep all his audience onboard, whether or not they knew of Freud. This was not difficult given that Freud's ideas had been endlessly presented in more simplified form.

With most of his audience apparently still tuned in Tim moved on from Freud and launched into an introduction to transactional analysis, a kind of everyman's version of Freud's theory of the psyche. Eric Berne the Californian founder of transactional analysis had the inspired and lucrative idea of substituting the accessible terms 'child' for 'id', 'adult' for 'ego' and 'parent' for 'superego': each of which referred to particular emotional states and related behaviours. Tim then added his own terminology to further explain Berne's model of the psyche: emotions (child), reason (adult) and socialised conscience or rules (parent): their dynamic relationship forming the mental state of a specific individual at a given time.

At this point Tim noticed an intense looking young woman in the front row, vigorously waving her hand.

'Go ahead with your question.'

'Thanks. Aren't two and three of Berne's and your interpretation the same; shouldn't rules be rational?'

'Good question. The short answer is that the rules of society are not always or entirely the product of reason, any more than individual actions always are. Some might be the result of prejudice or worse. Look at all the rules or laws Hitler introduced in relation to the Jewish population in Germany. All societies have rules but they're by no means always rational. Let me put a question back to you to consider. Are there any rules in our society that you would be prepared to break not necessarily simply because they are irrational but because you consider them morally wrong? Perhaps higher morality requires thinking beyond the rules of a particular society, being critical of them. As I say, this is the short answer the long one might need a full series of lectures.'

'Maybe you should give them.'

'Maybe but I better finish this one now. Also you could consult the reading list, of course.'

He moved into the final phase of his lecture. Consistent with Freud's model, Berne argued that the three functional structures of the psyche are universal but are variously expressed between individuals. Thus an adult who has experienced unmet emotional needs as a child, say a lack of love or acceptance, may seek to get them met by acting like a child in certain situations in later life. If the emotionally deprived person is unlucky enough to find a partner who is fixated on a harsh version of the parent role – perhaps also learned in childhood – the outcome might be constant criticism for 'childish' behaviour rather than gaining the craved for love and acceptance. Of course, another couple might experience the 'child/parent roles' much more constructively. As he was explaining this, it suddenly occurred to Tim that tortuous, dysfunctional and often painful patterns of interaction might be what the psychiatrist R.D. Laing was referring to when he used the term 'knots.' On the spur of the moment he floated this notion to the students. Glancing up he could see that most of his audience were interested but some looked lost. He dropped the Laingian digression and returning to his main topic clicked up a PowerPoint frame juxtaposing the three models for the purpose of review. Some students still looked perplexed and judging their frowns an indication of lack of understanding, Tim decided to attempt a final tricky technique of communication: audience participation. Unfamiliar with his young audience he had been uncertain about attempting this – there was a risk of a chaotic response.

'Right, it's time to illustrate the theory with some role play. I'd like six of you to volunteer to act out the various parts of the psyche: two each for the child, adult and parent. I won't force you. That's not my democratic way. But give me six volunteers. Come and join me on the platform.'

After a couple of minutes five volunteers had trickled forward, two men and three women.

The audience then seemed to reach a perverse collective decision not to throw up a sixth volunteer. Tim looked around encouragingly. The students avoided his gaze. The impasse lasted a further couple of minutes. It was finally broken by a voice from the back of the room.

'Why don't you volunteer yourself, Sir?'

'Don't call me Sir. I turned down the knighthood.' There was a thin ripple of laughter.

'Sorry, Sir... I mean sorry, show us how it's done.'

'Ok. That's a fair suggestion. Let's start with a child-parent interaction.'

'Why don't you be the child, Sir, er... Tim. That's gonna be the most difficult,' this from another disembodied voice.

'Ok, here goes.' He knew the suggestion might be a piss-take but he was keen to get things moving. He quickly allocated the parent role to one of the three women.

'Let's get into roles.'

'Ready?'

There was a murmur of assent.

'Off we go, then.' He braced him-self for a second before continuing in a plaintive tone, 'I'm upset. You never pay any attention to me. You seem to prefer going out with friends. I don't think you care about me.'

'Don't be silly. If you acted a bit more grown up perhaps we could have a proper relationship. You're too involved with yourself.' The tone of the voice was appropriately parental but with an unexpected hint of teasing.

Tim suddenly felt uneasy. There was something familiar about the young woman. He ploughed on. 'We never spend any quality time together these days. I never feel you want to listen to me.'

'I don't know about that. We had a great time together just a few weeks ago. Stop being miserable and perhaps we can have some more fun.'

Tim stiffened with the shock of recognition. It was Georgie.

'Oh my Lord!'

There was a brief moment of silence followed by a scatter of laughter and applause.

'What's Jesus got to do with it, Sir?'

Tim tried not to look Georgie in the eye, although he couldn't avoid noticing that she was grinning. He gazed out at the bemused faces of the students.

Panic sparked inspiration.

'Right! Sorry about that. I've just realised what time it is. Getting people to volunteer took longer than I intended. I'll be less democratic and quicker next time. We're going to have to scrap the role-play. If any of you really want to act out some of this, we'll do it eh... some other time.' He paused and added with emphasis, 'I really can't believe how late it is.'

The students' bemusement had more or less evaporated by the time he wrapped things up and unusually, there was even a spatter of applause as Tim swept into his peroration enjoining them to 'get in touch with their inner child' and have a carefree and enjoyable day.

Back in his office, mercifully empty of the loquacious Purfect, he brewed a cup of tea and opened up his copy of the *Independent*. He was settling down to read a piece on the winners and losers in the financial crash when there was a knock on his door.

'Come in.'

Enter Georgie, now looking more serious but still with the suggestion of a smile around her mouth.'

'Hi,'

'Hi.'

Tim folded his paper and dropped it onto his desk. He picked up his cup of tea wrapping his fingers around it. He leant back in his chair, receptive but feeling edgy.

'So grab a pew. I hadn't anticipated that we would meet again and certainly not like that. If I'd realised you were a student here I...'

'Tim, don't worry. I haven't come to talk about that.'

'We seem to be talking about it.'

'I didn't bring it up. When I'm a student I'm a student. Only a couple of best friends know about my... er... part-time job. The *Bombadier* is not a student pub. Hardly anybody here knows what I do there. If any students do go in, it's because they're gay. They wouldn't care anyway. Besides

I only have sex with people I fancy. It's not very often. You should take it as a compliment. I usually prefer my own sex.'

'Thanks. It was very enjoyable, but we'll have to leave it as a one-off. Even if it's no trouble for you, it could be big trouble for me. Really the best thing would be if neither of us mentions it again, either between ourselves or to any one else. Do you mind?'

'Consider it done.'

'Really? As easy as that?'

'Really? Why not? Obviously I haven't told anybody so far. I didn't know you worked here until today but now it will be a total, absolute and permanent secret.'

'Thanks a lot.' Tim hesitated for a moment. 'Look, just before we bury this thing for good. I mean, do you really need to make money in that way? There are other ways of...'

'Tim I don't have time to work for the minimum wage in a supermarket. I have to study. Right? Anyway it's not a job, it's more like sex with extras.'

'Georgie, you're a prostitute.' He could have cut his tongue out.

For a moment Georgie flashed anger. 'I know what I am and it's not that. What are you, a sad punter?'

'Georgie, I'm sorry. That was totally crass and insensitive. I'll take my own advice and forget the whole thing.'

'Like I said, consider it done,' she was quickly on side again.

'Thanks,' he relaxed slightly. 'Otherwise are things going ok for you?'

'So, I was going to ask you if you'd consider supervising my dissertation. I've got Professor Purfect and he isn't.'

'Isn't what?'

'Perfect.'

Tim smiled. 'That's not for me to say.'

'No. He keeps talking about life in Ocado instead of my dissertation. It's about the gay community in Manchester and I don't think he knows anything about it. You're from round there aren't you? But I guess I've worked out you don't think it's appropriate to be my supervisor.'

'No, no can do. It wouldn't even be ethical to grade your essays unless they happen to come to me for anonymous marking. By the way Whitetown is not around Manchester, it's a dynamic centre of technology and culture in its own right. Well, maybe not quite in Manchester's league. Anyway, no, it would be unethical to supervise your dissertation. Sorry.'

They held each other's gaze for a moment, sharing their disappointment. A shadow of realisation passed between them, that what might have been would not be, probably.

Georgie got up to leave.

'Georgie. Thanks… you've been terrific now and you were terrific then.'

The smile that seldom quite seemed to leave her face lit up at the compliment. 'You weren't so bad yourself. I might even give you a discount next time.'

'I might just take you up on that,' he murmured after she'd closed the door, 'but not yet a while.'

Chapter 13
Thank You for Coming

Tim felt a touch of melancholy after Georgie had left. He
didn't feel like work. He didn't even feel like going home.
Loner though he imagined himself to be, the thought of
its emptiness depressed him. He recognised the mood. He
was emotionally and sexually restless. And he was tense.
It didn't help that Georgie was so gorgeous and probably
willing. *Spring your arse from this slough of despondency!* He
decided to call Erica.

Calling Erica for a get-together was more complicated
than simply one partner, if that was what they were, con-
tacting the other. To call her would mean departing from
their established pattern in which she always took the initiative in setting up their meetings. In his unsettled mood
he decided he would invite himself over to her flat. So far
it hadn't bothered him that their liaisons were always at his
place: he was delighted to see her at all. But now restless and
frustrated he found himself balking at the rigidity of the routine - *her* routine. Besides he was curious to see what kind of
place she had put together. According to Freud or some such

luminary of the mind, a home tells a lot about the person that lives in it. He wanted to know more about Erica beyond the magnificent body and alpha performances. Ditching their routine might have unpredictable consequences but he was in a risk-taking frame of mind. Feeling grumpily assertive he decided that it was time to push for an invitation to play away, maybe to spend the night at her place.

He had an added reason to avoid asking Erica back to his place. Darren Naylor had begun to make sleazy comments about her. One remark triggered a suspicion that somehow Naylor had spied on their sexual activities, sneering that they were 'a pair of pervs.' Tim's riposte that Naylor 'was a pathetic peeping Tom' was a good hit, but added to his neighbour's festering store of loathing. It was quite possible that Naylor had managed to look into the house: the curtains on the windows facing Naylor's side were a poor fit and Tim didn't always draw them fully shut. Curtains were a low priority when he and Erica moved into top gear. So far his neighbour's offensive remarks about Erica had been directed to Tim but he guessed Naylor would target Erica if he got an opportunity. He would like to figure out a way to sort out Naylor. But today, tonight, he didn't want the hassle. And if possible he wanted to keep Erica out of it. Besides he was a born counter-puncher. He would wait for Naylor to make a mistake before knocking seven shades of shoeshine out of him. That was the fantasy version. He knew that in reality there was no predicting how this nasty situation might swing.

He picked up the phone and rang Erica's number.

'Hi, Erica, it's Tim…'

'Hi, Tim…You ok? I was planning to call you later. I'm kind of missing you.'

'Me, too, missing you I mean. I seem to be in a funny mood.'

Oh, why's that? Is something wrong?'

'No, not really… maybe work has caught up with me. To be honest I need a few hours' break. Can I bounce you out of your comfort zone? How about meeting up tonight? I'll treat you to an Indian. And then, I'd love to see your place.'

'My place?'

'Yeah, if that's ok? You keep appearing and disappearing like the lady in the lake or a being from outer space. It's great but it would be nice to see that you actually do live somewhere.'

There was a brief silence. Tim was unsure which way this was going to go.

'Ok, why not? But please don't compare me to a being from outer space.'

This was better than he expected. Erica had agreed with no more than a light-hearted rebuke.

'Great. Where? Would you like to eat first?'

'First? First before what?' Erica suddenly sounded less playful.

'I mean before we go to your place.'

'Just bring in a take-a-way for us and a couple of bottles of Cobra or something similar.'

'Ok. Is eight a good time to come over?'

'Fine, a bit earlier if you want. Say between half seven and eight. See you then. Take care.'

'Great. See you later.'

On his way to Erica's Tim stopped off to buy the food and drink. He thought of getting her some flowers but decided that this might strike an over sentimental note into their so far mainly carnal relationship. And in the past he had usually preferred to buy his girl-friends chocolates rather than flowers. It seemed better to buy something to share – especially if you could eat it as well.

Erica's apartment was in a modern block that was more up-market than he had anticipated. He passed through a colonnaded entrance zone before coming to some marble steps. He scaled these with his usual gusto before colliding with a uniformed security man of massive bulk and stature. Their long legs tangled together as they struggled to remain vertical.

'Ouch,' security gasped, 'you f... you f...'

'Sorry, apologies, your steps are uneven, sorry.'

Grimacing with discomfort, the security man managed to regain composure. He eyed Tim with aggressive scepticism, insisting on accompanying him to reception to check his status. Tim announced himself to a smartly turned-out yet bored looking receptionist and waited as she phoned through to Erica.

'That's fine Sir, Ms. Botham is expecting you. The lift is over there. Ms. Botham's apartment is on the top floor. It's a couple of doors down on the left as you leave the lift.'

'Many thanks.'

Tim turned to find the security man was still there. Slightly the taller and by far the heavier of the two men, security looked ominously confrontational.

'Stop being taller than me,' Tim opted for a touch of disruptive surrealism.

'What? Are you crazy?'

'Probably.' Tim stepped smartly round the uniformed monolith and hurried to the lift. He pressed the bell and the lift doors immediately slid open. He gave security a relaxed wave as the doors closed. The wave went unreturned.

Exiting the lift Tim found himself in a thickly carpeted corridor lit on each side by tastefully understated lighting. He was pleasantly aware of the soft tread underfoot as he made his way to Erica's apartment. Outside he put down the bag of food and beer and attempted to smooth his hair and clothes. In these surroundings, linen trousers, a clean white shirt and a well-worn jacket might undershoot the dress code on the informal side. Not that Erica made a habit of criticising his style – it was the place itself that suggested greater sartorial effort.

He pressed the doorbell. There was no immediate response. He leaned forward to ring again but held back on hearing movement and voices. The door opened and he was welcomed by a serious looking Erica. She was more dressed-down than he had seen her, wearing only jeans, a t-shirt and trainers. To his hungry eyes she looked better than ever.

'Tim, good to see you,' her welcoming kiss felt unexpectedly restrained. 'I hope you made it without too much difficulty.'

'No worries. Security gave me the once over but otherwise, no problem.'

'Security? If the big guy was on; he tends to be over-protective of female residents. Basically he's ok. Give me the bag of goodies and I'll put the beer in the fridge. I'll warm up the take-away later.'

Tim handed the bag over, expecting to be led into the flat. Erica seemed to hesitate.

'So you're not going to invite me in then?' he joked.

'I should have mentioned on the phone that... Look, come in.'

She abruptly stopped talking. It was apparent why. Immediately facing him as they entered a large reception room was Rachel Steir.

Rachel got up swiftly and strode towards him. To his surprise she held out her hand. The handshake was stiff and uncomfortable and perversely increased the sense of distance between them. The warm hand of friendship it was not. Tim wondered whether Rachel had taken pre-emptive action to avoid the kissing of alternate cheeks, now a fashionable greeting amongst all varieties of genders except heterosexual men. He was relieved to escape that ritual but disconcerted when for no obvious reason Rachel and Erica exchanged double kisses of the fatter kind. Was he being deliberately provoked? The women's display of affection struck a possessive chord and he planted a couple of kisses on Erica's cheeks, gauchely grabbing her backside as he did so. She quickly removed his hands but smiled broadly seeming to enjoy the outbreak of competitive attention. Rachel frowned but said nothing. It occurred to him that perhaps he had reacted with uncouth paranoia to a genuine effort at civility from Rachel. It was a relief when Erica moved matters on.

'Tim, do you mind if we eat later? Rachel has been looking for an opportunity to talk to you, informally at this stage. It's rather a sensitive matter and she doesn't want to raise it at work, at least not yet. So I thought she could come here and explain what she has in mind. It's not really about you, well not directly. It involves us all really.'

Agitated, Rachel interrupted. 'Erica thanks. I think I should take over now. After all, the whole thing is my idea. I should take responsibility for it.'

Tim tensed. His coolness to Rachel following his interview had diminished but he had no wish to share her confidences and even less to engage in clandestine intimacy. Besides he felt cheated. A lengthy conversation with Rachel was definitely not what he had in mind for the evening. A bad day was still on the slide. But he had little choice but to hear Rachel out. And he didn't want to risk upsetting Erica who inexplicably seemed to think the meeting was a good idea.

'Why don't you two sit down and talk. I'll brew up some coffee. I know how you both take it.' She clearly wanted to deliver Tim to benefit from Rachel's undivided attention.

As Rachel talked Tim's reluctance to listen evaporated. Her intense, authoritative tone grabbed his attention. It was clear she was on a mission. The gist was that as Head of Department she believed she had 'to tackle the problem of Henry Jones.' The ridiculous incident at the departmental meeting was merely symptomatic. More importantly she had received a steady flow of complaints about him from students. These included accusations that he was frequently drunk and incoherent when lecturing, failed to give proper feedback for assessed work, and had made rude remarks about other members of staff, particularly, as it happened, herself. One student had claimed that he had referred to her as 'an over-blown dyke.' His behaviour might affect the reputation of the department and quite probably student recruitment. If so, everybody's job would be at stake, not just Henry's. He had clearly lost all inhibition and had no consideration for colleagues. It was urgent either that he be persuaded to retire or, if necessary, be dismissed. Before raising the matter with the Dean she wanted to be sure she had the full backing of the department. She looked hard at Tim.

'Can I be sure of your support? I have everybody else's.'

Tim eyed Rachel coolly for a long moment.

'No.'

There was a moment's silence of the awkward variety.

'Do you mind telling me why not? Even in your short period here you must be aware that what I've told you is entirely consistent with Henry Jones' behaviour.'

'No means you can't be sure of my support at this moment. I need to think about this. Actually what you describe is not completely consistent with the man I know or, I should say, the man I'm getting to know. I'd describe him as kind, eccentric and brilliant, as well as drunken, unreliable and occasionally rude.'

'Timothy, whatever positive qualities he may have or perhaps once had, the defects you've just referred to demonstrate that he cannot possibly be allowed to continue in his job. To be honest we assumed he would ask for early retirement after he was demoted, I mean rotated or moved sideways.'

'Who are the 'we' who thought he would retire? By the way I think you do mean demoted.'

'I've already told you that everyone I've spoken to thinks that he should go. Surely you can see why people have had to give up on him?'

'What about Aisha Khan?'

'Well, yes, Aisha quite sensibly says she doesn't feel able to get involved and on reflection I agree with her. She recognises Henry is in a dreadful state but hasn't seen enough of him to make a judgement about what ought to be done about him. No doubt she feels able to leave it to senior colleagues.'

'I'm no more senior than her.'

'Your previous experience in education is recognised. Really I just need to know that you are in general agreement with us.'

Tim felt patronised as well as pressured. A familiar feeling of bolshiness was stirring. He decided to find out more about Rachel's intentions before making up his own mind.

'I assume Howard Swankie is part of "us"?'

'He believes Henry should go as soon as is practical. He's concerned that Henry is undermining the good work of the rest of us in building up the faculty. In fact Howard approached me about the matter although I had already decided I had to take it up with him. Howard's very keen that the initiative to get rid of, er... persuade Henry to leave should come from us. It would look bad for the faculty if this were to appear as a continuation of his feud with Henry. You can see his problem.'

'But however he wants things to appear Howard did start this off.'

'Don't be so literal.'

'Factual, you mean.'

'Timothy... Tim,' Rachel struggled to affect a softer tone. 'Tim, you surely recognise that what we're trying to do is the right thing. Surely?' She forced her face into a parody of a smile.

Tim felt cornered. All the good arguments seemed to be on her side. Better stall. 'Look, I get on with Henry. He's not as far gone as you think. Why don't I talk to him? See if I can persuade him to tone down slightly, sufficiently to get him through the next year or so?'

Rachel's face twitched swiftly from forced smile to horrified grimace. 'Please don't. We; all senior staff have talked to Henry at one time or another. You will only drag things out. There's no need for you to get involved. If you can't support us then please don't say or do anything.'

Rachel was beginning to sound panicky. Tim felt encouraged. Her hard logic had caught him cold. Now he was beginning to think of arguments to support his gut feeling.

'What about loyalty? Solidarity between colleagues? We give more and more time and energy to our jobs and less and less to the people we work with. Henry has given half a lifetime to his job. We ought to try to help him, not conspire to finish him off.'

Not wanting to sound too pious he toughened his tone. 'I don't intend to see Henry shafted without at least letting him know what's going on. We've become so obsessed with bloody targets and the rest of the paraphernalia that we've become desensitised to the consequences of our own behaviour. We think and talk within tramlines, we're getting too frightened to speak our minds.'

Rachel's voice was tight as she struggled to contain her annoyance.

'Tim, you're beginning to sound like Henry himself, full of impractical nonsense. Listen, Henry's situation has nothing to do with the high ideals you're referring to. The fact is he is unprofessional and dysfunctional. I regret raising this matter with you. I'd appreciate it if you would treat this conversation as confidential. Let those who know Henry well deal with it. It can't possibly do Henry or, for that matter, you any good if you interfere.'

Tim was about to challenge this remark when Erica who had been sitting quietly, a tray of coffee across her knees, cut in.

'Hey you two, there's no need to fall out over this. Let me pour some coffee. I'd have offered it you before but I didn't want to interrupt.'

'Thank you but I think I won't. I have things to do as I'm sure you two do as well,' said Rachel, giving Erica a reproachful look.

Erica looked crestfallen, almost contrite. 'I hope you're not upset, Rachel? After all it was you that wanted to meet with Tim.' This was a different Erica than Tim was used to: almost a mirror opposite.

Rachel ignored the question. 'As I said, I have things to do. I don't want to get in the way. I'll call you tomorrow, early if you don't mind?'

'Well, if you're sure you need to go.'

Rachel had already picked up her bag and coat. Tim contemplated remaining in his seat as a protest, but thought that she might miss the point. The expectation that a man would spring to his feet when a woman leaves the room is one of the many social rituals feminism has changed. In the end it was the residual politeness of his northern upbringing that prompted him to stand up. 'You can be too complicated,' he thought, as, rising to his feet, he tripped over Erica's Afghan rug, almost bowling into Rachel's arms. Rachel accelerated out of the apartment.

Outside the door Rachel turned to face Tim and Erica. Tim braced himself for more verbals. She settled for a thunderous frown before marching off down the corridor.

Back inside Tim and Erica looked at each other. Simultaneously they took deep breaths and burst into laughter.

'Jesus. Why was that so funny?' Tim grinned.

'It wasn't really but it's a hell of a relief to get it over with.'

'Yeah, but why did you?'

Erica moved in closer pressing a finger to Tim's mouth before he could finish his sentence. Relaxed now, she nuzzled up against his chest. The mood had slipped into intimacy.

'I can never decide what you smell of. Almost neutral but there's a suggestion of porridge.'

'Porridge?' Tim was not flattered.

'Or rice-pudding maybe.'

He was even less flattered.

'I doubt it. I did eat a lot of both as a kid but I don't think the aroma could still be hanging on.'

'I suppose not. It's a nice smell anyway. Very you. Some men smell sweaty or worse.'

'I can imagine. Spare me the details. What about women?'

'They're always fragrant. Like Rachel.'

'Quite.'

He ran his fingers through her hair and kissed her speculatively on the forehead. Feelings were stirring that he had not yet allowed himself to recognise. And if he did want more than lust and desire from their relationship he was not sure Erica did. He felt an unfamiliar pang of insecurity. It might help if he knew more about her relationship with Rachel, an issue they had previously steered clear of. Now he went straight to the point.

'So what is it between you and Rachel?

Her reply was equally candid.

'She's my partner, well, *a* partner. My other partner that is, in case you think I've got a stable-full. I'd assumed you'd guessed. Didn't you?'

'More or less, but I wasn't completely sure.' He was determined to keep his cool. Erica sounded less defensive than he'd anticipated. He decided to press on.

'So you're bi-sexual?'

'Yes, sort of, if you want to put a label on it. But my relationship with Rachel isn't mainly about sex.'

'So my relationship with you is mainly about sex then?'

'Tim,' she reached for his hand reassuringly, 'you mustn't get paranoid. I don't know what my relationship with you is about. I know we started with a strong sexual urge and that doesn't seem to have worn off. Anyway let's focus on Rachel first, seeing you ask.'

'Go ahead. Are you in love with her?'

'Tim, that's a bit simplistic.'

'Sorry, I wouldn't know.'

'I'm not in love with her romantically, if that's what you mean. She's my best friend. And neither of us sees any point in putting arbitrary limits on our friendship although it's not particularly sexual from my point of view. I mean my motive isn't sexual. Anyway I don't intend to talk about that side of our relationship. It would be disloyal'

'And I wouldn't ask you. But, so what do you get out of it? Are you attracted to each other?'

'Tim, you're still going on about the same thing. Of course we're attracted to each other but as people, not just as bodies... You're the body expert,' she added with a flash of annoyance.

Tim decided to ignore the jibe, suppressing the obvious retort that Erica was hardly lacking in that department herself. He wanted to hear more about Erica and Rachel.

'She must be twenty years older than you or more.'

'Yes. She was one of my lecturers, as you probably know. She was very kind to me when I needed someone to be. And she's a bright, interesting person.'

'So she was a cradle-snatcher. You still seem slightly in awe of her.'

The remark riled Erica. 'Tim for a psychologist you seem naively willing to stereotype us. Do you think I haven't thought about that side of my relationship with her? Well I have. I respect Rachel, but it's a pretty equal partnership,' she paused for a second before adding, 'anyway, more than at first.'

'I'm sorry. I don't mean to pry. I'm just trying to understand where I fit in. It seems like you've manoeuvred me into a very particular role.'

'How do you mean 'manoeuvred' you? Aren't you enjoying yourself? I'm beginning to think you're jealous of Rachel.'

Tim was half-inclined to back off. He wanted to get closer to Erica and he seemed to be achieving the opposite. But he needed to unload his feelings and at least he was getting some response.

'I promise you I'm not jealous. There's no point. Maybe I just want our relationship to open up a bit, perhaps see more of you, change the scenery a bit. After all I'm only here today because I invited myself.'

At the risk of annoying Erica he attempted some instant psychoanalysis.

'Are you sure you aren't applying Rachel-type control to our relationship? I know you see yourself as her equal now, but she's been your mentor for a long time and not just academically. Maybe you're imitating her behaviour without being aware of it. But you and I... I mean we could loosen up a bit?'

Erica's irritation flared again; more intense because she saw some truth in Tim's remark. 'I thought you men are only interested in one thing? Especially you. You have a bit of a reputation you know. It preceded you to Wash.'

Tim flinched. Now he was annoyed.

'Who dug that out? Rachel, I suppose.'

'No. Leave Rachel out of it.'

Caught up in their conversation they had not even sat down again following Rachel's departure. They stood starring at each other, stiff with tension, on the point of open anger. Simultaneously self-awareness dawned on them.

'Christ, look at us. All set for battle.' It was Erica who broke the spell. 'Tim, I didn't mean to upset you. Let's forget about all this for now. It's enough for one session. I'm going to get a bottle of wine from the fridge. Then I'm going to spoil you while we drink. Would you like that?'

He quickly agreed. He was in need of affection and it looked like he was about to get some. The change of mood was instant and total. 'Being spoilt' took the form of a leisurely massage to the gentle sounds of sitar-led music unfamiliar to Tim. He lay face down, closed his eyes and surrendered to relaxation. After several minutes Erica asked him to turn over. He watched her as she continued to massage him, his member on the rise.

Making love was not exactly the calm after the storm but they connected more tenderly than in their usual lust-fuelled explosions. Once inside her, Tim held back and kept holding back wanting to extend their pleasure and intimacy as long as possible. Slowly the warmth and pleasure in Erica's eyes intensified into fierce, shining desire.

Still, he held back before the rhythm of love took over, rapid and urgent. There bodies locked, immobile, rigid for a moment.

'Now,' cried Erica.

'Aaa...'

'Got you!'

'Aaa...'

Her body closed over his quivering cock as they released together. Their eyes open to each other in blue on brown-eyed wonder.

Desire slaked, they drifted together half-conscious.

Tim slowly eased away rolling onto the soft carpet, reaching for Erica's hand wanting to maintain intimacy. After a few minutes he moved closer again laying his head on her breasts.

'Phew!'

'Phew!'

'Thank you, that was...'

'It was...'

'Beautiful.'

'It was.'

Erica began to stroke Tim's forehead.

'Tim,' she was hesitant as she continued to caress him.

'Tim, I don't want to go back to what we were talking about before but I just want to say something so we don't fall out about it later.'

'Ok. Go ahead.' Tim was expecting Erica to say something personal, perhaps about her feelings for him or her relationship with Rachel.

'Tim, this Henry thing... I'm more in agreement with Rachel than with you. She exaggerates, but basically she's right. He's not doing the job.'

Tim was also reluctant to start again on Henry. But somehow he had become the man's defender.

'Erica, I don't know. Don't you think this is partly personal? Rachel and Swankie don't like Henry. And it's Henry that's lost out. They're banging him up really. I think he's been through enough. I'll talk to him, see what he has to say. Maybe there's some solution short of him being kicked out?'

'You can try but Henry's pretty stubborn. It's up to you. I just don't want us to fall out about it.'

She gave his hair a gentle pull. Shifting his head from her breasts he wriggled up to look into her eyes. For once they were face to face, albeit at floor level.

'I've got something else to tell you,' Erica smiled slightly coy.

'What's that then?'

'That was maybe the best sex I've ever had.'

'That's nice, but only maybe?'

'Not only but also. It was so good I can't wait for more.'

'You don't have to.'

Erica spread her long, Olympic class legs. Tim leaned back to get the full view. Abruptly she closed them again.

Tim groaned.

'Surely a cat can look at a queen?'

'Don't worry, it's not you,' she gave his perpendicular a friendly pat as she got to her feet. 'Can you hold that for a couple of minutes? I just want to pop into the bedroom for a second.'

Tim got to his feet pacing the room, aroused and impatient for her to return. It was worth the wait. Erica re-entered in full erotic regalia, her breasts bursting proudly through a cup-less bra and her backside and crotch bare through cut-out leather leotards. In six-inch stiletto heels she was almost as tall as Tim. If she hadn't been so drop-dead sexy Tim might have laughed. But desire overwhelmed any comedic impulse. The sheer beauty of her glorious body ensured that fantasy routed bathos. And that arse. You could travel continents and still not find its equal. Epochs must have passed without the appearance of quite so marvellous a bum.

Silently she walked to a low antique desk. Stretching

169

out her arms she touched its edge and bent over, her buttocks jutting high in the air. She spread her legs carefully, wobbling slightly on the stilettos, the perfectly etched muscles of her legs and rump clenching as she struggled to hold her balance.

The mind plays its own tricks. The phrase 'Don't look a gift-horse in the mouth' popped into his head. But perversely the ludicrous image intensified his lust - *ride a horse cock*. He gazed greedily on the smooth dipping contours of her bottom.

'I'll take you from the rear,' said Tim redundantly.

'From, not up, please,' she said quickly.

'Not an issue.'

He moved urgently towards her but curbing his lust began to stroke her upturned backside, feather light, barely touching. Erica felt as though static was crackling across its exposed surface. Her buttocks began to quiver, first one, then the other and then losing control, both together. Gripping the gyrating muscles, he eased his cock onto her warm, wet hole.

'Oh... Ah. Fuck me! Don't wait! Fuck me now!'

This was an invitation to which he was well poised to respond but still he played on the edge, teasing her. Erica was agonising for release. Finally she took the play away, dropping almost onto the full length of his cock. She shouted wildly, somewhere between ecstasy and execution. They bucked like animals, her rampant nates juddering like a pair of pistons, driving Tim to his roaring, cursing climax.

On the fuck/love spectrum this was off the scale at the fuck end.

Afterwards, sated and exhausted, they slept in each others arms. It felt to Tim as though some barrier had been shifted between them, not removed but jolted. It was a feeling beyond the intensity of carnal pleasure and Tim yearned not to lose it.

'I wish we could be as loving and affectionate as we are

now even without making love, just sometimes. Do you think that's possible?'

Erica thought for a moment. 'I don't know. I hope so.'

'I do, too. Let's see how it goes. But staying in the moment, I could murder that Indian.'

'Good idea. I'll give it a whiz in the micro-wave.'

It mattered to Tim that he got to stay the night. Two months previously it wouldn't have bothered him so much. They made easy love again as dawn spread its crisp light across the bedroom. They ate breakfast by a broad semi-circular window that gave a panoramic view of the city. But smiling and relaxed most of their attention was on themselves.

Tim put off leaving for as long as he could. At the door of the flat, bare-foot, Erica stretched to kiss him goodbye.

'Do you fancy one for the road, then?'

Tim smiled down at her.

'Come on now, give piece a chance.'

'Idiot!' Erica planted a giant kiss on his lips before they finally parted.

Tim felt a warm glow as he strolled back home through the city. He was pleased with himself, besotted with Erica and inclined to give the world at large the benefit of the doubt. 'Give peace a chance,' he repeated to himself as he beamed cheerfully at the passing public, 'she's certainly done that.'

Chapter 14
Henry and Tim
Play Golf

'Is that you Henry?'

'I think so. I'm not fully awake yet. Is that you, Tim?'

'Yes, no doubt about it. How are things Henry?'

'Pretty average Tim. And yourself?'

'Fine. Not to beat about the bush, how would you like to meet up for a drink and a chat?'

'The drink sounds good. Any particular reason for a chat? Are you in trouble or something; in need of solace and advice from a wise if fast fading colleague?'

Tim throttled a laugh. He wasn't quite sure how to take Henry's self-mockery.

'No, no more than usual. I just wanted to talk about a few work-related things with you, and see how you are.'

'Well yeah, good idea. Aren't we both free from teaching by late afternoon? I finish at three thirty. We could meet then. Do you fancy a round of golf followed by a barrel of ale? I seem to have run out of playing partners these days so it would be just you and me. Can you play the game, by the way?'

'Not really. It's always seemed like a slow way of boring yourself to death to me. But maybe I should learn. I'm about reaching the stage when I'll have to give up soccer for something less physically punishing.'

'I'll take that as a 'yes.' How about we leave from the campus shortly after three thirty? I'll come and get you from your room. Is that OK?'

'I'll look forward to it. See you later.'

'So you will. Cheers.'

On the golf course Henry was a revelation. He hit shots and sank putts to a standard that looked almost professional to Tim's untrained eyes. Without ever giving the matter much thought Tim had assumed that a man's physical strength was well past its peak by the age of sixty. At below average height and with a prominent beer-belly Henry looked even less athletic than many of his age. But this was deceptive. His wide chest and shoulders and low centre of gravity were well suited to golf and by no means all his muscle had turned to fat. He hammered drives in excess of two hundred yards with seemingly little effort. Tim knew from the first hole that two very different rounds of golf were about to unfold.

'Hell's bells, Henry, where do you find the strength to do that?' asked Tim as another of Henry's drives sailed majestically down the fairway.

'It's more timing than strength or at least strength isn't much use unless you've got timing. If club and ball come together on the sweet-spot you hardly know you've hit anything. Direction helps as well,' Henry added with a grin. 'Don't worry, you'll improve with practice.'

'That's some consolation, then,' said Tim whose own drives were a mixture of air-shots and random connections that flew off briskly at unhelpful if interesting angles. One pinged close to a dog of the square-headed, crocodile-jawed variety. The animal was about to make a lively riposte when its agitated owner managed to restrain it.

'Careful Mate, you shouldn't be playing if you can't hit

the ball straight, it's your own fault if the dog rips a piece off you.' Tim was about to contest this proposition when he was suddenly struck by a disconcerting resemblance between the snarling pair. If anything the dog was the less repellent of the two.

Confronted by two sets of unfriendly teeth he decided against a withering retort. Instead he waved an apologetic hand and hastened off in pursuit of his ball which had veered erratically towards a dense patch of brambles. Failing to find it, he took a drop and finished the hole in eight.

Their round had by now taken on a distinctive shape, or in Tim's case, shapelessness. Henry's opening drives invariably settled on or close to the fairway a hundred or so yards ahead of Tim's, depending on the length of the hole and the direction Tim's shot had travelled in. The two men then walked to Tim's ball usually to retrieve it from the long rough or even more remote locations. Tim then took the necessary number of shots to catch up with Henry. On the longer holes this routine was repeated a second or third time until they reached the green.

Henry was modestly enjoying his moment as top banana. He chatted and smiled encouragingly as Tim hacked round in his wake. He observed kindly that once Tim's ball was within a foot or so of the hole, he putted with 'an iron nerve.' Accepting that his round was beyond embarrassment and pleased for the older man, Tim took the piss-taking compliment with good grace. At Henry's insistence they abandoned any pretence of competition and treated the round as Tim's introduction to the game.

The eighteenth hole offered Henry a moment of transcendence and Tim one of partial redemption. The hole was a four-fifty yarder which dog-legged at forty-five degrees from about halfway. It was lined with thick-trunked trees on either side of the fairway.

'Tim, I've had the honour all the way, so you go first on the last hole. It might change your luck.'

'I doubt it. But ok. Make sure you stand well behind me. The one mistake I don't think I'll make is clubbing the ball backwards. But remember I have a long swing. I don't want to decapitate you.'

Tim selected a driver and squared up to the ball with renewed intent – a last chance to shine. He launched the club and himself savagely at the blameless orb. Seventeen holes worth of frustration cascaded through his long arms and the whirling blade. Man and ball left the ground at the moment of impact.

'Crack!'

Tim stumbled to the floor but the ball was motoring. A second crack rang out as it smacked into a tree trunk. It then angled back across the fairway cannoning into another tree propelling it a further fifty or so yards forward. The ball had reached the dogleg and came to rest in the middle of the fairway. The law of averages had finally worked in Tim's favour, aided by several touches of contingency.

Tim got up from the floor and waved his fists in triumph.

'Got you at last, Henry. You might equal that but you can't beat it.'

Henry nodded in appreciation. 'Cometh the moment, cometh the man.'

He carefully teed up his own ball before holding up a moistened finger to test the direction of the wind. Satisfied he selected a wood from his golf-bag. He loosened his shoulders and steadied himself as he addressed the ball. The club travelled swiftly in a perfect arch from one shoulder to the other, striking the ball almost noiselessly. The ball was still rising fifty yards short of the dogleg where it caught a gust of wind that carried it round the angle. They were just able to see it beginning to dip into the second part of the fairway.

The two men stood for a moment in awed contemplation, witnesses to an act of golfing perfection.

It was Henry who broke the silence.

'Tim, let's leave it at that. If I never play golf again, I'll live happily with the memory of that shot. Indulge me, young man, and give me an honourable draw. This is my Nicklaus-Jacklin moment.'

'Henry, the honour is all yours. You can call it a draw if you like but I'm calling it a lesson – and not just in golf. You're a model of sporting grace. By the way the next round is mine, in the bar that is.'

In the clubhouse the first pint of well-kept local ale tasted better than amber nectar. They talked sport before spending a few minutes effortlessly solving the world's major problems. Eventually Tim felt relaxed enough to bring the conversation round to Henry's difficulties at work. He had no clear idea of what he wanted their talk to achieve other than persuading Henry not to provoke the hierarchy into sacking him. On the other hand the fighter in him warmed to the fighter in Henry. But fight or flight he knew he was on the older man's side. This was the ethics of the gut but that was the way he felt.

He looked thoughtfully at his colleague: even as Henry relaxed there was nothing about him that suggested much capacity for compromise: the jutting chin, the belligerent brow, and a nose that looked as though it had battled its way through more than a few fist fights. The notion that Henry might lower his profile and stay more or less sober on campus was probably a non-starter. Tim broached matters tentatively.

'Some of us thought you got a rough deal in Swankie's job rotation exercise.'

'And others didn't. Steir's been out to get me for years.'

'I wouldn't know. But I think Swankie is your real enemy. I guess you're pretty pissed off.'

'You could say that,' a shadow passed across Henry's face. 'It's not just those two. The whole place is changing and in my view for the worse. I mean, I got an email from Swankie the other day asking me, well telling me, ordering me if you like, to go and see the Director of Learning and Teaching. I know there is such an entity but I'm fucked if I'm going to see him, or her - whoever it is. For God's sake, 'The Director of Learning and Teaching'! I thought academics directed learning and teaching. Not that 'direct' is the right word. I like to think I teach students, communicate with them. And despite what those shits think I still have plenty to say.'

As the beer went down Henry talked on. As usual his target of attack was 'the system' but Tim appreciated that a lot of emotional unloading was taking place.

'This isn't over yet. I'm not going to let my working life end in a humiliating shambles. They're trying to buy me off with a lump sum but I've no intention of making life easy for them. I might get a lawyer on the case to rough them up a bit. I've already talked to the union rep; she mentioned something about constructive dismissal. Or maybe I'll find some way of nailing them myself. I might enjoy that more.'

Abandoning any attempt to calm Henry down Tim reminded him of the likely outcome of any battle with management.

'Henry if you fight them they will probably suspend you or even sack you. They have the power and you don't.'

Henry was in no mood for realism.

'I'll think of something, believe me. I've nothing to lose.'

'Are you sure about that? Might they not mess around with your pension or your leaving package? I mean, I don't know, it's not the kind of thing I've looked into.'

'Tim I'm not going to be pushed out. If I go it will be under my own steam. Anyway, I don't think they can do much. My pension's opted out. I'm willing to suffer a bit if I can shaft them as well.'

'You mean Swankie and Rachel Steir?'

'Swankie mainly. She cosies up to him, feeds him the crap but he's the one that takes the decisions.'

'Henry, will a war of attrition do you any good? Why don't you just keep out of their way? Skip departmental meetings if you want. I'll feed them excuses for you.'

Henry gave Tim a stubborn look.

'I don't need excuses. The department was doing fine

before Steir and her mate came along. Who do they think they are: Butch Cassidy and the Sundance Kid? They've fucked up and now they're trying to mess me up, us up.'

Tim suppressed an impulse to jump to Erica's defence. It was best to keep the conversation on Henry's problems. Besides he didn't know the details of departmental politics of recent years. The conversation went round in circles for a few more minutes. Tim was about to suggest that they call a halt when he noticed that Henry's expression had changed. For once he looked vulnerable, struggling for words.

'Tim, look, I know I'm not the best advert for the things I believe in. When you get older you can see your mistakes more clearly, the opportunities you missed, the hurt you caused for other people. But you can't start again. You're stuck with what you've done. There's an analogy that I've come across that captures what I'm trying to say.

'Go ahead.'

'So, compare the journey through life to climbing a mountain, Every now and then you stop and look back. At every point you see more of the landscape or, in the analogy, more of the pattern of your life. The closer you are to the end of the journey the more you see and understand about what's gone before, especially your own part in it. It's all there in sharper perspective but set hard and immutable. You can't change anything. It's too late. There's no denying what's been done and there's no going back. Failed relationships of years ago that perhaps you gave up on too easily, can be seen for what they are, failures, perhaps selfish failures; culpable lack of effort in work, shrugged off at the time, clearly appears now as laziness or weakness. It's the same with failure to get really involved in the political causes you believe in.'

'Henry, you're being too hard on yourself.'

Henry brushed aside Tim's attempt to halt his lapse into melancholic nostalgia.

'No, I'm not, I wish I was. I know exactly what I've done

and not done, exactly where I am in my life. It's not pretty and I'm sorry for a lot of it: my penchant for fine words and feeble actions. But Tim, I want to say this to you. My inadequacies don't mean that my values and the causes I believe in are wrong. I believe that corrupt elites run this country and higher education has gone along with it. Academics have done almost nothing to stop it: a modern *trahison des clercs*. Ok... there have been a few protests and angry books and articles a-plenty but no serious action. We're a pusillanimous lot. And I admit I've been worse than most. There's not much I can do now. But I won't creep away and hide under a stone. If all I can achieve is a gesture then so be it.'

He shook his fist in rhythm with his concluding words, refocusing on Tim as he did so.

'Tim, I'm sorry. I'm banging on about myself again. I'm not a complete egocentric degenerate, you know. Well, not just,' he attempted a self-disparagingly smile. 'I should be helping you to settle in, not dumping on you. I know you have your share of personal problems too. Maybe more than I do. And you've walked into a bit of a maelstrom here – don't let it suck you in. But you've got youth on your side, a life still to build. It's harder when you're closer to the other end of things.'

He paused, resisting the temptation to return to his own problems. 'Look I'm sorry I've been more hindrance than help to you. You seem to be coping well but you deserved better than this. If there's any way I can help you I will.'

Tim was moved by the older man's unexpected apologia. But he felt awkward and uncertain how to respond. He seldom got emotionally close to other men and rarely seemed to want to. His air of independence and slight aloofness meant that it was not often that people confided their problems to him and he was even less likely to talk about his own. That was the way it had been for as long as he could remember.

'Henry, I enjoy your company, I wish I could be more use to you. And thanks for your offer of support to me,' he added, as he nearly always did to offers of help, 'but I'm fine.'

'Well that's ok then,' Henry gave a wry half-questioning smile.

Tim took this as a cue to check his watch.

'Henry. You're welcome to come back to my place for dinner? I can offer you a choice of ready meals or we can pick up a take-away as we go. I'm sure Annette won't miss you too much for one evening. Why don't you call her now to let her know where you are and I'll order a taxi?'

'No need. I doubt if she'd miss me if I disappeared for a week.' His voice dropped to a worried mumble as he added, 'she's been making threats to get me out recently.'

His words caught Tim by surprise. He had not realised that Henry's marital problems were so serious. The man's life was falling apart on every front. But now was not the time to play relationship counsellor. He gave Henry a sympathetic glance and called for a taxi.

Chapter 15
The Fight

Back at Tim's place a lighter mood returned. They washed down a meal of microwaved beef lasagne and instant chips with bottled beer. They continued drinking once the meal was over, still chilling after their heroics on the golf course.

'Henry, what type of music do you like?'

'Most: jazz, folk, rock and roll, especially progressive rock, even some of the better rap stuff. What have you got?'

'A pretty wide selection. How about something we can sing to? I've heard you can turn out the odd tune yourself.'

Tim played tracks from his collection of CDs and LPs most of them selected for them to sing along to. Well tanked up, they sang raucously and at maximum volume.

Just as they were launching into an attempt to accompany Leonard Cohen's *Hallelujah* there was a thunderous knock on the front door.

'There's someone at the door,' said Henry unnecessarily.

'Huh, I don't know who that can be, or maybe I do.' Tim got to his feet and walked slightly unsteadily to the door, humming as he went.

Opening the door he found himself staring into the hostile face of Darren Naylor. Tim was about to ask what he wanted when Naylor jabbed a stubby finger into his belly.

'Shut that fucking noise, you're keeping my kids awake.'

Tim stumbled backwards a couple of paces, briefly disoriented. As his head cleared he could see Naylor's point.

'Ok... ok, ask politely and we'll cut the noise for you.'

Naylor was not about to take a lesson in etiquette. He stepped inside the doorway shaking his fist under Tim's nose.

Tim pushed him back into the driveway, spinning him round. They squared up, sizing each other up.

In a flash, months of pent-up tension detonated.

Naylor swung a right cross that connected hard with Tim's left ear.

Tim staggered backwards but the blow had a sobering effect. As Naylor came after him he took a more controlled step back giving himself space to launch a long right hook in the direction of Naylor's nose. The impact was almost as satisfying as good sex. Naylor's nose spread like a squashed doughnut, blood and snot squirting across his face.

'Ah... shit... you fuckin' pillock. I'll get ye for that.'

Naylor wiped his face with the back of his hand. He raised his fists again ready to carry the fight back to Tim.

By now it had dawned on Tim that a serious fight with his neighbour could have all manner of nasty consequences. He decided to try to cool things down though he wasn't betting on Naylor's cooperation.

'Listen, we've landed a decent shot each, let's leave it at that. We're gonna have to deal with things by talking. Ok, I'll cut the noise down, just get off my property.'

No chance.

'Piss off, you lanky fairy. Ye're not gonna talk yer fuckin' way out of this one.'

Naylor had taken a bunch of keys from his trouser pocket. He gripped the key ring in his right fist fitting the keys between his fingers the sharper ends sticking outwards. A hard hit could take an eye out. It was soon clear he had another target in mind.

'How would you like to pick your teeth up with broken fingers?'

'Not a lot thanks, put those keys away. You're at risk of making a serious assault.'

Nothing infuriated Naylor more than, as he saw it, his neighbour's condescending arrogance.

'Who do you think you are you over-educated twat? You afraid to fight all of a sudden? No way, I have n't started on you yet.'

Naylor shaped up to attack again. As he did so Tim noticed Henry slip quietly out of the door. Before Naylor could launch himself Henry fixed him in a half-Nelson just managing to clasp his hands behind Naylor's thick neck.

'Shit! What the fuck?'

Naylor bent forward, shaking his arms and torso in an attempt to dislodge Henry. Swinging in mid-air Henry hung on, enabling Tim to step in and twist the keys from Naylor's clenched fist.

Cursing, Naylor turned to face away from the house and started to batter Henry against its pebbled wall. After thudding into the wall several times Henry was forced to release his hold. Suddenly free of his load Naylor reeled backwards cracking his head against the wall. Pebble and plaster exploded onto the driveway but Naylor's head appeared undamaged. The only effect was to further enrage him. Bellowing in anger he hurled himself at Tim who quickly sidestepped as his neighbour charged several yards past.

What the outcome might have been had the fight continued was not put to the test. Out of the blue came the blaring of a police car's siren - getting louder by the second. Naylor looked the most alarmed of the embattled trio. Without even a parting insult he swiftly exited through a hole in the fence. He was about to disappear through his front door when the police car screeched to a halt, veering giddily onto the pavement between the two houses. Three large male police officers tumbled out. Two made for Tim and Henry while the other retrieved the vehemently protesting Naylor.

Tim decided that it might defuse matters if he invited everybody inside 'to explain.' The senior policeman's response was that he himself intended to provide all the explanation required. Were they aware that he had the option of charging them with a number of offences and was inclined to do so considering the distress they had caused their neighbours; two of whom had called the local police station? At this point Tim and Henry adopted studiously penitent expressions. Naylor attempted to interrupt the officer's homily but was promptly told to 'shut up' unless he 'fancied a trip down to the station.' In the end the officer settled 'on this occasion' for giving them an informal caution as to their future conduct. The police had more important things to do than chase around after supposedly mature men behaving like juveniles. Didn't they also have more important things to do? Tim and Henry agreed that indeed they did and insisted that the current incident was entirely unique in otherwise scrupulously busy and law-abiding lives. Cornered, even Naylor nodded glum assent. The police officer concluded with a warning that in the case of any future incident there would be charges.

Nothing quite like it did occur again. Whatever it was that cowed Naylor he never threatened another physical confrontation. But his campaign to force Tim to sell up and leave carried on. Tim continued to experience nasty incidents that he was sure were Naylor's work but he could never prove it. The most dangerous was when one of his car-tyres burst causing a horrific skid. Fortunately there was no damage done to either the car or himself. Changing the tyre he extracted a shard of glass from it. Returning home he found a couple of more shards of what looked like the same kind of glass on the exit to his driveway. As he turned round after picking them up he noticed Naylor's van draw up. He found himself staring straight into Naylor's eyes. There was a cold hatred in them that carried a clearer message than any spoken word. Naylor would like to see him maimed or killed.

As far as the fence was concerned Tim woke up one morning about a week after the fight to find it flattened between the two driveways. He left it there. He had the feeling it might be his neighbour's last, self-defining act in their conflict. He was right. In the end it was Naylor who moved on. Tim cleared the old fence and built a new one fully six and a half feet high, entirely at his own cost. *You have to pay to get out of going through all these things twice.*

Chapter 16
Henry Receives
an Invitation

Henry had finished his morning's teaching and was pondering what to do next. His head was leaden and inspiration failed to spark. He was reluctant to go home where the atmosphere was now terminal. Annette was close to completing her chapter for Rachel Steir's edited collection of what he referred to in a moment of drunken provocation as 'old women telling young women what to do.' Hardened through years of emotional attrition, Annette gave as good as and often better than she got. She made it clear that his 'aimless presence' was an unwelcome distraction to her serious work. Twisting the knife she suggested that 'instead of loafing about' he might be better employed attempting to write something himself. His offer to provide a dissenting chapter for the women's book was met with contemptuous silence. Still, he didn't regret his taunt - it gave him belief that he had some fight left in him. But the days when Annette was in awe of his intellect were long gone. In desperation he began to reply to her clever jibes with choice selections from his extensive macho and toilet-based vocabulary. His coarser insults seemed to annoy her more than his attempted intellectual put-downs and he got an extra kick out of using politically incorrect language. Relief was temporary. To himself he admitted that he was hopelessly out of control and that many of Annette's comments were 'a fair cop.'

Occasionally he drifted from depression and despair into wishful thinking. He would pull himself together - eventually. Maybe he would get round to some writing. But for now the prospect of long hours running into endless days and months in front of a computer screen unsettled him. What was blocking him? Perhaps it was just a temporary loss of confidence. Or maybe, he conceded, it was the alcohol. He would cut down. What he didn't allow himself to think was that the cold, unyielding screen might bring him face to face with his own failure.

He left his office and wandered, vaguely pensive, towards the quieter part of the university grounds, still undecided about what to do next

He hated the way his image of himself had slowly begun to change. Like many sensation-loving romantics he had consigned the inconvenient matter of growing older and then old to the far recesses of his mind. *We were young so long it seemed we would never grow old...* 'Not now we're not,' he acknowledged. He had never quite believed in 'forever young' but the alternative was too depressing to contemplate. And too disturbing. Of course the 'never grow old' culture of his youth had come up with one solution to the problem of getting older: youthful death. *Hope I die before I get old...* For a few of the brighter lights 'hope' was not enough and one way or another they gave death a helping hand. Henry had always felt that in courting death the likes of Jim Morrison and Janice Joplin were really seeking to cheat it: self-destruction as the ultimate form of transcendence. Or perhaps dazzled in a haze of mass adulation they imagined they were on the brink of deification: *any day now, any way now, I shall be released.* More prosaically others like the American protest singers Phil Ochs and Tim Buckley made calculated decisions to kill themselves: idealists, they simply couldn't stand the sad, bad ways of the world.

Self-destruction, driven by excess or narcissism, still less through the slow drip of existential despair had no appeal to the younger Henry although he found the phenomenon interesting in archetypal others. Back then life was too much fun for him to seek an early exit. Better to be a campus king than a rock god worshipped by the adoring but amorphous mass. More than thirty years on, contrary thoughts occupied his mind. Self-awareness was catching up with reality and reality was not quite what it used to be. As Oscar put it, he had a great future behind him. Judged by the definitive Freudian tests of achievement in work and love, the unavoidable verdict was that he'd messed up. Or, in the brute win or lose terms of his re-set profession, he had failed his assignment. At sixty-two there was no chance of a resubmission. He had no children, his relationship was sliding into mutual loathing, and he had virtually nothing solid or permanent to show from his long professional life. Set against that litany of absence and inadequacy, an extended period of youthful and early middle-aged self-indulgence seemed flimsy in the balance. More so now that it was over.

To start again! But start what again? As far as women were concerned his easy charm of yesteryear had turned into a reverse charisma apparently so boring that few stayed around long enough to grant him a decent conversation let alone indulge him in the pretence of flirtation. Not much mileage there, then. Work was not quite such a dead end. Even if it was too late for him to publish he still sporadically enjoyed teaching. He could still put in a fair shift as long as the new model army of smart arses didn't try to tell him how to do it. He liked the students and he knew most of them liked him. Probably, most of them did. That was it! He would end his career on a teaching high. He'd show his detractors that he could still hack it. Fuck the technology! Fuck the jargon! Fuck the new fangled, bone-brained directors of this, that and the fucking other! He'd fucking show them! Then he would retire at peace with himself. The voice in his head was at full throttle: but not quite loud enough to drown out a quiet whisper – *Henry, you're kidding yourself.*

'Henry, stop talking to yourself.'

It was Bradley Purfect.

'You Brits are so eccentric. You were definitely mumbling to yourself. No doubt profound stuff. Why don't you share it with me? I'm in need of a good conversation. Why don't I join you for a walk and a chat?'

In normal circumstances Brad Purfect was not Henry's idea of someone likely to throw up a worthwhile conversation. He almost preferred the over-earnestness and aggressive egocentricity of American business people to the same qualities packaged in the form of a crude, Marxist pedant. Strident self-promotion elided with cultural myopia seemed to affect even American lefties and Brad more than most. But today Henry was willing to be more welcoming, if only to escape his own gloomy thoughts. He fell into step with Brad.

'Hi Brad. I'm sorry you're feeling neglected. So what have you been up to?'

'I've been trying to get a handle on the left in this country. I thought Britain was the home of real socialism but nobody seems to talk seriously about getting rid of capitalism. Oh, yes. I hear lots about how greedy capitalists are, but not much about how to replace the capitalist system or even what to replace it with. What we need is a good old fashioned revolution.'

Henry had no wish to discuss this issue, but any distraction, even in the form of Brad, was better than being left with his own company. He'd go along with it for a few minutes. Brad's gung-ho, roll on the revolution attitude had the unaccustomed effect of making him feel quite moderate and sensible. He made a few perfunctory remarks about the almost certain futility of attempting violent revolution in Britain: it wouldn't work and the vast majority wouldn't support it. Brad grudgingly conceded that 'the conditions weren't yet quite right' but was reluctant completely to dismiss the possibility.

They continued to bandy ideas about, Henry taking the opportunity to launch into a monologue on his pet theories of 'institutional democracy' and 'the industrialisation of the education system.' Unaware that he was doing most of the talking Henry almost felt that he was having a half-decent conversation with Brad.

He glanced at Brad, who wasn't used to being out-talked.

'Sorry, Brad, you've started me off. Let's drop the serious stuff. You didn't answer me when I asked you what you've been doing in your time over here.'

'No, don't worry. I agree with a lot of what you say. At least you've got some idea of how we might move forward. But talk about 'a long revolution', gradual change – I mean real change - could take forever or more likely just not happen. There's a need for leadership, some sort of vanguard, not violence necessarily. I'd go a lot further than...'

Brad was about to expand on how much further he would go when Henry abruptly stopped walking, giving him a perplexed look. As far as he could see the American had scarcely 'agreed' with anything he had said: rather the opposite. He remembered why he avoided arguments with Brad. It was not so much that the discussion went round in circles rather Brad's logic was highly linear and rigid, as if concession in argument personally undermined him. Henry decided to change tack altogether.

'Let's talk about something else. I'm taking time off from planning the revolution at the moment, "temporally like Achilles", as someone said.'

'Achilles?'

'Yes, you know, Achilles?'

'Not personally but I think I know who you're referring to. Wasn't he some ancient who had something wrong with his foot? Anyway who said they were temporally like Achilles?'

'Dylan.'

'Thomas?'

'Bob.'

'Bob Dylan?'

'That's right.'

'It sounds like the sort of thing he'd say or rather croak.'

'Don't tell me you don't like his Bobness. If it helps, Abraham Lincoln might also have said it.'

'I doubt that. It's not the sort of remark he'd make. But if he did he would have meant something different than Bob Dylan. Not that anyone can work out what Dylan does mean, assuming he means anything, which I doubt.'

The two academics had resumed walking. Henry was glad they'd dropped the testy topic of revolution but didn't particularly want to stay with the Dylans or Abraham Lincoln either. Typically Henry's conversation veered between the highly intellectual and the lowly vulgar. Deciding that the first was beyond Brad and the second would be seen as beneath him, he made a rare effort to hit the bland middle territory that he imagined was Brad's natural habitat.

'Brad,' Henry spoke with exaggerated emphasis as he tried to redirect the conversation, 'have you seen much theatre since you came over here? It's about the best cultural experience this country has to offer. Or what else have you been doing to entertain yourself?'

'Oh, the usual things.' Brad paused as if the switch in the conversation had sparked a reminder. 'By the way have you picked up your invitation to the party that Aisha Khan is putting on at her place? I must say it's very kind of her, quite a sociable gesture, especially as she's only been working here for a few months I believe. In the States it's usually senior colleagues that host departmental get-togethers.'

Henry was interested. He liked Aisha Khan but hadn't seen much of her other than when they had chatted in the so-called staff-room.

'No, nothing has come my way yet. If it had, I would have noticed, I checked out my emails last night.'

'The invitation came as a card. I picked up mine from my tray. You're sure to have been invited. In fact the card is a general invitation to all of us - partners and kids are welcome too. I'm sure your card will be in your tray.'

This piece of news gave Henry a convenient exit opportunity. 'Brad, as always it's been a pleasure to talk with you. Right now though, I want to check that I've been invited to this delightful young woman's party.'

'Sure, you're invited and you better behave yourself you old rogue. You realise she's married.'

'I'd be surprised if she wasn't.'

'How about a cup of coffee once you've picked up your invitation?' Brad called after the departing Henry.

Already well on his way Henry was almost out of hearing range. He decided to pretend that he was.

Henry used to look forward to checking his in-tray. As well as work- related bumph and publishers' catalogues, it served as a conduit for the odd personal message or letter. Now even personal communications came as emails – when they came at all. Sometimes he failed to spot them in the dump of official rubbish and global spam. Maybe he should get a mobile phone and learn to text properly. Otherwise he risked losing his younger friends and contacts.

He reached the bank of trays at a brisk geriatric jog. His tray bulged from neglect. On top was a bunch of publishers catalogues. He tossed them towards a nearby waste bin missing it by a handsome margin. Underneath he found a large mauve envelope with his name embossed on it in large gold italic script. Never since he had seen it inscribed on his PhD certificate had the name of 'HENRY JONES' looked so pucker. He opened the envelope carefully to avoid tearing the invitation card. Inside there was the expected invitation and an added personal message from Aisha saying how much she had enjoyed their recent conversation and that she hoped that they would talk again soon. Henry flushed with pleasure.

Chapter 17
Aisha's Party

Tim Connor had decided that Aisha's party offered him a
rare opportunity for a public display of his credentials as a
family man, diminished, as he conceded, though they were
by recent events. After much hesitation, Gina agreed to
come over with Maria. Reluctantly she also agreed to stay
over-night at Tim's place. Tim was pleased, though less so
when she emphasised that she would be sleeping in the spare
room with Maria. Still he had no serious expectation of a
recall to favour, temporary or otherwise. And there was his
slow burning relationship with Erica to consider. On reflection he realised that Gina's insistence on keeping a distance
between them made sense. In any case, her loyalties now lay
elsewhere. It was just that somewhere in the back of his mind
he kept hearing a barely audible whisper, 'you never know'.

The afternoon of the party found him making a determined effort to dress smartly – more for the sake of Gina
and Maria, who was beginning to notice and comment on
such matters, than to impress his assembled colleagues.

'What do you think I should wear for this party? I still have most of my clothes from when we were together.' Tim shouted for sartorial advice from his bedroom to Gina who was with Maria in the guest bedroom.

'It's not a formal do, is it? Wear something clean and comfortable. You used to look presentable in that white cotton smock and beige linen trousers. Wear them with those open strapped sandals you bought in Turkey.'

'I don't want to look too hippie, there'll be a squad of the suit and tie boys there, certainly the Dean and maybe others. Aisha Khan has been pretty inclusive in her invitations. And she and her husband are Muslims of some kind so this isn't going to be a let it all hang out affair. At least I'll be amazed if it is. There may not even be any alcohol.'

'Wear a suit and tie yourself, then, if you're that concerned.' Gina sounded terse. She still found everyday chat with Tim a strain. But she was determined to keep to their agreement to avoid post-break-up bitterness and sniping. And she wanted Maria to be able to maintain a relationship with her father. She reverted to faux cheerful mode.

'Tim, we're ready now. It's time to stop prettying yourself up. Maria, go and show your father how nice you look.'

Maria took a couple of steps and then hesitated. 'Why can't he come and see me instead.'

Tim overheard Maria's remark and quickly went over.

His daughter was dressed in a blue and red party dress with her hair tied back with a striped ribbon of the same colours. Her skin, almost as dark as her mother's, shone against the silk dress

'Wow! You look great, as pretty as your mum.'

Maria gave him an uncertain look but was drawn by the compliment. The moment hung in the balance. Then she tumbled towards him. 'Pick me up Daddy, I want to give you a big kiss.'

Tim swung her off her feet lifting her high in the air. They exchanged noisy kisses.

'Put me down now Daddy, you only deserve one kiss so far.'

'So far what?'

'I don't know, you might get another one after the party. Can we go now?'

Gina drove them to Aisha's place in Tim's car. There were already several vehicles, some luxury class, parked in the wide semi-circular drive. She managed to squeeze the old Volvo in between a gold Mercedes and a gleaming jet-black four-by-four.

'Well done, a scratch on either of those could cost the thick end of half a grand,' said Tim.

A tall Asian man with a head of hair like a lion's mane greeted them at the door. He was wearing a dark suit, white shirt and bow tie.

'Good afternoon, my name is Waqar Khan, I'm Aisha's husband. I assume you must be Tim Connor. Aisha has talked about you from time to time. She mentioned that you are rather tall which is how I recognised you.'

'That's right and this is Gina and our daughter Maria.'

'I'm delighted to meet you. I've been looking forward to putting faces to the names Aisha has mentioned.' He smiled down at Maria, 'That's a lovely dress you're wearing, beautiful colours.'

'Thank you, Mummy bought it for me,' Maria's face lit up.

'The party is in the extension at the back of the house and spilling out into the garden,' Waqar continued. 'We thought we would keep it as open as possible – there are a few children here and we want to give them space to play in. And on a decent day like this people enjoy gathering round the pool.'

The noise of the party got louder as they followed Waqar through the house. After passing through several rooms they arrived at a large glass extension that opened out onto a spacious garden area. Both were crowded, mainly with people Tim didn't know. Waqar called his wife over to welcome the new arrivals. She quickly left a group of women who were engaged in an animated discussion. Waqar then made his excuses, bowed politely and moved off to join a group of similarly formally dressed men.

'I'm so pleased to see you all,' Aisha smiled, opting to greet them with hugs rather than handshakes or a two-cheek kiss. 'As you can see there's plenty of food and there's lots to drink; non-alcoholic over there and there's some alcohol on a separate table if you want that. But I'd be interested to hear what you think of my homemade fruit and herbal drinks. Waqar is planning to trial them in the restaurants if we get a good reaction from our friends today. So far the feedback has been positive. But you must tell us what you really think. And please, no English politeness.'

She turned to Gina, adding by way of explanation, 'Oh, I should have said, my husband runs a chain of restaurants and we're always trying to think of new ideas to improve the business. My homemade drinks idea is probably a bit optimistic given that most Brits like a lager with "an Indian." Anyway let me take Maria outside so she can join in with the other children. My friend Caroline will look after them so Maria will be fine. I won't be a moment.'

Momentarily subdued by the occasion, Maria took Aisha's hand without complaint. They disappeared in the direction of a large French window.

'What a magnificent house,' said Gina, raising her voice above the noise, 'and our hosts seem to have thought of everything.'

'That's right,' Tim agreed, 'they've made it a real family party.'

Tim was impressed with Aisha's fluency as a host. At the university she quietly and un-fussily got on with the job but today, in her own home there was an easy confidence about her that he had not previously noticed. She was less reserved than he thought. On reflection he realised that her demeanour at work was also well measured. By working hard but being open about her lack of experience in an academic institution, she attracted the support she needed, sometimes more than she needed.

She was back with them within a couple of minutes.

'That's worked out well. There are one or two other children of Maria's age as well as my son Ali. He really loves playing the young host so she won't be short of attention.' She paused for a moment. 'Tim, why don't you pop over to the group I was with when you came in, a colleague of yours was asking where you were. I'll have a chat with Gina and show her round the property.'

'Ok, thanks,' said Tim. 'I'll just grab myself some food and a drink first.'

Having loaded up Tim took in the crowded scene. He hesitated for a moment. He was keen to locate Henry rather than join the group Aisha had indicated. Erica, Rachel and Annette were engaged in noisy and excited conversation and he decided not to interrupt. He could catch up with Erica at a better time.

Henry wasn't in the extension. Looking out onto the garden Tim spotted him just beyond the far end of the pool. He was astonished to see that he was sat almost knee to knee with Howard Swankie apparently in animated conversation. However their stiff body language did not suggest a love-in. Tim tensed. He had phoned Henry before the party to warn him not to spoil the occasion by indulging in another bout of his vendetta with Swankie. He pointed out that it would embarrass Aisha whom Henry claimed to like.

He stepped out of the extension and made his way along the edge of the pool. Noticing the children playing in a sandpit on the the far side of the pool, he waved to Maria.

'Hi Maria, everything ok?'

'Daddy can't you see we're playing,' came the reply.

Tim might have felt rejected had he not heard her proudly remark as he moved on, 'That's my Daddy.'

'You bet I am,' he murmured to himself.

It occurred to Tim as he approached the two men that

they might almost have been designed for the purpose of annoying each other: Swankie precise and self-important, Henry garrulous and wildly iconoclastic. From the sound of it, they had already hit their trouble spot.

Henry was the first to notice Tim. A flicker of guilt crossed his face.

'Hi, Tim, come and join us. Pull up a chair.'

'I will if you don't mind, just for a few minutes. Apologies for interrupting. You look like you're in the midst of an interesting conversation.'

'Oh hello Tim,' said Swankie, 'yes, it is rather lively, I'm trying to persuade this old traditionalist that times have changed and higher education has to pay its way now. Anyway, yes, do take a seat.'

As it turned out the conversation was less interesting to Tim than he had politely suggested it might be. As he had feared, it was yet another argument in the Howard and Henry saga. Howard was sounding even more superciliously didactic than usual, expounding on the need for 'cost effectiveness' and the importance of management having the power to 'weed out time-servers.' He wagged his forefinger reprovingly at Henry as he made the latter remark. Henry responded according to their standard script, ratcheting up the rhetoric as his irritation with Swankie grew.

Tim found himself nervously observing the dire emotional dynamic between his colleagues rather than listening to their often rehearsed opinions. As Swankie also began to lose his poise their language became more offensive and their angry interruptions more frequent. Henry's over-the-top response to the comment that his argument was 'perverse' was that Swankie's was 'morally perverted.'

The two protagonists knew exactly how to wind one-another up, revelling in mutual detestation. Henry's ploy was crude belligerence whereas Howard was more subtly sadistic. Howard was ahead on points having succeeded in annoying Henry more than Henry had annoyed him but he was treading dangerously. Henry was at his most unpredictable when ridiculed but for the moment he was still trying to hold down an argument.

'There you go again,' he snorted, 'your vision of education is determined by economic considerations, whereas mine is humanistic. I don't give a tinker's turd; no disrespect to tinkers, whether my teaching covers a bunch of economic and social 'competencies' or 'skills' dreamt up by some moronic quango. Social Science is already rich enough in intellectual and applied skills and it won't be improved by manipulating them so they can be checked off on some silly list. I'm fed up with this new army of educational semi-technocrats, blinkered crackpot would-be bloody realists constantly pissing about telling me what to do. How many ways are there to polish shit, anyway?'

'Henry,' Swankie's attempted interjection was ignored as Henry gathered momentum.

'All this bullshit is a huge waste of time and money. It's the likes of you that should be cut. Do you realise that the major area of expansion in higher education in the last twenty years has been petty office-holders, bistro-bureaucrats like your bloody self? You guys have even invented a posh name to justify your useless jobs: 'the third space.' Remember 'the third way?' What a cock-up that turned out to be; a fig leaf to hide Blair's lack of meat, a puff of ideological hot air. There was nothing there. This is worse. You can't escape from these 'third space' people. You can ignore a daft slogan like 'the third way' but these buffoons are all over the place, making a nuisance of themselves. We'd be better with an empty space. These people are just the foot-soldiers of the mad market extremists. They seem oblivious to the fact that they're implicated in the market swallowing everything. It's not just higher education but the arts, sport, you name it and there's the name of some fucking corporation plastered all over it. There's nothing left to the public good. It's time-servers like you, Howard, that are the worst because you could do something about it.'

'Henry, please.' Swankie's tone was more emollient as he

sensed that Henry was revving out of control. He enjoyed upsetting Henry but not to the point of goading him into violence, particularly if he, Howard Swankie, Dean of Social Science, was on the receiving end. But he feared any physical consequence less than damage to his reputation. Even though not at fault, involvement in a disorderly incident would hardly promote his career profile. 'Henry, perhaps we should talk about something else?'

Tim saw an opportunity to cool things down. He cast around for a safe topic. He recalled that both men had an interest in sport.

'As it happens, there's something I wanted to raise with both of you, and it's nothing to do with work. I need a bit of information. Wherever I've lived, I've always occasionally watched some local football. I used to watch my hometown team Whitetown South End and I saw some of the better teams around the Midlands when I lived in the potteries. Congleton were surprisingly good, I saw them beat Stafford Rangers 4-0 once. I haven't found a team to watch since I came down here. I've tried Wash Wanderers but they were, well a washout, not much better than a team I played for once, Tooting Urinals. So I need you to recommend a team worth watching.'

Henry guffawed into his beer. Swankie smiled sceptically.

'Tooting what?' They chorused in a rare moment of unison.

'Urinals. But only kidding.' At least his jest appeared to have diffused matters. 'Listen I need to check that my daughter is getting on ok, and then maybe percolate a bit. Why don't you two sort out a team within thirty miles of Wash that I could watch from time to time without jeopardising my interest in the great game? I'll drop back later to collect suggestions.'

Tim was surprised to find himself telling the two older men what to talk about, particularly Swankie, whose highly developed sense of status usually discouraged humbler souls from offering him suggestions. And Tim's proposed topic, though likely to lighten the mood, was, as he admitted to himself as he went to check out Maria, on the clunky side.

The party was still crowded although he noticed that the children playing with Maria and Ali had now gone, perhaps taken home. He was pleased to see Maria and Ali still playing together, the more so as she was carefully helping him to move his lame leg as he attempted to mount a small climbing frame. It was good to see that his daughter had inherited some of her mother's kindness as well as her brittle sensitivity.

He re-entered the extension and paused for a moment. Gina seemed preoccupied with a couple of guests he did not know and he opted to head for the group Aisha had directed him to earlier. As he approached he noticed that Brad Purfect had joined it and judging from the blank faces around him, was holding forth in typically drone-like manner. Still he could put up with Purfect for a few minutes. A trickier problem was Rachel Steir. He'd begun to notice that whenever he sat near her, she had a habit of abruptly leaving her seat. On a couple of occasions he had made the mistake of sitting next to her. She had shot off like a nun suddenly confronted by a flasher. He decided to sit well away from her in the hope that she would stay put. He was curious to see how she exercised her pull on others, not least on Erica who was sitting next to her. Annette, who had come to the party independently of Henry was still with the group and there were also a couple of middle-aged women he hadn't seen before.

'Mind if I join you?'

There was a murmur of assent. However it did not include Rachel, who was out of her seat before Tim was in his. He exchanged a mild look of concern with Erica.

'I was just about to say...' Brad Purfect did not reach the end of his sentence. He was interrupted by the sound of a loud splash followed by shouts of alarm.

'Shit!' Tim feared the worst. Without bothering to make his excuses he was out of the extension and running along the edge of the pool. He cursed at the sight of Howard Swankie, fully clothed, threshing around in the water.

'Help... help... I can't swim.'

The situation was simultaneously dangerous and comic. Suppressing an impulse to laugh, Tim tore off his jacket, preparing to launch himself towards his panic-stricken boss. He was beaten to it. Henry, stripped down to his under clothes, emerged from the crowd gathering around the edge of the pool and leapt towards the unfortunate Swankie. He landed plum on top of his senior colleague striking him on the head with his right buttock. Swankie sank under the impact. As he resurfaced rage briefly conquered fear. He lashed out at Henry who nimbly blocked the intended blow. Unbalanced Swankie dipped again. He reappeared looking desperate.

'Aah... Stop trying to drown me. Help someone! Save me from this oaf.'

Henry was in his element.

'Stop talking, stop struggling. Leave it to me. Bloody stay still or I'll have to knock you out.' He managed to turn Swankie round, grabbed the top of his braces and tugged him the few yards to the side of the pool. Several pairs of hands lifted Swankie onto the pool's edge. Amongst the sound of concerned voices there was a ripple of applause for Henry who swam a swift length of honour before emerging beaming from the pool. He was swiftly handed a towel as his sodden underpants dropped to his feet. A couple of jokers in the crowd applauded again.

'You deserve a medal,' shouted one of them.

Henry gave a nonchalant wave before gathering up his clothes and retreating to a wooden changing hut set back from the pool. He emerged a couple of minutes later to be greeted by the sound of Swankie's protesting voice. He was sat, draped in towels, on a poolside chair seemingly unharmed by his misadventure but indignant and embarrassed. He pointed an accusing finger at Henry.

'You did that on purpose. You deliberately tripped me.'

'Nonsense. That's a serious accusation. It was your own fault. For some reason you suddenly changed direction when we left our chairs and tripped over me. You struck my foot with your shin. Calm down. You should be grateful I rescued you especially after you attacked me in the pool.'

Tim was watching Henry closely for any sign of piss taking. For once Henry was playing it straight, milking his moment as local hero.

By now Aisha and Waqar Khan were fully engaged with the situation.

'Professor Swankie, I'm sure this was an accident. Surely it must have been,' said Waqar Khan. 'If you're certain you've recovered why don't we take you inside and we'll find you a decent change of clothes?'

Aisha Khan chipped in.

'I'm sure my husband's right, Professor. Let's get you a hot drink as well.'

Swankie was somewhat mollified by the attention of his hosts. With a vicious look at Henry he got up and was led off into the house.

Following the incident the crowd at the party began rapidly to thin out. Tim noticed that Gina had left the extension to be with Maria and Ali. She held both hands up, fingers spread wide, signalling to him that she wanted to leave in ten minutes. He swiftly did the rounds saying goodbye to colleagues and a thank you to the Khans who were still fussing over Swankie.

Finally he went over for a word with Henry.

'You alright Henry?'

'Sure, fine, I enjoy a dip.'

'I don't think our Dean feels the same way. But he seems ok. Mainly a case of wounded pride I think.' Tim looked at Henry thoughtfully. 'Quite the athlete, aren't you?'

'There's still a bit left in the tank.'

'Yeah, I can see.'

Henry, tell me something.

'Maybe. Go ahead.'

'*Did* you do that on purpose?'

'Tim, what do you think?'

'Henry, it's an effing good job you're not looking for promotion.'

Later they had a laugh together at Swankie's expense. But for Henry the journey on the long road down to the bad times picked up pace after the swimming pool fiasco. Swankie played a cool hand. He didn't make a public issue of the incident or even mention it again. He knew he had quite enough evidence to bury Henry without using this embarrassing episode. In any case it was one man's word against another's and if he was going to nail Henry he better not appear to do so on the back of a personal vendetta. It was much cleaner to rely on the complaints of Henry's peers and the students although to his surprise few were prepared to make unqualified criticisms. Nevertheless he was confident that the dossier he had painstakingly put together on Henry would do the job. He was a fan of carefully compiled dossiers.

Chapter 18
Thank God for
a Conference

Academic conferences are not exactly holidays but they can provide a welcome change of scene and a chance to recharge the batteries. Tim needed both. His energy auto-renewal system was beginning to falter and life seemed static on all fronts. For the moment work had settled into a tough routine and for a couple of weeks he and Erica had barely managed to get together. Banging his head against a brick wall understated things: he recalled the standard advice - it feels good when you stop.

The annual subject conference of the British Sociological Association offered the possibility of a brief distraction. The London School of Economics was not the most novel venue for a sociology conference but it was easily accessible and located in the centre of one of the great world cities. Tim was happy to leave his car behind and travel comfortably on a non-too-crowded train. It was a glorious sunny day. Interrupted only by the dull beige of Swindon and Reading the hundred or so miles of gleaming, green countryside to the capital flashed by in little over an hour. From

Paddington it was a short trip on the tube to the University. Once in the big city a sense of freedom gusted anarchically through the canyons of his mind. A good time might not be the purpose of the conference but that was what he intended to have.

As always he felt a frisson of excitement approaching the main entrance to LSE in Houghton Street. In his youth he imagined LSE as a citadel of pure learning, uncontaminated by worldly imperatives of practicality and compromise. He now wondered from where he had got that idea. Perhaps it was simply adolescent romanticism. But he still thought of LSE as his spiritual home, his *alma mater* that never was. An explanation for this imagined belonging lay in an incident of his school days. During the second year of his A levels he had been blocked from applying to take a degree at LSE by the head teacher at Whitetown College, an authoritarian Jesuit named Father Hannon. The bigoted cleric insisted that the university was 'dangerous and irreligious,' a description that sharpened Tim's desire to go there. It was to no avail. Instead he was directed across the Aldwych to King's College, considered by Hannon to be 'safer and more respectable.' He assured Tim that in twenty years time he would be thankful for this 'wise guidance.' Like most assurances given to him by Catholic priests Tim found this one to be as substantial as a yard of piss. As it turned out the priest's knowledge of the two universities was dated and inaccurate. King's had niches of radicalism and LSE was becoming less so. Nevertheless Tim still believed that his intellectual development had been delayed by a lack of radical ambience during a formative period. But he wasn't nursing a grievance. It had all helped him to define what he disagreed with. Discovering what he agreed with took a little longer.

Although he had arrived an hour or so before the President's welcoming address, the venue was already becoming crowded. He queued for several minutes before being able to register and pick up his conference pack – a bulky

cloth bag disappointingly full, mainly of publishers catalogues. More usefully it also included a list of 'conference
delegates.' He knew that several of his Wash colleagues
were attending, including Erica. He had suggested travelling with her but she insisted that she couldn't just dump
Rachel as the two of them always went to conferences
together. He was beginning to tire not of Erica, far from it,
but of the game of hide-and-seek that they had slipped back
into. He knew, though, that this was not the moment to
insist that they go public with their relationship. Too many
stressful things were going on without adding another. He
could put up with the 'now you see me, now you don't' routine for some time longer if it kept Erica happy. Checking
through the delegate list he noted that Annette was attending and he knew that Aisha was hoping to join them later.
Brad Purfect's name was also on the list. He felt a minor
pang of guilt about Purfect. Despite the American's bombastic manner he was a guest of the department and Tim
had done little so far to make his stay more worthwhile.
Perhaps the next few days would present an opportunity
for a friendly gesture without risking any extended entan-
glement. Finally he checked to confirm that Henry had kept
to an early decision not to attend. He needed a break from
the intransigent Welshman and his bunch of problems.

The introductory speeches followed by a plenary session on 'inequality and global finance' offered little new but
at least got Tim into the swing of the conference. When
they were over he made his way through a tangle of cor-
ridors to find his chosen 'theme stream,' *Youth and Protest*
that had been located in a remote part of the main building.
The group was a motley collection. Several of the thirty or
so who had opted to join the stream would have made a
good advert for its title, parading styles from post-punk to
electro-hippie. A couple of urban anarchists contributed a
darker presence. Roughly half the group were about Tim's
age or older, most having subsided into the low maintenance comfort of tea-shirts and jeans. An older man, per-

haps in his sixties stood out. He was wearing a kaftan and bandana. For a moment Tim thought he might be Henry: he had the same stocky shape and thinning, straggly hair. As he got closer he was reassured. The man was taller than Henry and had a leaner, fresher face. Tim mused that he was beginning to let Henry haunt him.

The group turned out to be lively and combative. The topics covered ranged from papers on 'the meaning or meaninglessness of youthful styles' to 'the recruitment methods of Al Qaeda among the young'. Eventually the theme of revolt morphed into a rolling debate on intergenerational justice. At times the sessions got fractious, dividing more or less along generational lines. 'You boomed, we bust,' shouted one youngster pointing an accusing finger at a couple of startled older members of the group. By the penultimate session of the second day Tim was beginning to feel that the discussions were becoming circular with the younger element fixated on expressing anger at the legacy left by the over forties and the later claiming that the current crisis was not entirely of their making, and cautioning that young people alone would struggle to change things. His own attempt to argue that the problems of contemporary youth were an important part of the still bigger issue of burgeoning global economic and social inequality failed to redirect the debate. As the arguments began to repeat themselves he contemplated skipping a session or two.

During a late afternoon break between sessions Tim found himself stood next in the coffee queue to the retro hippie he had briefly mistaken for Henry. The older man had sat listening quietly during the cross-generational debate but Tim sensed he might have something interesting to say. He introduced himself and suggested that they sit down together. The response was friendly.

'Thanks. I'm Calvin Frazier, Cal for short. Yeah, I noticed you, too. You were looking at me like you thought you might know me. I'm pretty sure we've never met.'

'No... no, we haven't. Well, I guess we have now.'

'Cool.' Cal reached out, catching Tim's hand in an awkward vertical grip. For a moment it looked like Cal was setting himself for a follow-through hug but a quick step backwards took Tim safely out of distance. This guy might look vaguely like Henry but he certainly didn't act like him. Henry was not the hug a stranger type. As they passed through the checkout Cal complimented the young female cashier on her beautiful brown eyes and expressed the hope that she wasn't finding her job too boring. The dark eyes smiled in amused surprise. She assured Cal that he needn't be concerned - she was a PhD student filling in at the checkout to make some pin money. She was confident that better opportunities lay ahead.

Cal looked ready to extend the conversation but thought better of it as impatient noises from the queue rose in volume. Queues are great places for impromptu chit-chat during the waiting phase but hopeless at the business end.

Aware that the next session was due shortly, Tim led Cal to an empty table. As they sat down Tim dived in with a question on the generational guilt theme.

'So are you on the side of those that blame the older generation for the plight of the current one?'

'You mean the boomers? My own generation? Some of them are pretty greedy and selfish but you can't generalise. A fair number are quite radical. Anyway, whole generations don't think and act collectively. No, I agree with what you were saying. It's the minority of the powerful and wealthy that control things and by no means all of them come from a single generation. Besides, many born in the decade or so after the Second-World-War are now quite poor and needy and were never particularly well off anyway.'

Cal's response was more down-to-earth than the 'peace and love' stuff Tim had half expected. Not that he was against peace and love. In fact he was curious to know more about where Cal was coming from philosophically. He was about to probe when he was interrupted by a familiar voice.

'Tim, you son of an Englishman, can I join you?'

It was Brad Purfect. He sat down without waiting for an invitation.

'Scottish, actually.'

'Scottish what?'

'My dad was Scottish not English.'

'My apologies. We Americans forget that you guys still have your local rivalries. You'd think the country was too small to cope with them. Anyway Tim how about introducing me to your friend?'

'Sure. Cal, meet Brad Purfect, he's visiting with us at Wash University from the States. Brad, this is Calvin Frazier, we're in the same theme stream.'

The two men exchanged brief gestures of acknowledgement.

'Brad, I've just met Cal,' continued Tim, 'we were just chatting for a few minutes before going into the next session.'

'Don't make assumptions, Tim. In the States hardly anybody attends the last session of the day. The best part of conferences are the breaks between sessions, and in the evenings when the formal stuff is over. And I'm not just talking about professional networking. What's the point of coming to these great cities if you don't take a look around? Anyway I...'

'Hang on a minute, Brad. We've only just sat down. Let's forget about re-timetabling the conference to suit our own whims for the moment. I was just asking Cal here...'

'Sure, let's talk now but it means we'll be late for the next session. Or, better still we can miss it altogether,' Brad persisted, 'How about...'

'Ok we can skip the next session as long as Cal is ok about it.' Cal gave a nod of assent. 'But let's relax for a few minutes. I was just asking Cal about his opinions on the current crisis.'

'Sure, of course, I was only...'

Tim cut Brad off. He wanted to hear more from Cal.

'Cal, I was interested in what you were saying about the

economic and financial crisis? Even as we speak the rich are getting richer, and the richer they are the quicker it's happening. And, of course, the gap between the very rich and the rest of us is widening. But what I'm really interested in is your moral take on the whole thing. How do you see things changing? You have the look of someone who might have thought about that side of it.'

'Well, thanks. I'll take that as a compliment. You're half-right in trying to second-guess me. Moral and cultural change has to be part of the picture. That won't come from the elites, the perpetrators and beneficiaries of inequality. Real change will have to be rooted in the actions of ordinary people. So, yes, there has to be a collective change of mind and heart, a change of culture. You do get such changes. Systems, regimes, empires, can be changed when enough people want it and are able to make their feelings count. The underlying process of change takes time but there are catalytic shifts and symbolic moments. For instance the freeing of Mandela accelerated the end of apartheid but the moral as well as the practical opposition to it across the globe had already underlined its credibility. Generally there have to be deep cultural shifts to prepare the way for radical institutional change. And the change in peoples' values and the way they relate to each other has to be sustained otherwise a reversion to elitism or even authoritarianism is likely. Maintaining genuinely democratic and humanistic systems can be as hard as establishing them in the first place.'

By now Brad was interested.

'As you say, the elites, I still prefer to call them the ruling class, cling on to their power as long as they can. They even resist the implementation of weak forms of liberal democracy until it becomes less trouble to implement than resist. When it comes to demands for real equality the wealthy and powerful will always resist because turkeys don't vote for Christmas. Or as Sartre put it more elegantly 'no man can condemn himself.' Very few do, anyway. Cal, no amount of cultural change will persuade these guys to share things out more fairly. They won't do it. They'll have to be removed by one means or another. Violence could play a role, maybe a crucial role. If a regime really does lose credibility, the armed forces, or some of them, sometimes defect to the popular cause, to the people. Sometimes violence is necessary.'

Cal waited patiently for Brad to finish before responding.

'The difficulties rule violent revolution out in technologically advanced democracies. Modern states have centralised the means of violence as well as increased their effectiveness. And the other part of the equation is that, however gross their inequalities, liberal democracies do allow for some expression of opinion, including dissenting ones. That decreases pressure for violent change and can even lead to some progressive social reform, although nothing much has been introduced by the neo-liberal regimes of the last thirty years. So, no; the bottom line is that if you want long-term change there has to be a change not only in people's values but in how they relate to each other.'

'You sound a bit like a preacher man,' said Brad half mockingly.

Cal looked at Brad sceptically but gave him the benefit of a serious reply. 'Not at all. I don't preach at people, I'm no priest. I have a philosophy of this life but not the next. If there is any conscious life after death I imagine it will be some kind of continuation of this one. That would seem logical but I don't know.'

'Now you're beginning to sound like a hippie. I bet you took a stack full of psychedelics in the sixties and seventies.' Brad seemed determined to needle Cal.

'I had my share but not now. They can take a toll on you and anyway these short cuts can leave people suspended in a counterfeit infinity believing all kinds of fuzzy-brained rubbish.'

In his efforts to annoy Cal, Brad had succeeded in annoying himself. He was beginning to look edgy and combative.

Tim decided to move in again. He shifted his chair closer to Cal.

'So, Cal, you're a lifestyle radical?'

'You can put it that way if you want. Capitalism has mugged just about every area of institutional life, even the arts, maybe especially the arts, and higher education. There's no alternative but to work with our own lives. 'The personal is the political,' as someone once said. Ultimately if enough people change their values and lifestyles, the old system will dissolve. Not that there's any guarantee.'

Tim leaned back, noticing that the room was now almost empty. People had headed off to the final sessions and the clatter of waiters clearing up was beginning to drown out their conversation. He took the opportunity to move things on.

'Look, we have to make a decision. Do we bunk the final session or not?'

'I'm for bunking,' said Brad. 'I'm looking forward to a guided tour of the great metropolis, or at least part of it.'

'That's fine by me. I don't know the city that well, though, so I won't offer to be the guide. Maybe Tim can do that,' suggested Cal.

'Ok, no problem. There's enough daylight left for a stroll along the riverfront and maybe through one of the parks. After that we could stop off in Soho for a meal unless either of you have signed up for the formal conference dinner tonight.'

Neither had.

'That's sensible of you,' commented Tim, 'it's expensive and you don't get a proper pudding.'

The three men made their way out of the university and onto the Aldwych crescent immediately to the south. The huge solid buildings amplified the crashing din of the traffic. Across the crescent was the massive edifice of Bush House, home of British public radio broadcasting and on the other side, the Strand. Bush House looked like the hulk of a vast beached ship. Traffic hurtled relentlessly round the one-way system regulated only by seemingly random traffic lights.

'Follow me you two,' Tim shouted above the cacophony. The three of them skipped across to the Bush House side of the crescent just as the lights let loose another barrage of traffic. A couple of car horns blasted behind them as they made it to the pavement. Tim shuddered at the mad, blaring noise; Brad shouted a generalised 'fuck off' at the oblivious vehicles; and Cal, kaftan flapping, just about preserved his trademark cool.

'Keep following, we can cut through here,' Tim gestured towards an open throughway between two sections of Bush House. Emerging at the other side they took advantage of a lull in traffic to cross the Strand. Tim waved a hand in identification of his old college, King's, confining his comments to an expression of regret that his favourite student drinking-hole nearby had disappeared.

Within a couple of minutes they had reached Waterloo Bridge.

'I don't want to drag you two all the way to the other side of the river but let's walk to the middle of the bridge, it gives a good view of the Thames and the surrounding city.'

As they made their way onto the bridge Tim attempted to recall items of historical or literary interest about it. Apart from mentioning Monet's stolen painting of the bridge, all he could come up with was the Kinks' *Waterloo Sunset*. It turned out to be a good call as both Brad and Cal knew the song. And as it happened the pale sun was just beginning to set, diffusing a diaspora of light blue, silver and gold across the evening sky.

'Waterloo sunset time,' Cal quoted a line from the song.

'Yeah, it's almost like I planned it,' said Tim, pleased with himself.

'Didn't Shakespeare write a poem about a bridge?' asked Brad.

'Could be – he wrote about most things - but you're

probably thinking of a famous sonnet by Wordsworth, *Upon Westminster Bridge*,' Tim suggested, 'it's a bit further up river.'

'That sounds right, you ought to know. Good name for a poet, Wordsworth. You know worth ...'

'No need to explain,' there was a hint of irritation in Tim's voice. He wanted them to enjoy the scene, not listen to feeble puns about it. Some phrases of Wordworth's sonnet came to mind.

'Wordsworth has a line in his poem something like 'ships, towers, domes, theatres and temples lie open to the fields and to the sky.' You can probably still pick out examples of all of those, apart from fields, even though most of those features are dwarfed by more recent stuff.'

'St Paul's still looks impressive despite the glass and concrete giants around it,' Cal commented.

'What's that? Brad asked gesturing to a point south of the river more or less opposite St Paul's.'

'That's the Gherkin.'

Brad puzzled for a minute.

'I've never thought of gherkins as beautiful.'

'What do you think of that one?' asked Cal.

'The same, it's not beautiful.'

'Postmodern architecture isn't necessarily beautiful. It's more conceptual,' Cal explained.

'What's the point of the concept of a gherkin?'

'I don't know. Maybe it asks a question.'

'It certainly isn't asking me a question.'

'Maybe not, but you asked one yourself a moment ago,' Cal pointed out.

'I know, anybody would, confronted by that dollop of...'

Tim decided to change the topic and the location.

'Let's just shift across to the west side of the bridge and look up the river. We'll see The Houses of Parliament and catch the best of the sunset.'

They crossed over and despite the rush of pedestrians managed to plant themselves against the west railings.

'Now that's architecture,' enthused Brad gesturing towards Parliament, 'that's no gherkin. That has elegance and style. It's almost as impressive as the Kremlin.'

'Yeah, true it's a great example of the mid-nineteenth century gothic but you wouldn't build something like that today,' Tim suggested.

'Maybe, maybe not but I'd rather see more buildings in that style than more gherkins. I mean, where do they go from a gherkin, a beetroot?' Brad looked genuinely perplexed.

Now Cal chipped in.

'They go even bigger, I guess, and even more arbitrary in shape. In fact new concoctions are already in the pipeline. Look at that half-constructed giant saltcellar like folly behind us. It's already dwarfing everything around it, an unintended monument to the sky-high egos of the age. Hubris signalling its own nemesis. Postmodernism's inadvertent satire on itself, its concluding exclamation mark, hopefully.'

'You've got a point there,' said Brad out of his depth. 'What's it called?'

'The Shard.'

'Shard to swallow,' Brad quipped.

'Puny, but you're right, it might well fail to pay for itself.'

'Capitalism is always shafting itself,' said Brad, feeling he was on a bit of a roll.

Cal looked mildly miffed at Brad's prosaic response to his flight of poetic social commentary. He decided to take a dig at him.

'Brad, you ought to develop your own style of Marxist gothic, an extravagant celebration of irrelevance.' He winked at Tim. Brad glared at them both.

Sensing that the quality of their architectural discussion was about to plummet even further Tim brought it to a swift close.

'Ok, let's wander across to Trafalgar Square and think about eating somewhere in Soho. I don't know about you two but I'm getting hungry. We're gonna have to give the park a miss. It's too dark.'

'Good idea,' agreed Cal, 'it's quite cold now the sun's going down. Let's move on.'

'Let's have a couple of drinks on the way. This walk has given me a wicked thirst,' said Brad.

Now that the idea of food and drink had been launched they moved quickly through the city, the day slipping into night as they went.

Brad was insistent that he wanted to sample the full 'London English pub atmosphere' and they stopped twice to knock back a few drinks. In practice Brad seemed to favour varieties of Eurofizz rather than English bitter but was still convinced that he was getting an authentically British experience. The effect was the same. The three of them were in light rococo mood as they made their way across Trafalgar Square.

Brad and Cal were fascinated by Chinatown, but the three of them failed to reach a consensus on whether to eat Chinese. Eventually they crossed Shaftesbury Avenue and settled for an Indian restaurant in Frith Street in the heart of Soho.

During the course of the meal the conversation turned to the other Wash sociologists at the conference. Tim was mildly concerned they might think he and Brad had ditched them in favour of the delights of the metropolis. It didn't reassure him when Brad pointed out that they had done exactly that. Tim was beginning to regret that he had missed a possible opportunity to spend some time with Erica, even if not on a one to one basis. It frustrated him that their relationship seemed suspended between the compulsively physical and tantalising intimations of something more serious. Diversions and interruptions constantly cropped up, mostly in the form of other people. Gina's image came into his mind. He smiled wistfully. He was by no means over her. Then he thought of Rachel, not so much a diversion as an obstacle as far as he was concerned. That was not

Erica's view. Frowning he drained off the dregs of his glass of wine. Putting the glass down he realised that the alcohol was beginning to go to his head. He'd rarely drunk so much so quickly since his student days.

'Wake up young man, you're in dreamland,' Brad gave Tim an over-the-top shove causing him to knock his glass across the table.

'Whoops, apologies,' Brad quickly retrieved the glass carefully replacing it the right way up. 'Good job it was empty.'

Annoyed, Tim glared at Brad who continued in his usual auto way.

'Listen, you guys, I like this Soho part of town. How about we spend a few hours here and take in a club or two?'

'Not for me thanks,' answered Tim. He felt he had paid his dues to Brad by chaperoning him so far. He thought again of Erica and concluded he was definitely in the wrong place.

Brad turned to Cal.

'How about you Cal? C'mon we could have some fun.'

Tim was surprised when Cal agreed, but less so when he explained why.

'Sure Brad, I'll spend some time with you in the fleshpots. I'm not going back to the conference anyway. I'm only paid up to today. I'm off to Spain in the early hours of tomorrow morning for a break. So I have a few hours to kill before I make my way to Stansted.' He gave Brad a considered look, 'Mind you Brad I'm not looking to do anything too exciting or tiring.'

'That's going to cut your options down around here but it's great that you want to come along.'

Tim was glad to get rid of Brad. He always felt more comfortable as a social outrider than as 'one of the boys'. A parting of the ways wrapped up things nicely and left him free to get back to the conference and search out his colleagues. With luck he might prise Erica away from the others.

Outside the restaurant Tim and Brad exchanged contact details with Cal. The three of them shook hands and said their farewells.

'Be careful how you go, then,' warned Tim, 'keep tight hold of your wallets and your trousers.'

There was an odd postscript to the jaunt. As it turned out Brad failed to take Tim's parting advice, at least as far as his wallet was concerned. In circumstances he was strangely reluctant to explain, he 'lost' it along with credit cards and a return ticket to Wash. Later he touched Tim for a bridging loan but adamantly refused to take his advice to report the incident – whatever it was - to the police.

Chapter 19
Ladies Evening

Tim returned to the university via the Strand; celebrated location of several theatres and top hotels, including the Savoy. For Tim this was a familiar stretch of London, although it would never mean as much to him as the streets of Whitetown. As a student the Strand meant no more to him than a crowded walkway between the London School of Economics and King's at one end and the myriad bookshops of Charing Cross Road at the other. Strangely his most personal memory of the Strand was linked to his hometown. He had walked along the famous street with his mother on her only visit to the big city in the mid nineteen nineties. She had behaved like an elderly Alice in Wonderland 'ooing and aaing' at the legendary sights from Nelson's Column down to Waterloo Bridge. He had kept several photographs of her trip, taken at a time when 'family snaps' reflected meaningful selection rather than automated habit. They served to connect the person to the place: 'look, I've been there.' His favourite was of his mother standing proudly at the entrance to King's where, as she frequently told her neighbours, 'our Tim passed his degree.'

She had no wish to venture past the college and into Fleet Street although she was happy enough to return along the Strand, oblivious to the frustration her slow pace caused. Stretching his long arm around her back, Tim steered her close to the walls of the Strand's massive buildings to protect her from being jostled. The walk back prompted her to recall a forgotten link with the Strand, the Irish émigré folk song, *The Mountains of Mourne*. The song featured a policeman, Peter O'Loughlin, who had risen from humble origins to direct the traffic 'at the head of the Strand.' The song tells how despite London's glamour the homesick singer 'might as well be where the mountains of Mourne sweep down to the sea.' She had sung the song to Tim when he was a child and now he sang it for her. She was a flutter of pleasure and embarrassment wondering 'what people might think' as he serenaded her down the mighty thoroughfare. He gently pointed out that they were most unlikely to meet any of these people again. And in any case, it wouldn't matter if they did. Had they been walking down the main street in Whitetown she would have rejected these arguments, but in the Strand she could see Tim's point. Released from her inhibitions she joined in the song's chorus harmonising a still serviceable alto with his bass. The incredulity of others passed them by. As Teresa commented 'the further you are from home, the dafter you're prepared to be.' Tim agreed that in general that had been his experience.

He had little time to savour these memories as he hurried back from his jaunt with Brad and Cal. Well juiced up, his attempt to weave his way between knots of evening pleasure seekers and tourists drew the occasional irritated rebuke. Spraying apologies with boozy abandon he waltzed on. Once back at the university he headed for the leisure and bar area provided for conference delegates. He was feeling edgy now that he was about to commit himself to an evening with his women colleagues. He was still sober enough to appreciate that he would not be at his sparkling best but too drunk to realise that he ought to forget about the whole thing. There was more than one way in which it could go wrong.

The room was large and punctuated by thick support pillars, making it difficult to see where the women were. He scanned it as best he could but failed to spot any of them. He decided to get himself a beer before resuming his search. Easier said than done. The area in front of the bar was crowded. Most people already seemed half canned and were energetically jostling for the bartenders' attention. Whoever coined the stereotype of the politely queue-forming British had clearly not observed them at the trough. He didn't feel like joining in the barging about and had resigned himself to a lengthy wait when he noticed a figure at the front of the queue apparently waving in his direction.

'Tim, Tim... Let me get you a drink. Otherwise you'll be here for ages.'

It was Rachel, in a mood expansive enough to stretch to buying him a drink. He put aside the ungenerous thought that she must be pissed.

'Rachel, yes, it's you,' he observed pointlessly, 'thanks. That would be good. Let me buy. After all I'm the gate-crasher.'

'Forget it, this is my round. Is it just you or are you with someone?'

'Just me Rachel, and it's a pint of whatever bitter they've got on.' He noticed a bartender move in Rachel's direction. 'Hey, don't miss your turn, you can order now.'

Rachel turned quickly and got her order in just as the bartender was about to turn his attention elsewhere.

Revitalised at the thought of a pint, Tim pushed forward and helped Rachel gather up the drinks and several packets of nuts and crisps, dropping a couple of them as he did so.

Rachel quickly picked them up. 'I'll carry these you look like you'll have your work cut out getting over to our table as it is.'

'Bossy bugger,' he thought, feeling his virility had been impugned.

There were four drinks: his pint and three shorts. Two of the shorts were presumably for Rachel and Erica but he was unsure about the third. It would not be for Aisha who as far as he knew didn't drink. Perhaps she had not yet arrived. He guessed it must be for Annette.

He just about kept up with Rachel as she bundled her way towards a far corner of the room. The group had found a niche behind a large pillar that partly shielded them from the surrounding hubbub. Both Aisha and Annette were there as well as Erica. They gave him a friendly welcome, only Annette striking a questionable note suggesting that Rachel's 'pick up' was 'a bit on the youthful side.' Relishing the irony, Rachel riposted that this was 'the best she could do.' Tim decided to let the jibes pass: he was not in the mood for lightly gendered piss taking.

Annette and Aisha were sat a couple of feet apart at a table already heaving with bottles and glasses. Aisha, a beacon of self-possession among the bacchanalia, had placed a large bottle of Buxton mineral water in front of her. It stood out as a statement of sober intent. Erica was sat alone on a faux leather couch. Once they had passed round the drinks and cleared a space on the table for the nibbles, Rachel plumped down next to her. Erica checked out Tim with a quick glance and a half smile. Masking a frisson of insecurity, he responded with what he imagined was a nonchalant wink.

Drawing up a chair he ignored the space between Aisha and Annette and instead squeezed in between Aisha and the sofa. He was within touching distance of Erica. Looking straight at Tim, Rachel stretched her arm round Erica's shoulders. Erica slightly shifted her body, Tim couldn't tell whether in welcome or discomfort at Rachel's possessive gesture.

There was a moment's awkwardness. Sensing Tim's unease Aisha tried to shift away from edgy personal dynamics by starting up a broader conversation.

'Our final session today was on the interplay of domestic and economic relations between the genders. It was interesting. You would have enjoyed it.'

Annette chipped in again, still sounding sardonic. 'Yeah, why don't you join us for the next session Tim? I believe your stream has got stuck in a generational debate with the young ones blaming the older ones for all sorts of things. Doesn't that leave you as piggy in the middle?'

Annette was already needling Tim. It was beginning to get to him, her innuendoes falling like piss disguised as rain. It crossed his mind that even if Henry was a mess of his own making a less spiky character than Annette might have handled him better. But maybe she hadn't always been this way. Probably the difference in their ages had played out badly over time as she wised up to his flaws. Something had soured her. He attempted a low-key response.

'I doubt if I need to change streams to discuss feminism. I'm sure you guys can tell me all I need to know? Anyway, what did you talk about today?'

It was Rachel who answered. 'We were discussing whether heterosexual partnerships break up so often because women no longer see it as their role to look after men while most men still expect them to. I believe you've been married and separated, Tim, what do you think?'

In his semi-addled state Tim had been hoping for a light conversation. This was not it. He was beginning to regret the amount of alcohol he had taken on board. He made a non-committal reply. 'That's probably a fair proposition although it's not particularly original. There are other reasons for the high rate of divorce and partnership break-ups, although I'm not sure I'm in the mood to discuss them now.'

'But don't you think men's dated expectations are part of the explanation?'

Rachel persisted.

'Yeah, it would explain some break-ups.' He decided to throw the question back to Rachel. 'But why do you think so many women have made paid work their priority. I believe about one in five women in this country now opt not to have children?'

Now Aisha intervened. 'It's obvious, really. They want independence. They realise it's not enough to live their lives only through others. They need something for themselves, something for their own fulfilment.'

Annette broke back in. 'Right but is most work *that* fulfilling? Especially the kind of work most women still end up doing? I don't see much chance of self development in cleaning or shop work or even routine white collar work which is still the kind of stuff most women do.'

'Agreed but it's a hell of a lot better than being stuck in the home waiting to service a man,' interjected Rachel. 'Anyway more women are getting decent jobs these days, despite being blocked for promotion at the top end.'

Tim was about to bring Erica into the conversation when he noticed that she appeared preoccupied with her mobile. As his attention was distracted, Annette took up the conversation again. 'The truth is that capitalists don't care about the gender of labour as long as they have a steady supply. My benighted husband is right in that respect. It's a vicious circle in which we're all involved. But Rachel's also right - things are better for women than they used to be. We're on much more even terms with men even if the system itself is unfair.'

Tim was surprised that Annette offered even a grudging compliment to Henry. He was on the point of responding when his mobile sounded the arrival of a text. Apologising for the interruption he was about to ignore the message and switch off when he noticed Erica adopt an oddly contorted posture. She had leaned forwards and slightly sideways, apparently to shield her actions from Rachel. Without turning her head she was slowly and repeatedly shaking her mobile up and down behind her back.

Tim stared in puzzlement. His first guess, feeble, but all he could come up with, was that she wanted to express her irritation at his noisy mobile. He switched it off just as she gave a quick glance in his direction. She raised her eyes in frustration as he did so. He had misread the script.

Realisation dawned. He recalled that a couple of minutes ago Erica had been fiddling with her own mobile. Suppose she had sent him a message that for some reason she wanted to keep from the others? If so it might not be too clever to open it now. There was an obvious alternative.

'Will you guys excuse me for the moment? I need to pop to the loo. Can I get anybody a drink on the way back?'

'It's certainly more sensible to get them on the way back than on the way there,' jibed Annette. Nobody laughed. Sensing she was over-doing the put-downs she attempted a more friendly tone: 'Thanks Tim, we all seem to be ok for now.' The effort proved too much and she added, 'you seem to have timed your round rather well as far as your wallet's concerned.'

Tim got to his feet. He hesitated, searching for a quick retort before heading for the gents. It was an unwise delay. He had begun to feel distinctly queasy. His gallop across central London had churned up several pints of beer, a couple of glasses of wine and a profoundly spicy chicken vindaloo. The effort of coping with the women had further bamboozled him. The gas was massing in his stomach. Control had passed from his brain to his baser self. It was either a belch or a fart. He prayed for the former.

As he battled with nausea he managed a befuddled smile to his colleagues. Bemused they stared blankly back.

There are moments when a belch can speak louder and more meaningfully than words. Tim surrendered to the moment.

Timing is all.

He let rip massively. And then again.

Rachel stared at him as though she had just received definitive proof that he was a moron. Annette's face was a mask of rigidity as she struggled not to react, Erica was laughing albeit with a hint of disapproval and Aisha, her lips parted in a faint smile, stared at him in wondrous disbelief. Surveying the effects of his gaseous interjection Tim decided that it would be a good idea to go missing. As he made his speedy exit he blurted an apology of extravagant insincerity.

No longer merely a convenient alibi, the trip to the loo had become an urgent necessity. *Oh Lord, give us relief!*

Once in a toilet cubicle he was comprehensively sick and soon felt much better for it. Within a few minutes he had recovered sufficiently to check his messages. The top one read: 'See you after twelve tonight. My room. Be there!'

He breathed the sigh of a man for whom affairs, having for some time been adverse, had at last taken a turn for the better. He decided not to return to his colleagues. If he was in for an all-nighter he would need a kip first. He texted Erica, asking her to explain to the others that he was too embarrassed to return. They might just buy that. He tapped out his message and then leant back on the pot, happy with the thought of what lay ahead.

Shortly before mid-night he made his way across the few blocks between his room and Erica's. He felt refreshed after a rest and shower. He stopped to pick up a bottle of champagne from a local pub. Take-away booze of any kind is nearly always more expensive in pubs than elsewhere, except in the bars of posh hotels but he was not about to mess around for the sake of saving a few quid. He was eager to get to Erica. The image of her vibrant body and the depthless blue light of her eyes shimmered in his mind. It wasn't just the sex he was looking forward to. Now that he lived alone he missed the emotional warmth and polymorphous closeness that he once could take for granted. Or so he had assumed. He could almost smell the scent of Erica's lean body. As he quickened his step his cock began to move in synchronicity with the swinging bottle of champagne. His heart beat faster... faster...

Erica welcomed him with a wide grin and the huge hug he had been looking forward to. He tossed the champagne onto a chair and as they hugged again swung her off her feet.

'Put me down macho man, you'll give yourself a hernia

just where you don't want it. That's if you haven't already sprung one through mega-belch strain. That was really pushing the limit.'

'Erica, Petaldust, I haven't come here to discuss my belches.' He returned her gently to the floor. 'But you're right, it would be a pity to put myself out of action.'

'And what action are you referring to?' She teased him.

'Well I assume you haven't invited me here to give me lessons in social etiquette.'

'No, not now perhaps, but I might give you a few tips some other time. You are a bit of an uncut diamond.'

Tim looked slightly taken aback and she added hastily, 'But a diamond nevertheless.'

'I thought you liked a bit of rough.'

'Tim don't be so crass. I'm not referring to your performance in the sack. It's your behaviour in public that lacks, how can I put it? A certain finesse.'

Things were not quite going as Tim had anticipated. He felt a stab of concern. He attempted to get things back on course. 'Let's pop the champagne cork and relax a bit.' He glanced around the sparsely furnished room. 'In the absence of any decent seats, why don't we drink it in bed?'

'Tim you're about as subtle as an air-raid sometimes? Ok, but I'm afraid I don't have any decent glasses. We'll have to drink it from the bottle. And perhaps we can talk for a while before we have sex. Maybe it's the atmosphere of this room or lack of it but I feel a bit disconnected just now.'

Tim's impulse was to respond defensively to Erica's mood. He was about to point out that their late night liaison was her idea when it flashed across his mind to take her remark seriously. He remembered that it was one of Gina's complaints that he rarely listened properly to her.

'Of course we can talk. We probably don't do enough talking anyway. We're both so busy that it's not surprising we get out of touch.'

'Thanks Tim, I just needed to slow you down a little. Sometimes you come at me like an express train. Anyway why don't we get into bed? It's not much fun standing here gaping at each other.'

Shrugging off an impulse to object to Erica's mechanistic imagery of him, Tim tried to stick with a sensitive approach. Perhaps he had misinterpreted her message on his mobile although it had read like a straight 'come on' to him. Maybe his oafish exit had caused her to change her mind. He ought to save such spectaculars for the lads. Or maybe drop them altogether. He did tend to regress under the influence. And he had missed an opportunity to get on more friendly terms with Rachel and Annette – something Erica wanted. Of course he had been provoked - especially by Annette. But the belch was unfortunate. It wouldn't have happened if he hadn't already been more than half pissed. Farting would have been even worse. Yet he had heard that women farted amongst themselves. Maybe farting was a form of same-sex bonding, but for some reason taboo in mixed sex situations. He reflected that natural though it was it was not particularly attractive.

'Tim what are you thinking about?'

'Nothing, Darling. I'm just sorry I seem to have upset you.'

'Well I'm not upset now,' replied Erica, still sounding slightly irritated. 'Let's get undressed.'

Usually they undressed for sex by hurling themselves at each other and tearing off each other's clothes at top speed. The exceptions were when Erica was in one of her more choreographical moods. This time they undressed separately.

Once they were in bed things briefly took a turn for the better. The bed was a single one and quite cold, encouraging a swift warm-up clinch. Tension eased as their bodies closed together. Tim rubbed his chest against Erica's breasts, her nipples stiffening in response. He was quickly erect. He remembered his promise 'to talk first.' His balls danced in protest as he made the effort to do so.

'Erica, what shall we talk about, is there anything you want us to discuss?'

To his chagrin Erica exploded with laughter. He preferred it when people laughed when he intended to be funny. Erica had wanted to talk and he had offered to do so. What could be more reasonable than that?

'Tim this isn't an academic seminar.' She lent back, now relaxed, smiling into his face. 'Maybe this isn't the best time for a heart to heart after all. I'm feeling horny again myself. It'll be fine if you just carry on as usual.'

Released from the coils of virtue, he was about to do just that.

There was a loud staccato knock on the bedroom door.

They gripped each other in alarm.

'Shush,' whispered Erica, 'it's bound to be Rachel.'

'Holy smoke and sunny Jesus! You're kidding.'

'Shush, she'll hear you.'

A second knock rang out.

They remained silent.

At knock number three Erica decided that she had no alternative but to concede she was in the room.

'Rachel, is that you? I was asleep. Listen, I don't feel too well. I need some kip. We can talk in the morning.' As a sweeter she added, 'we can have breakfast together.'

'What a coincidence,' there was irony in Rachel's voice, 'I don't feel well either. I was going to ask you for a couple of stomach settlers.'

'Let me see if I have any.'

After a credible pause she announced, 'Rachel I'm sorry I didn't bring any.'

'I happened to notice you had a packet in your handbag. I'm coming in.'

Her next knock loudly underlined her intention.

Erica was running out of ideas.

Realising that Rachel had no intention of retreating, Tim decided to register a protest.

His inhibitions lowered by his earlier breaching of polite custom, he ripped off a top range fart.

'Erica, there's no need for that,' Rachel remonstrated.

231

'Don't be disgusting, Rachel, it wasn't me.'

There was a moment of silence from outside the door.

'Then who was it? Are you being molested? Open the door or I'll have to call security. For all I know some man could be holding a knife to your throat.'

'Of course I'm not being molested. I would have told you if I was. It's Tim.'

There was a further, longer moment of silence.

'Tim! What a surprise. Is the man completely incontinent? Are there any of his orifices over which he has the slightest control? I'm still coming in.'

'Rachel, he's naked.'

'Tell him to put his trousers on,' shouted Rachel.

Having announced himself, Tim now joined battle.

'I refuse to be ordered to put my trousers on. Enter at your peril.' His resistance had no effect on Rachel but annoyed Erica.

'Tim, this is not funny. Please put your trousers on. I'm going to let Rachel in. We've got to stop this fiasco. Half the block is probably listening in.'

Tim sensed that the balance of power in their tripartite struggle had shifted. He pulled his trousers and shirt on and with a look of determination sat on the only chair in the room. It was to prove a meagre tactic.

Another thunderous knock sounded out.

Erica hastened to open the door. Rachel immediately walked over to the bed and sat on it. Without a struggle Tim had conceded the prime territory.

Once inside and in strategic control, Rachel's tone abruptly changed.

'Look, I'm sorry you guys. I just, I had to come up here. Erica understands. Tim, I apologise, I can't explain to you.'

Disconcerted by Rachel's sudden show of vulnerability, Tim was unsure how to respond. He looked across at Erica for some kind of indication.

Erica was silent for a moment, glancing from one to the other. Finally her gaze settled on Tim.

'Tim, the three of us can't spend the night here. I need to see what's wrong with Rachel.' She hesitated for a moment. 'Would you mind leaving us now and I'll call you early tomorrow morning?'

He looked at the two women and reluctantly decided he had no option but to retreat. There was no way that Rachel was leaving. And he certainly wasn't going to embark on a threesome. Sometimes it just isn't your day. He quickly finished dressing. Whatever was going through Erica's mind, her embrace as he left was full-blooded. But looking into her face for reassurance he saw only the image of his own confusion. *What the fuck is going on?*

Back in his own room he threw off his clothes and stumbled naked into bed. Through half-sleep he watched as Erica and Rachel drifted dancing and shouting, appearing and disappearing... Erica seemed to beckon him on. Stumbling after them, he fell.

Chapter 20
Decisions Have
to be Made

Howard Swankie was feeling faintly apprehensive as he finished off his breakfast of two lightly poached eggs and a single vegetarian sausage, washed down as always with a cup of decaffeinated tea. The Vice-Chancellor, Geoffrey Broome had set up a one-to-one meeting with him without giving any indication of what it was about. Not that he expected Geoffrey to send him an agenda for a short notice, unscheduled meeting but to be left completely in the dark seemed inconsiderate of his senior colleague. Reluctantly he acknowledged to himself that his well-practised persona of calm competence had been ruffled. It was particularly odd that the message had come via the Vice-Chancellor's office rather than through a personal phone-call. He had begun to think of himself as part of Geoffrey's trusted inner-circle yet this almost looked like a deliberate exercise in distance keeping. He couldn't help worrying if he had unwittingly made a mistake of some kind. Mentally ticking through recent events, he came up with nothing. Almost nothing. There was one matter on which he might be vulnerable but was virtually certain that he had safely covered his tracks. More likely the problem was something to do with the Social Science Department, his Achilles heal. The other five departments in the faculty were out-performing on all indices but the social scientists were throwing up one problem after another. He winced as he thought of Henry Jones. If there was one person capable of acting as his nemesis it was that antiquated poltroon!

He reached absently for the teapot to pour himself a second or was it a third cup of tea. His wife Heather saved him the bother. As usual when Howard seemed preoccupied she hovered in discreet attendance.

'Let me pour for you, Darling.'

She glanced at him as she did so, weighing up whether to keep quiet or attempt to reassure him. With years of practice she had become expert in reading her husband's moods but she was uncertain how to respond to the present one. It was inconsiderate of the Vice-Chancellor to leave matters so opaque.

'I'm sure there's no need to worry Howard. Your faculty has just about the best set of metrics in the university. And Geoffrey has said on more than one occasion that he would back you for promotion if you decided to apply to a larger institution. I'm inclined to think it will be good news of some sort. Who knows he may have called you in to tell you that you've been head-hunted.' She smiled, cheered by her own flimsy optimism.

She waited for his reaction. Despite their chequered history as partners, mainly due to Howard's extra-marital affairs, they had learned to work as a team both professionally and socially. As they progressed and prospered together a solid respect and low-key affection had developed between them. She genuinely supported Howard's career ambitions, although she was aware that by doing so she was also helping her own. The pragmatism of their current relationship bore little resemblance to the passion of their early days but she had no desire to revisit the instability of that time. It didn't worry her in the least that she couldn't remember when they last had sex, although she did sometimes wonder how Howard felt about it or rather the lack of it.

Swankie's mood lifted slightly in response to his wife's reassuring tone.

'You may well be right. But I don't like it when things are left vague. It begins to niggle not knowing what's going on.'

'Well you'll know shortly.' She glanced at the kitchen clock. 'It's time you went. Let me help you put on your jacket.'

She took his jacket from the back of an empty chair and opened it out for him to slip his arms into. He shrugged it onto his shoulders and turning round kissed her lightly on the cheek.

'What would I do without you, my love?' he whispered.

By the time Howard Swankie arrived at the university he had just about coaxed himself into a clear, business-like frame of mind. He prided himself that he had developed the confidence and discipline to cope with whatever might arise. In his private fantasies he imagined himself as a kind of academic sharpshooter – unfazed whatever the challenge. Although he preferred to keep it quiet he liked cowboy movies especially those starring Clint Eastwood, whom he considered he resembled in implacable character if not in physical stature. However, he had found it embarrassing to watch Eastwood's movies at the cinema where he might bump into students. DVDs at least allowed him to indulge his taste in private, although he rarely managed to persuade Heather to join him. That was her loss: he was convinced that the great man's acting talents were grossly underrated.

He recalled his favourite Eastwood quote as he nonchalantly triggered his car key instantly snapping the doors shut: *In this life there are those with loaded guns and those who dig.* He, Howard Swankie, was the man with the loaded gun or loaded brain, not to push the parallel too far. Soon, maybe today even, he would deliver justice to Henry Jones. Perhaps that was what the meeting was about.

He strode purposefully into the Vice-Chancellors office complex and knocked firmly on his secretary's office door. She promptly opened it.

'Good morning, Professor Swankie, the Vice-Chancellor is expecting you. He said you should go straight in.'

'Thank you.'

Swankie walked briskly across the room and knocked on his boss's door, more discretely this time. He waited for a few moments. He was unsure whether he had heard an invitation to enter. He did so anyway, not wanting to appear hesitant.

Geoffrey Broome rose from behind his office desk to greet him. A tall imposing man in his late fifties, he wore his chief executive status with self-conscious aplomb. As always when they met, Swankie found his attention drawn to Broome's impressive nose, the size of a Toucan's beak and the colour of beetroot. Swankie reminded himself not to stare at it.

'Howard, I'm glad you could make it at such short notice.' Broome paused for a moment. 'I need to resolve a couple of tricky issues with you concerning members of your staff. Do take a seat.' He gestured towards two expensive looking synthetic-leather armchairs set in an alcove at the far end of the room.

Swankie relaxed slightly. It seemed he was not the subject of Broome's concerns. Broome waited for Swankie to sit down and then, moving past the second chair, remained standing. He gazed ruminatively out of the window, taking his and Swankie's time. Swankie's unease stirred again. Broome was a master at signalling his authority with minor nuances of language and behaviour. Just when it was your turn to say your piece, there he was again reversing back into the limelight. Looking up at his senior colleague he waited for him to break the silence. Lowering his eyes Swankie's attention was caught by a vase of roses on the table between them, the petals compressed together in the style of mass overseas imports. He wondered vaguely if the flowers were artificial. Resisting an impulse to touch them, instead he spread his hands on his thighs, out of the way. In any case it wasn't always possible to tell the difference between cheap real and artificial flowers. Perhaps these were some kind of hybrid variety, half real and half plastic. Despite his nervousness he was pleased with this observation. Yes, he was definitely getting the hang of post-modernism.

He wished Broome would get on with things.

Broome turned round, ponderously dramatic, giving Swankie a smile of empty intimacy of the kind that the status conscious sometimes reserve for their senior acolytes. Usually Swankie found Broome's minor assertions of hierarchical gradation reassuring. They seemed to affirm his-own importance in the scheme of things. Yet on this occasion, uncertain of what might be coming, Broome's peacockery played on his apprehension.

Sitting down Broome started to speak. 'The degree classifications from your faculty were good again this year Howard, although not quite so good as last year. In any case congratulations. I don't doubt that the upward march will be resumed in the near future, preferably next year. I trust you will also manage to increase the number of full-time and full-time equivalent units in your area as indicated in your five year plan.' He gave another dead-eyed smile.

Swankie nodded a firm assent and waited for Broome to continue.

'But that's not what I wanted to talk to you about, at least not now. There are more immediate matters to deal with.' He paused for a second, exhaling audibly. 'I'm aware that the Social Science Department has been virtually reconstituted in the last year or so and on top of that you are coping with that rather eccentric exchange lecturer... What's his name? Burper.'

'Purfect,' Swankie corrected him, quickly suppressing a smile.

'Purfect, of course, an odd name for one to forget. These exchanges don't always work out. Strange types sometimes turn up. In any case he returns to the States quite soon, so any difficulties associated with him will disappear painlessly. There's no such easy solution with the other colleagues I'm concerned about, Henry Jones and Tim Connor. Let's deal with Connor first, as his is the less extreme case I think, though in certain respects more complex.'

Swankie relaxed, now the purpose of the meeting was apparent. It flickered through his mind that he might get more out of the meeting than he had anticipated: not only was Jones's neck on the line but it looked like Connor might be in trouble too. He had not been much impressed with Connor although he felt he still had some leverage over him, especially as he had not yet completed his probationary year. But for the moment his response was noncommittal. 'Yes, both are a challenge in different ways. They require quite some managing. As it happens I think they've struck up something of a friendship.'

'Have they indeed. Is this a case of the old corrupting the young? Jones has been a thorn in our side for the past ten years or so, ever since he succumbed to his drink problem. Hopefully he's the last of a kind, at least in this institution. Our selection processes are more robust these days. And as you know, they have to be. The technical and communication demands of the profession are much greater now than even fifteen or twenty years ago. We can generally filter out types patently unsuitable to the job. Even so, despite our safeguards, I understand from your interim report on him that young Connor might fall into that category.'

'Dr. Connor isn't that young, Vice Chancellor. He's well into his thirties – from memory, probably late thirties.'

'Really. I don't wish to discuss his age, Howard. Doubtless he's old enough to take responsibility for his own actions. In addition to your own not particularly enthusiastic opinion of him, I've received a couple of informal comments about him that suggest he may not be fully up to speed with the norms of professional conduct.'

Swankie was still unsure precisely where Broome's comments were leading. He was unaware of any serious issue in relation to Connor although he now regretted his own role in appointing him. Connor gave the impression of being slightly disorganised and at times adopted a confrontational manner that had not been apparent at interview and which suggested that in the long run he might be as troublesome as Henry Jones. But these matters could not be construed as misconduct and judging from the summary of student evaluations and peer reviews passed on to him, Connor was otherwise doing a reasonable job. Still, if there was a legitimate opportunity to get rid of him, Swankie was prepared to listen.

'Perhaps you could tell me what has been said about him and who said it, Geoffrey.'

Broome gave Swankie a measured look. 'For the moment the possible allegations must definitely remain confidential. It was made by three of his first-year students. It's unusual for such youngsters to seek me out. I presume they were unaware of the complaints procedure and came straight to the top. These days I don't keep an open door to students but if they insist on seeing me I will. That's their right as customers.'

Instinctively Swankie was uneasy at this. Of course students had their rights and much had been done to implement them in recent years, including giving them the opportunity to evaluate teaching staff. But their criticisms were not always well considered or informed. As was sometimes the case with imposed market mechanisms, one group's freedom could be at the expense of others.

'And what was the complaint, Geoffrey?' He leaned forward, intrigued to hear the proposed case against Connor.

'The students accused Connor of racism although I think they used the wrong term. In effect one of his lectures was apparently critical of multiculturalism.' Broome assumed a solemn expression. 'We are a multicultural society, Howard,' he shook his fist firmly, adding portentously, 'we are a multicultural university. There can be no sugges-

240

tion of, well racism is not perhaps the issue,' he struggled to find the right word, ending rather weakly, 'of opposition to, I mean, anti-multiculturalism.'

Swankie waited to hear more, but nothing was immediately forthcoming. On the contrary Broome looked as though he thought little more needed to be said. Swankie found Broome's blustering performance disconcerting. Racism was a tricky issue on which skewer anyone other than the most blatantly bigoted and, whatever his faults, Connor was certainly not that. All that Swankie knew about Connor suggested that he was strongly anti-racist. It was possible that the real problem was in the students' mistaken perceptions, apparently adopted by the Vice-Chancellor. Not for the first time Swankie decided that his role should be in guiding the Vice-Chancellor away from making an embarrassing cock-up.

Geoffrey's strengths lay in running the business and financial side of the university and Swankie had noticed that his grip of social and cultural issues was less secure. Yet perversely it was in these areas that Broome was most outspoken possibly to paper over his limited knowledge or, even worse, unaware of it. His pronouncements tended to be driven by politically correct positions that now shaped the culture of higher education rather than by his own intellectual grasp of matters. Usually his efforts were adequate to meet the expectations of the educational establishment but multiculturalism had become a complex and controversial area. Broome did not seem fully up to speed. It was one thing to support Britain as a multicultural society as both Broome and Connor did, it was quite another to understand the complexities of academic opinion about multicultural theory and policy which, Swankie knew Connor did and Broome apparently didn't. It was not unusual for some academics and policy wonks to oppose certain multicultural policies arguing that they had the opposite effect to what was intended, separating people rather than bringing them together. It was quite fair to criticise multiculturalism in that sense and Swankie guessed that Connor had made some allusion to this approach.

Broome's account was probably unintentionally distorted and inflated. There was little chance of Connor being legitimately disciplined on the grounds outlined. To try to do so might bring adverse publicity to the University and perhaps precipitate a court case that it would probably lose. He needed to persuade the Vice-Chancellor to take a less dramatic view of the complaint against Connor but without appearing to diminish his authority or, God forbid, making him feel foolish. Swankie's own professional ambitions required him to keep Broome onside but preferably not at the expense of implicating himself in a fiasco. He approached the matter cautiously.

'Vice-Chancellor, I believe the students may have misled you although I'm sure not deliberately. I know from my own conversations with Connor and my familiarity with his work that he is fully committed to Britain's multicultural society and he is certainly not racist. As you are aware there is legitimate academic debate about multiculturalism and multicultural policy and I am sure that Connor was merely reflecting this. In that context, he might also have identified his own views.' Swankie paused before making a tactical play, 'I'm sure I can take this matter off your hands and deal with it appropriately myself.'

Broome hesitated. He was half aware that Swankie had provided an opportunity for him to exit gracefully from what he was beginning to see might be an awkward situation. He hovered between relief and resentment. He disliked Swankie assuming the higher intellectual and moral ground at his expense. But he conceded that this area was one in which his colleague had superior expertise and in effect Swankie was advising him not to get entangled in this case. Yet he still felt uneasy about Connor even if he wasn't guilty of racism. He decided to raise a second complaint made by the students albeit in such vague terms that he had initially decided not to mention it to Swankie.

'The three students who complained to me also mentioned another matter about Connor. They suggested that he is inclined to be over friendly with female students. Admittedly they failed to come up with anything substantial but they did refer to an incident in one of his lectures when a student seemed to refer to a close personal relationship with Connor, perhaps an affair.'

'How extraordinary, Vice-Chancellor... Not the alleged relationship, although that is of concern enough, but that it arose as a matter of comment during a lecture. Has the young lady in question made a complaint herself?'

'I understand not and that she insists that she has nothing to complain about.'

'In which case, Geoffrey, we have nothing to complain about either.'

Immediately he regretted indulging in verbal finesse.

Broome looked more flustered than annoyed. His tone was defensively bombastic.

'Of course, I'm not suggesting that we do. I'm not illiberal, you know, Howard. I'm simply making a more general observation that we must appoint people who maintain the ethos of the university, the ethos that we've struggled so hard to create in recent years. We can't have young male members of staff or for that matter staff of any age,' his glance settled briefly on Swankie, 'rampaging around treating the female students as their personal harem.' Concerned that he had over-gendered the point at the expense of males he added 'or female members of staff rampaging either.' Finally in an attempt to cover every angle he concluded 'with either or any sex.' He leant back breathless but confident that he had covered the ground correctly.

Swankie struggled with a powerful urge to laugh, hoping that the silence he managed to maintain would be deemed as respectful. Broome composed himself, still unwilling to leave the subject of Connor. But it was with diminishing conviction that he floated a suggestion he had thought up earlier.

'I was thinking that we should at least require Connor to repeat his probationary year. If there is something in what the students say it will do no harm to serve him a warning. We don't want another Henry Jones on our hands.'

'Geoffrey, I don't think we can take action against Connor on the grounds that he might be a Henry Jones in the making. Hopefully Jones is a once in a lifetime night-mare – if I may use such unprofessional language. No, you can leave Connor to me. I'll talk to him. I could conduct his end of year appraisal. They're due very shortly. There may be grounds for requiring him to repeat his probation-ary year but I don't think we can go beyond that without risking a backlash.'

Struggling to reach a decision, Broome tried to find eye contact with Swankie. He failed to do so. Swankie, his hands together as in prayer, was gazing thoughtfully at his fingertips.

Irritated, Broome decided that he had had enough of this particular problem. 'Alright, Howard, I'll leave it with you but let me know if there is anything we need to be seriously concerned about.' He paused for a moment, taking a look at his watch. 'And now for Henry Jones, a more straight-for-ward case, I think you'll agree.'

'What do you have in mind, Geoffrey? I don't doubt we can soon reach a consensus for action on this one.' Swankie was beginning to enjoy the edge in the conversation he had acquired over his superior. He hoped Broome was impressed rather than annoyed. Egoist though Geoffrey was, he appre-ciated that he relied heavily on his senior colleagues.

Broome felt that he was now on more secure ground. 'I've had your report on him. It's clear that he's not doing the job he's paid to do. He's been in breach of contract for some time. As you know he refuses to submit any medi-cal information on his condition. We should dismiss him. I take it that is also your view?'

'In principle, yes. The only issue to consider is that he will be sixty-five in less than three years and we could require him to leave then as surplus to requirements without risking the kind of fuss that he might try to make now. On the other hand three more years of Jones in his present frame of mind is unthinkable. Of course he's entitled to due procedure but the case for his dismissal is unanswerable.'

'So we're agreed then. I'll set the necessary mechanisms in motion. But do recheck the details of your report.'

The two men relaxed for a moment, satisfied with their efforts. Broome leaned forward, clicking his tongue in apparent annoyance. 'Howard, we've been so preoccupied with these unpleasant matters that I've forgotten even to offer you coffee. Unfortunately I have another appointment shortly but would you like me to have something sent in for you before you leave?'

Swankie took the hint and politely turned down the offer. There was no point in hanging around when Broome had finished with you.

'Thank you, Geoffrey, but no, I have an urgent appointment to keep myself.'

'Well, if you're sure I can't get you something.'

'No, I'm fine thanks, really.'

'I'll say goodbye then and thank you for your helpful input.'

'Not at all, Geoffrey. Goodbye.'

The Vice-Chancellor's secretary had already left her office when Swankie passed speedily through. Broome walked over to the window facing the courtyard in front of the building. He watched his colleague get into his car and then adjust the driving mirror so he could look at himself. Swankie fiddled for a moment with his tie, already quite straight, and smoothed down his hair, in an attempt to cover his balding crown. Next, rather bizarrely Broome felt, Swankie appeared to practise smiling for a few moments.

'*Bloody vain bugger,*' thought Broome, guffawing to himself. As he did so, Swankie suddenly looked straight up at him. Broome swiftly converted his guffaw into a cheery smile. Swankie reddened and attempted to smile back.

Despite the minor embarrassment of his departure, Swankie felt thoroughly pleased with life as he drove out of the university grounds and towards Wash. He was finally getting rid of Jones and without any manoeuvring on his part had found himself in a strong tactical position with Connor. And he could claim to have done so without compromising his principles. Indeed, it was his principles that had carried the day. Admittedly delivering a tutorial on the complexities of multicultural theory to Geoffrey was a bit risky. *Bloody arrogant bugger, Geoffrey.* But overall Swankie felt he had negotiated matters with some panache. He may even have boosted his chances as a possible contender to replace Geoffrey when the latter quit. He stroked his jacket lapel in self-congratulation. What a card he was! What a winner! A good day, indeed!

And it wasn't over yet. The best was still to come. Or he hoped it was. He checked his watch. It was twenty-five to five. He had a few minutes to spare before his five o'clock date. There was just time to detour round Wash Heights before dipping down to his rendezvous on the East side of the city. Once on the Heights he pulled into a lay-by close to a golf course. He took out a bottle of water and a small packet of pills from his briefcase. Removing one of the pills, he bit it in two, swallowing one half with a draught of water. *That should do me despite lack of recent practice. After all I'm barely fifty-three.*

He checked his watch again. It was already ten to five. He hoped he'd timed the Viagra correctly. He was tempted to switch back and cut straight through the city to ensure he was punctual. He didn't want to appear anything less than razor keen. Caution prevailed. There was less chance of being recognised if he went by the less travelled back-road route. He threaded his way impatiently across the upper reaches of the city before turning right into a broad pebble-dash road flanked on both sides by large detached houses. He pulled into a small secluded side-road where he parked his car as inconspicuously as possible. Feeling more excited than for some time he locked his vehicle and walked swiftly towards an imposing Georgian mansion. The wrought iron gate was already open – he imagined in anticipation of his arrival. He went through and walked up the crescent drive.

His knock on the door was answered almost immediately. 'Hello Howard, do come in.'

'Hello Aisha, it's good to see you. You look lovely.' His attempt to kiss her on the lips was swiftly diverted to her cheek where it landed awkwardly. She drew back before he had a chance to plant a second kiss. Howard's optimism dropped a notch.

'You look very nice yourself, Howard,' said Aisha in a matter of fact tone. 'Have you come straight from work?'

'Yes, I've just had a long session with Geoffrey,' he replied, seizing the opportunity to impress.

'Geoffrey?' Aisha queried.

'Yes, Aisha, Geoffrey the Vice Chancellor, you know, the boss.'

'Yes, of course, he doesn't cross my path as often as he does yours. In fact he barely crosses it at all. Did you reach any interesting conclusions or is it all confidential?'

Howard was tempted to play the privileged insider and drop a few hints about his conversation with Broome but quickly decided on discretion. Besides he'd noticed that far from being impressed, Aisha seemed to react against anything implying self-importance.

'Nothing that won't be in the public domain in a day or two.'

'I see,' said Aisha flatly, quickly losing interest.

By now the distance between the scenario Swankie had imagined and what was unfolding was too apparent for him to ignore. It didn't help that his penis was making a determined attempt to break out of his trousers. The Viagra had kicked in a bit earlier than he had anticipated. He had also begun to feel slightly light-headed. He gazed at Aisha through a haze of frustrated longing. He decided to go for broke. *Don't go home with your hard on.*

'Aisha, I want to ask you if we can take our relationship beyond the platonic stage to a new level. We have a lot in common both intellectually and emotionally.' He was aware of how stiff he sounded despite his palpitating emotions. He strained to get across his feelings, to connect. What would Clint do in this situation? He would give it his best shot.

'Aisha, the truth is I've fallen in love with you and I believe you find me not unattractive. We both have dead-in-the-water marriages. Let's sleep together. Let's do it now.'

'Howard, don't be ridiculous. It's not possible. It could wreck both our lives. And I have a child to consider. I like you but that's as far as it can go or as far as I've ever wanted it to go. And you mustn't think that I find you unattractive... But, we can meet and talk as before. There's nothing wrong with that. I have several men friends. But it's not a good idea to meet here again. We are definitely not going to be lovers. Definitely not.' Aisha's expression was even more unambiguous than her words.

Howard was as miffed that his declaration of passion should be seen as 'ridiculous' as he was pole-axed by its flat rejection. There was no doubting Aisha's intent or rather total absence of intent. Looking wistfully at her it dawned on him that he had been playing way out of his league. He had imagined himself in the Premiership when his true form hardly made the Beazer League South. But if you don't try you don't know. He knew now.

Still, there was a cracker of a surprise for someone that night!

Chapter 21
In Some Other Lifetime

It was late one night early in summer term when Tim got a call from Henry. His voice sounded muffled, as though he was talking from some distant place.

'Henry, are you alright?'

'Not really Tim, I've been sacked.'

'I'm sorry, Henry, that's dreadful.' Tim had been expecting the news but still felt for his friend. 'When did it happen?'

'Earlier today. The VC wielded the knife but we know who held his hand.'

'Yeah, I guess so. Henry I'm sorry.' He felt his response was failing to match the seriousness of the news. Not that he underestimated the mess Henry was in. But he was stumped for what to say and even more for what to do. He decided the best he could do for now was to listen. Henry sounded badly shaken: dumped by Annette and now by his employers; a double termination. His battles with his wife and bosses had at least given him a sense of engagement. Now both had called time on him. He wasn't worth the trouble. Tim struggled to find meaningful words of support. 'Henry, you could appeal. Or, like you said, see if the union will take up your case.'

'No. I don't think so. I've had enough of all that. But believe me I'll find some way of getting back at them. They think they've got rid of me but I'll see them fucked.'

Tim's concern was beginning to turn to alarm. Henry was lurching between despair and a wild urge for revenge. A drunken and angry Henry was manageable, in a chaotic sort of way but in this mood he threatened to wreak serious mayhem. Tim decided that they had better meet up soon. He would try to conjure some way of salvaging the apparently unsalvageable.

'Henry we need to get together to see what we can do. Get a good night's sleep if you can and let's meet in the *Mitre* tomorrow. Can you make it by four-thirty? It shouldn't be too crowded at that time. We can have a proper conversation about how you can respond. Don't do anything that might make things worse. Hang on for a while so that we can think things through.'

'Thanks, thanks a lot. But you don't have to do this. I don't want my troubles to land on your back. As far as the hierarchy is concerned you'd be consorting with an undesirable person. They're a vindictive lot if you get on the wrong side of them. I don't want to drag you into the mire.'

'Don't be defeatist Henry, that's not you. Let's meet tomorrow. I don't want to be trite but things always look better after a decent night's sleep.'

'If you say so Tim... Thanks anyway. See you tomorrow, then - four-thirty.'

Tim was tired but he wasn't quite in the mood for bed. A beer might take the edge off his worries about Henry. He had others problems too – his own. And he didn't care to think about those either at the moment. Instead of a beer he settled for something stronger, a glass of calvados from a premium bottle he had brought back from Normandy some years earlier. He sipped slowly, rolling the heavy liquid on his taste buds, its vapour a comforting anaesthetic to his anxieties.

He resisted the temptation of a second glass before turning in. But the elixir had already worked its magic. He slept heavily and if he dreamed at all he remembered nothing.

Next morning at work he continued to mull over Henry's sacking without coming up with any further ideas. Almost on a whim he decided to call Aisha Khan. He doubted if she would be able to offer any suggestions either but she still seemed to like Henry despite his aquatic adventures at her party. She might persuade him from doing something that everyone but Henry would regret.

Tim quickly came to the point.

'Aisha, I have a problem or rather Henry has.'

'Go on.'

'Did you know he's been fired?'

There was a moment of silence.

'Poor Henry,' she said softly. 'No I didn't know, but on reflection I suppose I'm not surprised. I hope it wasn't that incident at my place. Maybe I should have steered the two of them away from each other but I thought it might help that they were talking. I didn't imagine they'd end up in the pool together.'

'No, don't worry it was nothing to do with you. Anyway, I don't think they could sack him for something that happened off campus, providing he wasn't breaking the law. And that fiasco may not have been entirely his fault. Swankie has a subtle way of needling people.'

'What then, is it his alcoholism? Surely he needs help with that, not to be thrown out?'

'No, it wasn't that. I don't think that's a sacking offence in itself. I'm not sure how they put it precisely but he's considered to be not adequately fulfilling the terms of his contract.'

'I see. Is it too late for us to do something to help? Assuming there is something we can do.'

Tim was not about to miss a chance to get Aisha on

board. 'Look, Aisha, I'm going to meet Henry later today, at four-thirty. I hesitate to ask but would you mind coming with me? Or joining us later if you've can't finish work in time? You might be able to influence him more than I can. To be honest I can't see a way out of this for him. I'm not sure there is one. He doesn't seem to have any notion of compromise, it's as though he'd rather fight to the bitter end. It's almost like he's got some sort of death wish.'

'Oh, I'm sure it's not that bad,' said Aisha quickly. But Tim's words had alarmed her. 'Of course I'll come, but I won't be able to make it until just after five. I'll get my friend Caroline to hang on to Ali until I can collect him later.'

'Hey, I'm sorry... I'd forgotten that you have to pick up Ali. I didn't mean to mess up your routine. Don't worry about it. I'll cope with Henry. He and I will come up with something. Bang two wooden heads together and produce a plank.'

Aisha laughed but resisted the offer of an easy escape. 'It's no trouble. Anyway, Ali loves going back with Caroline and Danny. It's a treat for him. No, I'll catch up with you just after five. Make sure you've got in a mineral water and a packet of cashews for me.'

'What terrible vices you have! No problem, see you later. And thanks.'

Tim made sure he got to the *Mitre* a few minutes early. Aisha would not want to be left waiting around on her own. In fact it was Tim who found himself alone, as Henry had not yet made it. He was slightly surprised. The pub was one place Henry usually got to ahead of time. But he was glad of a few minutes to himself. He found a discretely placed table and sat down. Depressingly, he had still not come up with any solution to the mess his friend was in. Henry was his own worst enemy. Deliberately or not the chances were he would torpedo any plan to help him out. Maybe Aisha could think of a 'Henry proof idea': a difficult trick to pull off given that Henry had to be at the centre of any idea she came up with.

Aisha arrived as she had said shortly after five.

'Hi Tim, sorry I couldn't make it earlier.' She looked around. 'Where's Henry?'

'Hi Aisha, it's good to see you. I guess Henry is on his way. I was just about to get you your mineral water and cashews and I may as well get a pint for Henry as well.'

'Thanks, that's kind of you,' she said, sitting down.

Henry had still not arrived by the time Tim delivered the drinks. He was used to Henry's habits but was unhappy at any inconvenience to Aisha.

'I think you said that you have to get back to Waqar and Ali in time for dinner.'

'I'm afraid so. Sometimes we get a cook in but I promised I'd make dinner tonight.' She sighed heavily. 'The joys of being a working mum.'

He looked at her in surprise. She always seemed so organised that he forgot that she must be under as much pressure as him. It was naïve to take her calm demeanour and seemingly effortless concern for others for granted.

'Maybe we should be worrying about ourselves rather than trying to sort out Henry. You'd think he'd at least turn up to cooperate in his own rescue, assuming he can be rescued. Anyway, Aisha, how have things gone for you this last year? It's really flashing by for me.'

'I've enjoyed the work. It's what I want to do. I couldn't believe it when I got the job. It's stretched me in other areas though. I don't see as much of either Waqar or Ali as when I was studying or doing only part-time work. I knew there would be adjustments but it's the effect on other people that's difficult to deal with, it's how they react.'

Tim sensed that Aisha was half-inclined to say more. He held back for a few seconds but she remained silent. He continued to make the running with the conversation. Scarcely aware that it was happening, Aisha's receptive presence was breaking down his usual reticence. He began to open up to her. 'I agree with you about how these big career decisions affect others. Coming here has really turned my life upside down. As you know I was already separated from my wife Gina, you met her at your party.'

'Yes, I liked her. She's was very friendly and good fun as well.'

'Yes, she is. Anyway I don't think she and I have completely let go of the each other. The way we feel, I mean. I guess that often happens with couples that were very close for a long time. There's still too much emotional baggage around for us to switch quickly into 'just good friends' mode. I thought moving away might help but it's not exactly been a clean break. It couldn't be anyway because of our child, Maria.'

'It must be difficult coping with things from a distance, especially for your relationship with Maria. At least adults understand what's happening, children can become very confused.'

An anxious expression crossed Tim's face. He put his hand to his brow, absently massaging his temples. 'I know. You saw Maria. I don't think she blames me for the break-up: it's more that she feels rejected. She's angry with me for not being around on a day-to-day basis. She feels insecure, doesn't really trust me anymore. I suppose she worries that if I keep coming and going one day I'll disappear altogether. She's not rejected me but I worry that it's going in that direction. It's a defensive thing and I can't blame her really. But it's easier to understand than do something about.'

He paused for a moment, aware that his habit of worrying about other people's feelings, even his daughter's, gave him an escape from confronting his own. He had been talking as if to himself, eyes glazed and opaque, as though trying to work things out. Refocusing he found Aisha looking attentively at him. They held each other's gaze. Simultaneously they smiled, retreating from the intensity of the moment.

'Sorry that was a bit heavy. I've been so busy I seem to have let things build up.'

'Tim, there's no need to apologise for having feelings.

You've been working so hard it's not surprising you're tired. You're in overdrive most of the time. You've done well to keep up with your daughter. And it's not all bad. As you say she doesn't blame you for the break up of your relationship.'

'I wish I could say the same for Gina.'

'She blames you, then?'

'Yes. Well... yes. But it's worse than that. Once she'd decided I'd betrayed her trust she closed down on me. I guess I didn't expect her to be quite so final about it. She was very disillusioned. She found someone else quite quickly after I'd...' He stopped mid-sentence.

Aisha did not push Tim to say exactly what had happened but she sensed that he might want to talk more. 'That must have hurt you.'

'It did but,' Tim went quiet. He seldom admitted to feeling hurt. Why was he doing so now? And why was it 'an admission'? *The trick is not to mind that it hurts.* Not a very clever trick after all: just driving the wound deeper. Either way, he decided it was time to retreat from the subject – the subject having become himself. A therapy session with Aisha was not the purpose of the meeting. His impulse was to turn the conversation around.

'Aisha, here I am baring my soul to you and as usual you're listening rather than talking. Maybe your life is free of serious problems. Or perhaps you cope so well that you don't need to talk about them.'

'Tim, it's you that's the dark horse. My life is normally pretty straightforward and so am I. Anyway I'm glad you've thrown some light on yourself. I was beginning to wonder how much there is behind the cool?'

Aisha was teasing but she had unsettled Tim. He was sticking with the idea that it was Aisha's turn to open up.

'So you have a life free of problems then, or perhaps you *really* don't need to talk about them.'

'Of course I need to talk about them, sometimes.'

'I suppose that's where your partner comes in.'

'Not necessarily.'

'Not necessarily?'

'No, as you know, partners can sometimes be the problem.'

Tim had managed to shift the conversation away from himself.

'So who listens to you when you need to talk?'

'Friends, mainly other women. I went to a counsellor for a few months once.'

Tim hesitated. Was he being helpful or just plain nosey? He trusted to his intuition that Aisha might want to talk.

'What kind of counsellor?'

Now Aisha hesitated.

'A marriage counsellor.'

'I thought...'

'You probably thought, like everybody else that I have an ideal life. Well it is pretty good in most ways, the obvious ways but...'

Tim waited, he was not going to push Aisha into giving confidences she was uncomfortable with.

'Tim, my husband is a great provider, a great protector and most of the time a good father. He's also, as you saw, in some ways quite modern and forward looking in his outlook,' she hesitated again, 'but he's quite traditional in his attitude towards women. It's something we've had to work on a lot.'

'How do you mean?'

'He believes that they're very different, very other, than men.'

'He could be right,' Tim grinned at his modest witticism. For once Aisha looked annoyed.

Tim back peddled. 'I only mean in certain ways. Difference doesn't mean inequality. I wasn't intending to be flippant.'

'Tim. Let me explain. I don't need a lecture in gender politics. This is an everyday issue for me. It hasn't popped out of a textbook. I can't believe I'm talking to you about it. I suppose it's because you seem to have a bit more 'university of life experience' than most of the men I meet. I hope it all hasn't turned you into a cynic.'

It felt odd to be simultaneously complimented and chastised. Aisha's feelings seemed conflicted. But if she did want to talk he would listen. He'd try to show some sensitivity. 'Aisha you've listened to me and I trust you. You can trust me, I promise. Maybe we should agree that this conversation is in total confidence?'

'I do agree but you haven't actually said very much in confidence to me yet. You said you were hurt about the break-up of your relationship, but believe it or not that is fairly obvious, especially from the way you were looking at your wife at the party.

'Was it that obvious?'

Tim shifted uncomfortably as the conversation swung back to him. Almost on auto-cue he came up with a diversion.

'Where the hell is Henry? There's a man who really has problems, and they could get worse given his Attila the Hun tendencies.'

'Tim, let's deal with Henry when he arrives. I was just going to say that to me, Gina looked as though she's still very fond of you. And she also seemed quite sad. You said she blames you for your break-up. Maybe she simply knew that emotionally she could not live with you after what had happened, whatever that was exactly; 'more in sorrow than in anger' as they say. That might explain why she found someone else so soon. Anyway, do you blame yourself?'

Tim was caught by the directness of the question. There was nothing for it but to flee into a moral abstraction. 'Blame isn't a very sophisticated concept. We live in an age of moral ambiguity.'

'Tim, that may be true but it doesn't answer the question. I think you're indulging in what the shrinks call 'avoidance.'

'Are you asking if it's my fault?'

'That's not quite the same question but...'

'Yes, I had an affair.'

257

'And obviously she found out.'

'Not exactly; she never had proof and I never really admitted to it.'

'Should you have done?'

'Maybe, probably… Yes.'

'If she knew or believed that you lied, maybe that was more the issue for her than the infidelity.'

'It could be. Anyway, I think it's too late now. As I said, she's found someone else. They're living together in our old place as it happens.' The thought reawoke his sense of loss and regret. He found himself reaching for some sort of self-justification. 'Maybe very occasionally dishonesty is justifiable in a relationship? Men have to deal with contradiction, you know. Most of them really want a decent home life and to be decent themselves but many – probably more than you think also succumb to the temptation of instinctual attraction. The two things don't gel well at all.'

'What makes you think it's so different for women? Most of us have to decide between loyalty and desire at some point in our lives. Anyway, the truth is the only fair basis on which people can decide how to relate to each other. At least you seem to have got some way to telling Gina the truth. Most lies are attempts to deceive others into doing or thinking something that they otherwise wouldn't so that the liar can gain some advantage, usually at the expense of the victim of the lie.'

'That's a very dispassionate and analytical way of looking at it. I'm not sure all lies are so calculated. Aren't they often the bastard child of passion? Anyway I bet you're glad that you have a stable marriage even if it's not perfect.' He was shifting the spotlight again.

'Perfect it isn't.'

'Tim gave Aisha a sharply quizzical glance.'

'It looked pretty good to me.'

'All that glitters… Lots of marriages look good from the outside. And to be honest I have a lot to be thankful for but…'

Tim waited.

'But I believe that I have the same problem with Waqar that your wife had with you.'

'Dishonesty?'

'Yes that, but firstly infidelity.'

'God! I'm surprised. Are you sure? I mean, you'd think he'd realise how lucky he is. I mean...'

'Thanks. That's very kind of you. He does treat me very well as he sees it. But he doesn't appreciate how much I've changed. He doesn't know how to react to it. He's quite a bit older than me and even now he 'daddies' me, treats me as his 'darling princess.' But that doesn't stop him having an affair in London. Two friends have separately warned me about it, so I'm pretty sure it's happening. Maybe he gets his real kicks down there. Sometimes it feels as if I'm just for decoration and status. Like the house, something to show off.'

'How long have you known about it?'

'Several months, almost a year.'

'I see,' Tim was pensive for a moment. 'You must have felt badly let down at times, quite isolated, lonely.'

'Yes,' Aisha looked vulnerable. 'As we're friends and you've told me something about your personal life, maybe I should confide something else to you.'

'Of course you can, if it will help. You can trust me. I swear to secrecy.'

Aisha came straight to the point.

'I have been lonely and as a result I've drifted into a friendship that may be unwise but it's not an affair. And I do mean *not* an affair.'

Tim hid his surprise.

'I've been seeing quite a lot of Howard Swankie.'

He could no longer hide his surprise.

'You cannot be serious.' Tim's effort at empathy was under serious duress.

'What do you mean, I cannot be serious?'

'I mean, Swankie! He's got as much charisma as a half-cooked kipper – and that comparison could make me unpopular with kippers.'

Tim frequently made the mistake of underestimating the attractiveness and sex appeal of other men. Ostrich like, because he couldn't see it, he assumed it wasn't there. But Swankie? Aisha put him right.

'Don't be so sure, Tim. Actually he's quite attractive in a mature, worldly kind of way. And he's intelligent, of course. He knows an awful lot about the education system and I find that quite helpful. Anyway I seem to go for older men: in love and in friendship.'

'That counts me out then, I guess.' The words were out before he could stop himself.

Aisha gave Tim a long look, edged with wistfulness but her response was reluctantly non-negotiable. 'Tim you have enormous charm despite your self-consciously rough ways and I like you very much but I haven't ever counted you in. How could I? The potential for personal and professional chaos if you and I got involved makes it unthinkable. So for me it has been unthinkable. I like and trust you as a friend. I assumed that was the way you thought about me.'

Few phrases are less welcome to the lusty male than '*I like and trust you as a friend*' followed as they usually are by '*but not in a sexual way.*'

Aisha's remarks disturbed more than Tim's macho pride. Semi-reconstructed romantic that he was, he felt a sense of sadness and regret for what would never be. But he knew that Aisha was right, that they had to settle for friendship. Besides, he had begun to believe he was falling in love with Erica. He had told her so even if they had not translated words spoken in passion into their everyday relationship. If that wasn't sufficient complication, his emotions were still raw and unsettled after the break-up of his marriage.

He suddenly realised that this moment might be the closest he and Aisha ever came to each other, as intimate as they would ever be. He wanted them to share and realise it fully. Words would not do it. He reached across the table and gently held her slim vulnerable wrists, kissing her hands with slow intensity. There was no resistance. She leaned forward, brown eyes wide and softly shining. She was so close to him he could see the grain and sheen of her skin and feel her breath on his face.

'I understand. Just one request, then,' he whispered.

'What's that?'

'A kiss.'

'Tim...'

'Please, a forever kiss.'

'Ok, just one kiss.'

'On the lips?'

'One kiss only.'

Finally, after the long kiss goodbye she slipped her wrists from his hands.

'Aisha,' Tim began.

She put a finger to his lips.

'Tim... in some other lifetime. But in this world and for now, I can't.'

Tim leaned back in his chair. He felt slightly dazed, as though lost in some half-remembered dream, engulfed by... As his focus returned he found himself addressing the banal topic of Swankie.

'So... so the Swankie thing then, is it sorted now? It sounds like he misunderstood what it meant to you. As long as you don't...'

Aisha anticipated where Tim was going. 'No, there's no chance of that happening. And there never was. I wasn't even tempted when he was trying to sweep me off my feet by being so helpful and, well... flattering, I suppose. I guess I was naïve about *his* intentions but believe me I never had any intentions myself, beyond benefiting from his supposed professional know-how.'

'Thank God for that, or whoever's up there. Swankie is an oily toe-rag as far as I'm concerned.'

'Tim, where do you get your language from? Stop judging everything on the basis of competitive egos. We can dismiss the Swankie-Connor contest as a non-score draw watched by a crowd of nil! It's not happening.'

Tim laughed, despite being cut down to size. He enjoyed the rare occasions when Aisha's calm broke and she gave vent to her feelings.

'Aisha I'm concerned about you, not him. That's what matters really although I can't deny I'm glad that Swankie has not had his wicked way.'

'Well he hasn't. Period.'

Tim finally levered his ego aside and focused again on Aisha's marital situation.

'That does make it simpler in terms of sorting things out with Waqar. I suppose by now you've begun to talk to him about some of this, including your suspicions of what he's up to.'

Aisha looked flustered and slightly embarrassed.

'No, no, not yet. There's a lot to consider, Ali for instance. And I've just started at Wash. Look Tim absolutely nothing happened with Professor Swankie but Waqar is incredibly possessive.' She looked defensively at Tim. 'I know what you're going to say.'

'Honesty you mean? Practising what you preach?' He smiled sympathetically. 'You make your own judgements, Aisha. If it was such a non-event you might well be right not to mention it. It's a complicated life,' he added, shrugging his shoulders.

He checked his watch. 'I'll tell you something else for free. I don't think we're going to see Henry tonight. I better call him now. He's probably still at home.'

He got Annette on the phone. Apparently Henry was asleep in front of the television and had been for the last couple of hours. Annette concluded the conversation by hinting that Tim might consider letting out a room to Henry in his recently acquired house. Tim opted to treat that suggestion as a joke. But it nagged in his mind. He wouldn't see Henry homeless, but the thought of sharing a house with him was alarming. Why was he always so drawn to irretrievably disastrous characters? Perhaps it was because he was one himself: a confederacy of the damned. He better be careful that he didn't ditch his own life into the pits. One seriously mistaken move and he was right in the middle of it.

At least Henry had not made a wild gut response to his sacking – not yet. Ironically he had cause to be grateful to Henry. His absence at the pub had completely changed the dynamics of the evening, creating a vacuum into which Tim and Aisha had poured their own pent-up emotions. In an hour or so they had slipped from a friendly professional relationship into closer personal intimacy. Admittedly it had to be of the confessional rather than the romantic kind but… Tim blanked out the latter possibility. Not that he was un-attracted to Aisha but the transpontine lunacy of doing anything about it made him feel almost giddy. He wouldn't, of course, not in this lifetime.

Chapter 22
The Grand Tour Begins

Tim welcomed the arrival of Easter as dry earth welcomes rain. Not that Easter offered the prospect of a complete break from work, but a few weeks without teaching flexed up his time. He intended to catch up with family and friends, taking student assignments and the rest of work on his travels. Inconveniently his teaching load had been topped up with two modules in which he was not a specialist and this was an opportunity to get more than one lecture ahead of his students. For a brief period he could do so where and when he wanted. The break changed the time-space equation.

He also hoped to make more progress with his own writing. Fortunately he wrote best late at night or in the early hours of the morning – time stolen from sleep. When things were going well or when he had a publisher's deadline to meet the late nights would close up on the early mornings. He could be half off his head with exhaustion. In his scale of priorities it was worth it. But there was a cost.

As he contemplated his personal life, it seemed under

pressure from all sides. There were moments when he wished he'd carved out a simpler existence but that option was now so far beyond the blue it was not worth thinking about. Far from being in control of his life he often felt he was the object rather than the author of events. Take Naylor for instance, self-confessed arsehole that he was. Buying a place next door to him was sheer bad luck. Why couldn't he have landed next to some kindly old lady eager to mother him: falling over herself to take in his washing and regularly passing home-made puddings over the fence? Instead he'd got Naylor, spoiling for trouble and hurling insults. Still, though he detested Naylor as a manifestation of humanity, a boil on life's backside, he couldn't help admiring a vocabulary richly vulgar enough to challenge his own best efforts. He had to concede that the East End, where Naylor was misconceived produced argot as vividly expressive as the North, serving the same good purpose of rude humour and even ruder insult. Still, he was relieved that for the moment he seemed to have silenced his troublesome neighbour.

And then there was Henry, not so much a disaster waiting to happen as someone stuck on disaster repeat. He feared that, sacked or not, Henry's potential for chaos still had much to offer. It was a dizzying thought that Henry's anarchic behaviour might attain even more vertiginous heights, that new pinnacles might yet be achieved. Even in a profession notorious for eccentrics and assorted escapees from 'the real world' there could be few to compete with Henry. He was a throwback to an earlier age – which one Tim wasn't sure, the early nutcracker time perhaps, or middle madcap-flutter period. Still, his sympathies were squarely with Henry rather than his critics. He felt driven by some perverse aesthetic to side with the stimulating and entertaining, against the dull and punctilious. If there were a battle to be joined over Henry's sacking he was with the old man. That, he realised, would not gain him any career brownie points. It wasn't even a question of principle over self-interest. He just didn't want to see Henry blown away by the system and the farts that fuelled it. Even so he had no desire to join his friend in some grand but futile gesture. He was in no mood to put his hard-earned job in jeopardy, unless some terrible issue of principle forced him to. He was not looking for a heroic conflict and hoped one wouldn't find him.

Yet, there were times when Tim wondered whether he was becoming as disaster-prone as Henry. There was plenty of scope in his life for further chaos, most of which centred on his relationships with women. After his conversation with Aisha in the pub he realised that far from living a cosseted life, hers was as difficult and troubled as his own. He now fantasised himself as her minder, guided by friendship, not passion. Was he kidding himself? Probably. But friendship with her was all he could or should permit himself or – and this was the protective bit, offer her. He had enough on his hands with his existing romantic relationships: Gina, now past (probably) and, Erica, still unfolding - hopefully. *Torn between two lovers, acting like a fool.* He corrected himself. He had only one lover, having been red carded by Gina, not to mention his refusal of a further dalliance with Georgie. He wasn't even coping with the one lover he did have. His relationship with Erica seemed marooned in a cul-de-sac of erotica. Nice if you can get it, but limited solace to the bleeding heart. They did connect emotionally from time to time but these moments slipped away even as he tried to hold them. Erica seemed to draw back – towards Rachel he guessed. He was determined that they should talk things through over the Easter break. He would try to persuade her to join him on part of his travels. The most serious issue though did not lie with the gorgeous women. It lay with himself and his child.

His life beyond Wash was as demanding and complicated as his life in Wash. He had to get a grip on things. 'Get a grip': a deceptively simple proposition. The separation from Maria had been tough for both of them. He was still unsure how well he was handling things. Perhaps his struggle to maintain a strong relationship with her was selfish - a failure to accept that he had forfeited his right to belong. He might even be an encumbrance, getting in the way of her adapting to a new life. Her welfare was what mattered. But he couldn't help his own emotions. What would she think of him in ten or twenty years' time? Would she think much about him at all? The best he could do was to keep making the long and sometimes apparently futile trips across the country. If nothing else his efforts would be on the record. After all, had he not tried?

His problems did not stop with Maria. Even with a battery of support, his mother was barely coping in her house. He planned to check out yet more care homes. He owed it to Teresa to get that right.

He decided he would plan most of the break around Maria and his mother. Admittedly the idea of spending an extended chunk of time with his daughter was not entirely his own. It was Gina who had initially suggested that he and Maria went on a holiday together. She pointed out that in over six months Maria had spent only three weekends with him in Wash. She added dryly that on one of these, she herself had brought Maria over and done most of the looking after. Tim had to concede these sparse but telling facts, but insisted that it was always his intention to spend time with Maria over Easter. But he realised that taking off with her for a week or more, as Gina suggested would require much more organising than the two or three days he had envisaged. Gina's comment that some people arrange their whole lives around their children came as a bit of a stunner. *Absolute beginner.*

Gina also weighed in with a suggestion for the Whitetown leg of his trip. At six years of age Maria had still not met Tim's mother. He explained this to himself as a matter of convenience: it was easier to leave Maria with Gina's sister or with friends rather than put her through a tedious five hundred mile round trip. But he began uneasily to wonder whether he was kidding himself, rationalising away an unconscious anxiety that his mother might react in a racist way to her grand-daughter. And was indulging this anxiety also racist? *Let he who is without guilt cast the first stone.* Even well into the twenty first century there was still much low key but deep-rooted, unearthed racial prejudice across the country and the North West was no exception. His mother shared in it. Was he genuinely protecting his daughter from any hint of rejection and seeking to avoid pointless distress to his mother or covertly endorsing prejudice – perhaps even sharing in it?

Gina cut through the double-think and prevarication by pointing out that if Maria never saw her grand-mother she would eventually come to see it as explicable, only in terms of avoidance and rejection, in short, as racism. Given Teresa's parlous state of physical and mental health they should deal with the situation quickly. Gina believed that Teresa would rise to the occasion. There was a promising precedent. Teresa had soon come to terms with Gina's own skin colour by insisting that she 'must be prone to catch the sun.' Bizarre as this mis-observation was it seemed to satisfy Teresa, allowing her to avoid confronting her prejudice whilst accepting Gina. This was not quite a conversion to anti-racism or cultural pluralism, but there the matter rested.

Appreciating that her reshaping of Tim's plans put greater demands on his parenting skills and stamina than he was used to, Gina offered a sweetener. She would link up with them for the Whitetown leg of their 'grand tour' and take Maria back with her after the three of them had visited Teresa. Tim swiftly agreed. He suggested that Gina join them in Moss Vale, a small village between Birmingham and Coventry where he and Gina had often stayed with their friends, Charlie and Rose. He intended to head there once he had picked up Maria in Peyton.

Released for the moment from academic routine, he drove from Wash across country in good spirits. He was looking forward to the next couple of weeks despite the challenges. Skirting London without any problems, in the early summer sunshine even the A13 seemed less dowdy than usual. Peyton itself, a long, lateral straggle on the map, would never prompt the description of attractive let alone picaresque but for him it triggered a satisfying feeling of arrival just by being there.

He parked as usual on the road outside the house even though the drive was empty. He guessed that Rupert had gone out to make it easier for them to load his car for the trip. As he walked towards the house he noticed Maria's face pressed against the front room window. It quickly disappeared as she spotted him. 'Good sign,' he thought, 'it looks like she's up for it.' He knocked out a cheerful rhythm on the door. Maria opened it.

'Hi Dad, we're going on a holiday in the car aren't we? Mummy says I'm to make sure you drive carefully.' Suddenly she looked and sounded bigger, a small child rather than an infant, flourishing newly discovered self-confidence. He even sensed a hint of calculated reserve in the hug she gave him; she was restoring her favours provisional on his good behaviour. Perhaps he was imagining all this, projecting his insecurities onto her innocent actions.

Gina stayed in the background as father and daughter re-engaged. When she did embrace him he thought he felt renewed warmth, probably in appreciation of the effort he was making.

As she stepped away he kept his hands on her waist.

'Do you miss me, then?'

'Be fair, Tim,' she said quietly, glancing at Maria, 'this is not about you and me.'

He lifted his shoulders in reluctant acceptance. Stepping back from Gina, he turned to Maria.

'Come on young lady, it's time to hit the hard nosed high-way.'

'Don't be silly Dad, the high-way hasn't got a nose.'

'True enough. Time to go anyway. I'll take your big bag and you take the little one with your playthings and reading books. Ready, then? Kiss Mummy good- bye.'

Gina waved them off from the roadside.

His drive across country from Wash had taken over three hours and Tim was glad that the journey from Peyton to Moss Vale was barely a couple more. Maria announced that she was 'going to do what mummy said and behave really nicely.' After all, as she pointed out she was 'actually six now.' As good as her word, she was no trouble. In fact for a time her chirpy remarks about the passing countryside and travellers in other vehicles helped his concentration. At one point they had a discussion about whether men or women are the better drivers, concluding that women probably drove more carefully and men more quickly. Showing early feminist potential Maria added that she thought women could drive more quickly if they wanted to, but they were 'too sensible to take silly risks.'

Maria's patter began to slow down and then stopped after about an hour. The sound of gentle and intermittently emphatic snoring confirmed that she had fallen asleep. He had intended to stop at the Watford Gap so that they could have a snack. Deciding against waking her, he pulled into the service station anyway. He stretched himself, drank some bottled water and made a call to Charlie and Rose confirming the approximate time of their arrival.

As he restarted the car Maria awoke.

'Where are we, Dad?'

'We're just leaving The Watford Gap. It's about half-way to where we're going.'

'That's funny.'

'What's funny?'

'Why is it called a gap?'

'There's probably a gap in some hills near here.'

'Near Watford?'

Tim thought for a moment.

'Good question. As it happens we're not that near the town of Watford which is quite close to London.'

'So why is it called Watford?'

Despite having passed through it innumerable times, Tim had suddenly become conscious of his total ignorance of how the Watford Gap, a good fifty miles north of Watford, had got its name. He reached for an escape.

'Maria, angel, we'll look it up on Google later. Maybe there's another Watford.'

'It doesn't matter Daddy,' Maria sounded sleepy again.

Moss Vale lies off the stretch of motorway that joins the M1 to the M6 – about halfway between the two. Fortunately for its inhabitants the village is sufficiently far from the motorway to allow them to ignore it other than in matters of commuting and supply. Once off the motorway, the approach to the village continues from the south-east by narrow roads, some without pavements, and heavily wooded on either side. Coming into a clearing of farmland the motorist dips into a broad, shallow valley where the village suddenly appears. Moss Vale is idyllic in a way that increasingly few English villages still are, lashed as much of the countryside is by concrete.

They had scarcely finished parking when Charlie and Rose were out of the house ready to welcome them. Charlie was a powerful, six-foot, sixteen stone. Next to him Tim looked almost skinny. Rose was about half Charlie's weight and almost a foot smaller. Both of them worked as social workers in Birmingham.

Tim got out of the car to receive his friends' usual warm greetings. Their attention though was focused on Maria who they hadn't seen for over two years. The star of the occasion was still half asleep and not quite up to the fuss. Lifted out of the back of the car by her dad and passed from the arms of Charlie to Rose she came over grumpily shy and reluctant.

'Put me down! Put me down!'

271

'Maria, say please,' Tim intervened.

To his surprise she did. Better still, once back on the ground she went straight over to him, pushing up closely against his leg. He ruffled her dark curls reassuringly. He felt relieved and a touch proud that in the absence of her mother he was her base point. It felt like a minor break-through. During the last year in Wash and even more in Peyton she was inclined to be untrusting or ambivalent. Gina was right that spending an extended period with his daughter might open things up for them. It had begun well enough despite her uncertain mood.

'Maria,' said Rose coaxingly, 'you must be hungry. We've got some lovely food for you and Daddy. Let's go inside now and settle you in.'

She reached out for Maria's hand. Maria declined to budge from her father's side but Rose had caught her interest.

'What kind of food?'

'Just one thing,' broke in Charlie, 'we have a big, friendly dog, Maria. He's called Stanley. He likes children. He's met Daddy already so he can go in before you.'

Stanley, more usually known as Stan, was a huge, black German Shepherd. He briefly bristled and growled at Tim before recognition flashed and he padded up to renew acquaintance. Maria was caught between fascination and awe at Stan, but once she had stroked his glossy back became besotted.

Rose and Charlie put themselves out to make their visitors comfortable and especially to give Maria a good time. They intended to do their bit to smooth the path of father and daughter. The food they provided for dinner was fresh and much of it home-grown or home-made, including the fruit drinks and ice cream that Maria consumed with such gusto that eventually she had to be restrained. The roast chicken that the four of them enjoyed came from a local farm. Faced with the evidence of two tasty helpings Maria agreed that it was better than McNuggets and even better than the long dead Colonel's KFC pieces. After a couple of hours she went contentedly to bed insisting only that she shared a bedroom with Tim and that the bedroom door remained open until he came up. The agreement was honoured but as she was asleep almost as soon as her head hit the pillow, she was unaware of this until the morning.

Charlie and Rose arranged the next four days so seamlessly and unobtrusively that Tim began to develop illusions of effortless competence about his parenting skills. He didn't yet appreciate how much easier and less exhausting it is for three rather than one adult to absorb and channel the energies of a child over an extended period. The four of them spent an afternoon together in a Safari park, and on other occasions rode on a steam train and took a rowing boat out on a local river. For Tim and Maria the area around the house provided as much fun as sorties into more distant countryside. There was virtually no garden at the front of the house, just a concreted yard for parking, but the garden at the back was huge. It was large enough to harbour two trees, an apple and a pear, and a galaxy of flowering shrubs. There was a small pond with goldfish that with the help of a protective-gauze survived the attentions of the local cats. A wrought iron table with matching chairs placed outside the back door gave the option of eating *al fresco*. On a couple of occasions they did so. For Tim it all knitted together as the ideal release from the tensions of the past few months. He even forgot about his writing. For Maria it was the perfect introduction to English arcadia.

Adjacent to the garden was an extensive wheat field. In mid April the crop formed an army of stiff yellowish stalks with green heads, not yet the rippling blond and gold of later months. There was some uncertainty about whether the public had right of way to the path around the field but Charlie and Rose sometimes took Stan for a walk along it. On the few occasions when they coincided with the owner, their over-cheerful greetings elicited a grunt and baleful stare. But it got no worse than that. For their part, they kept Stan on his lead when walking round the field and made sure he never strayed into it from the garden. It was different in the uncultivated land further to the north of the village where Stan roamed almost at will. Maria's friendship with him blossomed and it was a highlight of her stay when, under the eye of one of the adults, she took him out for walks.

Maria responded well to being a child amongst grown-ups, enjoying the extra attention without being too demanding. On the couple of occasions when she became restless, a chat on the phone with her mum was enough to calm her down. Only once did Tim have to spend a few minutes resettling her into bed. Even then the problem was not a major tantrum, but a mild attack of anxiety that didn't seem to have any obvious immediate cause. Tim stayed in the bedroom until finally she was well asleep.

Chapter 23
The Lord and the Lady

The one occasion when Tim took Maria out without the buffer of Rose and Charlie, his Walter Mitty life as a parent received a sharp reality check. Both his hosts were attending an in-service training course in Birmingham that they were unable to get out of. Tim knew Coventry better than Birmingham and decided to spend the day there with Maria. Although Coventry is something of an incoherent patchwork of a city, many aspects of it are individually interesting. It offers much from several periods of history. Its medieval cathedral was bombed to a skeleton by the Luftwaffe but a fine new one was built, not in its place but next to and intertwined with its remains. They stand together as symbols of destruction and renewal. Inside the new Coventry Cathedral, dominating the main altar and view from the central aisle is a portrait of the risen Christ. Its powerful presence symbolises resurrection, although as a work of art the tapestry by Graham Sutherland is controversial. In her own way Maria honed in on the debate.

'Why has he got such a big tummy and no legs?' she whispered.

'That's not just his tummy, it's a robe that covers his legs as well.'

'Is that why his feet are poking out?'

'Yes... Let's go outside now. There's something I want to show you.'

The 'something' was a massive Epstein sculpture of Saint Michael the Archangel standing astride the bound and defeated Satan. It hangs on the East wall close to the cathedral's entrance. Starkly dramatic its impact is immediate enough to impress a child. Maria was impressed and interested.

'What is it about, Daddy?'

Tim hesitated for a moment.

'It's about the victory of the good angels over the bad angels. You could say the triumph of good over evil. Saint Michael was a good angel on the side of God. Satan was a bad angel. He wanted to become more important than God.'

'I'm glad the good angels won. Do the goodies always win?'

'Not always, mostly maybe.'

Maria appeared slightly troubled by this answer. Tim was concerned that he might be introducing her to life's central moral conundrum too early. She was not quite finished.

'But in the end, do the goodies win?'

Tim decided to lighten the mood. He quickly lifted her up and face-to-face spoke in confidential tones.

'Listen. I'm going to take you to see something else that's special but first I think we should go and buy ourselves ice-creams.'

Maria took the bait. Conveniently there was a mobile ice-cream stall outside the cathedral grounds.

Clutching their ice creams they set off to find the statue of Lady Godiva, the naked women on a horse. In its own way the legend of Lady Godiva is another story of the triumph of good over evil or, at least, virtue over selfishness. Godiva, upset by her husband's penal taxation of his serfs, repeatedly pleaded with him to stop exploiting them. Finally, in exasperation he agreed to do so, provided that she rode naked on horseback through the city. Lady Godiva accepted the bargain but insisted that the city folk kept their eyes averted during her ride. According to legend, a character nicknamed 'Peeping Tom' famously failed to restrain him-self.

Telling the story to Maria in front of the six metres high statue of the lady on the horse was an easy pitch. But drawing a clear and simple moral message for her was more difficult than in the case of the Archangels, Michael and Lucifer. Even Godiva's compassion for the poor was demonstrated in an odd way as well as in a fashion that provoked salacious curiosity. Maria was not wholly convinced that she should have agreed to take all her clothes off, observing that 'she could at least have kept her knickers on.' Tim argued the lady's case, pointing out that she had used her long hair to protect her modesty. His own interest inclined more to the motives of her husband who had thought up the bizarre if picaresque performance in the first place. He arrived at the original diagnosis that his lordship was exhibiting 'exhibitionism by proxy,' a notion he did not share with his daughter. Aesthetically, though, it felt more pleasing that the lady, not the lord had ridden naked through the city. Either way it was not a stunt he would fancy pulling off himself.

'Daddy, can I grow my hair long like Lady Godiva?'

'It's already long, Darling.'

'It's only down to my shoulders. I want it down to my waist.'

'I don't think you can grow thick curly hair that far.'

'Yes you can.'

Tim was tempted to pass the buck by suggesting that Maria refer the matter to her mum. But his confidence in his own parental skills was growing. Instead he employed for a second time the technique of introducing an interesting distraction.

'Maria, it's time to buy Charlie and Rose presents. Maybe

we could get a small present for you as well. You deserve one. You've been very good this week. Think about what you'd like while we walk to the shopping mall. And I might get a new shirt or a pair of jeans for myself.'

Maria needed no further encouragement. In the shopping mall, fending off her eagerness to find a toyshop, Tim insisted that they first buy their hosts' presents. 'What shall we get Rose and Charlie?'

'Some flowers like you used to get Mummy.'

'Right. Why don't we get them a plant in a pot? It will last longer than a bunch of flowers and they'll think about us when they look at it.'

'We could get them a strawberry plant. I like strawberries.'

'We could, but they grow their own strawberries. They taste better than bought ones.'

'Why?'

'Because they're fresher, they pick them straight from the garden. We could get them a blueberry plant. They haven't got one of them.'

'Ok. What else shall we get them?'

'A bottle of wine. They sometimes like wine with their dinner.'

'So do you, Daddy.'

'Yes, well this is for them.'

'Ok, then we can get my present.'

By the time they had bought the plant and a bottle of *Chateauneuf du Pape,* Maria's excitement had built up a head of steam. They quickly found a toyshop.

'Have you decided what you want?'

'Yes.'

'What?'

Maria replied carefully, apparently having given the decision much thought.

'A dolly or a football.'

'A dolly or a football?' Tim repeated, struggling to get his head round the proposal.

'Yes,' she confirmed.

'Having got over his initial surprise, he had no doubt which way he wanted the decision to go, but she had to make it.'

'What made you decide on those two?'

I like dollies anyway and mummy says I'm good at football. Sometimes I play football with her. She's always telling me you like football.'

'That's true. My dad, your granddad, was a footballer.'

'I think I'll get a football.'

Tim continued to delay the final decision, pushing her to think it through.

'What about when you get back home? What will you need most, a dolly or a football?'

'I've got lots of dollies.'

'So what do you think?'

They ended up buying a full-size, panelled plastic football.

The next stop was a café. By now Tim was purring along in progressive parent mode. He was in the zone. He effortlessly persuaded Maria away from the rash of junk food outlets in favour of the healthy food café, *Giraffe*. Admittedly Maria still gorged herself on waffles, ice cream and lemonade but Tim was reassured by the quality of the ingredients. After first polishing off a couple of eggs on toast, he had the same himself.

Whether the blossoming success of the outing caused him to relax his parental guard or whether he was simply day-dreaming is unclear, but Tim's next move lacked lateral awareness.

'Maria, Daddy has to go to the toilet. Whatever you do, you mustn't go away from here. I'll only be gone for a couple of minutes. I'm leaving you in charge of the shopping. Make sure you stay in the restaurant. I'll be two minutes.'

He was as good as his word. In fact he was less than two minutes. The crass stupidity, negligence even, of his actions hit him half way through his pee. The job remained undone and so did his flies.

He cannoned back into the restaurant, virtually taking the toilet door with him.

No Maria.

Blood pulsed through his head and chest. A white flash of panic momentarily half-blinded him. He rushed staggering into the mall. *This must not happen. This cannot happen. Saint f...ing Anthony, help me find my...*

The mall rolled and shifted as he veered first in one direction and then the other.

'Has anybody seen a little girl? She's six with...'

He stopped, gripped by a feeling of unreality. People were gaping at him, accelerating as they passed, an older woman looked concerned, hesitating as though she might say something.

He felt a tug on his sleeve.

'Sir.'

He swung round.

'Sir, your daughter is inside the restaurant waiting for you. She wants to know why you're outside?' A young waitress from *Giraffe* was looking at him reprovingly.

Almost collapsing with relief he looked through the restaurant window. Maria was sat at their table, chatting to a second waitress who seemed to be serving her another ice cream.

'Mystical shit!'

'Pardon Sir?'

'Shit!'

'Sir, your flies are undone.'

Wrestling with his zip, Tim hurtled back into *Giraffe*. Lifting his daughter out of her seat he gave her a giant squeeze.

'Where the...Where have you been?'

'I went to the toilet too. You only said not to leave the café.' Maria had the grace to look guilty.

Later that day, as the four of them enjoyed a post dinner kick around in the garden, Tim reflected on a truth that he had never previously quite apprehended – at least not existentially – that it is possible to care more about someone else than about oneself. Even so, he was relieved that from tomorrow it would be Gina that would be doing the caring. Well, most of it. His occasional fantasy that he might manage single parenthood alongside his career had not exactly been extinguished, but it was now and forever deprived of its innocent glow. He was beginning to appreciate something else - it was possible he might not be up to it.

Chapter 24
The Grand Tour Continues

Gina's arrival changed the dynamics of the group. So far they had revolved around Maria. Now they refocused on Gina and Tim. Gina's striking physical appearance and natural extroversion meant that she was often a centre of attention among her friends. Tim used to take pleasure in her popularity whilst feeling relieved that it took the onus of conviviality away from him. His life out of Gina's aura had enabled him to indulge his introspective temperament, yet he was surprised how much he missed his role as her supporting act. Reluctantly he admitted to himself that occasionally he felt something like loneliness, less the pillar of self-sufficiency he sometimes imagined himself.

This was no secret to Charlie and Rose. Despite his recent career boost, Tim seemed unanchored and adrift, still trying to come to terms with his over-stretched life. And they were sceptical about Gina's apparently swift adjustment to a new partner and domestic set-up. They feared this might be a hastily thrown on band-aid over a raw wound. For them Tim and Gina together were more than the sum of their separate selves, but they understood that any reconciliation had to be on their own account. They had not given up hope.

Their feelings were not completely altruistic. The collapse of Tim and Gina's relationship had left a gap in the lives of their friends as well as in their own. For Rose and Charlie, spending time with a lively and likeable couple was more enjoyable than with two separate and wounded individuals. For now they persisted in sending their invitations to visit to Gina and Tim rather than to Gina and Rupert or to Tim and who-ever he might be likely to turn up with. They were unenthused by the thought of welcoming a series of Tim's girlfriends as they had done with good grace throughout most of his twenties. In Rose's rather clinical analysis that would be retrograde: socially awkward and emotionally stressful. In Charlie's more down-to-earth terms they were past that stage and they hoped Tim was too. They were determined to avoid a collective regression triggered by Tim's seeming obsession with finding the perfect partner. He claimed to have done that with Gina. Though they did not yet accept Tim and Gina's separation as a *fait accompli* they knew they could do little about it during the course of a short visit. After some discussion, they decided to create one decent opportunity for the four of them to talk seriously. Circumstances conspired to make this difficult.

Delayed by a breakdown of her train into London, Gina missed her connection from Euston to Coventry. By the time they had picked her up at the station it was late Thursday evening and a heavy conversation was out of the question. She was due to leave for Whitetown with Tim and Maria early Saturday morning. It was not until after a late dinner on Friday, with Maria already in bed, that the discussion took place. Charlie kicked it off obliquely.

'It's great to have you two with us again. We've missed you.'

'It really is,' added Rose.

Gina and Tim exchanged a wary glance.

'It's good to be here. Almost like old times,' Tim ventured.

'I suppose it's difficult for you to get together as a...' Charlie hesitated, already feeling he was in awkward territory, 'I mean the two of you, the three of you...' he came to a halt as his words failed his sentiments.

'We're past the stage where we're constantly bickering. We're generally quite civil to each other these days,' said a tired sounding Gina. 'Occasionally we both spend time together with Maria. She seems to want that, although she gets on quite well with Rupert.'

Rose sensed that Gina was steering away from the discussion she and Charlie were trying to set up. She hesitated, wanting to respect her friend's feelings but unwilling to give up on her agenda. It might be months before the four of them were together again, if at all. Gambling on Gina's habit of giving a straight answer to a straight question, she came to the point. 'Gina, Tim, why did you guys break up? Tell us to mind our own business if you want, but you're our best friends. It all seemed to happen so quickly. We were almost as upset as if we'd broken up ourselves.'

Charlie raised a quizzical eyebrow at Rose's final remark but offered a vaguely sympathetic murmur of support.

To Rose's surprise, it was Tim who responded first.

'It did happen very quickly. She was very angry with me. You're right, it would have been better if we'd given ourselves a few months to work things out. But it all went downhill very quickly when we were both messing around with...'

Gina cut in directing her response to Tim rather than Rose, 'Tim you've avoided the main issue. We had several months when we might have worked things out but you chose to lie to me instead. It was obvious from your emails that you were sleeping with... whatever her name was. You dragged it on and on without being honest with me about what you were doing.'

Tim was torn between wanting to assert some parity of

blame and satisfying Gina's insistence that he acknowledge responsibility for destabilising their relationship. His reply was a confused attempt to do both. 'You know, we both had affairs. Maybe mine did come first but Gina's got more involved. You can see that from what's happened since.'

'This is the first time that you've even got close to admitting that you were unfaithful. It's taken you this long and you're still fudging it,' Gina interrupted. 'By the way, my relationship with Rupert is not an affair.'

Stung, Tim shifted to attack. 'You keep on about my deception but how long had your relationship with Rupert been going on before I got to hear about it? Even if you weren't sleeping with him, as you claim? It looks even more suspicious now than it did then. And what about the ethics of reading my personal emails? Anyway, I still think you could have waited longer before you bailed out. It was the first time we'd had any serious difficulty in over seven years together.'

'So you say, but for all I know you've had other affairs. I can't trust your word now. I did *not* sleep with Rupert until several weeks after I was certain that you were having an affair. And remember you promised me when we decided to live together that you wanted a one-to-one relationship. As for reading your emails, we used to read each other's emails without worrying about it.'

Charlie quickly realised that whatever he and Rose had hoped for from the discussion, this was not it. He wanted to rescue Tim from the trouncing he was getting. He searched for less acrimonious ground. 'Listen, listen, I'm sorry... We didn't mean to start off a blame game. You'll have to resolve the infidelity issue some other time if you really want to look at it that way. It's too big a question to deal with now. But it doesn't have to be a zero sum exercise. I don't think quantifying degrees of guilt will get you very far. You need to look to the future.'

Rose picked up on Charlie's point, feeling bad that she had started things off insensitively. 'I agree. We're not saying that you should ignore your anger and sense of loss. You have to face up to what's happened and work through it. But Charlie's right, you also need to confront what kind of future you want, together or otherwise. Together we hope.'

Rose was uncomfortably aware that she was using the same routine psycho-speak she employed on a daily basis in her work. It seemed inappropriate for friends, even insulting. She attempted more direct and personal language. 'What do you want from each other going ahead? You're here together with us. You're travelling with your child. You're going together to help an old woman that you both care for. These things will not go away.'

Gina had a ready answer. 'I want the same as Tim said he wanted seven years ago, but which he didn't live up to – maybe he never intended to. I want a committed and honest relationship. He needs to decide what he wants not me.'

Tim looked at her in surprise. Was this a first hint of possible reconciliation? He was about to follow it up when she immediately backtracked.

'Besides it's too late for us now. There's another person in all this, Rupert.'

'How do you know you can trust him?' asked Tim flatly, his optimism quashed.

'Maybe I don't. Trust doesn't come so easily now. I'm not as naïve as I used to be. I take my risks more carefully these days.'

Tim listened glumly as Rose and Charlie attempted to resurrect his character in the eyes of his former partner. His friends meant well but their efforts seemed to be leaving him in a worse situation with Gina. It flashed through his mind that if he simply said he was sorry he might regain credibility with her. A clear apology might be the price he had to pay for any chance of reviving his relationship. But he still wasn't sure. He wasn't sure that their break-up was entirely his fault, not entirely. Then there was Erica, he loved Gina but he wanted Erica. Could he have both? Not without becoming a complete liar. He had become distinctly disenchanted with lies. He had learnt the hard way that they do indeed grow to have a life of their own. Most people tell lies, but to live a lie, that would define him as the kind of human being he refused to be.

He would not lie. Instead he prevaricated. 'Gina, you and I need to talk more about all this: just the two of us. I'm confused even if you're not. Rose is right, we have a future of some kind together. It's not as though we have the option of ignoring each other. Maybe we can find an opportunity to talk about ourselves and of course Maria at my mother's?'

'I'm sorry you're confused, Tim. I wonder why that is?' Gina smiled, unhappy at her own sarcasm.

'At least I admit to making mistakes. I can't aspire to your icy perfection.' Tim reverted to combative defence.

They continued to argue for a few more minutes. Almost the opposite of what Rose and Charlie had hoped for was happening. The knots of miscommunication and misunderstanding were tightening instead of loosening. They had re-awakened the gremlins of blame, dishonesty and pain. Reconciliation and healing would have to await another opportunity. Truth waited half forgotten in the wings.

Gina and Tim were about to embark on another circular tour of their problems when Charlie broke in. 'Tim, why don't you come into the kitchen with me and we'll do the washing up? That's what men do these days. It's replaced retiring for brandy and cigars. Although I suppose we could all wind down later with a brandy nightcap?' His humour fell flat but the atmosphere began to ease slightly. They'd all had enough.

Tim was glad to take the exit option. Once in the kitchen, he and Charlie spun out their escape into domesticity, chatting inconsequentially about their mutual interests of football and the problems of the world. Tim, tight and upset after his moral mauling, began to ease up. In the background they could hear the murmur of the women's conversation, now warm and intimate, unexpectedly interspersed with outbursts of laughter. Not for the first time it occurred to him that there was some wisdom in the occasional ritual social separation of the sexes.

Perhaps it was the effect of the brandy nightcaps but both Gina and Tim slept well, albeit separately. No favour was sought nor would it have been given. They faced the new day refreshed. Having done justice to a substantial early breakfast Maria was also bright and ready to go. After a more than usually demonstrative farewell, they headed north, a direction that, as Gina (not a northerner) observed is signposted as 'North,' seemingly however far north one goes.

From Birmingham the road to the north begins to open up, psychologically if not physically. The nominal change is from the M1 to the M6 and the sign-posted towns and cities are still those of middle England, such as Stafford and Stoke, but the names of the conurbations of the North West, Liverpool and Manchester and, on the other side of the Pennines, Sheffield and Leeds, begin increasingly to appear on the road signs. Eventually Whitetown begins to be featured and by then, 'home' for Tim is barely fifty miles away.

On this occasion Tim decided not to take the route of the grey concrete highway. He knew or thought he knew a more scenic journey along the leafy back-roads of Staffordshire. He was right about the scenery. West Staffordshire lacks the impact of the rugged landscapes to the east and north but its hedgerows and flatlands are neatly picturesque. For a couple of hours the three of them chugged along, the two adults enjoying the views and satisfied at avoiding the noisy motorway and Maria snuggled close to her mother finding plenty to comment on in the passing landscape.

It was only when they stopped for a snack in the village of Keele close to the eponymous university that they realised they were scarcely halfway to Whitetown. A call to Teresa, warning her that they would be at least an hour late – in fact, it was likely to be closer to two – elicited an anxious, barely coherent response. In recent years Teresa had begun to worry compulsively when Tim was on the road to visit her, and any disruption to the journey tipped her close to panic. He briefly considered trying to raise her spirits by reminding her that she was about to see her granddaughter for the first time, but dismissed the idea as likely to backfire. These days she found cause for worry in almost anything.

Now tense, Tim pocketed his mobile and turned to Gina.

'We'll have to get onto the motorway. It's much quicker. God knows what state she'll be in if we take another two hours.'

'Where's the nearest access point?'

'There's a service station about a mile from here. From memory it's possible to get onto the motorway from there, although technically it's not allowed.'

'You mean it's illegal?'

'Not exactly, it's just not flagged up as a numbered access point.'

'It's up to you, as long as you know what you're doing. But if we can't get onto the motorway we'll have wasted a few more minutes.'

Taking this as an endorsement Tim headed them off towards the service station. It was the wrong move. Where years ago there had been an open access point, there was now an electronically operated gate. About twenty yards on the other side was what appeared to be a control cabin. Tim shouted to attract the attention of whoever might be inside. There was no response. The gate remained shut. His stress level several notches higher, he turned the car round and headed back towards the scenic route, but with a much-reduced sense of enthusiasm.

'I won't say I told you so,' commented Gina.

'So I hear.'

'Well I did say,' she cut herself short.

Realising she was being unhelpful, on impulse she reached out and began to rub his neck and shoulders. 'Tim, you're absolutely rigid. I'll try to loosen you up.'

He leaned back into the movement of her hands increasing the intensity of her touch. 'That feels good. I'd forgotten you have healing hands.'

'Had you now?'

'No, not really, I just try to forget. It's not easy.'

She tugged his long hair – quite hard. He wondered if this was a rebuke for his original fall from grace or for his inability finally to let go of her. They lapsed into silence. She kept the massage going for several minutes, attentive and comforting enough for him to muse that perhaps, after all, the hair tug was a display of frustrated affection.

Gina's touch had taken the edge off Tim's tension, but he was still feeling troubled. He wished he had been more receptive to her the previous night. How many more opportunities would he get? He knew his mixed messages reflected his emotional confusion. His mood worsened again as they got closer to home, his thoughts shifting to his mother's depressing plight.

Maria had picked up on her parents' frustrations and pitched in for some attention herself. They were barely a few miles north of Keele and not yet even on the motorway when she insisted that she needed a pee. They pulled over at the sight of a glass verge. The outcome was a wind-blown performance of spectacular inelegance. Once on the motorway her urgent requirement was for a cold drink and later another pee. In between she was querulous and bored. Refusing suggestions that she take a nap she demanded instead to be told stories. Her parents were in no mood to do battle with her and resigned themselves to a holding strategy. As it happened by the middle of the second story their daughter was sound asleep.

Tim's ring of the doorbell was answered not by his mother but by an anonymous looking though anxiously friendly man who turned out to be Tony Smith, a social worker and his main recent point of contact.

'Mr Connor can I have a few quick words with you before you greet your mother?'

'Go ahead.' He paused for a moment turning to Gina. 'Gina would you mind waiting with Maria for a minute, it will be better for Teresa if we all go in together.'

As he said this, the thin, strained voice of his mother came from the living room. 'Timothy, is that you? I'm not very well you know. I'm glad you're here.'

Tim changed tack.

'Gina on second thoughts, do you mind going in and taking Maria? Why don't you introduce her to her grandmother? I'm sure you'll handle that better than me.'

'Ok but be as quick as you can,' replied Gina.

Tim turned to Tony Smith, who looked nervy but determined to say his piece. 'I'm afraid your mother's had a bit of a turn. It's the worse she's had so far.'

'For a moment Tim was nonplussed. The phrase 'a bit of a turn' sounded like something that might happen in *Strictly Come Dancing* rather than in his mother's increasingly sedentary life. Smith's next remark clarified matters.

'Yes, quite a bad turn. She fell over in her bedroom and was unable to operate the emergency communication system. It was a couple of hours before we caught up with her – when one of the carers visited. Your mother was quite confused and distressed. Fortunately though, she wasn't physically hurt. We had her checked by her doctor.'

'You're sure there's no physical damage?'

'That's what he said.'

'Did he say anything about her mental state?'

'He said she was disoriented. And as you know in the long term she's got irreversible dementia.'

'I know but I believe its progression can be slowed with activity and stimulation. I intend to help her choose a care home that provides that. I'll try to fix that up during this visit. It's unlikely that we'll be able to move her into a home immediately but we'll do so as soon as possible.'

'I'm sure you've made a wise decision. You just need to be aware that your mother is continuing to resist going into a care home. It's understandable. Even now she still wants her independence. We've done everything we can to enable her to remain at home but she simply can't cope with the adjustments we've tried to introduce for her safety.

She appears unable even to learn how to operate the basic emergency systems of communication that we've put in place. Frankly she's a danger to herself. She could easily fall down stairs or even set the house on fire. As you know she now gets three separate visits from carers every day but they can't provide the continuous level of support and protection she needs.'

'I see. That's bad news, but pretty much in line with what you've been telling me and I've seen myself. As I say, I'll try to move her into a care home as soon as we find a suitable place.'

Tony Smith looked relieved. These sort of conversations sometimes provoked far more difficult and sometimes angry reactions. 'Ok, Mr Connor, I'll call you late tomorrow afternoon to see how things are going. Perhaps by then you'll have managed to look at one or two of the homes we've listed for you.'

'I'll do that.'

'Right, I won't interrupt your family get-together. Perhaps you could say goodbye to Mrs Connor for me.'

'Fine, I will. We'll be in touch tomorrow then.'

'Goodbye then.'

'Goodbye.'

The two men shook hands and Tim saw Tony Smith to the door.

Tim paused for a moment before entering the living room. He wanted to listen in on how the three of them were getting along. It sounded like Gina had handled things well. As he listened, a remark of his mother gave him huge relief.

'Ooh, your daughter has a lovely complexion, Gina, just like yours. Isn't she lucky? Did you go abroad again for your holidays?'

It did not matter to him how his mother had reached an acceptance of his daughter. Whatever had got her there would suffice at this point in her life. If she thought that his daughter and ex-partner's skin was the result of sunshine, in her own idiosyncratic way and in the long march of evolution she wasn't far wrong. He felt an urge to sweep his mother off her feet and give her a quick whirl round the living room: the other kind of turn. He settled for a hug and a kiss.

His spirits lifted, he suggested that they go out for a meal - something Teresa had always loved doing with him and Gina. The four of them drove out for dinner to an up-market country pub. Teresa could barely cope with such an outing but wedged between Tim and Gina she entered the *Phoenix* determined to enjoy herself. For an hour she did just that before falling asleep on the strength of a 'gill of ale' and a fish pie dinner. Tim looked with affection and compassion at her worn and tired but still proud and pugnacious face. Her skin was drawn skull tight around her eyes and forehead, contrasting with the hanging, empty pouch of her neck. But the lines around her mouth belonged to a tough and determined woman. Her chin looked stronger than ever, still assertive through the loosening flesh. Luckily for him she was a fighter. She had often insisted to him that she had 'done her best despite everything.' Now 'her best' was close to being done. He had been on the wrong end of some of her destructive bouts of Catholic guilt but deeper than that was her unwavering parental love; her best was good enough for him. Who knows what his-own efforts might look like in thirty or forty years' time? *Judge not that you may not be judged.*

He reflected that this was probably the last time Teresa would be strong enough for them to go out to dinner together. He glanced across at Maria who had just discovered the delights of sticky toffee pudding, a substantial portion of which was decorating her face. Happy, she smiled back at him. He was glad for Maria that she had met her grandmother, even though for the moment it meant more to him than to her.

Gina had been observing his reflective mood.

'You alright then, Tim?'

'Yeah, thanks Gina, I'm fine.'

It took frequent visits from Tim and several more months of trying before Teresa was successfully settled in a care home. Teresa's first period of residence in a small religiously oriented home called the *Haven of Peace* lasted for just one night. By the next morning Tim received a call informing him that his mother was refusing to remain in the home and, indeed, on the basis of her current behaviour the owners had decided that she and the home was not a good match. Would Mr. Connor please come and pick her up? The owners were so keen to be rid of Teresa that they were prepared to waive the cost of the single night's residence in return for an immediate departure. By the time Tim reached the care home, his mother was sat on a bench in the communal gardens surrounded by her luggage. He didn't bother to talk to the owners or staff either then or later. Some things are best left to rest.

In the next few months Teresa came and went from a second care home before finally ending up in a third. Initially she had settled well in the second home. It helped that the start of her stay there had coincided with one of the trips that Gina had been able to make. She visited Teresa regularly over the period of her visit, trying to settle her into her new surroundings. However, within two days of Gina's departure Teresa had adamantly refused to return to the care home following a visit to her own home. Finally it became clear that the cause of this behaviour was not the quality of the homes, where staff seemed to do their often-limited best, but Teresa's dementia - that was worse than had been realised. A bizarre and inconvenient pattern gradually became apparent. When in a care home Teresa would insist to be returned to her own home, and after a day or two there, would then demand to be taken to a care home, protesting that she couldn't cope in her own home. In a care home she would accuse Tim of 'dumping her' and in her own home of 'leaving her without any help.' It became apparent that she had no memory of this pattern. The horror and helplessness of extreme dementia is not only the loss of memory but the consequent endless, meaningless repetition.

Tim was tangled in a net of filial duty and affection, until at the third time of trying Teresa managed, after a fashion to settle. Her fast progressing enfeeblement and greater firmness on his part finally bought the mad ritual to a close. It helped that the home was within sight of the parish church of Teresa's childhood. For that matter it was the parish church of Tim's childhood too, but it meant something quite different to him. 'Whatever keeps her happy and in one place,' he thought.

As it turned out the visit of Tim, Gina and their daughter to Teresa was the first and only time the four of them were together, a moment created from the fragments for Teresa and Maria. The fact that it happened was a matter of great satisfaction to both Maria's parents, particularly as Teresa and Maria got on well in a tentative, gentle kind of way. Tim stayed on for a couple more days after Gina and Maria left by train for Essex. Teresa did become restless at the prospect of moving from her house, but there was nothing to suggest the scale of the 'musical care homes' performance she was about to embark on.

Driving south after the visit, Tim found himself edging towards a more positive frame of mind than when he had set out. He believed he had taken the right steps for Teresa and that things would become easier for him and her. His relationship with Maria was now more established on a routine, taken-for-granted basis. They had enjoyed some good times together on the trip. He was less sure how things were with Gina, both about his feelings for her, and hers for him. She did not appear to have shifted from the firm stand off position she had adopted since their break up. Eventually you have to take 'no' for an answer, he mused sadly. But did he really know what he wanted? Did he ever? His thoughts drifted to his life in Wash. At Keele he pulled over into the service station and made a call.

'Hi Erica, it's Tim.'

Chapter 25
The Calm: Phoney or Funny?

Once back in Wash, summer term locked onto Tim like the squeeze of an angry bear. Henry's sacking meant that his end of year assessment load had to be picked up by former colleagues. Their protest that most of them were already working over hours soon got lost in the bureaucratic mist. Eventually a response came back that no financial savings from Henry's dismissal would be made until the next financial year, and so a temporary replacement was unaffordable. That was more or less that. The immediate needs of students requiring end-of-year assessments soon took over. The issue steadily lost momentum as despite a lingering sense of injustice the departmental team got on with the job.

Tim kept in touch with Henry as best he could. It was not easy. After his first angry response to his sacking, Henry became increasingly depressed as the finality of it sank in. His first wild threats of revenge gave way to brooding introspection at his apparent impotence and insignificance in the scheme of things. Years of lecturing on work and leisure proved to be no preparation for the reality of his-own workless life. Henry had usually initiated their get-to-gethers, but now Tim could barely persuade him to venture out at all. Claiming a need for advice, Tim used the fact that he was running revision sessions for students on Henry's option module, *The Accidental Anarchist,* as an excuse to contact him on a regular basis. The ruse had some effect. On one occasion Henry came briefly to life, urging Tim to try a class comparing Marxist interpretations of the 2008 financial crash crisis with the quasi-anarchist ideas of some of the students. But his offer to draft a few ideas on the topic never materialised and his moment of enthusiasm flickered out.

Tim went ahead with the suggestion anyway. In the event, the students were roughly divided between those who found the class interestingly current and others who fretted that it was just 'more stuff' to be included in the end of module examination. A couple of students, believing they had detected in Tim a sympathy for the anarchist or 'horizontalist' approach, criticised him for talking about exploitation while doing nothing to change it. He defended himself by arguing that his job was to teach people to think before they acted, something he tried to do himself. In any case he had done his fair share of protesting, adding almost straight-faced that he had taken part in a protest against the three-day working week of the Heath administration even before he had learnt to walk. He concluded by asking the students if they felt strongly enough about anything to protest about it. There was no lack of response ranging from criticism of British foreign policy to complaints about student fees. He was less happy when one student protested that Tim, not Henry was taking the revision sessions. Was Tim sufficiently familiar with Henry's material? The remark drew a scatter of support. Tim was stuck for a response as nearly all Henry's material was in the old man's head, but was saved when others intervened to praise his own efforts. The incident reinforced Tim's belief that Henry had given decent value to the end even if some students thought his own efforts lost-out by comparison. The real loss though was Henry himself, and the Henry that might have been.

Tim was aware that his well-intentioned reports to Henry of news and gossip about work might backfire, frustrating him rather than lifting his spirits. Henry wanted to be there and in the thick of it. He missed the daily buzz and rhythm of campus life: not only the teaching but also the chat and socialising. He didn't much care about some of his ex-colleagues, but he did miss others. But apart from Tim and occasional calls from Aisha he had heard from none of them. Ignored, he was lost in the swirl of his own dark emotions and imaginings: marooned on the small island of self.

Unexpectedly Tim noticed a marked change in Henry's mood about a month into term. They met as usual in the *Mitre*. Henry was first into the pub and when Tim arrived he found as usual a pint already on the table for him.

'Tim, man, how goes it? Sit down, sit down.'

'Thanks Henry, I intend to. Thanks for getting in the drinks. I'm fine and yourself?'

'Good, much better. More like my old self. I've been down so long it was in danger of becoming my new 'up' – to mangle a cliché.'

Tim leant back and gave his friend a sceptical look. Henry's moods could switch like strobe lighting. But any up-tick was welcome.

'That's good news Henry.' Feeling that his words fell short, he grasped Henry's hand and gave it a warm squeeze.

'Ouch, Tim! Thank God you didn't decide to give me a hug!'

'I will if you need one! No, seriously, it's great that you're feeling better. We've all been worried about you.'

It was the wrong thing to say. Nothing got Henry's dander up more than the suggestion that he was the object of general sympathy. Not that he was convinced by Tim's remark.

'Everybody? Don't kid me Tim, not that I've noticed.

Anyway I don't need pity. What were they expecting me to do, top myself? How inconvenient that would be for the hierarchy, what an awkward little scandal. No, I don't think that...'

'Hang on Henry, things are not that bad.' Tim quickly interrupted, keen not to allow the notion of suicide to hang around long enough for Henry to get interested in it. The possibility that Henry might kill himself had occurred to Tim. He had kept a careful eye on him in recent weeks as his moods swung between anger and depression. He hoped that by now Henry had passed the point of maximum danger to himself. He was less sure about how much of a threat he might still be to others. After weeks of trying to cheer him up, Tim now turned his efforts to calming Henry down.

'People care more about you than you think. Some of them might disagree with your views and lifestyle, but that doesn't mean they wish you harm. Even Rachel has asked about you a couple of times. And, I nearly forgot, Brad Purfect suggested that the three of us meet for a drink and a chat at some point.'

'Purfect! God preserve me from that premium gump.'

'Don't worry. If God doesn't, I will. But look Henry, I'm pleased you're feeling better. Seems like you've got your life back. Try and keep steady though. Sort out what you want to do with yourself, now you've got the time.'

'I don't know about getting my life back Tim. I've no intention of going back to my old life. I've got a different life in my sights, and a bloody good one at that.'

Tim was beginning to warm to the idea of Henry's revival, but was still not entirely convinced. He could see no obvious reason for the transformation. 'So what's brought about the change?'

Henry hesitated, his mood shifting from up-beat to cautious.'

'Well, I've decided to do other things, to move on.'

'That's good news. So what are your plans?'

'I'm going to travel.'

Henry's response seemed strangely normal, almost banal.

'Travel, where to?'

'There are lots of places I haven't seen. Maybe Cuba before it gets completely swamped by Western commercialism. Or China.'

Tim began to wonder if Henry was making this up as he went along.

'Are you planning to travel alone or with a friend?'

'I don't mind. I've got a couple of friends that are retired or near retirement. Fred, for instance. He might do a trip or so with me.'

Tim realised that it was perverse to doubt Henry on the grounds that he was at last talking sense. But sense, at least of the common kind, and Henry didn't go together, big ideas and wild emotions did. Henry sounded almost boring. They had once concluded together that boring was the cardinal sin – to be avoided on pain of death. But he had no choice but to go along with the new model Henry, as long as it lasted. At least it promised to be a lot less trouble than the crocked old model, if less interesting. He tried an up-beat response. 'I envy you. You've worked long enough to have built-up a decent pension, you've no kids and, despite all your efforts to the contrary, you're still in one reasonably robust piece. Lucky you.'

'Yep, young man, a second coming.' Henry leaned towards Tim, suddenly conspiratorial, 'you must occasionally join me on my travels. Anyway, I'll keep you posted, I mean bloody 'texted' about where I am.'

'Henry, why wouldn't I know where you are? You're not planning to take up a position with MI5 are you?'

'You never know, Tim. You never know. I could be the next James Bond,'

'Unlikely, Henry.'

'Cocky bugger! Anyway I'll let you know what I'm up to Tim.'

'Yeah, please do that, Henry.'

Tim's effort to go along with Henry's sudden enthusiasm for a planned retirement collapsed into teasing.

'Ok Henry, so now you've seen the light: Henry on the road to Damascus. You're a sudden convert to global travel. The prospect of visiting art galleries and miscellaneous sites of high culture has catapulted you into a mood of seamless optimism about the future.' He gave Henry a wry look. Henry smiled back, his expression blandly cheerful.

'Right Henry, what's different? What's really caused the change of heart?'

'You want to know?'

'Of course.'

'Well, don't laugh. I've been seeing a shrink, a counsellor.'

Tim didn't laugh but it was a struggle. This seemed like even more moonshine.

'I didn't think that was your thing. Never mind. Go on.'

'I'm not going to go into detail, but basically the shrink reckons I've been chasing an illusion.'

'An illusion of what?'

'An illusion of...' Henry hesitated, 'you're going to find this funny.'

'I'm doing my best to take this seriously,' said Tim, finding the conversation increasingly surreal.

Henry continued. 'The shrink thinks I'm suffering from a form of megalomania, that I believe I'm destined to be a hero, to pitch myself against the powers of evil, if necessary to the point of death.'

'Or against the hierarchy, to the point where you or it wins.' Tim suggested.

'Exactly.'

'So have the evil powers won?'

Henry looked annoyed.

Tim realised that he was handling matters ineptly. Henry might or might not be bullshitting, but it was a mistake to risk provoking him. Henry hated losing. The last thing Tim wanted was to re-ignite his fight to the death impulse. He quickly steered the conversation back in a more positive direction.

'Sorry, Henry, that was a stupid question. Tell me more about your sessions with the counsellor if you're happy to? What was it that has helped you into a better frame of mind?'

Surprisingly Henry responded calmly and reflectively. 'Tim, it became obvious that the only form of heroism still available to me is martyrdom. I've failed at everything else. But I've decided to fail at that as well. I don't want to self-destruct. I accept that I can't change the system. I didn't manage to do it in thirty years and now I'm not even part of the fucking thing. If I want to survive I've got to settle down, cultivate my own garden.'

'So that's what you're going to do?'

'Yeah, like any other loser, I guess I'm stuck with whatever's left. I might as well enjoy myself or try to.'

'Now I see where the enthusiasm for travel comes in. It sounded a bit far-fetched when you first mentioned it. It seemed to come out of nowhere.'

'I'll take that as a vote of confidence then.'

Tim was still less than half convinced by Henry's 'shrink' explanation. The disconnection between Henry's high mood and his unexpectedly conventional plans for the future persuaded Tim to remain vigilant. Counselling may have revived Henry's self-confidence and released his energy, but what Tim was witnessing seemed closer to a personality transplant. He was dubious. The whole thing could be an elaborate act or perhaps just a passing high mood. It was in these moods that Henry was most likely to rip into action mode, maximising his vast potential for chaos and disaster.

To keep an eye on Henry, Tim suggested they set up a game of golf some time in the next few days. It would give him an opportunity to get a clearer sense of Henry's state of mind and real intentions. Tim's doubts increased when Henry was unexpectedly off-hand about arranging a date for the game. Almost dismissively he agreed to give Tim a call about it. Nothing quite seemed to fit. Henry was different but perhaps not in the way he was presenting himself. The weekend game of golf never materialised.

After his conversation with Henry, Tim decided to walk to campus where he had some work to finish. Henry's unconvincing *volte-face* had thrown him into a mood of uneasy reflection. The pace and turmoil of the last few months had given him little time to consider how he might begin to shape his late-start career in higher education. He had gleaned few clues from Henry Jones or Howard Swankie in that respect. But role-models aside, it was in his blood to prefer a fighter like Henry to an effete careerist like Howard. He thought he knew from where his preference for the pugilist over the diplomat came: from his father through his mother's memories and stories about him. She had always presented Dominic as independent and assertive, a tough and intelligent working class Scot who could hold his own with the football authorities even in those more paternalistic days. So Tim conceded to himself that there was more than a touch of gut feeling in his support for Henry over Swankie. Still, he had no intention of following in Henry's footsteps any more than Swankie's although perhaps he could learn something from both.

He liked Henry, but only partly admired him. He respected Henry's intellect and ideas, but was unimpressed by his failure to get them into print and, though less so, to practise them. After all, Henry was a desperado. Perhaps his mad desperation came from self-dissatisfaction at his crucial lack of discipline and hard work. Perhaps it was due to frustration. But for all his practical irrelevance Henry had stuck to his beliefs in good times and bad. In the end, under siege he had the courage not to submit, to remain unbroken, bloodied but unbowed. Tim could aspire to those qualities, but had no wish to exercise them in the form of hopeless gestures extending, in Henry's case, over thirty years. It was not so much that Henry was a rebel without a cause as, in terms of making any constructive impact, a rebel without a clue.

But Henry was at least principled. Tim was unsure whether Howard Swankie subscribed to any binding principles, binding, that is, on himself as well as others. Swankie was some kind of pragmatic liberal. He believed in liberal democracy, modernisation and progress, more or less in line with the consensus in most Western nation states, at least amongst the political classes. Whenever Tim had heard them arguing the case, Swankie recoiled at Henry's ideas of extending democracy into everyday institutions. Swankie rarely swore, but made an exception when referring to Henry's 'notions', the phrase 'infantile bull-shit' being one of his choicer descriptions. As far as Tim could see Swankie had no interest in democratising the governance of universities, but operated comfortably within a management structure reformed to mimic closely that of business corporations. Swankie's elitism was well suited to the way the sector had been remoulded. Tim found it difficult to judge how much of an opportunist Swankie might be but if self-advancement was only one game in town, Swankie played it with an eagle's eye. No doubt he also sought to be effective even if within carefully calculated terms. Tim found it impossible to be enthused or inspired by Swankie. Perhaps Max Weber had the 'Swankies' of the world in mind when he spoke of modernity's 'loss of enchantment.' Tim was anything but 'enchanted' by Swankie.

But if he was much closer to Henry on values and ideas, he recognised that Swankie was far more skilful in acquiring and exercising power even, if only within pre-defined rules and objectives. As Tim saw it the price to pay for such 'realism' was high. Once people surrendered to the system, to the machine, it was difficult to see how they could find the resources not to be personally shaped by its instrumental culture. If Swankie was a model practitioner then there had to be something wrong with the model. At the heart of the new model -- its functional principle -- was the competitive market, the fulcrum on which the production of mass higher education would now be forged. The danger was that the pursuit of efficiency through competition plus technology would bleed humanity from the system.

It was a danger and challenge that Tim had decided simultaneously to live with and work against: a small part Swankie, a larger part Jones, and the rest his own alchemy. How the hell to turn the juggernaut around? Tim mused, as he approached the campus. It would be easier to climb the north face of the Eiger with bare hands. That was too bold and heroic an image! Grappling with an octopus gets closer to it.

But the system had been changed and it could be changed again. It had to be re-humanised. Human and qualitative values, not bureaucratic and quantitative ones should drive and control the battery of modern organisation and technology. He had no alternative but to rebel, but he would not indulge in futile self-sacrifice. He would find a way. With a jolt he realised that he might be looking at the project of a lifetime, over-arching his professional and personal life. Of course, he was neither alone nor unique in his thinking. Therein lay hope. Alone he could do little. There were many that felt and thought as he did. That was what made the project possible. He would draw strength from the others, and they from him. *It is the cause, the cause, my soul.*

As he walked up the wide campus driveway he turned his attention to the activity around him. He paused for a few moments to take in the scene.

The campus was resplendent with youth, stretched out with their laptops and mobiles on the grass or under trees in the cool of the shade. Summer term brings a mildly schizoid mood to higher education: the joys of the season jostle with the anxieties of examinations and assessment. The long, warmer days open up the physical world. Students and academics ease up, stop hunching and scurrying against the wet and cold and if they choose, slow down to enjoy nature revitalised. They begin to pay more attention to each other, pausing to chat and pass time together. Suddenly the campuses come to life again with the young and lovely, enjoying and flaunting what only they have and least appreciate. But youthful pleasure has to be matched off against the need to work: to finish essays, projects and dissertations and to revise for exams. Looking about him, Tim observed both work and pleasure going on side by side. Mostly it was impossible to tell which was which. The world of instant communication had collapsed access to work and leisure into the single medium of the Internet.

The scene around Tim was at once similar but different from his own experience as a student twenty years ago. He acknowledged it all with affection but recognised that he was no longer at its innocent heart. Times change and the dream of youth passes. He turned and walked on, wondering what the young people around him would make of their lives. The pattern of his own life was already heavily sketched in, but he sensed the definitive struggles lay ahead. A cool wind ruffled his hair as he squared his shoulders and walked briskly to his office.

Chapter 26
The Great
Disappearing Acts

Following Tim's conversation with Henry there were several days of what turned out to be a phoney calm. He was glad enough of a quieter period allowing him to get on with his work. A few weeks into summer term lectures began to wind down and there was more of the face-to-face individual and small group work that he enjoyed. His teaching was beginning to gain real traction as he got used to his new environment. Joining the lunchtime queue after a session advising a final-year student on his dissertation, he spotted Rachel Steir. She was sat alone on one of a handful of smaller tables tucked inside an alcove half secluded from the general noise and chatter.

Tim was beginning to feel that he had not been fair to Rachel. The personalised politics of the department were so intense that he had been drawn into them with little time for reflection. Even at his interview he had picked up on the fractious relationship between Henry and Rachel. It was fortunate that he had. His ability to exploit the torturous dynamics of the panel revolving around these two had helped him get the job. Quickly realising that Henry and Fred were his natural allies and that Rachel and Erica were apparently hostile, had enabled him to tilt his pitch towards Swankie whom, ironically, as it turned out, he didn't especially like or respect. Rebel he may be, but he did not regret this moment of compromise.

After seeing Rachel in action for a few months, Tim began to appreciate her hard work and commitment to students and younger staff. She was stubborn in pursuit of what she wanted, as he had discovered to his chagrin at the London conference. True, her efforts were selective and coloured by her radical feminist beliefs and tastes. Her blind spot was a failure to realise that in building up a coterie in her own image, she excluded those less like herself. There were many in the latter category and Tim was certainly one of them. The part-time appointments that the department now depended on to save money - or to make efficiency gains as the jargon had it - tended to be either female or gay, or remarkably often, both and the same was true of the students Rachel was closest to. Tim happened to fit neither category. It irked him that Erica had come to Rachel through this questionable filtering process. Even so, he appreciated that senior academics tend to seek and promote people with kindred ideas and ideals to their own. It was a way of developing research capacity and momentum in their area of interest. He hardly expected Rachel to search out academic equivalents of Hemingway or, for that matter, academics like himself. Group identity is demarcated in terms of difference from 'the other' and in this case he was content to be 'the other.' In contrast he found Henry interesting and amusing, an endless source of knowledge and anecdote. But he could see why he and Henry struggled to match Rachel in the increasingly over-determined micro-politics of academia: a pair of mavericks out-manoeuvred by a pragmatic enforcer willing to submit to and master the bureaucratic machine. He could not yet warm to Rachel but he had learnt not underestimate her.

As he put together his health-conscious meal of tuna, mixed salad and blueberry yogurt, he weighed up whether or not to join her. He had begun to seek a thaw in their relations. Virtual non-communication was impractical given how much their lives over-lapped. Apart from work, there was the matter of where each stood in relation to Erica. A sociable gesture on his part might provide a catalyst to better communication. Rachel had not been quite so hostile to him of late and a one to one chat in a safely impersonal public space might move things forward. She had just started her meal, so she could hardly barrel off as soon as he sat down without hitting record heights of rudeness.

In the event Rachel looked startled, but not particularly annoyed when he put down his tray of food on the table's small surface, almost touching hers. She shifted her own tray a couple of inches back. Tim sat down carefully making sure that his knees didn't collide with hers. Instead they thudded into the top of the table, causing her glass of water to spill and a couple of tomatoes to leap from her plate onto her lap. To his surprise she smiled indulgently, more relaxed now that she could enter the conversation with a mild put-down.

'Co-ordination isn't quite your thing, is it, Tim? Do mind where you put your feet I'm wearing a rather flimsy pair of shoes.'

Tim dropped his napkin over the spill of water, swiftly mopping it up. 'Apologies Rachel, I guess I shouldn't have interrupted you.'

'Don't worry I was going to get in touch with you in the next few days anyway.'

'Really?'

'Yes, now that Henry's gone we need to get together and plan for next year. I know he's a friend of yours but he wasn't exactly…'

Rachel's threatened rehearsal of Henry's deficiencies was abruptly interrupted by the sound of her mobile phone, a raucously up-beat rendition of the first few bars of *Walzing*

Matilda. She quickly plucked the phone from her bag excusing herself as she pressed connect. She greeted the caller familiarly but without mentioning a name.

Listening to Rachel's side of the conversation, Tim struggled to make sense of it. From her brief interjections it was clear this was more than just a social call.

'But this has happened before hasn't it?'

Her voice grew more concerned as the call continued.

'Have you had a serious quarrel? I mean worse than usual?'

'I wouldn't worry too much just yet.'

'As it happens I'm with him now. Hang on a second and I'll ask him.'

She put her hand over her mobile.

'Tim, it's Annette. Henry didn't go home last night and he's not turned up this morning. Did he spend the night at your place? Or, have you any idea where he might be? Annette's checked every other possibility.'

Tim dumped a large fork-full of tuna and salad back onto his plate, his alarm laced with frustration that his efforts to help Henry might have been thwarted. His scepticism at Henry's re-branding of himself as an enthusiastic senior citizen gagging to embark on a life of cruises and golf tours seemed about to be vindicated. It sounded like the real Henry had now turned up or, rather, not turned up. Perhaps he should have confronted Henry instead of humouring him. He found himself reacting defensively to Rachel's question.

'Rachel, Henry has never spent the night at my place. Look, I see a fair bit of him but there's no way I can keep tabs on him all the time. No, I don't know where he is.'

'Ok, Tim, obviously nobody's blaming you. But the fact is Henry's missing. It might just be his idea of a joke but he's not even answering his mobile. Mind you, it wouldn't surprise me if he doesn't know how to work it.'

They urgently discussed the situation for a few minutes. Rachel maintained that it was still too early to panic and that Henry would probably 'show up like a bad penny' in the next few hours. Tim suppressed an impulse to tell

Rachel to stop damning Henry with worn clichés and instead suggested that they join together to search for their delinquent colleague. Tim would scour the city in case Henry had met some mishap. Rachel offered to do what she could through calls and texts. They agreed to re-establish contact as necessary.

Tim had little idea of where in Wash Henry might have spent the night. Annette had already checked out the obvious possibilities. Twenty or thirty years ago Henry might have bumped into some friendly soul and ended up with an offer of warmth and shelter and in those days perhaps even more. Given the attrition of age and alcohol that was unlikely now. Deciding that speculation was pointless, Tim headed straight into Wash leaving Rachel to do what she could from campus. He was impressed that she was so willing to involve herself.

He began his search in the *Mitre*. In early afternoon the pub was almost empty. It was soon obvious that Henry was not there. Unusually the bartender had no recollection of having seen him for a couple of days. With diminishing conviction Tim tried several other pubs frequented by Henry. It was the same story: no Henry and no recent sighting of him. Plan A had been to look for him in the pubs, plan B was to look anywhere else. Tim quickly skimmed through the main public squares and a handful of cafes and snack bars. No joy. It was the same outcome as he tried less and less likely places, including even the Cathedral where there was just a chance that Henry might have repaired for a rest.

Tim's concern grew as his search continued fruitless. Images of Henry, bloodied and disoriented, flickered across his mind. He tried to ignore them, struggling to stay focused. Unsure of where to look next, he decided to check out some of the city's more downbeat back streets. Two hours later he had still found nothing and come up with no clues or information. Depressed and weary he returned to the river area, this time to search it.

As he walked along its pathway his eyes scanned the river's opaque waters and the shrubs and overgrown grass of its banks. The river was no more than two or three feet deep, but that was enough for someone to drown in if they were determined and desperate enough to try, or if they fell in helplessly drunk. Hot and sweaty, he gave a cold shudder as he caught sight of what might be a floating body several feet off the riverbank. With the help of a broken off branch he poked the bloated mass first tentatively and then more firmly, lurching forward as he did so. It swirled and collapsed under his efforts, a swollen bundle of discarded clothes. He breathed a sigh of relief. The bundle reformed and ballooned again above the water.

By now he was beginning to run out of ideas and he had heard nothing from Rachel. As his search faltered, suppressed fears resurfaced. Would Henry kill himself? He recalled that Henry had recently remarked that he 'may be going down but as sure as hell he would do so on his own terms.' Was this remark a hint of suicidal intent? Henry was an extreme character for whom suicide might have some logic and even bring a degree of resolution. It was perhaps the one act that might momentarily reconcile the poles of his character, a heroic high in the cause of self-annihilation: a last violent attention-seeking strike against the indifferent other. But this was all a bit melodramatic. The explanation for Henry's absence was probably more prosaic. His disappearance might be a misplaced hoax, or an attempt to provoke sympathy or guilt in Annette. Or, the whole thing might simply be a drunken folly.

Through all this, Tim tried to hold on to the slim hope that Henry's recent positive turn of mood was not a complete fabrication. Perhaps he had really come to terms with his career car-crash and the dereliction of his moribund marriage. It was just plausible that he had disappeared to do what he said he intended: travel, spend more time with his friend Fred and act more or less like other retirees. Not letting people know what he was up to may have been a gesture of indifference. It was plausible but unlikely. The notion of a semi-normalised Henry stretched credulity. Tim was becoming convinced that Henry's up-beat performance at their last meeting was just that – an act, an elaborate subterfuge to hide his intention to top himself.

He continued to search along the river pathway. The sudden erratic swaying of a cluster of heavy river plankton attracted his attention. He looked anxiously towards it. A shoal of fish swam out from under it, surprisingly large, not trout or bream, but a chunky, purplish species that he didn't recognise. Tired and demoralised he watched the fish swim slowly out of sight. With a cold shudder he decided on a temporary halt to the search and return to campus, to take things up again from there. He checked his watch. It was five-thirty. He had still not heard from Rachel. He left the riverside and hurried back towards the car park. As he entered his mobile sounded. The jazzed up version of *We Can Work It Out* told him that the caller was Erica. Without slackening his pace he switched it on. He was assailed by Erica's excited voice.

'Tim, have you heard?'

'Afraid so, Henry's missing you mean. Unless he's turned up since I left campus. That would be seriously good news. I've just spent the last few hours looking for him in the city. Zilch. Rachel's on the case as well.'

'No, yes... Henry is, but so is Howard Swankie.

'So is Howard Swankie what? You mean looking for Henry?'

'No, no, Howard is missing as well.'

Tim slowly came to a halt as he took in the news.

'Hells bells!' This put a wholly different twist on things.

'You don't think they've eloped together do you?' Erica giggled awkwardly, instantly embarrassed at her tacky joke.

Despite his rising alarm, Tim let loose an ironic grunt. 'I'm beginning to think anything is possible, especially where those two are concerned. No, it's far more likely that Henry has duffed up Howard and then made himself scarce.' He paused for a moment. 'Let's hope not, but it could be even worse. Henry seems to be back in his 'when you've got nothing you've got nothing to lose' mood. He could have done something unthinkably crazy.'

'Sorry Tim. You're right. This really isn't funny. It's so odd, though, both of them disappearing at the same time. I really don't think it can be anything too sinister. Probably a weird coincidence.'

'Some coincidence!' Tim interjected.

'Don't worry too much,' she tried to reassure him. 'Anyway the VC has got involved now. As soon as Rachel heard about Howard she got in touch with him. Geoffrey has called a meeting in his office for six thirty. He expects all of us to be there. Apparently he wants to solve the whole thing without calling the police if possible. Can you make the meeting?'

'Of course, I'm heading back to campus now. I was planning to meet up with Rachel.'

'She says go straight to Geoffrey's office. She's there now.'

'Shit, I hope she isn't making things worse for Henry.'

'She isn't. She says she intends to make sure people don't jump to conclusions until we know what's happened.'

'Right. Good on her.'

'Tim, you don't think Henry would do anything really malicious do you?' The seriousness of the situation was finally getting through to Erica.

Tim hesitated. 'I don't know about malicious. Not malicious. Not intentionally. He might do something pretty damn crazy though, particularly when he's blind drunk. We'll have to wait and see. Look, I need to get moving. I'll see you shortly. Oh, and there's one more thing.'

'What's that then?'

'Just the sound of your voice on the phone makes me want to fuck you.'

Tim had always been prone to the occasional *non sequitur*, intruding the pleasure principle when the reality principle should hold sway. This instance was spectacularly ill timed. Yet, such is the way of chance, that his crass remark goaded Erica into a moment of potentially relationship-changing spontaneity, creating a fissure in the defensive wall between them.

'Tim you're about as subtle as a landslide. Lust is not enough. Remember: 'want me a little less and love me a little more.' Think about it. See you soon.'

The connection went dead before Tim could deliver a riposte. It was just as well. The challenge was to reflect, not to be clever. He drove back to campus feeling even more unsettled than when he left. Henry might be in dire need of his full attention, but he couldn't get Erica's parting words out of his head. Did she really want what she said she wanted? Did either of them really know what they wanted? *Feathers in the wind.*

The sound of his mobile interrupted his thoughts, signalling the arrival of a text. He pulled over to the side of the road. The text read as follows:

'HAVE BUGGERED OFF FOR A BRIEF BREAK. WILL CONTACT YOU WITH MORE INFO. SOON. PLEASE TELL ANNETTE I WILL REPAY HER CARD MONEY IN DUE COURSE... DEFINITELY. BEHAVE YOURSELF, YOUNG MAN - HENRY.'

Tim was momentarily nonplussed by the chirpy triteness of Henry's message. It seemed to come from the hand of a man innocent of any great crime and untroubled by anything other than a debt loaded onto his wife's credit card. The debt might be tricky for Henry but was well within the scope of his routine marital warfare. Henry was clearly unaware of the chaos that his absence had generated. But at least he had not topped himself. The absence of any mention of Howard Swankie further eased Tim's worries. Apparently nothing too terrible had happened yet. In the circumstances, the text was manna from heaven. Tim's relief was only slightly marred by the thought of the anxious hours he had just spent in pursuit of Henry. It was still possible that Henry might do something stupid or even that he might be trying to mislead Tim. But on the face of it the situation looked like it might be containable. However he conceded that 'you could never be sure with Henry.'

At this point Tim's judgement might have been undermined by the attrition of an emotional and exhausting day. Back in the car, he had only a couple of minutes to think through his strategy for the emergency meeting. He decided he would wait until then to make public Henry's text, giving him-self some time to work out its implications. The text did not absolutely prove that Henry was innocent of any crime against Howard Swankie but its tone was not that of a guilty man. And the fact that Henry had sent it at all suggested that he had nothing to hide. If Henry did come under suspicion, producing the text at the right moment might tilt things in his favour. His reply to Henry read as follows:

'HENRY, THANK GOD YOU'RE OK. PANIC HERE ABOUT WHERE YOU ARE. EMERGENCY MEETING IN THE VC's OFFICE SHORTLY. SWANKIE MISSING TOO. HOPEFULLY I CAN CLEAR YOUR SITUATION UP. DO SEND MORE DETAILS - TIM.'

Chapter 27
Moment of Truth

As he swung the Volvo into the Vice Chancellor's courtyard he noticed Erica walking away from her Mercedes sports, its sharp, clean lines contrasting with his own battered wreck. He quickly knocked on his windscreen to attract her attention. She turned and gestured to him to join her. He caught up with her as they entered the building. Breaking their 'don't flirt at work' rule he planted a mighty kiss on her lips.

'Not now,' she said, looking pleased.

'Sorry, and apologies for my rude remark on the phone as well. So, any news of Howard?'

'No, not that I'm aware of, I thought you might be more concerned about Henry.'

'I am, but he's...'

By now they had reached a small lecture theatre that was part of the Vice Chancellor's suite of rooms and Tim dropped the conversation. The room was already almost full and there was a buzz of concern mixed with suppressed excitement. They threaded their way towards a couple of empty seats towards the back. As they did so Rachel waved energetically from the other side of the room at Erica. Jammed between Brad Purfect and a tense looking Heather Brakespeare, there was no way she could politely ask Erica to join her. Despite their recent mini-entente she barely acknowledged Tim.

Once seated, Tim looked around the room. All of the department were there and most of the rest of the faculty. Picking out Aisha, he gave her what he hoped was a reassuring look but avoided making eye contact with other colleagues. Most were more or less aware of his friendship with Henry and he wanted to avoid any curiosity. He would wait until he saw what line Geoffrey Broome took and play his own hand accordingly.

Normally punctual the Vice Chancellor was late on this occasion. As the minutes passed, expressions of impatience began to punctuate the low hum of intense conversation. One raised voice questioned whether Henry Jones was 'worth missing dinner for' and another complained that 'as usual' the pressures on those with dependents had been overlooked. It was almost seven when Geoffrey Broome entered the room, closely followed by his deputy James Flowers and Professor Richard Froggart, Head of the Department of Legal Studies. Flowers was an nondescript individual who saw it as his professional duty to support the Vice Chancellor, whatever the circumstances. Earnest and intense, if he wasn't born middle-aged, assisted by premature baldness, he had eagerly embraced that state as early as possible. Froggart was a pinched and precise looking man who appeared to see almost every aspect of life in formal procedural terms. Tim assumed that Froggart was in attendance to provide Broome with legal advice in respect to this complicated one-off situation. Tim settled down to listen to Broome.

From the moment Broome began his address, his anxiety was apparent. After briefly reviewing the situation he began to stress its potential gravity. Reluctantly he was forced to consider the possibility, perhaps the probability, that the two disappearances were connected. To believe they could be entirely coincidental stretched credulity. He then began to pick his words very carefully although their implication was clear. He still maintained the hope there was some benign explanation for what had happened. But he doubted it. What worried him most was that it was entirely out of character for Howard Swankie to go absent without explanation. He knew less about the habits of Henry Jones. What he had established was that the two men had a long history of conflict; on one occasion even involving violence. He would not speculate but the situation did not look good.

He went on to explain that he had called the meeting in the hope that someone amongst the two men's colleagues could throw light on where, separate or together, they might be. He paused for a moment to allow a response. None came. Tim remained silent waiting for him to finish. Despite stating that the welfare of the two men was his absolute priority, Broome stressed several times that it would be better for all concerned, especially the university community and the institution's reputation, if the matter could be solved at this early stage without involving the police. After again getting no response to an appeal for information, he opened the meeting to suggestions and questions.

Tim was quick with his hand up but was passed over in favour of a young man sat close to the front who had been vigorously trying to attract the Vice Chancellor's attention, even before he had concluded his address. In a state of some agitation he made an obvious and urgent point.

'Vice Chancellor, surely the police should have been called by now? It's possible that one or both our colleagues are in some kind of trouble, perhaps in danger.'

Broome looked uncomfortable. He turned towards Richard Froggart. 'Perhaps you could take this one, Richard?'

Froggart looked reluctant but offered a reply. 'It's a question of us doing what we reasonably can to resolve the matter, which may yet have an innocent explanation, before handing it over to the police. That will be the next step if nothing decisive is forthcoming from this meeting. If that is the case then, yes, the matter becomes urgent.'

He leaned towards Broome. 'Vice Chancellor, I think it would be very helpful if we try to establish when Professor Swankie and Jones were last seen, whether separately or together. It would be particularly useful to know if anyone has seen either of them in the last twenty four hours.'

Nodding assent, Broome put the issue to the meeting.

Determined to say his piece this time, Tim got to his feet and moved towards the front of the room.

'Listen, I've received a text from...'

He was interrupted by the thump of footsteps in the corridor leading to the room. The door swung open. In marched Henry and Fred Cohen. Among sounds of relief and astonishment among the gathering were some shouts of support for Henry.

Henry strode towards Broome.

'I believe this meeting concerns me. That's why I'm here, to clear things up.'

Broome was visibly shaken. His imagined scenario did not include Henry's dramatic arrival. There was an expectant hush as people waited on Broome's response. Instead it was James Flowers who spoke.

'Vice Chancellor, I suggest that we carry out a citizen's arrest of Henry Jones. Howard Swankie is still missing and the most likely person responsible for his disappearance is Jones.'

As Broome hesitated, Tim moved up to the front of the room and stood behind Henry and Fred. He intended his presence to act as a deterrent against any attempt to man-handle his friend. But as the two sets of men faced each other he offered some calming words.

'Look, Vice Chancellor, I was just about to say, before Henry and Fred arrived, that I received a text from Henry shortly before the meeting. It was obvious that he had no idea of the panic that has been going on. And if he had kid-napped Professor Swankie, as some seem to think, I doubt if he would be here now. Have a look at the message Henry sent me.' He pulled out his mobile, brought the text up and handed it to Broome.

Broome's expression was grimly sceptical as he read the text. He shook his head, manifestly less convinced than Tim that the text clinched Henry's innocence. Angry at Broome's reaction, Henry moved a couple of steps towards him. But the fleeting prospect of a physical confrontation disappeared as Richard Froggart intervened, his tone emollient and precise.

'Geoffrey, we can't make what James refers to as a citizen's arrest. Only a person actually witnessing a crime is legally entitled to do that. We are not in that situation. In fact if we incorrectly attempted to arrest Jones, we would be technically assaulting him and he could correctly arrest us. A quite ludicrous situation as I'm sure you agree.'

The ripple of laughter that this observation provoked was interrupted by the strident sound of a mobile. It was Heather Brakespeare's. She eagerly grabbed the phone from her handbag. The meeting's attention abruptly turned to her. As she listened to the call she flushed with emotion, seemingly relieved but also embarrassed. Conscious that all eyes were on her, she kept the call brief. She switched off her phone and stood up. As she composed herself it was impossible to tell whether the news was good or bad. After a few moments she broke into a smile.

'I'm delighted and relieved to say that Howard has been found. I mean he wasn't really lost. He was... I'll explain later. He's now back home. I'm sure you'll all understand that I want to join him immediately. Thank you all so much for your concern.' She turned towards Rachel. 'Perhaps you'd be kind enough to come with me Rachel, I don't quite feel up to driving at the moment.'

Her news was greeted with applause and a buzz of pleasure and relief. Most of the gathering spontaneously got to their feet, several surrounding Heather. Rachel, her arm around Heather's shoulders, steered her towards the exit, firmly batting aside efforts to elicit more information about Howard's reappearance. At the front of the room, the two sets of men, the point of their confrontation suddenly resolved, didn't immediately join in the general good feeling. For a moment they stood solid regarding each other awkwardly. The whole affair had taken on a surreal aspect. Suddenly they were eyeballing each other for no good reason other than mutual collective dislike. Just a hint of disappointment hung in the air, a sense that they had been deprived of a set-to, *bellum interruptum*. The thought of an all-round handshake to defuse matters briefly occurred to Tim, but he was unsure of Henry. Instead he reached across and offered his hand to Broome.

'That seems to be it, then, Vice Chancellor. No victims and no villains.'

Still slightly fazed Broome responded on auto, shaking Tim's hand. Tim's firm grip on Broome's slack hand seemed to reawaken the Vice Chancellor to his sense of authority and status. He attempted to regain control of the meeting that was already beginning to break up. The occasion, which he now decided he had managed with characteristic sensitivity and skill, required a conclusion of some import and panache.

'A moment everybody please.' There was a slight dip in the happy hubbub and a trickle of people already leaving turned to listen. 'A moment please,' Broome repeated. 'I'm delighted that our local problems have been resolved. I think our softly, softly approach has been justified.' Henry was not alone in registering a raspberry to this sentiment. Recognising that interest in his comments was fast dwindling, Broome abandoned his attempt at a rhetorical finale. 'I won't delay you any further. I know many of you have pressing commitments. Thank you all for coming.'

At this point Erica and Aisha moved up the room to join Tim, Henry and Fred. Broome perfunctorily acknowledged them without appearing to recognise them. Ignoring Henry and Fred he granted Tim a more engaged and thoughtful look before turning to his senior colleagues. The two groups moved away from each other.

The intensity of the last few hours quickly evaporated. Tim suddenly became aware of his own needs. He was tired and dehydrated. It was time to replace the fluid. 'Right, guys, we're... Henry and myself that is, we're still not sure what all this was about but it feels like it's time to celebrate. You all ok to have a drink or two in *Doctor Syn*? I'll buy the first round.'

In the pub they managed to piece together the story of a strange day. Tim was right in his interpretation of Henry's email. Far from kidnapping and making off with Swankie, and thoroughly fed up with Annette, he had decided to take a break with Fred. He saw this as part of his new assertive and up-beat lifestyle. After spending the night in London the next day, the two of them went to Reading, Fred's home city, to watch the eponymous football team which Fred still supported despite years of frustration when the team played yoyo between the leagues. The arrival of Tim's text put a swift end to that plan. Henry realised he would be chief suspect in the mystery of Swankie's disappearance and he and Fred immediately headed for Wash. Hurtling down the M4 at roughly the speed of light, they were just in time to make their dramatic and decisive entrance.

As they were celebrating, a call to Erica from Rachel added the last piece to the puzzle: the explanation of where Howard had disappeared to. The tale was an unlikely combination of coincidence, ill luck and a moment of dozy abstraction on the part of the main protagonist. Howard Swankie was an enthusiastic member of a local drama society of which he was Chairperson. On this occasion he had gone to the local church hall where the group usually performed, to close it down after it had been used by a visiting drama troupe from Kazakhstan for a rehearsal of *A Day in the Life of Joe Egg*. Expecting the chore to take no more than a few minutes Swankie did not even mention his absence to his wife who in any case had repaired early to bed after a hard day at work.

Having closed the hall he decided to check out some scenery stored in the attic of a small adjacent building too run-down and sub-modern to be used for much else. Entering the attic he put on the light and absent mindedly shifted the attic trapdoor back into place. He had locked himself in. The metal ring handle on the inside of the trapdoor was embedded in rust and resisted all his attempts to prise it loose. It was not until the following evening when the local vicar heard his cries for help that his ordeal ended. Fortunately Swankie was little the worse for his experience although according to Rachel once released he spent a considerable period restoring himself to pristine elegance. In time, Swankie was able to embroider the tale to present himself as something of a cool, unfazed hero, coping seamlessly with the dirty tricks of fate. Few were convinced.

Once they were reassured that Swankie had been safely returned to the mainstream, the group in the pub launched into a long night of conviviality. The mood escalated further when Henry announced that he intended to leave Wash and go to live with Fred in London. He laid great emphasis on the fact that since his divorce Fred's place had a spare bedroom. Apparently he was keen to quash any notion that they had taken a late queer turn. Fred added that everyone would continue to see plenty of Henry and probably also more of himself, offering an open invitation to visit them in London. Tim reciprocated, only making the proviso that he might sometimes have to work while they were enjoying themselves.

The Henry-Howard drama had developed so rapidly over the day that it was not until well into the evening that they began fully to reflect on the bizarrely coincidental nature of events. For both Henry and Howard to go missing simultaneously without explanation and for entirely unconnected reasons was one chance in infinity. Henry's behaviour was understandable because it was more or less in character. In his own words he had simply indulged an impulse 'to bugger off.' Belatedly he decided he ought to tell someone what he was up to, unhelpfully, but again understandably, choosing Tim rather than his wife. Howard's case was quite different. He would never intentionally stay out all night without Heather's knowledge and agreement. He did so, only as a result of a careless mistake. It was not surprising that people connected the two disappearances and speculated against Henry. Attempting to mitigate Howard's foolishness, Aisha recalled that some years previously a famous actor had got similarly stranded after wandering into a theatre 'props' room and falling asleep. By the time he woke up the room was locked and the theatre closed. Coincidence aside, as the evening wore on it was the lighter side of the whole affair that surfaced, not least the bumbling performance of Broome and his acolytes.

If possible, a five-star night got even more galactic when Rachel unexpectedly arrived. Aisha and Erica who were sitting next to each other made room for her and she sat between them. Tim was about to offer to buy her a drink but was beaten to it by the resurgent Henry. Surprisingly Rachel accepted. Even the unlikely things were going right: even the long-time bad things were coming good. It was as though the resolution of the Henry-Howard incident had catalysed a powerful and pervasive restorative energy. As the vibes rippled out they seemed to generate only positive feeling. Tim was caught in the flow. He looked across at the two beautiful women sat either side of Rachel. He thought he caught the shadow of a smile from Aisha – with a tinge of regret he remembered 'in some other lifetime.' As he glanced at Erica she mouthed something to him. He wasn't certain but the words seemed to say: 'Tim, do you love me?' A shiver of excitement passed through him. *Trumpets sound and I hear thunder boom, every time that you walk in the room. You know I do.*

'Tim, you're dreaming. Wake up, and tell that villain Jones to get me some peanuts with my drink.' It was Rachel, secretly piqued at being by-passed as Tim's gaze alternated between Aisha and Erica. Not that, as she reassured herself, he had a pig in a poke's chance of getting anywhere near her.

'No problem Rachel, if anybody has earned a few peanuts, it's you. I'll get them for you myself.'

As he waited for service at the bar, still revelling in the euphoria of Henry's triumph, a single contrary thought crossed his mind. *That's the mad genius sorted, how about sorting yourself out?*

Chapter 28
There's a Price You Pay

After the excitement of the Howard-Henry saga, routine kicked in again. Facing a mountain of scripts to assess, Tim had planned to spend the weekend working in Wash but unexpectedly Gina pressed him to come over to Peyton. She had something important to say and insisted on a face to face. Despite his efforts she refused to explain further, adding a shard of anxiety to his heavy mood. The thing he feared most was any attempt to reduce his access to Maria. He would fight that, although he had no reason to think that Gina intended this. Keen to keep her on side he agreed to ditch his plans and drive across country.

Determined to reach Peyton before Maria had gone to bed, Tim pushed the old Volvo to a decent lick on the M4. His mind wandered to the events of the last few days and he smiled at the thought of Henry's shenanigans. Against all odds, Henry had departed Wash University on an unexpected high. In Henry's own eyes his unscheduled farewell cameo was an unmitigated triumph. The incident had already been given prime place in his grand narrative of Henry versus the plods, a finale in which he had bowed out as the undefeated victor, beaten down again and again but back on his feet to deliver a last round knock-out. This single event enabled him to reshape his life story into an unyielding struggle in which his diamond will at last triumphed. He now added to the tales of his fearless youth and effortless routings of Swankie, the definitive moment when the Vice Chancellor and his acolytes had been rumbled. Finally Henry the rebel had defeated 'them', 'the system', 'it'. He conceded modestly that his victory was only one battle in a never-ending struggle. The war goes on: fight, fight and fight again, above all, never surrender. If you want proof that it's worth it he would say: 'look at me.'

Tim grunted in acknowledgement of Henry, pleased for the old bruiser, appreciative even, but sceptical. Henry was no longer merely a legend until closing time, but his triumph was largely symbolic. True he now had a good story to tell but he had made little impact on 'the real world' as defined by Broome and Swankie. 'The more is the pity,' thought Tim. Henry appealed to Tim's streak of romanticism but to something more substantial as well: his sense of fairness. Instinctively, both of them threw in their lot with the oppressed majority and distrusted the power-seekers. There was nothing precious about this: it was more a gut than a brain thing, despite all their theorising about it. In their 'big ideas' conversations they agreed that the democratic and humanistic post-war consensus established in the West was being slowly eroded by self-seeking elites. What was emerging in its place was a corporate-driven popular culture cloaked in a shallow and deceptive rhetoric of competitive individualism, a parody of true individualism that respects the rights and welfare of others. Increasingly people could see the sick selfishness of it all, but as yet there was no constituency big enough and willing to confront it head-on. Somehow the world had stumbled into a new age of greed, more resembling the spectacular inequalities of feudalism than modern social democracy.

Tim took in a deep breath: he had thirty or so years of his career ahead. There were many ways to fall short of aspiration. He would try to harness values to action more effectively than Henry had managed. Watching and listening to Henry had been a kind of education – in hanging onto ideals but equally in how not to achieve them. It was easy for him to criticise. It was a relief almost that as well as his commitment to 'big ideas' he had more ordinary responsibilities – but demanding enough: a child and an aged mother, as well as his job. On top of all that, a lone campaign to change Western society might be a bit of a stretch! So how many others felt like him?

Realising that he was about to overshoot the turn-off for the M25, he quickly cut short his bout of pondering and shifted sharply across the lanes to make his exit. For a mid-Friday evening the M25 was unusually clear, and he skirted the north of London without any delays, arriving in good time to spend half an hour with Maria before her bed-time. She was now more at ease with his comings and goings. Their grand tour had sealed their re-bonding and she had begun to look forward to his visits and her trips to Wash. Once he had seen her into bed he returned to the living room, uncertain whether Gina wanted to raise her issue immediately or to wait until the morning. She gave him a warmer hug than usual and asked him if he would mind staying on for a few minutes so that they could talk. As he settled into an armchair she called to Rupert, who was in the kitchen asking him to make a pot of tea for the three of them. Tim sensed that this courtesy might be setting the stage for something less pleasant. Already tense, the thought of Rupert joining them ratcheted up his anxiety another notch. Rupert must have been on stand-by because he arrived almost instantly with tea and biscuits. Having poured the tea and offered Tim a biscuit he sat down in an armchair opposite him. Gina had settled herself on a large sofa between them looking self-consciously composed and purposeful. She did not waste time coming to the point.

'Tim I wanted you to be the first to know: Rupert and I are going to get married later this summer. We thought of waiting a little longer but I'm thirty-six now and well, we'd like to start a family in the not too distant future. You're the first person that we've told. I thought you should be.'

She looked strained as she waited for Tim to react, but she knew there would be no histrionics. He was more likely to hide his feelings altogether.

'Married?' He paused for a moment, numbed rather than surprised. 'Congratulations,' he added dully, ignoring a flash flood of chaotic feelings. 'I guess it's what you wanted.' It was the best he could do.

'Yes it *is* what we both want.' Gina looked across at Rupert and smiled - a knife to Tim's heart. There was no doubt she was happy. Tim searched for a trace of regret in her face. *Stop kidding yourself.* Rupert returned Gina's smile with interest. Turning to Tim, he gave a not unsympathetic nod: the unspoken message was 'sorry, mate, that's the way it goes.' Tim denied him the satisfaction of a response but he understood: 'Nobody to blame but myself.'

'Tim,' the kindness in Gina's voice felt like a blow, sharpening his feeling of loss. Kindness was no solace.

He wanted to walk out, but could not risk even that gesture. 'What about Maria?' he asked.

Gina was quick to respond. 'That's why we wanted to talk to you face to face: to reassure you that nothing needs to change between you and Maria. I know how hard you've worked at your relationship with her. And you've succeeded. That won't change as far as we're concerned. You could see more of her if you like. She's always talking about going to see Daddy now. Anyway it's up to you. Nothing will change from our side.'

Tim looked palely towards Gina, his emotions still contained: frustration and anger at himself rather than Gina; painfully confused that she was to have the second child he knew she wanted, envious of Rupert despite himself, but massively relieved at Gina's reassurance about his relationship with Maria. He understood now that this was the turning point. In the end Gina had decided matters. Her decision would irrevocably change all their lives.

'We're hoping you'll agree to a quick divorce.' Tim barely heard Rupert's voice as he continued to gaze at Gina.

'Rupert, please, not now. We can talk about practicalities later,' interrupted Gina. She understood well enough how Tim was feeling. 'Tim this news has come to you out of the blue. It's a big thing for you to take in all at once. You could sleep here tonight if you prefer? On the sofa bed in this room. Rupert's happy with that.'

'Perfectly,' Rupert agreed, 'although Tim might not want to hang around.'

Tim declined the offer but saw it as a good omen, a sign that Gina's disillusion with him and the related rise of Rupert would not lead to a complete communication breakdown. Gina seemed to have reassured Rupert to the point where he could accept that Tim had a permanent place in the scheme of things, albeit on the well fenced periphery.

Tim spent most of the next day with Maria, who had already been told that she was going to have a baby brother or sister. She was excited, but not yet at all concerned about the child's provenance. Tim was glad to pass on that issue. The questions would come soon enough and he knew that she would not rest until she was satisfied with the answers. But this was a different kind of day. Two fingers up to fate, he had decided that they would enjoy themselves. After kicking a football around together for a few minutes he took her along to the tennis club that he had been a member of in his Peyton days. He was pleased to get a friendly welcome and find a free court. Looking at her across the tennis court he suddenly noticed that Maria had recently put on a growth spurt. She had always been strongly made, but she was now also quite tall for her age. To his delight she showed an instant aptitude for the game. As long as he fed her the ball at an appropriate speed and height she was able to return it well, on both the backhand and forehand sides occasionally knocking a shot past him. With a lighter racket she was even able to hit one or two half-decent serves – almost a sign of prodigy in a six-year old beginner. On the strength of her performance Tim renewed his lapsed club membership and promised Maria that he would coach her on a monthly basis until she could play the game better than him.

After showering together they ate a healthy lunch at the club followed by a less healthy ice cream as they walked into town. They spent the afternoon at a fun fair that had pitched down locally and then indulged in a little light shopping. It was only later, on his return journey to Wash well into dusk that Tim realised the subtext of what he had been up to. He was attempting to show himself such a great dad that his beloved daughter would lock onto him forever. It had been hard work, but they had both enjoyed it. And, as he admitted to himself, it showed how much of a dad he could be when the stakes were high. If only Maria didn't look quite so much like her mother. *When you think you've lost everything, you can still lose a little more.* A lot more, that is.

After returning Maria to Gina, Tim decided to take a walk before driving back. It was not so much that he needed to think about Gina's decision to marry Rupert. Her recent announcement really only told him what, in his heart he already knew. He hated it, but he would have to live with it. Confirmation of their break-up was at least one clear marker in a time of restlessness and uncertain transition. Never mind Henry's ups and downs, his own life was in flux. Professionally he thought his first year at Wash had gone well. Whether the hierarchy thought the same was another thing. He had got on the wrong side of Swankie and no doubt Broome, but that was par for the course, at least, his course. Despite himself, he always somehow backed into the attention of management but he should be ok. No, it was his personal life that lacked a stable centre other than his own powerful and cussed sense of self. He was missing the steady affection of a committed relationship and, if he dare admit it, the love. He was secure in his mother's love, of course. He had yet to meet or hear of a mother that did not love her son. And he had consolidated his re-bonding with his daughter. Their time together over Easter and since had gone well. But Gina, as he had known her, was gone.

Erica? If he was honest with himself his relationship with Erica had been unsettling him for some weeks. It was stalled at half-in/half-out. He was convinced that they were more than just a pair of hedonists, but there was no developing sense of secure belonging, just fleeting moments of reaching out for each other. Of course Erica had Rachel, or, he assumed she had. Perhaps he really was on his own.

Stability! Security! He surprised himself. He was slightly embarrassed. He rarely thought much about security, or not for long. In his twenties and early thirties he had thrived on excitement and risk. With Gina he happened upon stability and security without conscious effort or even much awareness that he'd found them. Until their destabilising crises he had never given much thought to ontological security. But he was thinking about it now. Was he insecure? It was a novel thought. Or lonely? An equally disconcerting notion.

Lost in himself he had wandered into an unfamiliar part of the town. It was clearly not a wealthy area, the terraced houses built of plain but functional London brick reminded him of the old working class houses of the north. A small church caught his attention, the kind of place he would normally not give a second glance to, if he registered it at all. It was a squat building with mottled walls and a small, white stone steeple with a plain iron cross. Two narrow windows and a dark wooden door with a black painted handle and hinges punctuated its front wall. It bore little resemblance to the big, ornate Catholic churches of his childhood, other than both offered space for reflection.

On impulse, he reached out and grasped the door handle. The door was shut solid.

He turned away, more disappointed than he could explain.

As he walked on he heard the crash of a bolt and the heavy sound of the door being dragged open.

He swung round.

'What can I do for you? Are you looking for something?' It was a middle aged, informally dressed man whose profession was only apparent from the clerical collar he was wearing.

The man's friendly demeanour encouraged Tim to talk.'

'I don't know that you can do much for me. On a whim, I was going to pop into your church. I think I might have been about to reflect for a few minutes. Praying is not really my thing.'

'Perhaps not but it *is* mine. Come in for a moment.'

'I don't want to take up your time.'

'No problem, I was about to take a few minutes break from composing my next talk.'

Tim followed the pastor through the simply laid-out church, into what looked like a small assembly room. An oval table with perhaps a dozen or so chairs tucked in around it dominated the room. There was a smaller table at the far end with a kettle and some crockery on it.

'Take a seat. My name is Thomas, by the way. But please call me Tom. I'm the one-man band around here. In fact I'm also pastor to another small church in Woodham. The way we're heading we're soon going to have more churches than clergy.'

'Hi. I'm Tim, Tim Connor.'

'Good to meet you Tim. You look a bit down. Why don't we talk a little?'

'I am a bit down but it's under control Tom.'

'Can I get you a drink? Tea or coffee?' offered Tom.

'Tea please.'

'Me too, tea for the tiller-man as someone once said.'

'Donavan, maybe.'

'Could be. It certainly wasn't Cliff Richard.'

The two of them chatted as Tom made the drinks. Tim decided that this was as good a place as any and better than most to air his feeling. Tom listened but said almost nothing until Tim had finished.

'Tim you sound like a decent man and far too sensible to expect me to produce some sacred alchemy to solve your problems. But praying is like talking you know, as you and I have been doing. You can believe you're talking to God, your dead relatives, or into the void. Whatever or whoever else, you're certainly talking to yourself. It can bring some emotional comfort and maybe even some answers. A lot of people like to pray together but that's not necessary. But if you pray on your own don't count on hearing a responding voice. I don't myself.'

Tim smiled at Tom's idiosyncratic take on praying.

'Thanks. It's some time since I heard a sermon.'

'I wouldn't call that a sermon. Anyway, sermon or not it will have to stop there. I have to go off to Woodham,' he paused. 'Oh, just one more thing. I've read that praying, especially with others, can help you live longer.'

Tim looked at Tom quizzically.

'Is that true? I'm always reading about things that will help you to live longer, even half a glass of wine a day according to one expert.'

'That sounds frustrating, I prefer half a bottle myself. But prayer? Maybe... I have noticed that most of my parishioners live to a ripe old age.'

'I see. I'll bear it in mind.'

Both men looked at their watches. Time was up.

Thomas saw Tim to the door. They shook hands and said goodbye with neither feeling the need to suggest a further meeting. Why try to improve on serendipity? A one-off chance meeting was enough, although what it was enough for Tim was not sure. A few yards on from the church Tim turned round intending to give a friendly wave. But noiselessly the pastor had gone.

Tim continued on his way, still in reflective and unhurried mood. Dusk had fallen by the time he reached his car and he drove steadily across country without making a stop. Back home, he went to bed in better spirits than he could account for.

Chapter 29
It's Staring You in the Face

Tim unravelled from his sprawl on the couch to search for the remote. He had no wish to watch the same cycle of news items repeated again, and again. After scouting around for a few seconds the elusive piece of equipment caught his eye. It was deeply embedded in the cushion he had been sitting on. Annoyed, he picked it up and squeezed hard on the off button. There was a flash, a moment of darkness and the television resettled to another channel. He resisted an impulse to launch a karate attack at the insouciant piece of equipment. Revenge against a machine only hurts oneself: injury to insult. Regaining his calm, he pressed the button again more carefully. This time the set clicked off. The silence was welcome. Life across the world seemed no more cheerful than his own: corrupt politicians, a government swamped by financial crisis, a train crash in Pakistan, and Liverpool out of the Champions League for another year. Not a chink of light anywhere. Minor earthquake in Blackpool, nobody injured, was the good news.

He regarded keeping up with the news as part of his job.

Usually the news didn't much affect his mood, one way or the other: mostly it was selectively bad, but he didn't take it personally. Apart from his on-going project with Henry of global utopia, there was little he could do about the state of the world other than vote conscientiously and protest against the more iniquitous cock-ups and self-seeking of the great and good. The arrival on the internet of petition-protest groups like 38 Degrees and UK-UNCUT had made a level of political participation easier, although clicking a 'yes box' didn't carry the same virtuous charge as joining a street protest.

Still, the world, the universe and whatever else aside, he was feeling the need to get a better grip on his own life. He had learnt as a child to believe that individuals should take responsibility for themselves: for good or bad you make your own choices, his mother repeatedly insisted, and you live with the consequences. As with all her advice this was framed in terms of her earnest, guilt-driven Catholicism. Quite early in his childhood his own understanding of free will and circumstance had become more secular than his parent's and as he grew up he began to buy her books with titles such as *The Power of Positive Thinking* and *Your Life in Your Own Hands*. There was nothing patronising about this; the books provided grist for a lively dialogue between the two of them and helped to keep Theresa sharp. She read the books or parts of them though regarding them as cheap change in comparison to 'the truths' of her religion. Tim was unsure whether his own strong will, bordering at times on wilfulness, came from nature or nurture but he continued to believe that he could achieve some control over his life, despite the play of chance and the unpredictable intentions and interventions of others.

Before he could get the desired grip on things, he needed to sort out exactly what was bugging him. He could switch off to the state of the world, but not to the state of self. In that respect meditation had never quite worked for him. He had never got past the stage in which random thoughts block the arrival of a state of total suchness, if, indeed, that was what did come next. The transcendence of the Buddha was far beyond his experience: unless being stoned was some kind of counterfeit enlightenment. He was residually pious enough to doubt that. His was the oyster of the still irritant grain of sand, not that of the pearl of wise acceptance. Still, he understood enough about the workings of his psyche to realise that personal troubles often lurked behind his moods of philosophical angst. He felt a nagging need to disentangle the threads of his anxiety. He was determined not to rush. It was as though for the previous nine months he had been living out a script, that everything, even the seemingly spontaneous and pleasurable, had been pre-de-termined. Despite all his frenetic action – the intense work, domestic commitments and upheavals, the sexual adventures – he felt he was driven, not the driver. Odd that the more he rushed, the less he felt in control. A familiar image returned to mind: banging heads, brick walls and it being good when you stop. He needed more than head-bang-ing; what was missing was a gentler counterpoint to the arrhythmic beat of his life.

He decided to take Pastor Tom's advice and pause for an internal dialogue, a chat with himself. As aids to cogitation, he got a beer from the fridge and rolled himself a joint. He stretched out again on the couch, head propped up on a cushion at one end, legs dangling off at the other. He suspected he knew what was troubling him but he allowed his mind to choose its own direction of travel.

He took a thoughtful drag on the joint, followed by a pleasantly rehydrating mouthful of ale. As he mellowed his mood began to shift. At the edge of his awareness, shadowy images and notions were beginning to take shape. He closed his eyes and took another slow pull. He began to sense that out of the maelstrom of his 'problems' he could draw new energy and fashion a way forward. *All people dream, but they do not dream equally, some seek to live out their dreams in the light of day.* And when Tim dreamed he dreamed big – of beautiful women and of saving the world. This time it was the women.

To put it at its most expansive – and he had begun to feel expansive - there were three intelligent and beautiful women in his life, all in their early to mid thirties: Gina, Aisha and Erica. Slowly... slowly he was coming to terms with what each of them meant to him and he to them. His difficulty in getting there was emotional, not intellectual. He still hadn't fully caught up with the fact that two of these women seemed to be out of his reach. In his guts and gonads he had not accepted what he knew to be true: *a walking contradiction, partly truth and partly fiction.* Rationally he understood that his relationship with Gina as a partner was over. He was ninety nine per cent sure of that. He had just been told so in no uncertain terms. And even before she announced her intention to marry Rupert, she had not wavered in her loyalty to her new partner. He believed now that he had lost any chance of reconciliation, not because of his infidelity but by choosing deception rather than truth. He had felt remorse, but lacked the honesty and humility to express it to Gina. It was not so much that he obdurately didn't 'do' humility as that it had simply never occurred to him to 'do' it: he lacked practice. By the time he had almost got hold of the notion, the right moment, if there was one, had gone.

Gina had finally cut the knot. For months a sense of loss would sometimes invade him. The thought of it dizzied him, the chasm where their life together had been. He would always love her. But love, their love, was not what their lives would now be about. What was left to them was shared responsibility for a child. Yet love lost or unwanted is not the end of love. It takes refuge until its time comes again. *Even if you lose your love and don't know what to do, the memory of love will see you through.* He was not so sure.

Aisha? Other than in his own imaginings and, so he liked to think, in hers, they had kept love at bay, apart from a single hello-goodbye moment: a few seconds of time out of time. And there were compelling reasons to do so. But for now he was allowing himself to think in ideal, 'what if' terms, to dream in a realm of free choice in which there were no consequences. A flâneur of fantasies.

Supposing Aisha was available, how much would he want her? More than Erica? He could not say that. He would not say that. Thinking in this way would plunge him into the cruellest of crosscurrents. He was almost glad that in reality Aisha was unattainable. He was no ritual respecter of conventional constraints but he had come to recognise the damage that the careless indulgence of desire can cause. Aisha should be protected. He had promised himself to do that: not out of convention but because... for *her*. The Great Protector.

It wasn't easy. Aisha was a sensitive and delightful, as well as a beautiful woman. So! She was no more accessible to him than other women in her situation. Get used to it! Had he become unhinged by his sudden ejection back into life as a single man? Did he imagine that every attractive woman was the legitimate object of his... of his what? Lust? Ego? No, he did not want to go the way of a middle-aged Lothario. He took a deep drag on the joint, again washing away the dryness in his mouth with a long draft of beer. He sucked on his tongue thoughtfully, his mood of self-rebuke softening. Of course Aisha was not 'every' woman, she was a woman he was close to and... what were his feelings? Supposing... He let out a low guttural growl of frustration. He was going round in circles, not to mention in psychoanalytic clichés. He had set up a pointless hypothetical situation. Forget it. In the non-ideal world of real consequences he had no intention of riding roughshod over Aisha's life – her family, her child. *You can't always get what you want.* And sometimes you should not try. He remembered now, you can choose not to do, as well as to do. Like Gina, Aisha had made her choice: 'in some other lifetime.' What right did his charm and lust have against such purity of the mind and heart?

Now he came to the crux of his problem. It was Erica. It was himself. Or rather it was his uncertainty about Erica's feelings for him and his confused feelings about her. That, he conceded, amounted to an uncertain and confused relationship. His deepening feelings for her were fraught with a sense that she had locked him into a narrow role in her well-ordered life. In flashes of paranoia he wondered whether sexual gratification on tap was all she wanted from him: controlling him for her pleasure whilst keeping him at an emotional distance. Why would she need or want to do that? But was this also what he wanted? Their relationship was fun, more than that, it was pure, exquisite sensuality but was it enough? Was that it? Control freak meets free-wheeling hedonist. *In the end I know, I'm just a gigolo, life will go on without me.*

He could be wrong about the whole thing. He wanted to be. There were hints, long moments even, when it seemed that they were on the edge of something reassuringly ordinary and blissfully un-dramatic: perhaps a stable, loving relationship. That was the point; he wasn't sure what Erica did want from him. Much of the time it felt like they inhabited separate plastic bubbles. Occasionally, usually at Erica's say-so, they would burst out and come together in frenzied delight. Then, usually sooner rather than later they returned to their bubbles. True, there had been emotional break-throughs, real enough at the time but not sustained. Once the period of closeness had passed, they reverted to the usual routine: 'wham, bang thank you man.' And during the in-between times at work or in social situations their relationship went unacknowledged by others and by themselves.

Tim's reverie had bought him to the realisation that it was time to put his relationship with Erica to the test. How, he was not yet sure. It was a risk. If Erica rejected his move the whole theatrical fabric of their relationship might implode. Was it worth the risk? He did not even consider the question.

The drifting was over. It was time for action. You can

only dream for so long. Then events take over. You either make things happen or things happen to you. He stubbed out the remainder of the joint and drained the bottle of beer. He checked his watch. It was seven o'clock. The chances were that Erica was at home. He would surprise her. As high as a kite and still on the way up he decided to break out of his habitually laid-back, understated self. He brought up Erica's number on his mobile and pressed connect. The call was answered almost immediately.

'Hi Tim. I can see it's you. How are you, lovely man?'

'Fine. And yourself?'

'Ok, missing you, though.'

This had started well. But it hit Tim that a phone call was not the best way to say what he had in mind: especially as he wasn't yet quite sure exactly what that was. Face-to-face with Erica he would find inspiration. For now he improvised.

'Erica, I've been thinking about us. I know we're both incredibly busy but we never seem to spend more than a day and a night together, usually just a night. Let's sort out some serious time together. How about going away together for a weekend, preferably next weekend?'

There was a pause.

'We can do that. Next weekend is fine as it happens. I might have to take some work with me but otherwise I'm free.'

'Great.' This really was going well.

'Have you any ideas about where we should go?' asked Erica.

So far Tim hadn't thought of anywhere but inspiration struck.

'Bognor.'

'Bognor?'

'Yes Bognor Regis. I have a friend there. He has his own house, lives on his own. I used to share digs with him at university.'

'Bognor Regis? Isn't Brighton or maybe Bournemouth

more attractive than Bognor? I don't know anybody that's actually been to Bognor. Are you sure it's worth visiting?'

Tim did not want to get bogged down in a discussion on the merits of the old seaside resort. He reassured Erica of the town's undoubted charms and added that his friend was even more colourful than his name, Delaney O'Toole, suggested. Staying with Delaney would also make for a cheap weekend although he didn't mention that aspect to Erica.

'Ok, Bognor it is. See how easily I submit to you when you get assertive?'

Tim was in no mood for psycho-banter of the dom-sub kind, but was glad they'd agreed on the weekend.

'Ok. I can do even better. I'll arrange the whole break for us.'

'Great, Tim,' Erica hesitated, 'there's one more thing. Could you come over tonight. I've had a fall out with Rachel and I'm feeling a bit low. Would you mind?'

Tim opted to walk rather than drive across the city. He would avoid the butt-end of rush hour and the cooling evening air might clear his head. On his way he bought eighteen yellow roses, full, with broad petals, faintly glowing. Once at the flats, Security and then Reception, used to him by now, nodded him briskly through.

Erica looked plaintively beautiful. She managed a pale smile as he presented her with the flowers. Putting them carefully aside she gave him a hug, gentler than usual. As he eased her away she held on for a second, rubbing her blond head against his chest.

'Tim those flowers are lovely. Thank you. Do you know they're the first you've ever bought me?'

'The first? You should be so lucky. They might be the one and only.'

It was a paltry jest. Erica's face fell.

Annoyed at himself, Tim tried again.

'Erica, I'm sorry. Let's relax and just be together, watch a film maybe, after we've had something to eat. It feels like a night for talk and TLC. We don't have to have sex tonight, if you're feeling fragile.'

She gave him an uncertain look.

'Tim, I hope you're not saying that because you're not attracted to me anymore.'

'Erica, you must be bloody joking.'

He never did get to hear what Erica's falling out with Rachel was about but as he snuggled up close to Erica that night it occurred to him that maybe their quarrel had done him a favour.

Between the night of the yellow roses and their break in Bognor they spent only one more full evening and night together. With assessments piling in, they ratcheted up their workloads to create space for their weekend away. The night they did spend together was as passionate and rude as the night of the roses had been calm and comforting.

It also revealed that Erica's sexual imagination was not confined to the role of dominatrix. As soon as he arrived and without a word she thrust a leather strap into his hand. Removing her jeans and panties, she bent over, her hands gripping her legs just below her knees. Tim gazed in awe at the perfect contours and dipping valley of her jutting arse.

'You sure you want me to strap your bottom?'

'Yes please.'

For a moment Tim was torn between his taste for raw sex and his sense of the ridiculous. The sight of Erica's legs from heaven and her upturned rump cut short his hesitation. She was ball-bustingly sexy.

Slowly and rhythmically he gently plied the strap, first across her left buttock and then the right. As her arse turned from golden brown to rose, Erica remained statuesque, barely moving under the steady smack of shiny leather. As the spanking gathered pace she obstinately thrust her backside upwards to meet the relentless strap, even in this position struggling to exert some control.

Tim was now quivering with excitement. Tossing the

strap aside he started to mount her. But for Erica the play was not over. She abruptly closed her legs.

'There's a cane in the bathroom cupboard Tim. Please, six of the best.'

Tim was reluctant.

'Tim, please.'

'Ok, but I'll decide when this stops.'

Poised above her, he ran the cold cane across her hot behind.

'One firm stroke on each buttock and that's it. We'll pause after the first stroke but you stay where you are so I can enjoy the view.'

It didn't work out like that. Tim broke the cane over his knee and grabbed Erica's hips. Lifting her off the floor he quickly entered her. Taken by surprise, she dangled on his cock. It was not in Erica's nature to dangle for long. She tipped forward planting her hands firmly on a table in front of her.

'Tim, keep hold of my hips.'

Levering her legs upwards, she crossed them behind his back. Tim's cock remained tightly gripped inside her. Suddenly she pushed backwards precipitating a joint explosion followed by a slow collapse to the floor.

They remained silent for a few minutes, when Erica spoke.

'You enjoyed that then, didn't you my lovely animal man?'

'Yeah I did, but let's keep the props as an occasional treat for feast-days and holidays of obligation, that kind of thing.'

'And it doesn't stop us making love in other ways, does it?' Erica sounded anxious.

'Not at all, not unless you, we get addicted. But I don't think that's too likely. What do you think?'

Oh, I agree, absolutely not. I love doing it the ordinary way as well.

Tim looked deep into her azure blues, 'Erica you're priceless, one in a million.'

'And you Tim.'

'That makes two of us.'

'Clever man, not just a pretty face, then?'

'Apparently not.' He was beginning to feel that in his quest for the love of Erica he just might be pushing on an open door.

Chapter 30
On Bognor Sea-Front

They decided to take the train to Bognor. Erica had not previously made this journey and they opted for a slow train so she could take in the long stretch of countryside that opened up once they were clear of Wash. Erica enjoyed the rural landscape but Tim, adopting his 'our lad from the North' role claimed to find it flat and tame compared to the rough terrain of the Lake District and Pennines. On the strength of his regionalist bluster Erica tied him down to a promise of a guided tour of the North West. Tim didn't mind at all. Chalk that one down to things moving in the right direction.

They were met at the station by Delaney, a rotund Irishman with a shock of prematurely white hair that shot perpendicularly from a massive head that could have been lifted from a Rodin sculpture and dropped, slightly askew, roughly between his shoulders. A great crescent beard covered the lower part of his face, further adding to his messianic air. As if nature had not rendered him conspicuous enough he wore a long purple cloak over a multi-coloured kaftan and a pair of claret velvet trousers. Emerald eyes twinkled in welcome. Pausing to wink at Erica, he gave Tim a fierce bear hug, half lifting him off the ground. Erica got a smack of a kiss on each cheek and, suddenly enveloped in the purple cloak, a slower, gentler embrace than Tim had to endure. Grinning Delaney stepped back from his guests.

'Holy Saint Cuthbert! Where in the name of Jaezus did you find this beautiful creature? Even more amazingly what possessed her to pick you out of the bunch?'

'Good taste,' Tim replied. He was keen to keep the banter under control. He enjoyed his friend's sharp wit, but on this occasion he planned to rope him into supporting his from-lust-to-love project with Erica. He wanted Delaney to boost his image, not demolish it. He had briefed him ahead of the visit to assist his romantic endeavour or at least not to mess things up. There was a good chance Delaney would deliver. Underneath the blarney he was a sensitive soul, softened rather than embittered by his own experience of lost love, peaking in a vicious divorce barely two years into a marriage in which he was far more sinned against than sinning. In the depressing aftermath he had given up his job as an IT consultant and now made his living as a session musician. He also played saxophone in a local jazz band, quaintly named 'Just East of Chichester': so far it had been a 'for love not money' affair.

As they walked from the station Tim glanced across at Delaney who was chatting with Erica, giving her some background on the historic town. He was soon telling her one of Bognor's more famous stories. It was the kind of tale Delaney enjoyed, vulgarly piss taking of those who were more accustomed to pissing on other people.

'Erica, do you know why Bognor is called Bognor Regis rather than plain Bognor and why the words most associated with the town are *Bugger Bognor?*'

'No, I have no idea, but I think I'm about to find out.'

'You are. King George V visited for a health cure in the

1920s and was so grateful it seemed to work that he added 'Regis' to the name of the town. Thus, 'Bognor Regis.' That's the polite bit of the story.'

'Interesting, but that doesn't seem to fit with 'Bugger Bognor.'

'No. There's more.'

'Ok.'

'Roughly ten years later, when he was seriously ill his courtiers reminded him of the reviving effects of Bognor and suggested a return visit. What do you think he replied?'

'I don't know, but I'm pretty sure I can guess.'

'Right, 'Bugger Bognor': his final utterance.'

Laughing Erica gave Delaney a sceptical look.

'That's a good story, but it sounds like a piece of blarney to me.'

'Not so, check it out for yourself on Wikipedia.'

Its tragic denouement aside, it was the light-hearted aspect of the 'Bugger Bognor' story that set the tone for the next couple of hours. Delaney proposed a drink before they set off to walk the couple of miles or so to his house. In the event this turned into a guided tour of the town's best watering holes. Tim and Erica made no attempt to keep pace with Delaney's drinking, but after an hour or so and having visited several pubs they were both were lightly sozzled. Wanting to sober up they pressed Delaney to take them to a coffee bar. They ended up at a rambling establishment that set itself out as a coffee and teashop, although in a couple of niche rooms alcoholic drinks were on sale. Tim and Erica ordered black coffees and Delaney a black coffee and double brandy. They found a small room with armchairs and, even though it was a mild day, a pleasantly smouldering log fire. Delaney eased back in his chair and thoughtfully sipped his brandy.

'To walk or not to walk, that is the question...'

'Definitely to walk – to your place you mean? Neither of us have much luggage. A walk will clear our heads,' Erica suggested.

'Definitely,' Tim agreed. 'We're only here till midday Sunday, so we might as well get an early taste of the sea front. Erica's never been here before.'

Delaney concurred.

It turned out that the Bognor seafront was more impressive than the town itself which had appeared slightly worn and tired looking. The wide esplanade that skirted the seafront offered a vista of ocean and sky, as inspiring as the town was not. They strolled along, almost in silence, drawn into nature's massive presence, listening to the weird, metallic cries of the gulls and the whip of the wind on the sea.

The sight of a large holiday complex brought them back to earth.

'Butlins,' said Delaney, 'although I think it acquired some posh new name a few years ago. We don't have to stay on the esplanade. There's a stretch of beach ahead. Why don't we go down there?'

'Sounds great,' enthused a slightly drunk sounding Erica.

Switching from the esplanade to the beach took them even closer to the elements. Hot from exertion they removed their shoes and socks, dragging their feet in the cool wet sand. Aroused by the sounds and movement around her Erica suddenly shed her backpack and began running along the edge of the sea, occasionally shouting wildly and pirouetting with stunning virtuosity and grace. Neither Tim nor Delaney felt they had the attributes to follow suit. Even less so when she made her next move.

Erica began to shed her clothes.

'Christ on a motorbike, I think she's going for a swim,' cursed Delaney.

His fears were confirmed as she swiftly removed her remaining clothes down to her panties and shouted across to them.

'I'm off for a quick dip, why don't you join me?'

Exchanging looks of pure panic Tim and Delaney attempted to close the fifty or so yards distance from her in sub world record time, Delaney a whirling ball of purple and claret as he rotated after his more athletic friend. They were too late. Erica danced gleefully into the water seconds before they made up the ground. Tim followed her in but was left treading water. Sodden to the knees he lurched back to the shore.

'Don't worry, I'm a very strong swimmer,' Erica shouted as she plunged into the deeper water.

'We may need to go after her,' said a much sobered Delaney, 'there are some nasty currents out there.'

'Right, let's strip off and be ready to do that. But she should be ok, she *is* very fit.'

'She's also seems to be very drunk.'

'Yes, well... I can't think why that is. Anyway, how well do you swim?'

'Pretty well, got a tin pot somewhere to prove it.'

By the time they were down to their underwear Erica was a good hundred yards from the beach. She then started swimming strongly in a lateral direction having apparently decided she had gone out far enough. The two men continued to urge her to come ashore. She shouted back that it was warmer in the water than on the beach, so why didn't they join her? They ignored the teasing and remained on uneasy orange alert. Erica's next move was to embark on a series of water acrobatics, including a display of flashing leg-scissors.

'What a cracking pair of legs,' exclaimed Delaney, 'how the hell does she manage to do that?'

Tim was less impressed. 'Right, but I'd prefer to see them back on dry land.'

They remained suspended between anxiety and admiration for several minutes when Erica abruptly concluded her extravaganza.

'I'm on my way back,' there was an edge of anxiety in her voice.

'Thank God for that,' Tim exploded in relief.

'And the fucking quicker the better,' Delaney agreed.

They watched as Erica turned towards the shore. Delaney, cold despite his bulk, started pulling his clothes back on.

'Wait a minute, there's something odd going on. She's swimming but not getting any nearer,' said Tim.

Looking around, Delaney quickly worked out what was happening. 'Shit, the tide's going out! She's probably hit a contra current.' He immediately began tearing off his clothes again.

Tim was already in the water. He was not about to wait for Erica to shout for help. Her pride in her athleticism might deter her until she was in serious difficulty. He shouted reassurance as he started to swim.

'We're coming for you, Erica? Stay calm.'

'I, I'm not moving. I'm cramping up.' Her voice was tight and strained.

As he got near her he could see she was in real trouble. Her arms were pumping ferociously but her legs were virtually immobile. She was almost vertical in the water, her head bobbing up and down. Her face was taut and her eyes dull with fear.

'I can't move... I'm not moving.'

Reaching her he put his arms under hers, resting the back of her head against his chest to keep her from going under water. By then Delaney was with them.

'It's going to take both of us to get her to the shore,' shouted Tim. 'Delaney, you take the front and I'll take the back. Erica, grab Delaney's shoulders and hang on. I'll push from behind. Don't try to do anything yourself.'

Once they had manoeuvred into position, the makeshift carriage worked well. The moment of horror quickly evaporated as, resembling a Bognor version of the Loch Ness Monster, they proceeded steadily to the shore. Out of the water, a relieved and grateful Erica submitted to a towelling down with the men's shirts and a vigorous leg massage to stimulate circulation. Having sorted themselves out, they headed straight for Delaney's place fortunately now only half a kilometre away. Other than a bemused elderly couple and a gaggle of derisively amused teenagers, the bedraggled trio made it to the house without attracting too much attention.

The after effects of the episode hit them in an unexpected way. Once inside the house, instead of collapsing with exhaustion they found themselves in a zone of collective exhilaration, talking excitedly, almost babbling, smiling and laughing, marvelling at how life and death can turn on a moment, delighted that fate had nodded kindly in their direction. All this did not prevent them from noticing that they were fiercely hungry. Delaney had excelled himself having already semi-prepared a meal of fish and local vegetables. He hadn't prepared potatoes but produced a loaf of the size and appearance of a small log and a large wedge of butter. They cut off chunks from the loaf as they waited for the fish to grill and the vegetables to warm up.

Delaney's place was a good reflection of his personality, chaotic but friendly and colourful. They agreed to eat informally: Tim and Erica sitting on a heavily cushioned couch and Delaney on what was obviously a favourite armchair. Delaney spent little money on décor but regularly indulged an expensive taste in wine. 'That unscheduled dip has sobered me up. This snapper deserves a couple of bottles of premier cru burgundy and you can have whatever drink you want with your afters. I can offer you a fair choice.'

Gradually the food and alcohol brought Tim and Erica down from their highs. Exhaustion began to set in. Even Delaney, so far impervious to the vast amount of alcohol he had shifted began to look tired. By the time they had finished eating they were ready for bed.

'Listen you guys,' said Delaney, 'I've got a gig in Portsmouth tomorrow afternoon, nothing special, just filling in for the band's regular saxophonist, so I'll leave you two here to relax and enjoy yourselves. Get up when you want. There's plenty of food in the fridge. I'm playing locally tomorrow night and you'll enjoy that better. I'll go upstairs ahead of you so you can have the bathroom to yourselves in a few minutes. Tim will show you around, Erica.'

As he left the room he turned round, grinning. 'By the way you guys, next time we'll get a taxi from the station.'

When Tim and Erica woke up the following morning Delaney had already left. They got up lazily, showered sensuously and then enjoyed a long, slow, deliciously unhealthy breakfast. Their pleasure and sense of intimacy was sharpened by their recent close skirmish with the Reaper. Refreshed, they were now more reflective about what might have happened. Erica had the grace to be penitent.

'Tim, I'm sorry, I put you and Delaney in danger as well as myself with my crazy behaviour.'

'I don't think either of us is thinking about that, all that matters is that you're safe.' He paused for a moment and then added more seriously, 'but you do have to be aware that moments of danger can occur. They can come out of the blue. You have to be alert to the risks around you.'

This sounded too drearily inhibiting for Erica. 'But you can't predict what's going to happen. You'd lose all spontaneity if you tried,' she opined.

'Listen Erica, what we nearly lost yesterday wasn't just your spontaneity it was the rest of you as well. But yes, we have to trust that the world is a secure place most of the time, just to get by. But I'm right too, you need a kind of mental alarm system, an awareness, that kicks in when there's real danger, or when you're about to do something that might harm yourself or others. You didn't have that yesterday.' He paused for a moment, surprised at his own intensity. In a quieter voice he added 'I should know I lost my marriage in a mad moment of passion. I wouldn't want to lose you too, would I?'

Erica smiled, pleased at Tim's concern for her but sensitive to this rare expression of vulnerability. She tried to lighten his mood. 'And I certainly don't want to lose you, my knight in shining armour,' she reached across to kiss him but he wasn't ready to let go of his argument. His lips briefly brushed hers as he continued. Unsure that he had convinced her he attempted a more anecdotal approach.

'In the days of the Wild West, cowboys used to sleep with one eye open. You know, keeping an eye open for trouble.'

Erica saw this folksy reference as an opportunity to bump him out of his serious frame of mind.

'Tim, that's ridiculous. It's not possible to keep one eye open all night. At the least, they'd have to rotate eyes. Anyway, in all the Westerns I've seen, sleeping cowboys cover their eyes with their hats.'

Aware that he was on the wrong end of a leg-pull Tim decided to conclude his homily. 'Alright, then but just take care of yourself.'

'Tim, I will. How about going out for a walk now? I promise not to dive into the sea or even dance along the beach, if you promise not to give me another good behaviour lecture.'

'You've got yourself a deal,' he replied with a wry smile.

Chapter 31
A Get-Together at
Rachel's Place

Rachel was quietly pleased that Annette was unable to make it to the modest mid-summer social get-together she had arranged for the department's women. She was getting tired of listening to Annette's endless complaints about her husband, her delight at his downfall and then her chagrin at his apparent revival. She winced at Annette's fierce cruelty: 'Let's hope the fucker cracks up properly and gets himself institutionalised, finally out of my way. He never could cope with himself, pathetic.' She had some sympathy for Annette but to her Henry was no longer relevant. Her conflict with him had been essentially professional. Henry had to go and now he had gone: job done. He was no longer around campus and didn't even live in Wash. From time to time she did wonder whether he really was as demented as Annette believed and she herself sometimes suspected. Mad genius? She thought not, but she recognised, with a tinge of professional regret, that he had squandered a decent talent, depriving the department of a much-needed boost to its profile. She even allowed herself to wonder whether

Annette's brittle, niggling behaviour had tipped Henry over the edge. She dismissed the train of thought. It didn't matter now.

Annette's absence meant that her only guests were Erica and Aisha. And she could hardly think of Erica as a guest as she had a house key, came and went as she wished and occasionally slipped into Rachel's bed. Rachel could not help noticing though, that lately Erica's comings and goings had been less frequent and that her bedroom visits had almost dried up. She knew why, of course. It was her involvement with Tim Connor. To be fair Erica had been frank about the matter. In any case, her relationship with Erica was an open one and given Erica's youth, it was hardly surprising that it was occasionally tested. Rachel was confident in its resilience. She herself had affairs with men when she was younger before deciding that on balance they were not worth the hassle. Still, she recognised that she felt happier and more secure when there was no third party attracting or, as she saw it, distracting Erica's attention. She recalled how upset she had felt at the recent London conference when Erica had seemed to prefer Connor's company to her own. It had made her physically sick, forcing her to realise that her hard won confidence and assertiveness was not quite as secure as she liked to believe.

Erica was always guarded in her remarks about Connor but from what she did say Rachel guessed that the relationship was mainly sexual and would in due course probably smack into the buffers or just fizzle out. When that happened she intended to ensure that any of their subsequent personal problems did not spill over into work. She knew from experience that it was in the bitter break-up of a relationship that the serious trouble could kick off. She could see the appeal of Connor. He had the edgy, brooding demeanour of an outsider combined with a raw sensitivity, transparent to everyone but himself, that might attract the female romantic. In other words he was a recipe for disaster as she suspected Erica would discover. Either way Rachel would remain on stand-by. The fact was she loved Erica. This was the one aspect of her life that she recognised as being beyond the dictates of logic. She was quite willing to play a waiting game.

In any case, on this occasion her focus was Aisha rather than Erica. She had, of course, no wish to develop anything other than a positive working relationship with Aisha, to bring her fully into the departmental ethos. She was puzzled that this was taking longer than she had expected. Not that she was dissatisfied with Aisha's work or had clashed with her in any way. Her teaching was going very well, effectively engaging the ever-widening ability range of students, and her contributions to the women's research group were impressive. In fact, Aisha was a perfect professional.

The problem, if it was fair to call it a problem, was that she seemed to be holding back from full commitment to the group. It was her apparent lack of that extra element of identification with the team that concerned Rachel. She knew that she could not demand this but it was something she always looked for and usually found in women colleagues. It mattered because Rachel wanted to create a working environment built on a spirit of collective commitment to shared projects. She believed that this was the foundation of authentic performance, of 'excellence', rather than merely observing the proliferating regulatory rules. She could play the top-down institutional game well enough – you had to if you wanted to survive and get anything done – but it was her feminist values and purpose that made her tick.

At first she worried that Aisha's reticence was a response to her ethnic minority status: that as a British-Asian member of an otherwise white group of staff she felt inhibited, perhaps without even being aware of it. However, she had to concede that Aisha's poise in ethnically mixed social gatherings and her easy relations with a diverse body of students seemed to belie this explanation. Rachel was well aware that contrary to one stereotype of Asian women as

rather muted and subdued, many could be quite the opposite. Only the unobservant would mistake Aisha's demeanour as withdrawn or lacking in confidence. She carried herself with an unaffected dignity and sense of self-worth that
commanded the attention as well as the respect of others.
True she seldom showed the remarkable sparkle she had at
interview but that was a one-off, winner-takes-all situation
when she had to distil and dramatise what she had to offer.

Another possibility was more troubling for Rachel.
Despite Aisha's commitment to the women's writing group
and to feminism more widely she seemed less of a feminist in
her everyday life than Rachel had assumed. It was almost as
though Aisha suspended her criticisms of patriarchy outside
of an academic framework. For Rachel, men's tendency to
selfishness and lack of reliability were realities that women
needed to be aware of as a matter of course, in a lived way.
Of course, there were individual exceptions to the predict-
able patterns of male behaviour, mostly among gay men, but
men had created a society in which they routinely practised
their unpleasant and destructive behaviours.

Yet, if anything, Aisha seemed to prefer the company of
men to women. She certainly spent as much time with them
as with women colleagues. This was particularly unwise
given the men immediately around her. It was understandable that she might seek informal advice and support from
Howard, although even his track record was hardly pristine. In her early days at Wash he had even tried it on with
her. More worryingly Rachel had also noticed that Aisha
quite often socialised with Tim Connor and, when he was
still around, even Henry. From time to time she had seen
Aisha and Henry in quite animated conversation. Again it
was tricky to bring this up with Aisha, but it puzzled her.
As a black feminist Aisha was a potential star in the kind
of department Rachel wanted to develop. It was important
that she was 'one of us': Rachel could have kicked herself as
the tainted cliché came to mind.

Aisha's own thoughts could hardly have been more

different from Rachel's as she turned into the pleasantly secluded mews where Rachel's house was situated. She had just got the news from her doctor. She was pregnant and healthily so, as far as could be assessed at this stage. She had immediately called Waqar. His great, laughing roar of delight almost blasted her ear off. Unlike the day she was appointed to Wash, he had honoured his promise to return early from London to celebrate the news. He stopped only to buy her and 'both juniors' something 'special.' Aisha had pretended to dissuade him from 'making a fuss' but was secretly pleased. She knew her husband's priorities and children were top of the list – along with her, of course, but in his mind the two were inseparable. She wasn't too happy with this fusion but she was sure that a second child would strengthen their marriage. Not that she had any intention of reducing her work and career commitments. On the contrary having delivered for Waqar in his terms, she was well positioned to insist on her own. She might even persuade him to take a part-time course in Social Science. His views had always been quite progressive for a self-made business-man and recently he had begun to take a greater interest in Aisha's work. Their partnership was renewing itself, more mature, more equal and more genuinely shared than when they had first got married. She was glad that she had kept her faith in Waqar, not that it had ever really wavered.

High on cloud nine, she found that she had breezed past Rachel's place. It was easily done. The house was a mid-terrace bijou property, beautifully presented, but petite enough for a daydreaming mother-to-be to miss altogether. Aisha backtracked a few yards and pushed open the wrought iron gate to Rachel's garden. The flowers were in colourful early summer bloom almost bursting out of the neat beds Rachel had planted. Their abundance reassured her that she had chosen well to buy Rachel a small gift of dark chocolates of the high cocoa content Rachel loved rather than yet more flowers. Pulling the chocolates out of her bag it occurred to her that if she held them conspicuously in front

Tim Connor Hits Trouble

of her Rachel might be deterred from delivering her usual crunching hug. It didn't work. As soon as she answered the doorbell Rachel was squeezing the breath out of her much slighter colleague.

'Lovely to see you. You look so well, positively blooming. Oh!' as she released her, Rachel noticed the now severely dented box of chocolates, 'Are those for me? Oh dear. I'm sorry I...'

'Don't worry, they'll still taste the same,' smiled Aisha.

'Absolutely, we'll eat them this afternoon.'

As they were speaking Erica appeared at the garden gate. Rachel prepared to launch herself again.

Unlike Aisha, Erica usually welcomed Rachel's hugs but she quickly intercepted this one.

'Rachel, just a kiss on the cheek please. I'm feeling slightly nauseous.'

Rachel settled for kisses all round and then led the way into her living room. She gestured Aisha towards one of the armchairs of a dark-leather suite, expecting Erica to join her on the sofa. Erica went purposefully to the other armchair.

'I see you're rejecting me, then. What have ...'

'Not at all, I really am feeling nauseous,' Erica interrupted her.

'I'll get you a glass of water, then.' Rachel had now twigged that Erica was genuinely a bit off colour.

Sipping the glass of water, Erica soon announced that she felt much better. As the three women settled down their conversation turned, as is often the way in single-sex groups, to the other sex. Henry was the prime candidate, his recent adventures, still the hot topic. They each rehearsed their views on his dismissal: Rachel reiterated her opinion that his sacking was necessary but insisted that she had no wish 'to dance on his grave.' Erica also took the view that Henry had to go, but felt it would have been better to wait until the end of the academic year to fire him – granted that it had now become difficult to know if the academic year ever did end. Aisha agreed with Erica, adding that the possibility of keeping him on next year could also have been left open should he become more settled. Rachel's response was to insist that it would be much better to start next year with a clean slate. In any case, that was Howard and Geoffrey's view: 'the patriarchs have spoken,' she quipped.

'That's rather disingenuous of you, given your part in his downfall,' commented Erica.

'We really don't want to be wasting time and energy on the Jones problem next year,' Rachel repeated, 'and with him out of the way we're in an excellent position to motor on, especially if we get a new appointment, perhaps in the gender area. From now on we should look forward.'

Keen to avoid further discussion of Henry, Rachel suggested that it was time for tea and cakes. The whole idea of this get-together was to cement relationships, not to argue over dead meat. She had a gourmet selection of teas and had made a chocolate cake for the occasion that she was eager to sample herself. Having sorted out the tea preferences she rotated off to the kitchen.

The two younger women looked at each other and grinned.

'She loves doing the maternal bit,' said Erica leaning forward towards Aisha. 'Aisha, it's so good to see you away from work. Somehow we never seem to get the chance to spend any time together.'

'I know, I've had the busiest year of my life. I think we mostly teach at the same times and when I'm finished I'm usually off to the library or to pick up Ali.'

'We must make more time for each other next year. Things should be a little easier for you.'

They continued to chat for a few minutes until Rachel reappeared, barely coping with the huge tray she was carrying.

Erica and Aisha quickly rose to assist her, Erica taking the enormous cake from the tray and Aisha removing a jug of hot water. Her load suddenly lightened Rachel wobbled backwards. As the crockery cascaded around the tray, she managed to stabilise herself by plumping down on the couch. The moment of near disaster passed and the three women swiftly set things out for tea.

Rachel was soon in charge again. Having offered her guests a choice of tea-bags, she began to cut the cake.

'I'll cut up the whole thing, knowing you, Erica, you'll want a second piece. I don't know how you manage to keep that figure of yours, the amount you eat. Aisha I think you might be back for more as well.'

'Rachel, no, actually I don't think I can eat any cake at all. I seem to be feeling slightly sick again,' said Erica looking awkward.

Rachel put the cake knife down and, hands on hips, stared almost belligerently at Erica. 'No cake! That's not like you. What's wrong with you? I don't think I've ever seen you even slightly off-colour. If I didn't know you better I'd think you might be pregnant.'

There was a moment of silence for which the word 'pregnant' is the best description.

'I am,' said Erica.

Rachel looked puzzled. Aisha was stunned.

'You are what? Ill? Finish your sentence,' Rachel demanded.

'No, pregnant,' Erica insisted.

Rachel gaped, her mind frozen in pre-response mode. Erica got to her feet and gripped Rachel firmly by the shoulders. Eye-ball to eyeball Erica said in slow staccato:

'You're supposed to congratulate me.'

'Congr... whooo...' Rachel appeared to be hyperventilating, 'whooo...'

At this point Aisha decided that, as nearly as possible, the announcement of the pregnancies should be simultaneous. She joined Erica and Rachel in the middle of the room.

'Erica, Rachel, I was going to tell you this later – after tea – but, well, here goes. I'm pregnant too.'

Erica quickly let go of Rachel and gave Aisha an almighty

hug. The two of them then attempted to scrum up to Rachel who, far from wanting to cavort around sank to the floor in a state of semi-collapse. The two younger women helped her to her feet and led her gently to the sofa before embarking together on an enthusiastic jig.

The rest of the afternoon took on a different aspect from Rachel's original intention. Once she had established, with as much sensitivity as she could muster that the two women were as happy about their pregnancies as they appeared to be, she began to adjust to the situation. By the time they left she was more or less on board to the idea that her brave new future would encompass the needs of her pregnant co-trailblazers. The first thing she would do was to check out that the university crèche was functioning properly.

Erica had not intended to announce her pregnancy just yet and certainly not in the impromptu manner that had just arisen. Not that she ever doubted that she would have this baby. She had decided that she wanted at least one child some years ago and at nearly thirty years old this seemed about the right time. She had not particularly planned to get pregnant, but had allowed herself to be as careless as Tim sometimes was about contraception. If Tim did not want the child she had the resources and support to bring it up. She had kept quiet about her pregnancy because she wanted to get used to the idea of becoming a mother, especially if she was to be a lone parent. Having a baby might mean, surely it would mean, a massive change of lifestyle. The pregnancy was now almost at three months and she knew that in fairness she ought to tell Tim soon. Her concern now was that he might hear the news from someone else even though Rachel and Erica had promised not to tell anyone until she gave them the go-ahead. She trusted them but felt that once three people were aware of her condition it didn't make sense to try to keep it quiet for much longer. She decided to talk to Tim immediately after she had left Rachel's. She got him on his mobile and arranged immediately to go round to his place. He was puzzled at her urgent and mysterious tone but delighted at the prospect of an unexpected visit.

She decided to walk the couple of miles or so between Rachel and Tim's houses. She needed some thinking time. She knew that she wanted the child even if Tim did not, but the imminent prospect of hearing what he actually felt was nerve-wracking. His intentions would have huge practical consequences for her and the child but just now it was his emotional response that mattered. And how she felt about him was just as important. She had come to realise that she not only found it difficult to trust men but that she had not really given it a try, except briefly as a child with her father but never since. As Rachel hinted from time to time, Tim might not be the best man to start a serious, trusting relationship with. But they had been getting closer in recent weeks. She enjoyed their intimacy and did not want to lose it. Their break in Bognor had been something of a turning point. It was not so much that he had been prepared to risk his own life to save hers but afterwards they had opened up to each other in a deeper way. Perhaps it *was* cause and effect: it felt quite natural to be open to someone who has just saved your life, especially if they were also your lover. They had enjoyed moments of intimacy before, but their closeness now was different, more a state of being, part of her life. It was a new experience for her. She supposed this was perhaps what happened when people were 'in love'. She wasn't too fussed about the words but the notion appealed to her. Yes, she loved Tim. Very soon, she would know for sure if he loved her.

Keen to get to him as quickly as possible she left the main pedestrian route to take a shortcut through a dedicated zone of small-scale industry and miscellaneous warehouses close to the river. She was making her way through an alleyway at the back of a row of workshops when she was accosted by a familiar voice, sardonic and with a hint of threat.

'Hello blondie, aren't you my f...ing ex-neighbour's piece?'

Erica froze. It was Darren Naylor. He stood a few yards in front of her, his van and large bulk almost blocking her way. Instead of moving aside to let her pass he shifted across, blocking the remaining space. She could attempt to squeeze past him or retreat. Either way there was a risk she would not be rid of him.

'Come on darlin'. There's nothing to worry about. I always did take a liking to you. I fink there's about enough room for you to wriggle by. Come on then.'

Backing off she pulled her mobile out of her pocket.

'I'm phoning the police.'

'Naw, why ye doin that?' Naylor edged forward a couple of steps.

His move made up her mind. She turned and ran. She didn't look back until she had reached a main thorough-fare. There was no sign of Naylor. She was still clutching her mobile. Checking the panel she saw that that the numbers were scrambled – her attempted call would not have brought help. Still breathless and upset she decided to call Tim. For now she wanted the reassurance of hearing his voice, she would tell him about the Naylor incident later.

'Tim, hi, I'm on my way.'

'That's great. How long? You sound a bit out of breath.'

'I'm fine. Ten, fifteen minutes at the most. Look I wanted to say something. I couldn't wait until I got to you.'

'Go on.'

'I love you.'

'I love you too.'

'Really?'

'Sure. Definitely.'

'That's good. I hope you don't change your mind when you hear what I'm on my way to tell you.'

'I know what you're going to tell me and it doesn't change my mind.'

'You do?'

'Yes, you – we – we're pregnant.'

Erica was silent for a moment.

'Are you sure you're ok about it?'

'Of course, 'ok?' I'm totally paradisiacal.'

She felt a rush of pleasure and relief.

'Me, too, I'm so full of everything, mainly baby! But how did you know?'

'Well you've missed two periods. And that stomach of yours isn't quite as perfectly flat as usual. It's perfectly not quite flat. Anyway get yourself over here and we'll celebrate. I'm as happy as you are.'

'Right. Get out the teabags and biscuits. I'll be with you soon. Bye, then.'

'Bye.'

She patted her stomach, the worst, best kept secret of her life. Her smile was pure sunshine.

Moving into the preparation for baby phase consolidated Tim and Erica's relationship. Their delight with each other was strengthened by their delight at the prospect of the child to come. Pooling their resources enabled them to consider buying a decent sized house together close to the Khan's also awaiting their new arrival. Having confirmed with Erica that he was 'number one' in her life Tim decided not to worry about her relationship with Rachel. He had limits to what he could accept in a relationship but they were more flexible than most. That was just the way he was.

Chapter 32
Great Transitions

Teresa's death, although it came as no surprise and though she was ready to go, hit Tim hard. In the three years she spent in the care home he had finally found for her, she had drifted further and further into dementia. There were moments of tragicomic confusion. The most frequent was Teresa thinking that Tim was Dominic, her long dead husband. Tim was tempted to play along with it: from childhood he had sought to fill his father's shoes and he was inclined to take Teresa's conflation of him and his dad as some kind of endorsement that he had made the grade. On one occasion he indulged her illusion. His cameo was so convincing that Teresa seemed to believe that she had been reunited with her husband in heaven: a moment she had long ardently anticipated. After that, whenever she mistook his identity for Dominic's he thought it better gently to convince Teresa that he was, in fact, himself. This proved satisfactory to Teresa although often within minutes she was again addressing him as Dominic.

The doctor who signed her death certificate was presented with several ailments as the cause or contributory causes of death. He chose respiratory failure and dementia but the reality was that she had simply 'conked out.' She was intermittently sufficiently aware of what was happening, that she was dying, to come to a terms with it. Physically she was ready. Her own words, spoken without self-pity but with a touch of irritation, were 'I've had enough.' A combination of drugs and sensory decline meant that she experienced little pain but she was beyond exhaustion in her increasingly feeble attempts to make the brain-body link function. Due to her diminished and erratic state of mind Tim found it difficult to judge how she embraced death spiritually. He had no wish to project his own spiritual uncertainties onto her. She was long past attempting to fit herself or the world into any framework of divine intent, intelligent or otherwise. Her readiness for the great transition reflected a habitual state of mind rather than a conscious reaching out. In any case, the final resolution is the most personal moment of all, unknowable to those on this side of the veil.

Those around her made sure that the support and comforts of her faith were there in her final days. The parish priest and the chaplain to the hospital visited her regularly. As she had always wanted, she received the last sacraments fully aware and in good time before she died. What difference they made in the great scheme of things, she was now in a better position to know, than those she left behind.

Tim was round and about Teresa throughout her last few days. Gina and Erica shared the vigil with him, Gina mainly out of loyalty and affection for Teresa and consideration for Tim, Erica mainly for Tim. The younger women had not exactly become friends but they got on well together. There was no cause for animosity between them. They had plenty in common, both working in the educational sector and each the mother of a two-year-old boy. It helped that Tim and Gina had slowly managed to establish a friendship that neither of their new partners found threatening.

This was not merely the result of the passage of time, they both worked at it for Maria's sake. For his part, Rupert had the good sense not to challenge Tim's role as Maria's 'real' father, as the child herself put it.

Teresa faded so slowly that it was difficult for Tim to know the precise moment when she was gone. He and she had been alone together for some hours when a nurse came in. After a couple of minutes attending to Teresa she turned to Tim and told him quietly that she thought his mother had died. A doctor was called and quickly confirmed this. Tim reached for her hand, heavy and rough in his own, the hand of someone who had worked hard and unselfishly, mostly, as he had come to realise, for him. His tears were his first since his father's funeral. They came as silently and unbidden as the angel of death.

Dealing with the practical matters following his mother's death helped him with the first pain of loss. The sadness that followed would linger, fade and from time to time return. Immediately, he had the funeral arrangements to get under way. His first stop was the presbytery of the parish in which his mother had spent her life, apart from the few years when she had moved around with Dominic as he made a couple of late career transfers. The priest, Father Canon, a confident youngish man, sporting hair evocative of a wild cactus, was up to the demands of the occasion. He offered Tim a choice of whisky or tea and some quality chocolate biscuits, as well as providing him with the information he needed to organise the funeral. They agreed that the church service followed by the cremation would take place in five days time. Father Canon also managed to raise Tim's spirits by recounting tales from his own quite varied and eventful life. At one period he had been a steeplejack and, as he pointed out, had finally landed safely in the right place. Tim was in too subdued a mood to pass on the thought that 'it all depends on one's point of view.' Still, he was in better spirits as he left the presbytery than when he had arrived.

The church service celebrated Teresa's life as well as mourned her death.

There was pretty much a full house despite Teresa outliving most of her contemporaries. Among the more sombre hymns and prayers, the congregation also belted out Teresa's favourite, the tuneful and bittersweet Star of the Sea, 'pray for the wanderer, pray for me.' *You and me, both,* he thought. In his homily Tim wove together the lives of his mother and father expressing his hope and his mother's expectation that their relationship, cruelly terminated over forty years ago, could now be resumed. After the service an elderly couple approached Tim, keen to share a memory of his parents wedding at which they had been guests. They agreed that 'two such lovely people, perfectly suited to each other, deserved to be together now.' *Amen to that.*

Amongst the wreaths for Teresa were two that Tim had not expected. One was simply signed 'To Teresa Connor and her beloved husband, Dominic, together at last. From the Parish.' The other, as Erica commented, was 'a bit of a turn up.' It was signed 'Henry, Fred and Rachel'.

The day had begun cloudy and overcast but the congregation came out of the service to find that after a freshening shower the sun was now shining and a pleasantly cool wind was stirring. Gradually the family and friends invited to attend the cremation ceremony separated themselves from the rest of the congregation and gathered round the cars making up the funeral cortège.

The cortège was a short one. Teresa had outlived all her relatives other than two distant ones, and only one of her remaining friends was well enough to attend, a doughty old woman named Mary Atkinson who was determined to accompany Teresa to her final destination. 'I'll be next,' she said, not seeming to mind in the least. Tim and Erica followed the hearse in a hired black Mercedes, Tim's Volvo and Erica's sports car failing the test of appropriateness on contrasting criteria. Mary Atkinson sat in the back, her posture as proud and erect as a Grenadier Guard's. Gina and Rupert followed in their family car with Maria, now nine years old, in the back. After some discussion between Tim and Gina, they had decided not to bring along their respective boys, Dominic and Alexander, to the funeral. At two years old they would remember nothing of the occasion and might just create minor mayhem. In the third car were the two relatives, a brother and sister, James and Florence Nixon. Although they were elderly pensioners they had done their best to help Teresa during her last years at home. It was only after bumping into them several times in Whitetown hospital that Tim realised how much concern they had shown for Teresa in her last years. The least he could do was to invite them to see her off.

The cremation was functional and business like – too much so for Tim's liking. The small party entered the cremation area to the piped strains of *My Way*, a tune they were required to listen to several times as the cremation ahead of them ran behind time and they had to wait. The knock-on effect was that there was some pressure on them to hurry along when 'their turn' came. A leisurely last goodbye it was not. Tim hadn't been expecting an assembly line set-up, the industrialisation of cremation. He resisted the attempt to push them along and suggested that everybody touch the coffin making their own, silent farewell to Teresa. He had half a mind to suggest a rendition of *Lassie from Lancashire*, a song his mother often used to sing, to counter the repeats of *My Way*, but respect prevailed.

In her prime, Teresa had a way of putting other people's happiness and interests ahead of her own. True to form she wanted the meal following her funeral to be an occasion for celebration rather than mourning. She had insisted on giving Tim a generous sum of money for that purpose, asking specifically that they go to the *Phoenix* for the meal. It was, she said, her 'way of being there with the people I love.' The death of a loved one can bring those left behind closer, putting conflicts and ill feeling into perspective. Life is short, why spend it taking chunks out of each other? A wake especially provides an opportunity to consider whether long standing rifts and quarrels are worth continuing. Tim and Erica and Gina and Rupert enjoyed the meal together in a reflective and conciliatory spirit. They even began to discuss the possibility of visiting each other as families, something that had not so far happened. The sense of bonding was intensified by the awareness that although they were marking the passing of a life, both couples had quite recently brought a new life into the world. Erica pointed out that recently Aisha and Waquar had also had a child, a baby daughter much loved by her brother, Ali. Tim's thoughts slipped back to how fragmented his life had felt when his marriage had broken down and he had moved to Wash. Now new bonds were being formed and he could again look forward to the future. Fully compos mentis Teresa would have taken pleasure in all this, although she might well have observed that 'our Tim has a funny way of doing things' very likely adding 'but he's a good lad really.'

As they ate and talked an idea came to Tim. He had already decided to remain in Whitetown for a short period to deal with matters relating to his mother's death. It happened to be school half-term holidays. He looked across at his daughter Maria. Why should she not stay up with him for a few days? At nine years old, noticeably independent-minded and self-confident she would take it in her stride. He had never wavered in his determination that they should fully share in each other's lives, but so far they had spent little time together in Whitetown and the region around it, the part of the country that he thought of as 'where I come from.' Apart from the two elderly relatives who along with Mary Atkinson had decided to spend the meal making a fuss of Maria, there was no family left to introduce her to, but the place itself was part of her history as well as his and his parents. He wanted to give her a feel for the area. Enthused with his plan he put it to Gina and Erica. As usual Gina was happy to encourage anything that promoted the father-daughter relationship. Erica was in any case less affected, expecting to return to Wash on her own while Tim remained in Whitetown for a period. After a brief discussion she and Tim agreed that he would get back to Wash within a week and with that she was happy.

'Great! That's decided then,' Tim concluded.

'Aren't you forgetting somebody, Dad?' It was difficult to tell whether Maria was upset or just teasing.

'Maria, I'm so sorry. I forgot to ask the main player what she wanted.' Uncertain how serious his daughter was Tim's tone was mock penitent.

'So?' said Maria, milking her centre-stage moment.

'Maria, I would love you to stay up here with me for a few days so I can show you the beautiful North.'

There was a theatrical pause.

'I'd love to stay too,' Maria leapt off her chair and delivered a giant kiss on her father's nose.

'Good. No problem, then, Maria.' Tim smiled ruefully, aware that she had been taking wicked delight in playing his feelings.

True to his intention Tim took Maria around the North West and even added a brief foray into Yorkshire to see the Dales and the tumbling, rock-scattered rivers that intersect them. They rowed on Windermere, climbed half-way up Helvellyn and exhausted themselves on a trek along the Ribble Valley. To avoid Maria becoming surfeited with the 'green and pleasant' Tim spliced in a few urban delights, including visits to the Cavern, the first venue of the Beatles, and the football ground where her grandfather used to play. It was all good stuff for Tim as well as Maria, keeping him in the present when he might have been pre-occupied by the past.

The last act of their stay was one of generational communion. Tim wanted to share with Maria the scattering of some of Teresa's ashes on Dominic's grave. They collected the urn together as they had done everything that week and drove to the cemetery. The sturdy granite Celtic cross of the tomb was visible almost as soon as they were through the cemetery gate. As they parked the car and walked towards the grave, a single shaft of sunlight seemed to pick it out.

'Your grandma's saying hello to us,' Tim said, 'she's arranged for the sun to shine on her husband and to welcome you and me.'

Maria, who had become quiet, smiled up at Tim.

'And soon it will be shining on her.'

Once at the graveside it was Maria that suggested burying some of Teresa's ashes in the soil around the grave as well as scattering them on it. Tim was glad to do both. It was as close as he could ever get to reuniting Teresa and Dominic.

They knelt in silence by the grave for a few moments before Tim spoke.

'Your granddad, you know, Maria - he was a good man. And your grandma, she did her best, she was a good woman.'

As they got to their feet, a question occurred to Maria.

'What about you Dad, are you a good man?'

They looked at each other for a moment, smiling.

'Maria, that's a very good question.'

CPSIA information can be obtained at www.ICGtesting.com
Printed in the USA
BVOW05s1003190515

400973BV00004B/83/P